THE WEATHER MAN

SAM HAYES

to my father,

who believed in the American Dream, woke it up, and kept on dreaming

THE WEATHER MAN

ONE

"LOOK ALIVE."

Jonathan Harvey, head of the National Weather Commission, stood up from behind his onyx desk and wandered about his highrise nest, surfing a waterfall of pent-up thoughts spilling from his weathered old mouth. "I don't know how else to say it Adam—we need you to be happy."

Adam stared down at the dim reflection of his face in the desk and saw a statue of himself. His speckled green eyes had darkened to black in the onyx. They looked back at him as though they had been trapped in that stone since the dawn of time, waiting for a chance to break out and see in color.

"This isn't just a strong suggestion anymore," Harvey went on. "And it shouldn't be so damn hard. We've had this conversation a few times now. I've given you a raise. I've changed our shooting schedules to best fit your needs. I've recommended shrinks. I've gotten you—"

"I told you I don't need a doctor. I'm not depressed." Adam looked out the gaping window over the great gleaming city. A ray of sunlight blinded him, and as his eyes shifted he could see Harvey's reflection in the glass. He was shaking his head.

"That's...whatever. Sure." Harvey sputtered back into his monologue, slowly approaching Adam from the far reaches of his excessive office. "I've...I've...I've gotten you pills. Prescriptions. I've thrown every perk at your feet. But no matter what I do," he gritted his teeth a little and squeezed Adam's shoulder a little too hard, "you continue to sink into whatever self-destructive mindset you've created." Harvey swooped around the desk and glared at Adam, waiting and waiting for Adam to say something until he

1

couldn't take the silence anymore. "Wake up!" Harvey burst out, slapping his open palm onto the desk.

"I don't know what to tell you Jonathan. I don't know anything about a self-destructive mindset. I haven't changed. I get up there and put a smile on my face and do the broadcasts the same way I always have. I'm not sad. I'm a *very* level-headed guy. Nothing fazes me; you know that. That's why I'm consistent; that's why my ratings are always high."

"Were."

"Nothing's changed."

"No." Harvey shook his head. "No. That's not what the data says. And I can see it in you too. You're not the guy I hired." He stopped in his tracks. He squinted. He was mourning now. "You... you had this big, blind hope in your eyes. You just, you never had bad days, not even when you fell flat on your face, over and over again. That's what I wanted for the broadcast. That's why I hired you. You had these eyes, see? These forgetful eyes. Eyes immune to the lulling comforts of failure." Harvey peered into them, but that blind hope was all but gone. These were eyes that had seen, and moved on with their search.

"Not anymore." Harvey looked away. "Something's off. It has been for some time now and it's only getting worse. You just can't see it. Your goddamn silver-spoon generation doesn't understand. Look at this." He stepped up onto the window ledge in front of Adam and peered over Chicago, watching hundreds of skyscrapers striking like silver lightning into the clear blue sky. "Really look at it," Harvey urged, squinting with the proud nostalgia of a father watching his son at graduation. "All this man-made beauty. But you didn't fight for this." He turned back to Adam suddenly, and an age-old rage fell into his voice. "You were born into this. You haven't the slightest clue what we've given you. I wish I could send you a few dozen years back in time," he shook his head and slipped behind eyes missing in action, "just for a day or two. I'd put you on the ground with me. In Russia. China. Let you taste your own blood, maybe somebody else's too. Maybe then you'd see things how they are." He tapped his finger on Adam's temple. "You'd have no choice but to be happy—you'd be so damn grateful."

Adam swatted his hand away.

"You understand?" Harvey pressed. "You understand what you have?"

"I mean, as best as I can." Adam searched for words as Harvey turned away, looking at the ceiling. "What do you want from me? I'm grateful. Maybe I don't feel it as intensely as you, but I try to—I hope to. I know I'm lucky to be here, lucky to have this job, lucky to live in this time, this country. I'm lucky. I get it."

"No you don't Adam," Harvey whipped around, chest puffing out like a bulldog. "Let me explain something to you: they're not bored. The guy before you, the gal before him, and pretty much every face we've ever had—we eventually fired them because they got boring. People still watched because they wanted to know how their day would go and they wanted the news beat, but after a couple months or a couple years, engagement levels in their brains decreased drastically, and with it our value to advertisers. But you," Harvey looked at Adam like a curious exhibit at a museum, "you're the opposite. You're the luckiest guy on earth. Five years and you're still not boring. You're not. I look at the charts every single day. You're still logging the highest engagement of any weatherman we've ever had... when people watch."

"So what's the—"

"*The problem*, Adam, is that no one's watching anymore because when they do, when they see your face, they don't get bored—they get anxious. Oh, engagement is soaring for our remaining viewers! But the pleasure centers of their brains aren't lighting up; it's a rise in stress hormones we're measuring. So what they're connecting with can't be joy anymore, can it? It's not hope. It's fear. Loneliness. Melancholy. Everything that no one has fucking time for. We're losing money every goddamn day. I just sold a banner for half what I sold it for six months ago to the same company," he fumed. "Because no one else would take it! And those designer threads—yeah, you'll have to start paying for those. See, they're not paying for you to wear them anymore. No, no. They're asking us to pay *them* if the logo is visible in the broadcast."

"Why...," Adam stood up, grabbing the back of his head, "why didn't you tell me any of this?"

For once Harvey paused before answering. "Are you so dim? Because I couldn't hurt your feelings and make you even more of a crybaby. This is all a game Adam. The only reason I'm telling you now is because you've already lost."

"I don't know where this is all coming from." Adam was baffled. "I give the job everything I've got, every single day. I'm trying, I really—"

"Trying?" Harvey mocked. "*Aw*," he brought his fists up to his eyes like a wailing baby. "It's not conceptual physics Adam. You just have to cheer up. Get a hold of yourself." He grabbed Adam by the shoulders and shook him. "You have a responsibility to be happy. This isn't a joke. People wake up to you every fucking morning. If you aren't making their day, you're not worth their time. They're closing the damn hologram before it even pops out of their wrists and for fuck sake I would too." He ripped off his coat. He was sweating now. "I built this company with everything in me. I begged borrowed and stole, lied cheated and killed for this company. And for a while," a loathing laughter bubbled up from of his mouth, pushed out by anger swelling within him, "picking you was one of the best business decisions I ever made. But it's quickly become the worst. You are *wrecking* everything I've built faster than I can fix it!" He slammed his fist against the window and a big empty thud swallowed the surge of his voice. "This 'level head' of yours … it is destroying my life's work."

"Jonathan, whatever you're describing, I'm not feeling. It's just not there. I mean, fuck, I'm not an emotional guy, and, and … and I'm as happy as I've ever been."

"The data doesn't lie!" Harvey drilled his finger into his own head as he tried to catch his breath. "You may know how to fool yourself, but your smile's not fooling anyone else. What they're feeling is real. We pull it straight from their PIDs, straight from their fucking brains, and it's all pain. What does that tell us about you? Huh? You were happy to accept that data when it proved you were priceless. Now it tells me you're worthless."

"What do you want me to do? Crack a few quick jokes to start the one-minute broadcast? I feel fucking fine. I don't feel anything!"

Harvey stood there with his arms crossed, each breath practically bursting them loose from his chest. And as Adam carried on, looking around the room searching for himself, the echoes of his own voice finally began to rattle into his soul. "I...I don't even know what people really mean when they say they're depressed. When people get so sad they cry, or so happy they cry—I don't even understand how that happens. I've never...I'm just here—good old straightforward me. Nothing has changed. Nothing will."

"You're so numb you don't even realize you're depressed. But I don't give a shit anymore. I've already decided I'm letting you go," Harvey boiled. "I'm just looking for an adequate replacement. If it weren't for your fucking fan club of teenage girls I'd have just picked one by now. But they won't save you for long. We'll find the right guy in time."

"In time, huh? How long?"

"Maybe a day. Maybe a month. I'll let you know the moment I fire you. You can go be an actor on some moody drama. Maybe that'll cheer you up, you ungrateful bastard."

Adam stood up. "Well Jonathan, I wish I could tell you I cared. I really do. I wish I could get all fired up and demand my job back...but I just don't fucking care. And I'm not just saying this. I really, really don't care." Adam turned and walked toward the door.

"Don't care...?" The words barely escaped Harvey's quivering mouth before he exploded—he picked up a porcelain bust of his own head and chucked it past Adam. It smashed into a million screams, scattering an eerie silence across the room in their wake. Adam stopped. He slowly turned toward the sound of Harvey's heavy breathing.

"You're a fucking disgrace to this company," Harvey muttered, leaning over his knees. "To your audience—to the whole country. To your generation. To your friends, if you have any real ones. To your mother." He looked up, nodding. "To your father."

Adam shook his head. "You don't know my father."

"Neither do you." Harvey propped himself back up and looked Adam in the eyes. "But I know your father fought. And now I understand why he left you."

Adam didn't speak, didn't break eye contact, didn't even breathe for a little while. He just stood there, still as stone, staring back at Harvey until he felt a tear slowly rolling down his face. He reached up and let it melt onto his finger. He looked at it like he'd just discovered water.

"Crybaby, see?" Harvey smirked. "What are you looking at?"

Adam said nothing, but as his eyes dried they widened a terrifying distance.

"What the fuck are you looking at? Speak up," Harvey berated, until he realized Adam wasn't looking at him at all. He was looking past Harvey, through the window, beyond the city, over a bright blue Lake Michigan quickly turning dark grey.

Harvey rushed up to the window. Adam slowly followed. A massive inky storm cloud was moving swiftly over the lake and toward the city, drowning everything in its path with waterfalls of rain.

"What, what is this?" Harvey whispered. "This wasn't in the forecast." He looked at Adam. "What is this!"

Adam could barely hear Harvey over an enormous groan of thunder like a mountain toppling down. A shadow darker than night fell first. Then came the rain, pounding the glass with such authority that Harvey stumbled back from the window. But Adam leaned forward to feel the glass shake on his forehead and watch the drops splash against his eyes.

"I thought we had this under control." Harvey glanced at the display on his wall—*68 and Sunny*. "What the fuck is up with the forecast! What is this!" Harvey threw his hands up at the storm like it would answer him.

Adam fell back from the window as the fear on his face melted into awe, and the terrifying feeling inside of him produced the most shocking smile. "It's gorgeous," he said.

Harvey stared into the great black beauty and then back at Adam. "Get outta here," he said.

But Adam couldn't take his eyes off the white lighting cutting through the heavy sky. "Get out!" Harvey thundered.

Adam strolled out of the office and into the elevator. He stood and he blinked and he breathed as it descended, and he couldn't stop smiling.

He walked through the lobby and straight out the doors to feel the rain. But when he got outside, the sky had only maintained a thin layer of wispy clouds, spread aimlessly like a puddle of wine around a shattered bottle. The wet streets and the warm fullness of the air muffled the sounds of the city starting back up again. Adam shut his eyes and let the scent of fresh rain wash over him.

The sun struck his eyelids; he opened them to see streams of gold breaking holes in the sky. And flickering back into the air between the buildings, high above the city, Adam saw his own smiling face as a holographic giant, relaying the forecast to the masses below. He closed his eyes again. With another deep drag he chose the rain.

Maybe this was how it felt—happiness. He didn't know for sure. He was as limited by his own experience as everyone else, but a little more aware of it. Adam was never convinced he felt things like others felt them, never rising quite as high or sinking quite as low, and always wondering, like a bronze statue watching the crowds stroll through the grass and stare at him in reverence. They wanted what he had—the ability to endure rain and shine, standing tall, unmoving and unmoved. All he wanted was to know why. Bronze may rust forever green, but grass, though it dies every winter, gets so much greener.

●

N.N.N. BREAKING NEWS – *Weather Commission Wrong!*

CHICAGO – A completely unpredicted, severe thunderstorm formed over Lake Michigan, moving over downtown Chicago and surrounding suburbs with heavy rain and constant lightning. Strangely, the storm appeared at approximately 3:07 p.m. but dissipated by 3:15 p.m.

For the first time in 20 years, the National Weather Commission has missed a forecast.

Stay tuned as investigators figure out why.

Published at 3:34 p.m., April 1, 2076.
© *National News Network, Inc. All rights reserved.*

TWO

YOU PROBABLY KNOW the story of Adam Anderson, but not like I do. I nearly lost my life for this story. Several times. Mostly in the spirit of fun. We tried, very hard, to have fun—to be happy. For a time, Adam's strange situation afforded us lives in the vein of ancient kings and modern trillionaires.

But I didn't always know Adam. It took twenty-three years for our paths to cross. I should say collide, like a bird and a window, while I stood with my face plastered to the inside of the glass and watched beautiful feathers explode into the air. I didn't know him until our snow-globe world had already started to crack in 2076. Or, he didn't know me. I knew him as the ever-present fixture of pop culture that he was.

Every morning, millions of people spread across America's biggest cities woke up to Adam on their PIDs—personal information devices, that is—1.618/1 inch screens built into our wrists, rising smoothly just about a millimeter above the skin. In addition to mediating communication and information by projecting holographic displays, PIDs connect to tiny speakers planted in our ears, and constantly measure body chemistry. They even connect to the brain through the nervous system, and pretty much run our lives from dawn till dusk and dusk till dawn.

For a long time, Adam served as America's alarm clock, delivering the day's need-to-know headlines, and then the only bit of news most of us really cared to hear—the weather. To be the face of the Weather Commission in the 2070s was to be the country's constant—the one person so charming or mysterious or interesting that no one got tired of seeing him or her, at least not for a minute. Adam's job wove him intimately into our lives. It was hard to go a day without seeing his face, whether standing on your wrist like a toy, or sprawled across the sky, floating above the major cities he covered like a weather god. He stood tall in either place, unflinching on an athletic frame. His eyes seemed ancient but alert, perched vigilantly above a jaw cut like stone. And his tan skin had a golden hue, like he had seized just the right amount of sunlight and was content. A marshmallow cooked just right.

Adam's broadcast stayed on the surface of things, but you could tap in for more on any of the headlines, or see minute-by-minute forecast details in your specific area. If you wanted to look up the weather on any day or hour within the next year, you would check the pre-records. Forecasts inside of a year, anywhere in the United States, except for poor old Alaska, carried 100 percent certainty. If you wanted to know the weather somewhere on a day two years out, you couldn't count on more than 75 percent accuracy.

Adam did nationwide weather reports too. Hurricanes and earthquakes and tornadoes—he always gave warning reports a year out. He didn't actually know anything about the science behind predicting the weather, but Adam's was the face we loved, so when he told us about an upcoming earthquake or a hurricane, we felt like he alone had saved our lives. He had a way of saying things, a sureness and a solidness, as if his words didn't just predict the weather, but brought it into existence. I guess that would make him a criminal when there was a bad storm, but we were always very well prepared. There was typically little damage, and reportedly no one had died due to weather in more than twenty years, if you don't count the growing trend of people who deliberately put themselves in the path of a storm just to feel the rush.

Other than that, weather was not a problem for America. The inclement impact of global warming on other parts of the world seemed far more severe. I've heard storms are twice as large as they used to be and happen twice as often, but very little of that damage was ever covered in the news. Authorities credited our safe situation to the mastery of weather forecasting and preparation, and noted that for whatever reason, we'd been geographically fortunate not to be in the path of quite as much extreme weather. They said global warming has affected the vastly different parts of the world in vastly different ways, and acted like anyone who hadn't been our ally in World War Three had it coming like karma. They tended to blame the climate crisis mainly on the massive developing countries who refused to reform their pollution laws from the early 2000s onward, even when we knew of the impending effects.

That's what they said, but I'm no expert. I figured it wasn't likely the truth, the whole truth, and nothing but the truth. I know we played a part as well. How large, I have no real way of knowing. It's difficult to find reliable facts in the virtual world, tucked behind beautifully simple platforms that select answers for you, drowned under miles of links and distractions in an endless sea of information washing all around us. We float so effortlessly atop it, there's never a need to dive in. Computers piece together immense amounts of information to instantly answer any factual question you could possibly ask—even things that had never been known until that very moment. You don't question their answers, because you're wrong—you're always wrong. Realities are presented to us in transient images that cannot be held, and we move tirelessly from mirage to mirage. All our technology, our whole world— everything just keeps getting simpler. Except for us. We take on every complication left behind. We become the clean interfaces hiding miles of complex code beneath our skin, and we are not to be left alone with ourselves. We expect our happiness to be as immediately accessible as everything else, and a psyche as refined as the purest laws of science.

Well, people were pretty psyched about America's 300th birthday coming up, and politicians seemed pretty damn happy with how far we had come as a nation. They liked to call our time "The Age of Power," because all of our knowledge brought about all kinds of predictability and ease. We rose from the ashes of World War Three like a great glorious bright white angel of death—now we find ourselves living lives of options. Options and options and options. We just know everything; we know all the options. All that's left to do is choose between them. We've been fighting for freedom in this country for three hundred years, and at this point we've overdosed. You can always try to be anything you want to be, because at worst, failing means you are given a decent home printed in a day by the government and fed decently healthy food until you are old and not that gray. The safety net is so large there's little you can do to miss it. We are left to figure out exactly what we most want out of our lives and live them. It is as beautiful as any impossible thing.

●

At this point you might be wondering who I am.

Me too. My name's definitely Clark, and I'm not sure what else to say. Never have had a whole lot to say. I've always had trouble getting out of my own head, so I write, and the trouble winds up on the page. What else should I tell you? Do you want to know my eye color or something? Brown. Hair—brown. Skin—kind of white, kind of brown. Classic stuff.

Sports are good. The outdoors—absolutely. I'm really no different from anybody else except that I know I'm the same. Back in high school I wasn't exactly killing it. You could tell I wasn't crushing it, definitely not putting it away or packing it in, mostly just keeping it to myself. I certainly wasn't making a splash. That's just out of the question.

In college I was told to find myself, so I tried, maybe a little too hard. I found a whole lot of things I could become and lost track of what I actually wanted. My school offered 88,000 different customizable degrees. I felt like I'd been set at the bottom of the Pacific Ocean and told to swim around until I found the one fish I liked the best, the grand happiness waiting for me somewhere like sunken treasure. "It's in there alright Clark! Just gotta find it." You're about to grow up—what do you want to be? What do you want to be? Try this. Try that. Try something else. Say please; say thank you. Don't ask too many big questions. If you find yourself sad you just haven't found the right thing yet. If nothing's working you just suck. There's no reason for depression and there's absolutely no room for it, and there's pills for that anyway. Unhappiness is unacceptable. Just keep trying things, don't be so anxious, and take your time dammit! We're all supposed to live till we're at least 150 anyway, or maybe forever if things get even better. They call our generation The Forever Young, and I was starting to wonder if it might take me the whole forever just to decide what I wanted to be—never mind anyone asking you *who* you want be when you grow up. We're all a little undereducated in that department.

But none of that matters, because this story isn't about me. In fact, none of this has anything to do with the story, but now you know me a little, and I hope it's enough to trust me. My grandma used to tell me seven out of ten people are liars, and the other four do their best to keep the facts straight. Well, I'm one of the four trying to keep the facts straight, because it's the one thing I know I'm pretty good at. When I'm paying attention, I remember just about everything. The only genetic modification I received in the womb, besides the basics like longevity and fast metabolism and resistance to most ailments, was enhanced memory. My folks could only afford to buy me one, and memory was the one enhancement that felt morally sound to them—the only one that might benefit me without disrupting who I am, or am meant to be, naturally.

Well, with recent advancements in the PID, it turns out having this much naturally accessible memory is already as outdated as writing a book. And while it's not generally desirable, I guess you could say it worked. I've got a great memory, and I'm grateful for it, but I can't say it didn't affect who I am. It affects me every moment. It makes for a lot of thinking, a lot of moving pieces rattling around in my head. The reminders and connections between everything brim out the borders of my mind until I am pushed out with them and lost in space, spinning in a black hole of thoughts and feelings about those thoughts and feelings. That's when I don't create new memories or really notice anything at all. Ironically it's all my damn memory, yanking my attention inward, that allows external realities to fly right over my head. You've got to understand, I'm a space cadet, often caught up in the swirling place between my ears, and in between the facts you're bound to swirl with me a little. But I'll tell you everything important that I remember, and everything Adam told me. At this point, I don't have the luxury of asking Adam to search for a memory on his PID, but any memory he showed me or told me, I remember clear as day.

●

I didn't graduate with some big goal or dream like everyone else. Without one I was floating, drifting with the wind, and would keep floating until I could find somewhere to land. But I hadn't figured it out yet and I was suspended on nothing, and somehow that didn't feel like freedom.

I guess I was waiting for an idea that felt significant. Something that might lead to a little happiness if possible. But happiness is a heavy word. It's held in such high esteem, and when you find a little of it you soon wonder, "Wait, so ... is this it? This is it, right? Is this the thing we're all going for? Do I have it? Did I have it? Do I need more of it? Is it already gone?"

At least I do. I'm a wonderer. And a bit of a wanderer for it.

So I wandered. Odd jobs here and there, but nothing serious Susan. No commitments or careers. I'm not ready to start anything here. It's not that I wasn't driven, or capable of being driven, I just didn't know what I wanted. They say not all who wander are lost. Not *all*. Well, I was definitely one of the lost ones. And I probably would've had more fun wandering if I wasn't trying so hard to figure out where I was going.

I lived in downtown Chicago that year. With my grandma. The fast lane. She had an open bedroom in a pretty nice apartment not far from some of my friends.

Her balcony perched right across the street from the entrance to the National Weather Commission building—a giant color-changing glass tower of strange, angular shapes—a new building without a spec of nostalgia, except that it seemed to reach back to us from the future.

With an invisible arm, it held a large banner celebrating "Twenty Years of Perfection." It was a big stamp of approval for themselves, a playful little slap on their own behinds. Well-deserved.

All that time and they hadn't missed one raindrop. The last time they had gotten anything wrong was another unforeseen thunderstorm here in Chicago twenty years ago. It had come up suddenly. Hardly anyone was affected. I saw a documentary on the whole perfection thing. They had the one and only Goodman Washington doing the story on his show, *Anchored in Answers*. He sat there with his sharp suit and his black hair straightened and slicked back to no tomorrow, talking with all the grace and force of a powerful river. He asked Jonathan Harvey how they do it. With a cock-eyed smile splitting across his stern face, Harvey said, "There are only so many variables on this planet. It's not infinite. As big as the earth feels, in the end this world is quantifiable. Once you've mapped it all out, directions aren't so hard to come by."

"Then why only a year, if I might ask?" Washington replied.

"Well, we haven't quite mapped out everything. Of course, we have researchers and engineers on the ground and in the sky, even underwater, even in space, working hard to extend the prediction time. I imagine by the time my grandkids have grown up, we'll be forecasting ten years ahead, maybe more."

"Amazing," reeled Goodman. "But Mr. Harvey, how? Please, explain."

"How..." Harvey pondered, gearing up for a look of sudden resolution. "Because, Goodman, we have to. It's our godforsaken duty I tell you. The only appropriate response to our world's quickly changing climate is mastering how to predict it. It may grow more volatile every decade, but we'll always be ten steps ahead."

They kept the whole operation under wraps. They would never tell anyone specifically how they predicted the weather so perfectly, or where all these sensors were, or how exactly they worked. Though they reportedly hoped to one day offer the service to rest of the world, they hadn't managed to expand their geographic coverage outside of the USA. They were in some way a private company, but heavily supported by and connected to the government as a public service. They said they weren't willing to share any information that might help the wrong people get their hands on powerful technology. Top-secret stuff. I would wonder about it as I looked out Grandma's windows at that beautiful National Weather Commission building looming over us.

And then I'd go off to work at a restaurant nice enough to staff real waiters but not nice enough for real tips. Or I'd hop on a train and head to some warm and sunny place for a day. I wasn't doing a whole lot until my dad came up with an idea.

Ned Norman, chairman of the Department of Public Wellness, had been a fraternity brother of my dad's. I knew this, but didn't see myself anywhere near Washington, DC. Not until my dad called me up one day.

"Listen," he said, "Ned's a little bit of a tool, but he's a really nice guy. Maybe a little too nice. Most of what he says is hot garbage, but he's very well connected, and if you work hard, you're going to learn a lot about the world and about yourself. Ned very well may help you get the job you really want down the road. Got it?"

Had it. It was about time I try something, and the old fraternity brothers had an internship set up in no time. A rare opportunity like this could not be passed up, whether I was in any way cut out for the job, or just lucky. April 1—that was the big start date.

THREE

LOOKING BACK, I have to say I find it very strange that I saw Adam on the morning of April 1—the first time I'd ever seen him in person. Granted, it was the first time I had gotten my ass out of bed early enough to see him since living downtown with my grandma.

In fact, I woke up far earlier than I needed to. I was afraid I'd be late to my first day of work, and a pit in my stomach wouldn't let me get back to sleep. I went to the kitchen and noticed my grandma out on the porch with her tea. The sun hadn't risen, but a dim light grew from Lake Michigan and hovered foggily in the air. Her tea steamed into it.

"Morning kid," she said.

"Morning," I mumbled groggily.

"Joining us in the real world today, huh?" she said with a knowing tone, that remembering tone that casts warm hues over everything like old photographs. "Well it'll be fun, and then it won't be, and then it will be, and then it won't, and that will keep going on for about a century. Ready?" She laughed and pulled me in for a hug. I laughed and died a little, leaning over the fourth floor balcony with her as we watched the sleeping city.

Across the street, a night-black Cadillac pulled up to the front door of the National Weather Commission building. The car door slid open, and Adam flowed out in one clean brush of life across the dead early morning. As he walked toward the building the car pulled away, to go wherever cars go after they drop us off to find solace and wait for the master's call.

"Grandma, is that Adam Anderson?"

"Huh?" An unbreakable dead stare.

"Oh my god—that's the guy."

"Honey quiet down!" She bounced whispers off her cupped hand, accidentally dropping her mug off the fourth floor balcony.

The sound of it shattering on the moving part of the sidewalk startled Adam. As the smooth walkway carried the little disaster swiftly away, Adam turned around and looked up at our balcony. I nodded and waved as my grandma covered her eyes and froze. He smiled, then went inside to wake up the world as we knew it.

Grandma had always called herself one of "Adam's apples." I tapped her on the shoulder as Adam disappeared into the building and she cracked to pieces like the mug, shards of memories and reflections on the weather and how things used to be. We sat on the porch for a while. The sun crept toward the horizon's edge and gradually illuminated the expressions on our faces—mine mostly surprise, hers pure nostalgia.

She talked about her outdoor wedding sometime way too long ago, when an unforeseen storm blew up during the ceremony and she got married in the pouring rain. Everyone danced on the beach in their suits and dresses. That's the kind of stuff that just doesn't happen anymore. I mean, you could plan a wedding in the rain, but that kind of crushes the serendipity of it all. But lots of stuff was like that. She used to go to Cubs games at the baseball museum and sometimes they had "rain delays," where you would just wait at the field for hours until it stopped. That was a riot for me. They'd been scheduling baseball seasons around the weather for twenty years by the time I was going to games. Outdoor games when it was nice; indoor games if there was too long of a span without a nice day. It helped that springs and falls were a little warmer than they used to be.

●

Well, it was a ten-minute walk to the slingshot platform and then a twenty-five-minute ride to New York and then another fifteen minutes on a slower train down to DC, which is a pretty long commute if you ask me, and I spent the entire time reading up on Adam Anderson. Seeing him that morning had sparked some curiosity about the weatherman. I had seen him almost constantly for the last five years yet knew almost nothing about him. Lately I had been shutting off his broadcast before he even got into the daily weather, and I almost never made it to the news beat, but I still loved waking up to the quote of the day, and I never understood why so many people opted out of it. I knew Adam simply as the friendly face who delivered another quote to get my brain going and me get out of bed.

What I had never known was how and why he had become that guy. When I asked my PID, it pulled up a Willy Williams segment from a couple years ago. It was the Valentine's Day special, and that year the show had elected Adam as America's sweetheart.

The crowd cheered and whistled as Adam walked out on stage and shook Willy's hand. Willy sat down, licked his palm and ran it through his hair, as he does, and then knocked back a shot of bourbon with Adam, as he does. I tapped the top of my ear a few times to turn up the volume. They toasted and began to chat.

●

TRANSCRIPT EXCERPT: *Tonight Tonight! With Willy Williams*
Ep. 587 - 2/14/2074

Willy: So you've been at this three years now, Adam. We've all gotten very used to you; you, you haven't gotten fired yet. (Laughs.) (Crowd laughs.)

Adam: Well I think maybe people are a little too used to me. At this point, they can't fire me, even if they want to. (Laughs.) (Crowd laughs.)

Willy: Smart. It's kinda like dating somebody—you make it through Valentine's Day, well you probably said some things, and now you can't really break up for a while. Well, we've made it this far with you Adam. Now we're in it for the long haul, like it or not!

Adam: As long as I don't break your heart. (Laughs.) (Crowd cheers.)

Willy: Now hold, hold, hold up, everybody, hold up! Adam, are you telling us you may be quitting? Leaving us? On Valentine's Day of all days!

Adam: (Laughs.) No, no, not at all. I love what I do. They'd have to toss me out kicking and screaming.

Willy: Well I don't think your "apples" are gonna let that happen anytime soon. Have we got any of Adam's apples here tonight? (Crowd cheers. Adam covers eyes.)

Willy: So, Adam—
(Crowd cheers.)

Willy: Enough of this, enough. (Shushes crowd, laughs.) He's already getting way more love than a weatherman is ever supposed to get! Don't give him too much—he'll dump us! (Crowd laughs.)

Willy: Anyway, (laughs), Adam, you are, in my understanding, the youngest weatherman ever hired by the National Weather Commission. You are the most loved weatherman of all time. And of course, you're the only weatherman we've ever had on the show.

Adam: I'm honored.

Willy: Please, we are. You're twenty-six now—so tell us, at twenty-three, how the hell did you land the job? Don't spare the juicy details. We won't judge.
(Crowd laughs, cheers.)
(Adam laughs, shakes head.)

Willy: I'm kidding; I'm kidding. But seriously, how'd you do it?

Adam: It started with an internship. Unpaid.

Willy: Unpaid?

Adam: They weren't hiring, so I offered to work for free.

Willy: That's ... geez, good fucking gracious. That's wild. (Laughs.)

Adam: Some said desperate.

Willy: Not how a blossoming love affair generally begins.

Adam: (laughs) Yeah, I mean, I had just graduated school, and I knew I wanted to be a
weatherman—that's all I wanted to be. So I—

Willy: How'd you know?

Adam: I've always known.

Willy: Really?

Adam: Always.

Willy: Like, *always* always?

Adam: Always and forever, Willy.
(Crowd cheers.)

Willy: A man who knows what he wants! (Slaps
table.) I respect that. Anyway, please, go
on; I interrupted.

Adam: You're fine. So, I had just graduated
school, and they wouldn't hire me, so I said
I wasn't willing to work anywhere else and
that I'd show up every day until they let me
work for free. Except at night—I bartended
at night.

Willy: So they took you?

Adam: For free? Sure they took me. Well,
actually, they ended up creating a volunteer "public service" job for me because
I wouldn't stop showing up. I worked the
lobby of the National Weather Commission
building as a "greeter." (Laughs.) They told
me I had a good smile, so my job was just
to stand there and say hello and answer any
questions visitors might have.

Willy: How did you move up so quickly from
there?

Adam: The head of the commission—Jonathan
Harvey—every day I would see him walk
through the lobby bright and early. I'd say,
"Mr. Harvey, how are you this morning?" He'd
say whatever he said, and then I'd always
say, "Mr. Harvey, I'd like to be considered
for a weatherman position." Every single
day, for a year, and finally—

Willy: He didn't get annoyed?

Adam: Of course he got annoyed! The guy hated
me for a while. I was his nightmare. He
kept going in different doors to avoid me!

But, he could never get away from me for
more than a day or two. (Laughs.) I'd track
him down, all chipper, and say my line, and
he'd say, "I know! I know! You tell me every
damn day. Adam, I know! And the answer is
still no!"
(Crowd laughs.)

Adam: But I thought, "At least he knows my
name." Right?

Willy: (laughs) A year of this? I don't know
how you kept it up. You must have been practically delusional!

Adam: Gotta keep one foot in a fantasy world
to make your dreams come true, right?

Willy: So they say. And others call that crazy.

Adam: Honestly, I kind of was. I just decided,
early on, that every time I failed I would
try to forget entirely, and start fresh the
next morning. Like I was meeting him for
the first time all over again. That was my
outlook. To keep beginning.

Willy: Hey, if it worked it worked!

Adam: It became sort of this weird, annoying, tongue-in-cheek joke between us. Some
days he'd be like, "You really phoned it in
today Adam. More enthusiasm next time." And
finally, one day, just when I was starting
to feel worn down by it all, just when I was
starting to question myself, Harvey comes
down to the lobby and he goes, "Adam, Adam,
we need a new guy. Come upstairs at noon;
you've got an audition."
(Crowd cheers.)
(Willy gets up, high-fives Adam.)

Willy: So that was it? You aced the test?

Adam: Essentially. There were a few...dozen
more tests and statistical studies on my
performance with the audience and so on,
but I didn't pay much attention to that
stuff, and it all worked out.

Willy: (laughs, shakes head) That's an amazing
story.

> **Adam:** I mean, look, we do what we have to do
>   to have what we have to have.
> **Willy:** We do indeed. So, so Adam, to that young
>   kid watching out there who wants to be the
>   weatherman, would you recommend an unpaid
>   lobby boy gig?
> **Adam:** Shh! I don't want anyone taking my job.
>   (Crowd laughs.)
> **Willy:** I think you'll be just fine Adam. We're
>   all in a perfectly happy relationship with
>   our weatherman.

●

And as the crowd cheered and Willy laughed and the camera closed in on Adam smiling, I couldn't tell if he really believed any of it deep down, even at the peak of his popularity.

The slingshot swooshed into the station in New York, and I shuffled out with a clumsy abundance of elderly people, each small step a small step further into their real world. And as I walked between the high buildings toward my next train platform, stuck at a snail's pace behind a coagulation of the slowly dying, I wondered if they really had anything figured out—with their anti-aging treatments and organ regeneration, lobbying for free preventative care and longer youth-spans, as if they had been cheated out of whatever they felt life had promised them and needed decades more to recover it. "Fight aging. Defeat death," the billboard floated above the entrance to the next platform. You see the mantra enough and you start to wonder if the magical powers of science might really beat us to the grave. I'm supposed to be excited, but it scares the shit out of me.

When I arrived at The Department of Public Wellness a few blocks from Capitol Hill, the door into the grandiose white building was locked, and Ned Norman had not yet come out. Great white pillars stretched a good five stories up to an overhanging roof. I attempted to lean against one of them but fell right through it. They were all holograms, which are cheaper than real pillars and never get dirty or wear away. And I'll just tell you, falling down by yourself is really something. I felt like I'd gotten away with a crime, conspiring with inanimate witnesses—trees and grass and bricks—swearing never to tell a soul. Ned stepped out just after I stood up.

"Ken," he beamed with bouncy, rosy cheeks that screamed positivity, "first thing's first: memorize our mission statement. Repeat after me, 'We exist to provide positive stability for the physical, emotional, and social lives of American citizens, through intentional community dialogue and development.'"

"It's Clark," I said, and only spat out the first half of that slippery glob of meaningless words before he cut in energetically.

"Good," he nodded, and his giant bowtie flapped like lazy wings. "Great. Now go at it again, like you mean it."

Public Wellness seemed to be a division of government that was involved in everything and did nothing—the kind of department that a president somewhere along the line had formed in order to get elected with only his own wellness in mind. "Ken," rallied Ned. "It's Ken, right?"

"It's … it's Clark." He seemed so excited about me being Ken I felt like I was apologizing.

"Ah, Clark, right. I'm so sorry. I think your dad told me it was Ken. Is your middle name Ken?"

"I think my dad probably told you Clark … since that's my name."

"Right, of course. Or maybe he was messing with me—that son of bitch. Good old rowdy Ray Bell. Legend. I've got stories. Someday I *won't* tell them to you. Anyway, Ke—Clark, we have the best job in the world. Do you know why?"

"I'm not sure. Why?"

"Because our job is to make people happy. Our job is to make people's lives better, however we can. And you know what else? We can't make people happy … if we're not happy! So c'mon, ranger. We got a brand new printer in the office; you can grab a coffee and whatever you like. The thing makes a mean egg-white spinach wrap, with a garlic pesto I would literally murder a man for, even a good man."

Geez. I didn't print a coffee because caffeine makes my head explode, and I felt like eating the wrap would make me an accomplice to Ned's garlic murder, so just I sat down at a desk and started answering phones. There were three other interns, all young, attractive women, and I had a feeling Ned maybe needed me more than I needed him, to dilute the general sense that he was a wannabe womanizer, however unsuccessful his attempts. The intern who had been assigned directly to Ned had just left, and that's where I fit in.

But I really was excited to be Ned's assistant, because as absurd of a human being as he immediately made himself known to be, apparently he was a big deal. I hated politics, but I guess I was up for trying a job that felt like a big deal, even if Ned was a hell of a lot to deal with. Let me give you an example.

"I've got messages from Sterling Gym Company and LiveRight Fitness," I told Ned. "They're both still wondering if they got the contract on the Public Fitness Expansion Bill."

"Great," he smiled.

"Well, what should I tell them?"

"Thank them both for their interest."

"Oh, did you give it to someone else?"

"Nope."

"So…what should I…who will you give it to?"

"Can we give it to both?"

"I don't know, can we?"

He pet the gnarly dimple on his chin. "Well, no. No, we can't. That's a ridiculous idea, Clark."

"Okay, so what do you think?"

"I think they're both great companies. Fantastic. Terrific."

"But, which one? How do I reply?"

"However you want," he chuckled fatherly, as if doing me a favor.

"Can't you just decide on one and tell me?"

"How about you just decide on one and tell them. Yes, you decide. Tell them I didn't have time to make the decision—that my associates made the decision."

"But I'm just an intern; you're barely even paying me, and I have absolutely no experience."

"Tell both of them I hardly even knew about it, just didn't have the time. Delegated. That's what good politicians do; they delegate."

"Got it."

"Son, don't ever be afraid to delegate." But Ned Norman was afraid, so he delegated his whole life to make everyone and everything else responsible. He turned in his swivel chair, put his feet up, and continued playing solitaire on his PID while dipping his hand, ever so slowly, into a small bowl of carrots, munching and munching so they would never run out and he wouldn't have to face the facts of life after lunch.

You would think this would make being his assistant very easy, but it didn't. Work still needed to get done, and he wasn't doing it. Ned paced back and forth in his extremely fit fifty-five-year-old body, smiled under his vaguely balding but thoroughly repaired head, and shook lots of hands, occasionally kissing asses, whenever he got the chance. He was always leaning back in his healthily-shaped, sitting/standing chair and talking to some politician's head popping out of his wrist, words exploding through his bombastic red cheeks. "N-squared here! What can I do for you friend? Let me guess; you're hoping to bake up something good, but you need some fresh dough. Well, you provide the recipe, and I'll see if I can get you the ingredients. You bring the flavor; I'll do the favor. Throw me your best pitch."

No one ever knew what the hell Ned was talking about, but he controlled a lot of loosely purposed government money, and he had a lot of his own. His philanthropic work and the campaign donations he probably made had gotten him his position at the Department of Public Wellness. Ned came from a family whose old oil money had been invested and multiplied beyond belief into new biotech money. Naturally, politicians liked them, and naturally, they became politicians themselves.

●

By three in the afternoon, I was beginning to get a grasp of the kind of nonsense my job assisting Ned would entail, so the breaking news alert that caught the attention of the whole office only threw me into a deeper state of shock.

Had I still been in Chicago that day, I would've experienced the massive, unexpected storm myself, but I caught the last few minutes of it through a buddy's eyes in a high-rise. He, like just about everyone I knew in Chicago, was live-streaming what he was seeing on his *Fix* profile. The PID connects to the nervous system to interpret visual stimuli, so broadcasting what you're seeing to all your friends is effortless. You can tap your temple to take a photo with your eyes or press down to start recording video. Save as much as you want to the cloud, but if you record everything, you'll have a hell of a lot of material and a tough time finding anything, unless you remembered the date it happened. Well, April 1 was a date to remember.

Sure I'd seen some intense storms roll in from Lake Michigan, but never anything unpredicted or anything stirring up so quickly. The sky looked so black I couldn't see a thing unless my buddy was pressing his eyes right up to the windows. Everyone watching had to keep commenting for him to move closer, to which he said, "I would, but I feel like the window is about to break!"

I had practically the whole office standing behind me watching the storm unfold from my PID, with the projection set to ten feet high. What was even more shocking than the storm was how quickly it disappeared, as if nothing had ever even happened.

But boy did it leave a mark. The short fall from perfect to flawed is a painful one. Mother Nature had pulled a fast one on us. Here we thought we had things under control, but her first unforeseen act in twenty years broke ground like an earthquake. Suddenly we knew we were human, and shook.

We didn't get back to work for the rest of the day. We couldn't stop talking about it. A shockwave of curiosity plowed through popular culture, and before the day was done, the National Weather Commission had Adam making a statement. Adam's hologram stood there in front of us in the center of the office. The "20 Years of Perfection" insignia had disappeared. Adam paused and let the suspense build, folding his hands up to his chin.

Rarely did I see him life-size like this, standing just a few feet in front of me, and with his hands raised I couldn't help but notice his watch. Adam wore a different watch every day—it was his thing. Lots of people collected watches, but very few actually wore them. Well, this one caught my eye. It was a unique, rustic sort of gold, thin and hugging his wrist tightly. Gorgeous, but the hands read seven o'clock. It was only five where I stood, four where Adam was broadcasting.

Adam began to speak with all the sternness of a tragic news report. They had him in sharp black suit, as if he were attending a glamorous black-tie event—or a funeral.

"On behalf of the National Weather Commission, I would like to apologize for our failure to predict the storm in Chicago this afternoon. Thankfully, no one was hurt, and no real damage was done, but we are sincerely sorry for not keeping you informed. We thank you for trusting our forecast, and we guarantee another twenty years of perfect prediction, starting right now. We have top-notch scientists working hard to find out exactly what went wrong with the forecast, and we will get back to you with those answers shortly. Thank you."

FOUR

BUT NO ANSWERS came shortly, or the next day, or the next day. Writers and reporters speculated about what could have happened, but the Weather Commission simply had no answers.

●

N.N.N. *Weather Commission Suspects Digital Terrorism*

CHICAGO - As the National Weather Commission continues to scratch their heads over what could have caused the weather malfunction on April Fools' Day, they're turning their investigation in a new direction. In a statement released earlier today, the commission pointed to digital terror as their best explanation.

We have yet to uncover any errors, even abnormalities, in our weather systems. The surrounding atmospheric conditions of that area on that day provide no indication of how such a storm could have occurred. In the absence of any reasonable chance of miscalculation, we are entertaining the possibility of what we are calling the 'April Fools' prankster' and investigating internally to find out if anyone was tampering with the data. Unpredictable storms are dangerous, and we are taking this one very seriously. We are thankful that no one was hurt, and we are doing everything

*we can to ensure our systems are bullet-
proof going forward, immune to this kind
of reckless digital terrorism.*

Thus far, the National Weather Commission
has suspended fourteen employees on suspi-
cion, but not yet determined any guilty of
misconduct.

Published at 5:05 p.m., April 3, 2076.

●

Well, the Weather Commission was never able to prove anyone had
hacked into its already airtight system, but if someone was messing
with it, they were awfully good, because things only got worse.

●

N.N.N. *City of Boston Sues Weather Commission*

BOSTON - City officials announced they would
be filing a civil lawsuit against the National
Weather Commission this morning after unpredicted
thunderstorms rocked the region last night.

Without such severe weather programmed
into the transportation grid, the system was
unable to adjust for the high winds and heavy
rain that cropped up suddenly and intensified
for over an hour. More than 50 cars crashed,
some sliding into city property. Three people
died, while 8 were seriously hurt. Damage
estimates and reports of emotional trauma
have not yet been released.

With the National Weather Commission's
promise of perfect forecasting falling far
short after just three days, the people of
Boston are angry, demanding reparations and
answers. The Weather Commission has refused
to release a statement thus far.

Published at 7:03 p.m., April 4, 2076.

●

My daily commute to the Department of Public Wellness became a zoo of anxious people breathing like animals as they all read the same articles and watched the same videos on their PIDs. When the doors of the slingshot opened, they would look up at the sky before stepping out. Weather was no longer a predictable thirty-second start to our days, but an issue taking over all of the air-waves, all the time. And by April 6, watching it unfold wasn't even a choice anymore. It seemed Public Emergency Alerts from the government were popping up on our PIDs all the time—so often, I began to feel too overwhelmed to even tap in for the full story.

●

P.E.A. EARTHQUAKES IN SOUTH CAROLINA AND NORTHERN MICHIGAN

Out-of-place earthquakes with magnitudes of 5.4 and 6.2 erupted near Charleston, South Carolina, and Iron Mountain in Northern Michigan. Dozens of structures were dam-aged. Casualties are still being assessed. Scientists are puzzled over seeing earth-quakes in these areas, advising citizens everywhere to be on their guard and remain in earthquake safe environments until fur-ther notice.

4/6/76 - 6:15 a.m. - Public Emergency Alert
U.S. National Safety System

●

P.E.A. TORNADOES IN WESTERN KANSAS

Seven unforeseen tornadoes have been spotted in western Kansas. Citizens living in areas susceptible to tornadoes are advised to stay

prepared to move to the nearest underground
shelter.

4/6/76 - 6:29 a.m. - Public Emergency Alert
U.S. National Safety System

●

P.E.A. *SEVERE THUNDERSTORM WARNING*

Unpredicted thunderstorms are breaking out
randomly across the country. Stay indoors.
Stay alert.
  Tornadoes in Kansas have ceased. Eleven
people are confirmed dead in the wake of fourteen violent tornadoes ranging in intensity.
Twenty-five people are dead in Charleston and
Iron Mountain, where most structures were
not built to withstand earthquakes.

4/6/76 - 7:15 a.m. - Public Emergency Alert
U.S. National Safety System

●

I hobbled into the office on April 6 drenched and shivering. Ned
was waiting for me with his arms crossed. "Clark," he demanded
over the low groan of thunderstorm outside, "first of all, you're
late. More importantly, people want to know what we're going to
do about all this weather. The phones are already ringing off the
hook, but I don't want you to answer any calls. I need you to come
up with a list of fifty ideas as to how the Department of Public
Wellness will respond to these new natural threats and ensure the
well-being of the people of this country.

So I spent the whole morning brainstorming, and at noon I
gave him the list of ideas, some of which I thought were okay, none
of which were used.

After lunch it was sunny again, and Ned told me to start
answering calls with the statement he had landed on. "Here at the
Department of Public Wellness we will continue to ramp up our
fitness expansion bill, offering our nation's beloved citizens more

and better opportunities to relieve the stress caused by unpredict-able weather through healthy physical exertion. There's nothing like a good sweat to alleviate tension and sharpen the mind."

Ned Norman, author of the poetically hefty obesity tax on all public transportation, the man who essentially made fitness our national religion, to the rescue, once again.

●

As I rode the slingshot home that day, Goodman Washington was doing a live segment of *Anchored in Answers*. He was staking out the National Weather Commission building, hoping to surprise someone who knew something, giving them no choice but to tell truth. His cameraman filmed as Goodman stood behind a large pillar by the door, occasionally turning back to say, "Anchored in answers, I'm Goodman Washington. We're live at the National Weather Commission Building, and I'm willing do whatever it takes to uncover the truth."

I must have watched for a solid fifteen minutes while Goodman fidgeted and looked around. He was even more zeroed in than usual, just so ready to get fully and deeply anchored in answers. At one point it began to drizzle. Goodman looked back at the camera shaking his head. "This wasn't in the forecast. This was *not* in the forecast. We're seeing it live. It's pervasive. It's everywhere. It's all the time. They've completely lost it. I won't stand for it any longer." A couple minutes later Jonathan Harvey himself strolled out of the building. Goldmine. Goodman practically tackled him.

"Excuse me Mr. Harvey, Mr. Jonathan Harvey. I'm Goodman Washington and I need some answers right now."

Harvey ignored Goodman and kept walking toward a car waiting for him a few hundred feet away on the busy street. "Mr. Harvey, will you please give me your attention for a min-ute? You're on a live broadcast to fifty million viewers as we speak."

"Shut it down," Harvey yelled back. "You don't have the right."

"You are on public property. You are a public figure. We have every right." Goodman surged ahead of Harvey, trying to block his path as they hustled down the sidewalk. "Do you presently have any idea what's causing these forecasting failures?"

"No," Harvey grunted.

"You're telling me you have absolutely nothing to say?" Goodman glanced back at the camera, indignant.

Harvey stopped for a moment and finally faced him. "Goodman, we're doing the best we can—this, this, this is an incredibly unique display of Mother Nature's power that is baffling everyone in the scientific community, not just us. It's a whole new beast, not something we've dealt with before. There's simply no reasonable explanation for these atmospheric events that are frankly...popping out of nowhere. Understand? Out of thin air, Goodman, literally. So no, I don't have anything to say." Harvey walked onward.

Goodman stomped after him with a sense of righteous rage. "I'm sorry Mr. Harvey, but the people of this nation want answers and they want them *now*. They've experienced destruction, death— they are living in danger in a way we haven't seen in a hundred years. The fact that you are evidently not doing *anything* to put an end to this," Goodman propped himself right in front of Harvey's face and vigorously nodded to the sound of his own words, "it's repulsive."

"Nothing? We are doing absolutely everything we can," Harvey threw up his hands. "You can't possibly understand what this company has done for the last two decades to protect the people of this nation from Mother Nature, and we won't stop damn it! We're rebooting everything. We're checking and re-checking. We're deconstructing every single protocol in practice to find the chink in the armor. And as soon as we do I promise you," Harvey looked into the camera, "and I promise everyone in this country, we'll be even more effective than before, having learned a few things along the way, like how to prevent a previously unstoppable series of anomalies like these."

Harvey marched the last ten steps toward the open door of his car, but Goodman thrust himself in front of it. "We're not done yet, Mr. Harvey. There are human lives at stake, and we need to know how and when you expect to get things back on track."

"All I can say," Harvey took a deep breath of frustration all over Goodman and slowed down, "is that I don't think this will last very long. It's a brief spell, that's all, and we are well on our way to finding exactly what we need—a completely fresh start. That in mind..." Harvey looked down and paused. "That in mind, this is as good a time as any to announce that Adam Anderson will be leaving the broadcast in the coming days. But I promise you'll be even...," Harvey shook his head, searching for the right word, "happier... with a fresh new face."

"Why the sudden change, Mr. Harvey?" Goodman pleaded as Harvey shoved him out of the way.

"You don't quit, do you? Adam and the Weather Commission have simply chosen incongruent paths. That's it. He needs a fresh start. So do we."

Goodman shoved his arm in the doorframe to prevent it from closing. "But what's the reasoning for that? This seems like a horrible time to rock the boat even harder."

The cameraman pressed the lens right against Harvey's window to try to get a clear view as Harvey slapped Goodman's hand away and fired back, "The ship is sinking, and the captain's going down with it. Got it?"

"I'm not sure that I do Mr. Harvey. That's very cryptic."

"Then get a fucking decoder!" Harvey erupted, bits of spit flying into Goodman's face. "The job isn't making him happy anymore, and he's certainly not cheering anyone else up. It's time he moved on. Now get the fuck out of the way and let my car move. This is ridiculous."

Goodman stepped back and the car pulled away. He turned back to the camera, panting with a borderline crazed look in his eyes. "Anchored in answers, I'm Goodman Washington."

●

As I rode the slingshot the next morning, I was relieved to see that nothing major had happened overnight. I had watched the forecast for that day in the morning, and so far it was completely accurate. So instead of news, I found myself catching up on opinion. My thirst for answers could not be quenched. The mystery of it all raged through culture. We weren't used to not knowing what would happen like this. Everyone wanted everyone's opinion, and everything was a possibility. You had rowdy conspiracy theorists claiming the Weather Commission did know these weather events were coming, but chose not to forecast them in order to drum up viewership and ad revenue. Or you had top-level scientists making wild speculations, even the most revered in the country, like conceptual physicist M-Dr. Dobbins.

> When you consider the raw energy needed for these storms to form so quickly out of nowhere like this, there must be an unknown force involved. It could very well be that these anomalies mark the definitive beginning of extra-terrestrial communication with humans. What better way to get our attention? I'm eager to find out what sorts of messages they're hoping to send, and frankly, a little anxious. If these are in fact alien signs, they feel somewhat pushy.

Or you had me—clueless as fuck, freaked out and not afraid to admit it. I was getting ready to get off my train in DC when I saw a miniature Adam suddenly appear on a few dozen wrists, and I looked to my own. He was making an emergency announcement. The Weather Commission itself was beating the government to the warning.

"Excuse me," Adam cleared his throat, struggling to get the first few words out behind wide, blinking eyes. "This is an emergency weather warning. A Category 3 hurricane has formed in the Gulf of Mexico, fifty miles from Naples, Florida. We don't know which direction it's heading, and we're asking everyone near the gulf to prepare for the worst."

I'd never seen Adam so frazzled. In fact, I'd never seen him visibly worried at all. Someone off camera got Adam's attention. He held his finger up to us while he waited for new material. We all held our breaths.

"It, um …," Adam struggled to speak through a choked-up throat. "It appears the hurricane is heading toward Naples rather quickly…" He stumbled back until half of his body wasn't even on the hologram anymore, then covered his mouth as he said, "The hurricane is strengthening rapidly as it gets closer to shore, now well into Category 4..." He stepped off the screen, and he never came back.

We were so glued to our PIDs, watching the hurricane rock the western coast of Florida, we didn't notice what was going on outside our windows. It had been perfectly sunny in the morning, but the air temperature had dropped twenty degrees, and the sky had turned to a solid gray. Ned sent everyone home for the day, worried that it would get worse and we would all get stuck in the office for the night.

When I stepped off the train in Manhattan, the air didn't feel right. It wasn't just cold; there was something deeply unsettling about it. There was a certain energy in the air, a tension I couldn't describe. I only knew that I needed to make my way four blocks to the slingshot platform as quickly as possible, and I wasn't the only person who had this idea. People surged through the streets at unusual speeds, even for New York. Some were flat-out sprinting.

I had only made it a block when the first baseball-sized chunk of hail clobbered a man in the head five feet in front of me. I knelt down to help him up, but he was out cold. I dragged him into a shuttle stop, and so many people crowded in after me, I had to tuck him underneath the bench to keep him from being trampled. Not a minute later the entire glass shelter shattered to bits all over us. Only the unconscious man under the bench was remotely safe—the rest of us joined the mad dash toward the nearest subway station.

Above us the whole sky broke apart like a frosted window and fell down in icy daggers. I sprinted for all I was worth, covering my head with my arms. I was struck several times before hobbling into the subway staircase. Unfortunately it didn't turn out to be any safer underground. When I got to the bottom of the stairs I was pushed flush against the wall by the mob. I looked up the stairs, and chunks of ice weren't the only things tumbling in. People who couldn't hold their footing surfed the crowd of bodies down to the floor. Those who couldn't stay afloat were trampled to death.

●

The following week, Adam never once showed up on the Weather Commission's forecasts, which were simply text banners full of asterisks alluding to the bottom of the screen, which read "*All predictions are uncertain and subject to change due to the current weather forecasting crisis."

The violent storms had taken a break that week, but a cold spell swept over the entirety of the Northeast and Midwest. Spring temperatures dipped into freezing temperatures the day after the hurricane and kept getting colder. Some areas dropped all the way to zero.

Adam broke his silence on an unsuspecting Sunday with a brief hologram posted to his *Fix* page. I saw it an hour after he posted, and the view count had already reached 550 million. He looked into the camera for a few moments—I mean really looked into it—with such a transparency that I found myself looking away, as if the eye contact were uncomfortably real. His eyes seemed to have left something behind, and now listened to everything in search of its replacement.

When he finally spoke, he said, "I'm so sorry about all this weather. I believe I've figured out what's behind it, and I'll be holding a press conference to share my thoughts tomorrow evening."

Immediately after he made the announcement, the cold clouds above me began to fall down as warm rain. My spry old grandma and I took to the streets, letting the rain wash the cold off us, reclaiming the piece of spring we had lost. A breeze blew in the blue sky, and the sun shone down to dry us off. The whole country warmed up, and there wasn't a cloud in the sky for a little while.

Later that afternoon Mother Nature told us how she really felt again. The temperature kept rising, and before we knew it, that cold streak had turned into a hot spell. High winds created dust storms and tornadoes. Earthquakes continued to shake the foundations of this country. I don't think anybody got any sleep that night. By the next afternoon, we'd seen a few dozen more casualties spread across the country, and some people had started to wonder if this was the beginning of the end, some kind of environmental Armageddon.

The press conference was scheduled for seven o'clock. I couldn't find a single station that wasn't broadcasting it, nor did I know anyone who wasn't watching it live. But by half past, Adam still hadn't arrived.

FIVE

WE HAD BEEN ANTICIPATING the press conference all day and I couldn't take the anxious waiting anymore, watching an empty podium while Ned breathed loudly in my general vicinity and Goodman Washington speculated wildly at everyone.

I jumped outside for a swig of fresh air and fell over. I wasn't prepared for sixty mile-per-hour winds and gusts up to one hundred. Tree branches and somebody's hat flew through those holographic pillars as I curled up next to them with some false sense of safety.

A minute after I crawled back inside, the next in a long series of PEAs lit up my PID.

•

P.E.A. *30 FT. WAVES OFF COAST OF NORTHERN CALIFORNIA*

People are advised to stay away from the California Coast between San Francisco and Eureka. Waves are 30 feet and growing. Harbor and coastal home damage is extensive.

4/17/76 - 7:46 p.m. - Public Emergency Alert
U.S. National Safety System

•

Just then, Adam finally walked on stage. It was odd to see a room of reporters go silent instead of chirping up when the man of interest walks in. Goodman Washington welcomed him over-enthusiastically. "Finally, folks, here we have it; the man we've been waiting for. Adam Anderson, we're ready for answers. Begin when you please, but please, begin. Thank you for coming this evening. Anchored in answers, I'm Goodman Washington."

He stood in contemplative silence for a moment, glints of shaky resolution in his bright green eyes. "I'm going to tell you something wild, okay? Okay, okay. I know what's been happening, but more importantly, I know why. The conclusion I've come to is not something you'll... want to accept. It's not something I wanted to accept either. I stayed in denial until very recently. I've gone back and forth on even making the announcement. But I just... I can't bear it any longer. You all deserve to know the reason behind the tragedies—I know that, though I fear what may come of it. So, I'm going to... um... I'm going to tell you a story.

"Alright." He rallied and breathed deeply, looking down, building a false confidence until he could wear it as a mask.

"Growing up, I was always known as the kid who never cries. Whether I got hurt, or picked on, or didn't get what I wanted—I just never felt the need to cry. Never even felt close. The last time I had ever cried was when I was eight years old, on a very painful day. Of course I remember the day well, and it so happens that the moment I began to cry, the Weather Commission experienced a very rare malfunction—a large thunderstorm that came out of nowhere, here in Chicago. I felt the rain myself. Well I stopped crying, and the thunderstorm went away. That failure to forecast, twenty years ago, that was the last time they missed a prediction, that was the beginning of twenty years of perfection... until the next time I cried. For twenty years, I hadn't cried. And until April 1st, I didn't think crying was still possible for me.

"But some tears took me by surprise just before that first forecasting malfunction hit—that thunderstorm in Chicago. I had been reminded, rather suddenly and brutally, of that painful part of my life, and without expecting it, I began to tear up. Before my eyes, I saw the thunderstorm form over lake Michigan and descend on us in a fury. It was terrifying.

"But for me, it was kind of therapeutic to watch, I guess. Before I knew it, I felt good, and the storm was disappearing. I went outside to smell the fresh rain. That made me pretty happy. That was when the skies cleared. I took it as a strange coincidence—the two incidents. I had just gotten fired from the Weather Commission, and I thought the incident was a nice little touch of fate. Poetic bookends to the beginning and ending of a large segment of my life. But I'm here to tell you those tears were just the beginning. I don't know why it's happening again now, but now it's all happening, and there's nothing I can do to stop it."

"Mr. Anderson," Goodman rubbed his forehead, "I'm sorry to interrupt, but we're not here for story-time. We're not here to be poetic. We're here for answers."

"Let's get to the point," an anxious woman in the front of the fidgety pack of reporters echoed Goodman.

"If everyone will just listen, I'll get there as soon as possible. I have to tell you everything I'm telling you." He paused, and it seemed everyone was on board. "So after that, well...I started to feel things. I mean really feel things. In ways I hadn't ever before. Life started to feel more...real, like I had just woken up from a very long sleep. Like I had only been dreaming most of life and I didn't know it. Well now I was starting to feel the pinch, if you know what I mean. I guess I had been set on some things, cemented into a certain way of thinking, and, and, well, it started to crack.

"A few days later, my grandma sent me some pictures from my childhood, photos I had never seen. Some, um, hit me pretty hard. For god sake, I found myself crying like a little kid, like I was making up for years of childhood, making a fool of the kid who never cries. I wouldn't have had it back then, but now, all of a sudden I...I just felt so angry all at once. I'm not going to explain. Nor will I take questions after this. But those are the facts. That's what happened, starting at around 11:30 p.m. I didn't notice the alert about the huge storm over in Boston until it had already been going on for a while, and hearing about it didn't make me feel any better. It was weird. I tried to back off from it."

"Mr. Anderson, exactly what are you trying to say—that you have some sixth sense for weather anomalies?" One reporter belted out from the back, followed by the murmurs of all the others.

"I've asked—"

"We're not here for your sob stories," another reporter broke in.

"Just let me talk," Adam pressed onward. "After that we had the earthquakes. I woke up early to get ready for work that day. When my alarm went off, I had a message waiting for me from my grandma. She's like a mother to me. Well she's been sick for as long as I can remember, and it's always been manageable. But she told me the treatments weren't taking so well. She was finally running out of options. Doctors were telling her to tell anyone she loved that she would only be around for another year at most. Well that shook me. Deep down. Here my life had been pretty easy, and I hadn't thought much about death, but there it was, right in front me. Things got real, real quick.

"Then I heard about the strange earthquakes in Charleston and Northern Michigan. The coincidences—they were too much to bear. I could hardly prepare my report that day. And just as I was freaking about it, all these tornadoes starting forming in Kansas—I was a mess. It was all a blur. I couldn't stop thinking my emotions were causing the weather. By the time I got home, half of me had convinced the other half that I was crazy. And I started to get angry, the kind of anger you feel when you've been lied to, or tricked. I was mad at myself for thinking my emotions actually controlled the weather, because I knew it wasn't true—I was scared I had lost my mind. That frustration, of course, is what created thunderstorms around the nation that day. As the day went on, I slowly convinced myself it was only another coincidence. And as I calmed down, so did the storms. When I had finally relaxed enough fall asleep, they were gone.

"The next morning I walked into the studio, and my boss was...furious. He goes, 'You know you've gotten to be a really bad weatherman, Adam. I should've brought somebody new on weeks ago.' Of course, he had no clue what was going on, but it started to make my mind race again. Before I even got on the air, a hurricane had started forming off of Florida. Now I was really starting to believe it was me. The truth of it all clawed at me, and as I became more anxious, the hurricane strengthened. When they changed the prompt because the hurricane had become a Category 5, I couldn't take it anymore. I left. I couldn't digest any more thoughts about it. I froze up with bitterness, toward myself, toward the whole thing.

"I didn't know at the time that these strange, cold clouds were building high above New York. And then it all fell down. The hailstorm. I am so sorry about that. I am so sorry about all of—"

"Are you actually claiming to be the cause of all this!" a short man interrupted, charged with emotion.

Adam spoke loudly over the chattering crowd, "I'm doing the best I can here. I won't answer questions. I'm making all the information I have available right now. Many of you know what happens next. The cold streak—because I knew it was me, but I couldn't do anything with that. I had gone completely bitter over the whole thing—paralyzed. But when the cold got to Chicago, I was forced to actually feel it, and I started to feel it inside too. One day, I went outside in the cold. I took off my jacket. I let it in. I stood there shivering, and I came to terms with it. I made my post on *Fix* to do this press conference. Finally I had some sort of peace, whether I'm crazy or not. And then it all turned into rain, this weird warm rain. I saw people dancing in the streets, and I was so relieved. Just like that, things cleared up. The rain was evaporating off of the streets in the sun. I dropped my coat and walked to the beach. That was the happiest I'd been in a long time. But then I started to think about this announcement, and I started to worry, and things have been bad out there. But it feels so good to get this off my chest; things should be calming down outside right now."

And they were. I saw it myself. I opened my window. Trees had stopping keeling over. Doors had stopping whistling. As people in the pressroom peered out the windows, they wore that same expression Adam had described, like they were angry after being tricked. Adam tried to keep talking over the murmurs, to keep explaining.

"These last couple weeks have been the most emotional time of my life, and the weather has proven it." The murmurs grew louder as Adam paused. "I know that hundreds of people have died. I feel horrible, and I want to say I'm—"

"What is this?" the angry, short man burst out louder than everyone, stepping up onto the stage next to Adam. "He's a liar!" he yelled to the camera, then turned back to Adam. "How gullible do you think we are? You think just because you're Adam Anderson we'll believe every word you say? We're not stupid. It's probably some scheme you cooked up, some publicity stunt! Some way to let the Weather Commission off easy for this, distract us with your insanity, throw us off their trail. How much are you getting paid for this! You're not fooling anyone, you pompous ass!"

The room was about to explode. Adam had to yell as loud as he could to be heard. "No! No! This is the last thing I wanted to do! Are you kidding? Making this announcement is embarrassing, horrifying. I still wonder if I'm crazy, if I'm hallucinating this whole fucking thing! You don't think I wonder? I knew what would come of this—I knew you would react this way, but I had to do it! It was the only way to relieve my stress and stop all these storms! It was the only way! I did it for you! I did it to ..."

It got so loud, we couldn't hear anything. The short man was toeing up to Adam now, grabbing him by the collar, yelling in his face, hunting for any kind of guilty confession.

Adam was much bigger than the man. He grabbed the man's shoulders to push him out of the way and leave. But the man jumped onto Adam's back, trying to bring him to the ground. Adam nearly fell, but he dumped the man over his head onto the ground. Adam tried to step over the guy, but he grabbed Adam by the feet and brought him tumbling down. The shocked crowd had quieted some, I could hear the man screaming, "My brother died in that hailstorm, hotshot! Explain! You will explain! You will!"

Security was trying to rush in, but was only slowly making their way through the dense crowd closing in on Adam. The man had Adam's neck pinned down with his forearm. "Answer me!"

But Adam kicked and rolled so than now he had the man pinned. He reeled back his fist and smashed him square in the face. Blood squirted out of his nose. The man was out cold. Adam stood up, wobbling around like a kid with his shoes on the wrong feet, as horrified as everyone staring at him.

"Somebody get this guy a doctor," he said, and walked out of the room. He pushed open the glass door so forcefully it slammed against the wall and shattered. The reporters didn't start yelling again until the glass had finished its symphony of tingles, every last note.

They switched back to the press box, where Goodman Washington talked into a microphone over the chaos. "Folks, you've heard what Adam said, but can we believe it? Has he gone insane, like he himself wondered? Until we can get some specialists in here to analyze what we just heard—"

A violent ripping sound scared Goodman out of his chair. Behind him, a giant tree crashed through the ceiling. Shards of wood and building materials exploded across the room, leaving a thick cloud of dust in the air. As it settled, you could see that several people had been crushed. The coverage ended.

The storms in Chicago that night raged on for an hour or so. Everyone wondered if it really was because of Adam's anger, but no one believed it. We needed time.

Six

ADAM BASICALLY WENT INTO HIDING. At first he stayed completely offline, not wanting to even receive any messages. He remained quiet, holed up in his apartment, with his windows tinted and fogged. But on the second day, he dropped a handwritten note out his window via paper airplane. It read, "I need time alone, away from the controversy. I'm keeping a close tab on my emotions and the weather they create."

The more psychiatrists went on the air and tried to analyze and diagnose him, the worse the weather got. The more explanations people proposed, the worse the storms. It wasn't long until Adam began posting exactly how he was feeling to his *Fix* page, often in reaction to the things he would see on the news, and we started to see the same correlations that had convinced this evidently insane man that his emotions controlled the weather. If he said he was angry, immediately after he posted, thunderstorms formed. They varied in intensity, seemingly matched with the same degree of anger he alluded to experiencing. Sometimes he didn't specify, or maybe didn't know, just how frustrated something had made him, but we could tell by the severity and size of the storms. More people began to believe him without admitting it—a "who knows" here, a "you never know" there. Even media outlets started entertaining the idea by interviewing mystics and philosophers who refused to dismiss the possibility, because the scientists and meteorologists had nothing to say.

I imagine these reports were a comfort to Adam, and on the rare occasion that Adam reported feeling generally at peace or happy or even excited, the weather was predictable again. It was exactly as forecasted or sometimes a little better—a few degrees warmer where it was going to be warm, a heat wave taking a breather, some fresh rain where the climate had been too dry, sunny skies where the forecast was partly cloudy.

But the more Adam proved himself able to predict Mother Nature's flare-ups simply by being transparent with his emotions, the more some people thought Adam was simply in on an elaborate plan, collaborating with digital terrorists in a huge, destructive hoax. Politicians were calling on the government to forcibly remove him from his apartment, question him about his knowledge of those working with him, and test him psychologically. But when Adam reported to feeling disgusted or embarrassed by these jabs, we would see an ornery earth wrought with sinkholes, rock slides, and avalanches. And when Adam shook deep down, so did Mother Nature. These things were just too strange for forecasting issues alone.

And he just kept posting. When Adam said he was feeling sad, enormous black clouds wept like babies. When he felt fearful or uncertain or confused or conflicted about his own claims, the wind threw violent fits and tornadoes twisted up towns. When he was angry, lightning like rain lashed out from the sky, whether it was raining or not. Of course, Adam often felt more than one emotion at once, whether he knew it or not, and you'd get a mixed bag of wild weather from unidentifiable feelings, or a big fat hurricane beating its chest and stomping to shore until it wore itself out. Sometimes Adam would post a new feeling, and it intensified or modified whatever weather was already going on. For instance, a low-key mood of sadness would have the skies gray all day, but then Adam would be surprised by something and suddenly they would turn darker and begin to rain or just go away. Mapping out which emotions created which weather was more of an art than a science, and there was a lot of debate. But the longer this went on, the clearer it became: Adam was a force of nature.

Obviously Goodman Washington was on the hunt for some good solid answers, relentlessly seeking out anyone with an inside scoop. The first person he was able to track down was Adam's childhood best friend, Steven Bumpton, outside of the *Fix* building in San Francisco, where Steven held a somewhat coveted programming job.

Goodman introduced Steven to the camera, then leaned into his face. "Do you believe Adam's emotions control the weather?"

Steven tilted back as he thought, letting his chubby belly jiggle into view. He cleared his throat and scrubbed an anxious hand through his knotty hair. "I don't know. I believe there is something strange about Adam. Always has been."

"What's so strange? Give us examples."

"Um, I'm not sure. I actually haven't seen him in a couple years. I haven't really seen much of him since college. What..." he scratched his scruffy beard, looking the other way, "six years ago now. Wow."

"Sounds tough," Goodman pressed, "why is that?"

"No, no reason, just fell out of touch. He lives like an hour away; you know how it is...," he pleaded through forgotten eyes, darting this way and that, "he's been busy. He's had his weather-man job. He's famous."

"What was it, if I may ask, that struck you as strange when you were close with Adam?"

"Well, that's... that's the thing. I never felt 'close' with Adam the way you're saying it. We spent lots of time together—he was a loyal friend, a good friend, just closed off. It always seemed like he was still waiting for his life to begin. Holding back a bit, even in college. Here I was, young and spending all my fun, spending it wherever I could like everyone else. But Adam was saving his energy. Like a runner before a race. Studying for his tests. Staying in shape. Getting good grades. He had this dream since the day I met him when we were seven—he wanted to be a weatherman. He needed to be *the guy*, you know? That never wavered. He never even considered anything else. And I never knew why he wanted to be the weatherman, but he craved it like it was his destiny. I guess it was. He made sure of it."

●

Goodman found Adam's grandmother next. When he knocked on her front door, she replied, "Come back in an hour." So he waited just outside of her front yard in the western suburbs of Chicago for what ended up being two hours. It was a small, government-printed home, but it was quaint and carefully decorated. She had raised Adam there since he was nine years old, and she had grown old there.

Finally she came to the door, politely motioning Goodman inside. She had tea set out between two chairs, where she sat quietly beneath smooth makeup. Neatly styled hair poked out judiciously around a fluttery purple hat. Her dark eyelashes could have poked out an eye. She kept her head high and stable while a flurry of impulses bounced helplessly inside of it. An energetic and well made-up face mediated a woman of few words and many thoughts, which flaked off in blue-eyed blinks and gratuitous sniffles.

"Lilla," Goodman spoke tenderly, "lovely Lilla, we're so sorry to hear about your illness from Adam's announcement, and we wish you well. But tell us, did you ever foresee Adam doing something like this? Saying something like this?"

"The announcement," she paused and thought, "was only surprising because Adam has always been good with his emotions. He was always so strong. And he always chose happiness. My boy is a man of choice."

"But, Lilla, if I might ask, why would Adam choose to do something so crazy like this, to cook up some elaborate plan like this?" His eyebrows crinkled around the sharp edges of his words to soften their blow and keep them warm.

"Only as a last resort. Adam has chosen to overcome very difficult obstacles before. Only as a last resort. Only," she pointed, "if it's the truth."

"The truth…," Goodman pondered. "Lilla, I don't mean to offend or disrespect you, but I'm struggling to stomach that kind of hocus-pocus. It sounds like magic to me. Doesn't it sound like magic to you too?"

"Sure. Then again the whole world is magic to me," she chuckled as she spoke. "The way we live. Each day beginning. I don't know the difference between magic and science anymore. But I'm old. I've witnessed the changes that you were born into, Goodman Washington."

"The world we live in… it's full of possibility. It's an amazing time to be alive. But in the end, it's all explainable. But this, Lilla, how can this be possible?"

"I haven't the slightest clue how it is possible," she began to speak with a wild-eyed conviction, "but have you seen what's happening? Have you opened your eyes and looked outside and really considered the madness we're seeing from Mother Nature? Have you seen what she is doing?" Lilla stared into Goodman's eyes, and with the questions now turned on him, he seemed to have run out of words. He fell into a trance listening to hers. "The clouds, they huff and puff and no they won't quit until they've spat everything out. Every last tear. Until they are black and blue and groaning and lashing out no more. Until it all happens and the earth can breathe again."

Goodman sat silently for a few seconds until he could finally peel his eyes away from her and back to the camera. "Anchored in answers, I'm Goodman Washington." He turned back to Lilla. "That'll be all for now. Thank you so much for your time."

The broadcast ended abruptly.

●

Still, we hadn't heard a peep from Adam. But Goodman Washington was relentless. He devised a plan where he would follow the delivery bot from Adam's favorite restaurant to show up at his loft. The camera crew followed Goodman live as he tailed a drone carrying a pizza through the hallways of an apartment complex. Goodman ran down the hallway to keep up with the drone as it neared Adam's door. This was all very dramatic, and some kind of legal gray area.

When the drone stopped at the door, Goodman grabbed the box of pizza from the drone, and having made its delivery, it flew away. Goodman waited for Adam to come to the door, pizza in hand. He turned his excessively stern face to the camera and whispered raucously, "Reporting live on WBC, diving deep into the heart of the Anderson scandal, anchored in answers, I'm Goodman Washington!" He said "Goodman Washington" like it was a rocket exploding into the sky. Suddenly Adam opened the door. "Oh fuck," he said as he tried to close the door quickly. But before he could, Goodman burst through.

"What are you doing?" Adam was simply dumbfounded as Goodman and his cameraman stood panting in his living room, not sure what to do next.

"I ... I have your pizza, Mr. Anderson. I'm here to deliver it. So sorry to disturb," Goodman offered as he meekly held out the pizza.

Adam took the pizza and opened the lid to give it a look. "Are you sorry Goodman? Are you?"

"Um, no, I'm just—"

"I'm guessing this all happening live?"

"Yes, Mr. Anderson, I'm so—"

"You know this is illegal. I don't know how you even got into the hallway without permission."

"Right, Adam, I'm very sorry to barge in like this—technically I was hired by the restaurant as a delivery supervisor, giving me the right to—"

"I don't care. What do you want?"

"Okay. The truth is, we, the people of this nation, are desperate for answers. We need some face time with you, and we need it now."

"Fair enough."

"Wait ... yes?"

"Sure. What do you want to know?"

"Well, um, wow. Thank you. Okay then." Goodman couldn't hold back a smile breaking up his words. "Okay, where do I begin?"

Adam walked into the kitchen and set the pizza on the counter. He sat at a barstool and started eating. "Sit down," he said. "Have some pizza."

Goodman studied Adam and the pizza, vigilant for any trace of insanity. "I'm quite alright, thank you." He sat on the barstool next to Adam and the cameraman swung around the island to face them. "Well, Adam, thank you for agreeing to this interview on such short notice. It's really a great—"

Adam waved him on. Goodman hesitated, not used to being cut off, but quickly found his stride. "Adam, the last couple weeks have brought more wild and unpredictable weather. But today, the forecasts have been correct. What do you make of that?"

"The last few times I've been very upset were because I paid too much attention to the media. People like ..." Adam squinted at Goodman, shaking his head. He took a bite of pizza and restarted.

"Anyway, most people have started to come around a little bit, and today I decided to stop paying attention to the media completely. I found some peace. Until you showed up, which, was very...surprising," Adam answered honestly with a chuckle. "You should probably check the weather."

"I see." Goodman looked down at his PID for a moment and then smiled like you would at a child. "No alerts yet."

"It takes them a minute to notice it."

"Of course it does." Goodman stared blankly at Adam. "Adam, I think you have wonderful intentions, and I believe that you really do think you're telling the truth, but tell us—"

"You believe I *think* I'm telling the truth?"

"Yes. But are there any other—"

"Out."

Goodman recoiled.

"Just get out please." Adam stood up and motioned his head toward the door.

Goodman walked a few steps and then turned back. "What I'm trying to say is that—"

"Please leave. The longer you stay, the angrier I'll become, and the worse the storms will be. Go."

Goodman hustled past the camera, quickly and quietly reminding it, "Anchored in answers. I'm Goodman Washington!" It followed him out to the hallway and then turned back just in time to see Adam slam the door after saying, "Hunker down."

●

P.E.A. *METEORITES IN NORTH DAKOTA*

Dozens of small meteorites have made land-fall across North Dakota. One parked car was struck. Hundreds of livestock were killed instantly, and several farm fires are ongoing, but no human casualties have been reported. People in the region are encouraged to find their nearest bomb shelter until further notice.

5/3/76 - 6:05 p.m. - Public Emergency Alert
U.S. National Safety System

●

P.E.A. *THUNDERSTORMS IN ARKANSAS AND OKLAHOMA*

Violent thunderstorms covering much of
Arkansas are spreading west across Oklahoma.
Stay off the roads and find secure shelter.

5/3/76 – 6:08 p.m. – Public Emergency Alert
U.S. National Safety System

●

Goodman was still on the air, standing outside of Adam's door, as the alerts pinged his PID. He was shaking his head and blinking as he read them. "Seeing it happen for myself," he looked up, "I don't think I can deny it anymore. I'm starting to wonder if somehow, somehow..."

Seven

THE NEXT DAY the government released a study. They'd been tracking Adam's biochemical state through his PID ever since the press conference, and their measurements had been entirely consistent with the correlation between his negative emotions and the weather anomalies. He had really been feeling what he said he was feeling, and the timing was 100 percent undeniable, down to the very moments these storms would form, intensify, and taper off. I doubt Adam was too happy they'd been hacking into his brain, but he must have felt vindicated. And despite the fact that doing something like that was highly illegal, the government does pretty much whatever the fuck it wants in times of emergency.

And they did. They stationed defense teams around Adam's apartment to let themselves in, to force him to take some drugs. I suppose some guys with guns and a team of doctors shot Adam up with all kinds of happy. They had erased any measurable trace of negative emotion, anything that might create bad weather.

•

N.N.N. The Anderson Affect – *Government Efforts Backfire, Drought Intensifies!*

CHICAGO – As a team of psychiatrists hired by the Department of Homeland Security continues to maintain Adam's complete happiness with a powerful and complex array of drugs, supernaturally strange climate conditions continue to spiral downward.

The DHS has been forced to renege their "simple solution" due to the puzzling effect that Adam's seemingly perfect emotional state has had on the weather.

"We have created conditions where the brain chemistry behind Adam's emotional state mimics exactly the chemistry we measured when Adam was entirely happy—moments when the weather was perfectly predictable and safe," said head of the Emergency Psychological Task Force, world-renowned psychiatrist M-Dr. Martin Scheff. "When the rain first stopped, we thought we were onto something. Obviously that is not the case. We've tried elevating his emotional state to a perfect euphoria, but that has only made conditions much, much worse. We have two or three chemical modifications left to try before we bring Adam back to his original state of mind, and we will be doing them as quickly as humanly possible."

They must move very quickly, as even another day of the devastating drought could bankrupt the nation's water supply. The disappearance of all predicted rain across the country has turned into something much stranger, as lakes and rivers everywhere evaporate at impossible speeds. Water levels in the Great Lakes have lowered three feet in the last hour.

Published at 12:37 p.m., May 7, 2076.

●

In Chicago, I could see the water evaporating from Lake Michigan like rain traveling upward. A heavy mist rose from the water. People kept saying, "It's impossible." And it was, but it was happening anyway.

This only went on for ninety minutes or so before the DHS pulled the plug on the whole brain chemistry operation, and the government set out to find better ways to protect the nation from Adam's wild weather. The basic idea remained; we had to keep him happy.

There were a few storms and mishaps while he adjusted to life without extra chemicals and sorted out his resentment, but the water that had evaporated poured back down in heavy rains, and things improved. They had to take him off every drug that alters your mind and emotions in a really serious way. Adam could only take mild over-the-counter mood-enhancing drugs like X-4, which he already took sometimes, along with X-1 through X-7, like most of us.

The consensus was that Adam needed to be genuinely happy for the atmosphere to remain safe and predictable. Scientists pointed out that there was no clinical difference between happiness with the drugs and happiness without them, but Mother Nature said otherwise.

One group got a lot of media attention. They wanted to kill Adam. They said he was guilty of killing hundreds, and we needed to end his life before he ended thousands more. It made sense.

Then again, it didn't. After seeing what happened with the government's happiness experiment, most people didn't want to mess with Adam at all. They didn't want him killed; they wanted more defense teams assigned to protect him. There were some who felt this way because they felt he was not guilty, as he never intended to hurt anyone. But the majority of people feared that killing Adam would bring on some kind of Armageddon. If Adam's emotions caused this much damage, and the drugs didn't work, we couldn't imagine what his murder might do—how he, or Mother Nature, would haunt us. Some thought the emotions would simply end, and all would be fine, but most people saw this as something far more mysterious. The risk of killing him was just too great, at least for now. There were other ways to keep the weather at bay.

That's when President Douglas Powers called Ned.

●

A thick fog hovered in the air, making all of DC look fuzzy through the conference room windows of the Department of Public Wellness. I never foresaw myself standing in the same room as the president, but Ned needed someone to keep him supplied with his super tea and organize recordings while he had meetings.

Ned and I waited while President Powers used the bathroom—something I somehow never considered presidents doing.

We sat around a big glass table with a number of top-level people and their assistants, from various departments of government and fields of study. Jonathan Harvey leaned back in his chair, staring out the foggy window like there was something to look at. M-Dr. Martin Scheff hunched over the glass table, fogging it up with his breath as he tapped to an inconsistent beat and tried to hold up his viciously old shoulders. He was a maven doctor, making him one letter better than everyone else, an expert of the experts in the field of psychiatry. I had learned about this man in school, both in Psychology 101 and Modern History 101. I had never seen him in person, and it kind of made me wonder if he was already dead. He looked like something out of a comic book—wiry, white hair that sliced the air and formed a thin halo around his shiny, bald head. His hair was connected to a white beard encircling his flimsy, purple-red mouth. His large glasses constantly tried to slide off his molten face. His thin-ish body seemed to be entirely made up of some anonymous, soft flesh that only wildly old people get to have, something even he couldn't explain. He was 121 years old. Holy fuck.

President Powers burst through the door like an exploding trophy. He wore a black suit laced with gold all over, gold in places it had no business being—gold thread connecting all the seams of the jacket, gold buttons, gold pocket panels, a gold coat lining, a gold stripe paving down each pant leg like a satin tuxedo stripe, and a gold goddamn collar, and it was all actual gold. It must have been a heavy suit—a terrifically, tremendously heavy suit. His pale white face burst out of it red and roaring like the fires of hell.

We all rose, or tried. "Sit down," he barked, and immediately waved us back into our seats. "We're getting to work. I have protesters piling up in front of the White House, demanding something be done. You're all here because you're part of a special task force I'm assembling to keep Adam Anderson happy, and in doing so, keep our nation safe."

He asked M-Dr. Scheff to lead off the meeting with his thoughts on Adam. Scheff began to speak about his confidence in the immediate relief Adam would feel once a solid plan for his

happiness was in place. Powers firmly nodded his stern face as gold
hair celebrated all around it, cheering him on no matter which way
his head was moving. He listened intently with the kind of dead-set
eyes and ever-adjusting mouth that rip the words out of you before
you say them.

"Jonathan," M-Dr. Scheff stopped and wondered, "if I might
ask, do you know exactly what triggered Adam's initial emotional
outburst? In his announcement, he mentioned having been fired
just before the first storm, and we know he was in your office."

"Yes, I watched the whole thing happen," Harvey admitted
while he cleared his throat and looked around at everyone. "But,
no, I have no idea what triggered it. Adam's a mystery, maybe even
a basket case I'm afraid. He had been sinking into a strange, careless depression for months, with no awareness of his own state
at all. We had a hard discussion, but he seemed just as content
to quit doing the weather as he was to keep doing it. He said he
didn't care."

"I see. It's no matter what triggered it. What matters is what's
triggered. I am certain that something, something very deep-seated,
something he has been avoiding and repressing, has come back to
the surface. I know he mostly grew up with his grandmother, but
I'd like to know more about that history. I have on medical record
here that his mother died in an accident before Adam could even
remember, and that his father—well, there's nothing substantive
about his father really. A veteran with no psychological or physical
injury, and then a career pharmaceutical researcher. Seems to have
been a perfectly standard citizen until his disappearance, which I
would like to know more about."

"We've looked into Paul Anderson," a woman from the NSA
spoke up, "but we haven't been able to find anything conclusive
about his disappearance, or anything at all. No record of death,
imprisonment, re-identification, emigration, or even any kind of
police report regarding his sudden absence. He simply fell off the
map. No explanation. I haven't see a case like this one … ever."

"Curious," said M-Dr. Scheff. "Please, keep searching. Alert
me to anything you find."

"But why drive down a dark road?" Harvey postured thought-
fully. "Who knows what you'll find. I know Adam very well, and

he's at peace with his father's disappearance. It's not really a big deal to him, not anymore. Why make it one? He's never even talked about it."

"You know him very well, and he has never talked about it?" Scheff wondered out loud.

"Exactly," Harvey reassured.

"Then I can assure you Adam is not at peace with it, because—pardon my French, Jonathan—it's a big fucking deal."

"Hmm." President Powers paused. "But Martin, regardless—Jonathan has a point. Is this really a can of worms we want to open for Adam?"

"It would certainly be messy, but yes, I think finding concrete answers would be worthwhile, whether just for us or for him as well, depending on whether the answers would help Adam deal with his issues and become a happier person or not."

"A messy situation is by no means worthwhile on my watch," President Powers responded. "We've got a big enough mess on our hands. It's time to clean up."

"But...how? You must understand," rattled M-Dr. Scheff, "I'm sure I can help Adam. I've studied endlessly to help—but I'll have to bring out the pain before I can really make him happy."

"Oh, oh my. No, that's not going to work." President Powers stammered. "Don't break him. Fix him."

"Mr. President, if I may—the heavy drugs failed for a reason. Human emotion remains one of the great mysteries of modern science. It is not like modern medicine. You cannot simply inject someone with happiness, or kill a person's loneliness like a virus. These things are not independent entities in the brain; they are more like the nervous system of the conscious mind. They are a vitally connected aspect of consciousness we do not fully understand."

"Nervous system of the—what the fuck are you trying to say Martin? Let's stay grounded here."

"Think of it this way—you can ask your PID amazing questions, right? How many steps you've taken in the last ten years, what percentage of sleep you spent last night in REM, blood counts, levels of nutrients. You can even ask about stress and pleasure levels in the brain. But you cannot ask your PID, 'Am I happy?' You cannot ask it what happiness really is. You cannot ask why you feel unfulfilled despite feeling pleasure. You cannot ask it to tell you about your self-worth, or your guilt, or what you truly want. You cannot ask it if you're lonely, or bitter, or ashamed, or longing, or what levels of joy and sadness and anger are all battling within you. And you can never ask why. It doesn't know. Emotions are not so empirical. Sometimes, the only way to deal with them is the old fashioned way. To dig into their roots. Adam needs therapy."

"Well," President Powers raised his hand to his chin, "I can't let you make him sad. Actually, you would get in big trouble for that."

"But the longer Adam avoids these feelings, the stronger they will become. We have to deal with these things now, while they're fresh, or they may grow, unchecked and unhindered, into monsters."

"I'm already trying to tame the monsters. I'm not about to willingly release them into my country to wreak havoc until they get tired. This is a very unique situation, Martin. I brought you on to help with a very unique solution. We're going to keep the monsters at bay. We can't afford to deal with them now, or ever. Just do what I said. Keep him happy. No more storms. No more destruction. Don't ask him all those weird personal questions and try to make him cry it out or something. Yuck. If you make him sad, and someone dies, you'll wind up in the slammer. Mark my words."

"Then... what do I do?"

"You tell me. You're the big psychiatrist. Find ways to keep him happy without making him sad first. Is that so much to ask? Happiness is a choice. We all know that. I choose it every day," he said simply, though I hadn't seen him genuinely smile since the election.

Scheff cleared a throat that had been vegan since 1990, thoroughly jostling a body that had been thoroughly old since 2030, like a tornado hitting an old barn that just won't fall down. "I'll... see what I can do."

●

A few days later I found myself sitting behind a press stage on The White House lawn next to Ned, while President Powers took the podium to address the nation.

"My American friends, from the outset of this great nation, we have believed in life, liberty, and the pursuit of happiness. We are all entitled to these rights. Adam is no different, except that for some strange reason, his happiness seems to determine our safety, and in turn, our happiness. For that reason, I am commissioning the Pursuit of Happiness Project. The Department of Public Wellness, in cooperation with the Department of Homeland Security, will give their full attention to this new task force. Members of my cabinet and I will oversee operations. The sole mission is to keep Adam Anderson happy at all times. We will go to great lengths. We will reach great heights. We will do anything and everything to make this man happy and keep him happy. We have great expectations for what's to come, as does Adam, as you might imagine." Douglas looked over at Adam and apparently blessed him with a grandfatherly nod of teasing approval, chuckling out loud.

"We have full confidence in our team. My longtime close friend and trusted colleague, Ned Norman, chairman of the Department of Public Wellness, will be in charge of running the Pursuit of Happiness Project on the ground, taking all of Adam's requests, watching out for Adam's well-being day in and day out, with virtually unlimited resources at his disposal. Ned continually upholds the kind of winning attitude that will keep Adam on the up and up. Adam's safety, therefore your safety, will be in the hands of an extensive defense team dedicated solely to protecting Adam from any and all threats.

"All aspects of the project will be overseen by experts in their fields. Most notably, world renowned psychiatrist M-Dr. Martin Scheff has signed on to the project and will be consulting the entire task force in the interest of Adam's personal happiness.

"From this point forward, matters of the Pursuit of Happiness Project will be private. This is in accordance with Adam's wishes. Any member of the media or private citizen caught spying Adam or the Pursuit of Happiness Project will be arrested and punished. We will never inhibit your freedom of speech in speculation, but any media outlet broadcasting unapproved footage or maintaining unverified facts will be punished even more severely.

"Together, as the Pursuit of Happiness Project task force, we're eager to bring in the bright future. We may have experienced some April showers, but we are headed securely toward May flowers. A chance has fallen into Adam's lap, one that has first brought destruction, but will soon usher in perfection. A chance to become the true embodiment of this notion we proudly call the American Dream. Forget the good life, Adam; we'll give you the perfect life. You don't have to dream anymore; paradise knocks at your door. My American friends, Adam Anderson will so happy, so consistently, that our weather will be better than our forecasts, better than ever. Thank you."

A crowd of press and government officials cheered incessantly and President Powers absorbed it all into the cracks of the wrinkles doctors couldn't quite keep off of his face. He shook Adam's hand and then leaned back toward the podium. "My fellow Americans, I'd like to make good on my promise right now. Let's hear Adam's first request. Adam?"

Adam strolled out from the side of the stage, smiling a little sheepishly as the crowd cheered.

"Well, first, I just want to say sorry for the storms that have already affected so many people. I'm terribly sorry. But I'm grateful to have the problem more under control, and for the Pursuit of Happiness Project. And listen, I know the old adage: money can't buy happiness. I know that. But I have a feeling it can be pretty entertaining while I'm searching for it," Adam grinned. "And, god, do I love my country."

"You and me both, Adam," Douglas said as he smiled. "So go ahead, what would you like? Anything you want is yours."

"Anything?" he sincerely asked.

"Anything."

"Is anything off limits?"

"For you, Adam," Powers looked at him, "there are no limits."

"Well," Adam looked pensive, "I'd like a new place in Chicago. I know just the one I want. I've dreamed of living of there. To be honest, it's extremely expensive."

"Well we have a lot of money. Consider it done," President Powers nodded, unfazed.

"You can do better than that!" A giddy reporter in the back shouted. Adam laughed and looked up while he thought. "Go big!" the reporter egged him on.

"I mean, I like Miami a lot. I suppose a nice room at the Raleigh wouldn't be so bad while the movers set me up at my new place." Adam looked to Douglas as if asking permission, not realizing how powerful he had become by the end of the speech.

"Of course," he nodded vigorously again, "we'll get you the very best room, and the biggest, for as long you like."

"Wow, thank you." Adam laughed. "This is incredible. I wouldn't mind inviting some friends down to kick off the project. I mean, can we rent out the entire hotel?"

"Say the word and it's already done." Douglas looked over the crowd, probably hoping Adam wouldn't say the word, and smiling for a little too long as he and Adam awkwardly stood next to each other.

"Okay, I guess we'll do that then. Oh, and how about a yacht anchored just off shore. That'd be nice, so," he looked around at the laughing crowd—a little shy, a little proud—like he had gotten away with a bank robbery, "we'll add that on too. Why not?" Adam looked at the president, pinching himself. "Thank you so much."

"Don't thank me," he said plainly as it dawned on him just how expensive this project could become. "Thank the taxpayers."

I swear Adam could've killed a man, looked around, and everyone would've been smiling and clapping and throwing their own damn heads on the chopping block asking who's next. For Adam, and for President Powers, there was really only one sin—unhappiness. Because when Adam wasn't happy, nobody was.

So, guns blazing, crowd cheering, unlimited funds at his disposal, and absolutely no rulebook to follow, Adam set out looking for happiness. And yours truly, the lowly new assistant to Adam's new glorified assistant, got to go along for the ride.

EIGHT

A FEW DAYS LATER, Ned called Adam while the limo hummed gently in front of his new building, the old John Hancock building. The tall tower seemed to undulate between old and new. The original Hancock rose as the center stake, but the tower had been built out on either side with much lighter and stronger metals, both supporting the old building and adding to it a supreme modernity, a jagged harmony of dramatic transitions. These kinds of buildings were a growing trend.

Adam's face popped up on Ned's PID, "Hey Ned. I'm not quite ready yet. Come on up and see the place."

In the elevator I pressed "P" and felt like a prince perched above a hundred little numbers. We waited a few seconds until Adam allowed a light to turn from red to green, and suddenly we were rising so fast I thought my head might fall out my ass. The doors opened in a private foyer, where a giant mirror greeted us with our own clumsy reflections. Mine told me to get a haircut, and Ned's just smiled like an idiot.

Two military guards waved us through the door. I pushed it open slowly. "Mr. Anderson?" said Ned. "Mr. Anderson?"

"Just a minute," Adam replied from a bedroom. "Have a drink, explore. I'm just trying to find a few things to pack." Through the open door I could see him rifling through boxes of stuff. There were moving boxes all over the place, and a few workers were helping to unpack them.

"Great thanks thank you thankyousomuch," Ned blurted through a smile. "Take your time," he chuckled. "Take your time Mr. Anderson!"

Ned moved to the kitchen and began worrying and laughing out loud, like a tight string that had been plucked and wouldn't stop vibrating. He looked down at his PID. "Well," he wobbled, "it doesn't say I'm thirsty or hungry, so I, well, what the heck—gotta live a little sometimes, right?"

"Sure," I said. I had never seen Ned eat or drink without direct permission from his PID, reporting based on his body chemistry. He even followed the PID's suggestions on what to eat. That's why Ned looks like a wrinkly twenty-five-year-old.

Ned bustled through the cabinets and knocked over a glass but managed to catch it. "Should we get a drink? We'll get a drink. What should we have? Too early for 'drinks' drinks. Right?"

"Um...," I shook my head and forgot to continue speaking. I wandered off, strolling between moving boxes as I cautiously looked around the enormous loft.

"Can I help you find something, Mr. Anderson?" The woman in charge of the move stood at his door, scrolling through a list emerging from her PID.

"No, no, that's alright. It's in one of these boxes, just need to keep opening them."

"We have everything catalogued. I could look it up right now if you tell me what you're looking for."

"I'm good. I'll find it myself. Thanks. Why don't you guys take a break until I do; you've worked hard." Adam walked out of his room and started opening stacks of boxes in the sunken den. He noticed me standing across the vast main living space of the loft and looked up. "Welcome! I'll be with you guys in a minute. Check out the views."

"Hi," I said, awkwardly waving. I ambled around the space as Adam continued his search. In the corner of that room Adam had his own 3-D printer, and not just your run-of-the-mill Walmart wannabe. I walked up to it and gave it my bowtie, which Ned had given it to me earlier that day in attempt to craft my appearance to his liking. The printer broke down the tie and told me what else it could create for me with those molecules. I selected a beanie with a blue paisley design. I put it on, still warm, and began exploring the massive penthouse.

The loft sat atop what used to be the roof of the Hancock building. It was a modern addition, like a fancy new hat on an old man's head. They had left the two giant old white antennas intact, which rose from the floor up through the high ceiling like support beams. One had been hollowed out and turned into a fireplace in the sunken den. And if that wasn't enough to warm such a cold antique, cozier relics wandered about the space—hand-carved wooden furniture, old lamps that glowed like open treasure chests, marble statues of ancient heroes, and a rustic dining table big enough to seat about thirty people. There was a working record player in front of a whole shelved wall of classic albums, most of them over one hundred years old, all in mint condition. Adam had an old Simon & Garfunkel album singing songs warm and scratchy, singing just the right song it seemed. *"Oh I can gather all the news I need on the weather report. Hey, I've got nothing to do today but smile. Do-n-do-da-n-do-da-n-do, and here I am, the only living boy in New York..."* I kept listening while I looked through the other albums. Across the room I could see Adam humming the song as he rifled through boxes. *"...Half of the time we're gone but we don't know where, and we don't know where. Tom, get your plane right on time. I know that you've been eager to fly now. Hey, let your honesty shine, shine, shine..."*

The song went on and the words *"Here I am"* kept echoing in my ears like a distant dream, slowly fading as I ventured away from the record player. I headed down a hallway that ran against a wall of windows above the city, where the glass floor beneath me, extending a few feet out from the building, meant I was walking through the sky. It took me to an oaky office that looked like it belonged to some CEO in the 1960s, complete with a spin-dial phone and humidor. It seemed every room was either a nostalgic reach into the past, or a bright present pregnant with the future. The place had a dozen decades living in it at once, because our time had not its own identity, but borrowed from dreams and memories.

I stepped gently down another entirely glass hallway lined with watery walls and floors, where giant bubbles floating to the top occasionally spanked the colorful fish swimming between them. Surprised to not break through the glass like thin ice, I passed by several guest bedrooms and eventually washed ashore on red shag carpet as unsettling as quicksand. It filled the floor of a spacious holotheater, one where the characters could play out their stories all around you. It was dark, and I couldn't find the lights. I squeezed my fist three times to activate the flashlight feature from my PID, and kept squeezing until the light was shining full blast, which you're not supposed to do because it drains energy from your PID faster than your body can replenish it, eventually causing the PID to sleep, if only for a few minutes. But that's exactly why I abuse the feature.

The light illuminated more boxes and racks upon racks of hanging clothing, outfits of every kind that designers had given Adam over the years to wear on the broadcast or promote on *Fix*. The clothes represented practically every time period since the twenties, and they were all in style.

But as I thumbed through the endless fashions in the silent room, I began to hear a soft pitter-patter like a billion ants marching. I turned and held my breath to get a better listen. The strange chatter grew louder in my ears. It drew me toward an unopened box as high as my chest, squatting there in the shag carpet. I put my ear right up to the side of it and listened to what sounded like an aluminum rainstorm striking a plane of glass. I shined my light on the top of the box, wondering what the hell could be in there. I knew shouldn't open it, but that sound—that overwhelming high-pitched sound—it drove me to insanity in seconds. I tore open the box.

Hundreds of timepieces were piled high in little glass cases, indiscriminately filling the box to the brim—wristwatches, pocket watches, old watches, new watches, watches that looked rare and expensive. My flashlight shimmered off the metal and glass, bouncing in all directions like light off a disco ball, and hypnotizing me to the impossibly fast beat of all those little hands. My gaze was met by hundreds of faces staring back at mine, whispering with ticks and tocks, waving their tiny hands, all trying to tell me one thing—time was passing. I felt millions of seconds moving all at once, and I had never felt more helpless to their unforgiving speed. They would never stop, never even slow down. They would keep running around those clocks and disappearing. And where do they go? I would never see them again, never find them, never catch up and never catch them.

But in the corner of the box, something stole my attention—a wooden lockbox, hiding something away. It must have been due to the move that the brass key was already plugged into the lock, not wanting to lose it. All I had to do was turn it.

Resting on red velvet was a watch I recognized. The worn leather, the weathered golden face—I had noticed this watch on the broadcast that day Adam apologized after the first storm. I gently picked it up, and when I did, I uncovered a small handwritten note, folded up and worn at the edges.

Dear Adam,

Remember me in those rare moments I was at my best. Take my watch and never lose it, because it doesn't count the days or the years. It can't see more than twelve hours ahead, but it keeps on ticking just the same. It never runs out of beginnings so long as it does not run out of time. Keep it with you. Keep beginning. I will see you again, in time.

Love,
Dad

P.S. Don't bother trying to become a weatherman. It's just too predictable. There's no fun in that. Do what makes you happy. Aim for the stars kid, because if you miss you'll land on a—never mind, they're only vapor. Don't miss.

But when I looked closer at the watch I noticed it still read seven o'clock. Its golden arms had stopped above its golden face, where the fine engraving of a lion's head stared past them as if through prison bars. Maybe it had run out of time just after some golden sunrise, or maybe just before a glorious sunset, but was forever frozen either way. It did not tick anymore. It did not tock. It remained still, always waiting for seven o'clock to come around. As my light dimmed, the shadows made that lion look sad, like he could hear the sound of time striking, swift as ever, and retreating with him into the darkness.

Suddenly I heard footsteps coming closer from down the hallway. I put away the watch and the note and I shut the box. But my PID shut down; my light shut off. Now I couldn't find the key. It had fallen out somewhere. I ran my hands through the thick carpet as the footsteps drew nearer.

The lights came on. I was still ducking behind the box searching for the key. It was nowhere in sight. I stood up.

"What are you doing?" Adam stared, every bit as alarmed as me.

"I was just... exploring."

"In the dark? Where did you find that?"

I looked down; I was still holding the box. "I, I couldn't find the light. I had my flashlight on. I mean, well it ran out of juice. I was just noticing all these watches."

"But why do you have that box? I've been looking for it."

"I don't know. I'm sorry; it was with all the watches here. I just—"

"Who put that there? That shouldn't be in there. Did you open it?"

"It's locked," I said without thinking.

Adam reached out. I handed him the box. He tried to open it but he couldn't. Thank god it had self-locked when I shut it. "Where's the key?" he asked.

"I don't know." It was a relief to tell the truth.

He looked into the giant box of watches and found it lodged between two cases. "Geez," he muttered, and slipped the key into his pocket.

"Quite the collection you have," I said, trying to ease the tension.

"Yeah," he barely replied. "Thanks."

"I've noticed these watches on the weather—so unique."

He nodded and, rubbing his chin, walked away with his locked box of time. I was sure that he hated me, that I had caused some catastrophic weather event, and that I would be fired as soon as I emerged from the room, where I watched the time pass as my breathing slowed down. Suddenly my PID lit back up with an alert. "Dramatic rise in stress hormones! Send emergency medical services or law enforcement?"

Of the options it presented me, I selected "neither." I walked out of the room, down a few hallways, and through the main area without looking at anyone. I stepped onto the massive porch, where the building's other white antenna reached into the sky, half plugged into a wall behind the hot tub. I walked past a powerful telescope to the edge of this urban perch. Only a thin glass wall kept me from joining one thousand feet falling below me. A stiff breeze ran up the side of the building and rushed across my face. I looked out, squinting. A garden of silver and shine angled and curled up in all directions, continually outdoing itself, intermingling with shorter older buildings. It pulled my eyes in a frenzy of directions. The blinding sun gleamed from hundreds of sharp faces, ricocheting about the city. The buildings nearly brimmed over into Lake Michigan, which spread its bright blue body over the entire eastern horizon unapologetically.

A rectangular skyscraper with a square cutout in its center sat right across the street, facing the balcony. From the top of the square hole, a massive poster hung. A giant display of Adam's face in uproarious laughter made up most of it, and next to his face was a regal key, painted like the City of Chicago's flag, and shaped like its skyline. Above the key, the word "Adam" beckoned. Below the key rang out a simple plea in proud letters. "Enjoy!"

"What's your name?" Adam stuck out his hand, smiling in a small but real way. I had been lost in thought, and suddenly there he was standing next to me, like he had jumped right out of the poster. Ned tootled indecisively out the porch door toward us.

"I'm Adam," I said. "I mean, I'm Clark, sorry." He laughed it off. When you've always known someone as a hologram, shaking his actual hand doesn't feel real. He had for so long been a fixed image in my mind. Meeting him felt like talking to a moving statue. How he could move without crumbling, I do not know. He nodded at my silence and waited for some words, not feeling the need to say anything. I think he was used to this. "Nice to meet you," I said. "I'm Ned's assistant."

"Great to meet you too," he smiled. "Happy to have you along." He didn't seem to remember the awkward moment we had endured just a few minutes before. He had already pushed so far beyond it you couldn't see it in the rearview mirror or even know if it had ever really happened. He had an impressive power either to let go or to ignore, though I wasn't sure which, or what the difference was, or whether he had simply learned to keep up with time.

"Nice poster," I said.

"Wild, right?" he echoed. "Kind of embarrassing, but I can't complain."

"It looks like it's even real too," I mentioned. "Like it's real material—not a hologram. Look at how it sways and flaps in the breeze."

"Oh, wow." He peered across at it. "I hadn't even noticed that. How strange."

"Pretty cool though," I said. "They went all out for you."

"Right, but it will wear away eventually, especially in the winds way up here."

"I'm sure they'll replace it when it does," Ned beamed. "You've got the key to city now! Key to the whole country if you ask me." Ned reached out for a fist bump. Adam didn't really know what to do, but nodded, and eventually gave it to him.

●

P.E.A. EARTHQUAKE WARNING IN CALIFORNIA

Highly unusual seismic activity has been reported all along the San Andreas Fault. All Californians are advised to prepare for a major earthquake.

5/15/76 - 10:35 a.m. - Public Emergency Alert
U.S. National Safety System

●

Ned and I saw the alert at the same time. We didn't tell Adam what it was, and he didn't ask. We just silently hoped nothing would happen and went on chatting with Adam in his current happy-go-lucky demeanor.

Traffic stopped for over an hour across California. People ducked in doorframes and hit the ground in parks. Buildings were evacuated. But nothing ever happened. People went on living their lives, a little more fearful than before, but a little happier to be alive.

Adam's PID was now specifically programmed not to receive any kind of weather or news updates, even the government emergency alerts that couldn't be disabled. So he would never know what catastrophe had tucked itself back into the vacuous darkness inside of him to go back to sleep. It was better that way. They couldn't risk upsetting him. Adam wouldn't even be receiving any alerts from his PID about his own health and safety—they would keep tabs on that, and everything else, for him.

NINE

NO ONE IN MY GENERATION had the chance to see Venice, Italy before it sank. Miami, however, was only half underwater. So it was considered the world's new Venice. Coastal cities across America had each responded a bit differently to the rising sea levels and storm surges of global warming. Small towns were slowly abandoned and cleared away as water moved inland. But big cities, like Manhattan, built walls and levy systems all around their shores.

Miami, which relies so heavily on tourism, took advantage of the rising ocean, even welcomed it. They built up infrastructures to channel the water through the streets of South Beach and preserve the buildings in it, flooding themselves slowly, before nature could do any damage. The streets became canals, and most of the old art deco architecture was preserved and expanded.

We floated down the canals in a fancy water taxi, discreetly passing between the old hotels and the people walking on sidewalk docks. When we pulled into the Raleigh, most of the friends Adam had invited were already there, indefinitely excused from work and flown down by the Pursuit of Happiness Project. They were fulfilling their American duties as they reclined on giant, man-made lily pads, which sauntered about in the calm of the sea walls like floating beaches. We waltzed straight through the empty lobby, barely absorbing all its antique glory as we headed out back to the ocean. A swarm of hotel workers at the docks, with no one else to help, shook Adam's hand and smiled. "Anything you need, Mr. Anderson, just ask." They set us up with little personal jet boats and pointed out all of the lily pads they owned.

"Come on out with me and meet some of my friends." Adam motioned for us to follow as he started up his engine, and the three of us glided swiftly toward a floating island full of people so beautiful they made me nervous from hundreds of feet away. I could hear the music growing louder as we drew closer. I could see the cocktail waiters dancing with trays of tropical drinks and the people in swimsuits jumping in and out of the water. I could see the sun striking the ripples on the water, and I could feel it pouring over me. I could see Adam smiling as he glanced back from his boat in front of me before speeding ahead. And I could see fluffy white clouds stacked up at the end of the horizon like mountains, bound to turn gold before the day was done.

Adam landed his boat along the soft shoreline with some speed and hopped off to a gathering of fifteen or twenty friends shouting and hugging and spilling their drinks all over each other.

I found myself rolling up the pants of my suit and wandering along the squishy green shore, trying to keep my distance from Ned as usual, but also not ready to intrude on this new group. They were a few drinks ahead of me and a few notches above my social pay-grade. I looked at the bubbling crowd and watched *Fix* match the faces with their profiles on my PID, each of their first names and their numbers popping up over their heads. Everyone seemed to have a social influence number of eight or nine, except for Adam, who had, in recent weeks, been catapulted to an extremely rare ten. There were a few more women than men, all soaring through their twenties or thirties with self-expressive jobs: a popular editorialist, a model, an actress, a music producer, a couple other weather broadcasters, people in fashion, people in entertainment, an ad executive, an entrepreneur or two. I didn't recognize any of them except for Steven, Adam's childhood best friend, another average three like me, who normally had to pay for things instead of just getting them shipped to him for free by advertisers, and that was comforting. He stood on the edge of the crowd looking in, holding his scruffy face like it might fall off.

I became distracted by the enormous cargo and cruise ships in the distance, and stared out to sea until I felt a tap on the shoulder. It was Adam. "Hey," he said, "come say hello."

As I strolled into the group with Adam and Ned in my suit, I felt like an ill-equipped chaperone, no more mature than kids, getting ready to blindly turn my head at a whole lot of misbehavior.

This was a happy crowd, and if happiness was the purpose of all this, I didn't see a random low-level government employee fitting into the equation. Yet there I was. Ned moved from person to person, vigorously introducing himself with a handshake that squeezed too tight and lasted too long. "Hi, Ned Norman, running the project for Mr. Anderson. Call me Ned," he repeated ten too many times.

As I made basic small talk, I began to realize none of these amazing people had known Adam for more than a couple years, or had really spent that much time with him. They were people he met along the way after becoming "the" weatherman. They were party people. They seemed like really good people; they just didn't seem very close to Adam. I think he preferred it that way. He surrounded himself with busy, beautiful people with too much to worry about to ever dig deep into his life. Many of them had gotten the works in the womb—athleticism, facial symmetry, intelligence, creativity. Everything everyone wants; everything money can buy. But I can always tell, because even though these people seem perfect in so many ways, the ways don't always work so perfectly together, and many of them end up with an oddity what wasn't engineered. Scientists are still figuring it all out, and sometimes traits conflict—things that shouldn't naturally occur together. You can wind up having everything except cohesiveness as a person.

June Dafney was one of these perfect people, though she seemed more like an expensive piece of contemporary art than a painstakingly refined design like the rest of them. She didn't rush to greet Adam; she pretended she didn't even know he had arrived. She was tanning, curled up with a cocktail right by the water, watching something play on her PID. I noticed her when Adam was trying to introduce me to his buddy Steven, but kept looking over our shoulders, across the pad. "Steven, this is Clark. He works for the project, for Ned, my um... my assistant, I guess."

"Good to meet you," Steve exhaled with a hint of relief and nodded like we shared a secret. Finally someone could hear his SOS transmission—*not cool enough to be here*—even if it was just another flimsy boat in uncharted waters with no solid ground in sight.

"You too," I replied. "Where you from?"

"I'm going to, um—," Adam interrupted, looking over at June again. "That's my friend June; I'm gonna go say hi. Wanna come?"

We sauntered across the squishy green surface with Adam. I wasn't sure he actually wanted us to join him, but he asked, not wanting to be rude. So, not wanting to be rude, I wasn't going to say no. "June," he yelled out when we were midway there.

June looked over her shoulder and took off her shades. "Adam," she mouthed, and blew him a kiss. She stood up in her white and gold swimsuit as we approached. Her skin looked like some flawless close relative of ivory. Her hair shined even brighter and whiter. She was taller than most girls, but not too tall, and she was very slim, but strong, exposing the most-subtle curves in muscles that drew the eye. She was a world-class ballerina and a part-time fashion model, tenaciously trying to become a full-time celebrity. She was twenty-five, though she looked eighteen, and would work hard to stay that way for the next twenty years. June had not only been given the works in the womb, but done up with little tiny surgeries whenever she got bored, so that she looked perfect right down to the intentional imperfections that made her stand out—an ever-so-slightly sharp nose; fake freckles on the side of her left eye; eyelids expanded to make her frosty blue eyes slightly oversized; a pointy, man-made widow's peak in her hair.

When Adam introduced us, I don't think June even noticed me or Steven. She spent the whole time looking straight at Adam with the kind of innocent eyes that wreck homes, and pursed lips that wouldn't tell a soul, and little ears made for small whispers.

"It's so good to see you again," June cooed. "You've had such a tough go at things lately." She pecked him on the cheek before she picked up a tone of having something good up her sleeve. "I'm so happy things have turned around for you."

"Well I'm glad you made it."

"It turned out I had nothing too important on the schedule this week, so why not?"

"Funny, you've been too busy to do much of anything until right now," Adam smiled and regarded the surrounding paradise.

"Oh, I know how it must seem," she blushed, "but I haven't taken a day off in a couple years. I work very, very hard."

"I know you do. You could use a break. I've got a feeling this will be worth your while."

"Bold to predict anything with your forecasting track record."

"Wow," Adam laughed out loud. "You went there. I'll tell you this much, I predicted you'd wind up coming when you told me you had to 'check your schedule,' and I was right about that."

A reluctant smile broke across June's face and she giggled. She never really laughed without being a little bit embarrassed that she was laughing at all, like she was hiding a sweetness you could never have, to go easy on you, or maybe just exposing a pride that made every subtle moment a power struggle. But whatever it was, for some stupid reason, it made her endlessly appealing.

●

But the best part of Miami wasn't what floated on the surface. It was what was sunken beneath. Much of what used to rest firmly on the ground—ornate hotel lobbies and fountains and statues—Miami had sacrificed to the sea as beautiful monuments.

People at the hotel set up our whole group with oxygen converters, goggles, and flippers. We headed under, starting right out front of our hotel. Twenty feet down we found ourselves in front of the old entrance, swimming over the circle drive. When I reached the bottom I looked across the submerged avenue beneath Collins Canal. The shadows of boats passed by overhead, and across the canal were other half-submerged hotels, sticking out of the water with the support of steel reinforcements, their first floors where the third floors used to be.

I grabbed onto the reaching arm of a stone mermaid and pulled myself over the original front steps of the Raleigh. She looked content, resting underwater after being stuck in the hot Miami sun since the 1940s.

A school of clownfish wandered out of the wide open doors as I swam into the main lobby. Crabs scurried about on the gorgeous marble floor. It was darker in there, but Edison lights glowed on the walls so that the place felt like midnight on a Saturday, only the rushing crowds dressed to the nines were tropical fish. It was eerily calm inside the hotel; we were the only real disturbance to the still waters. There was the old front desk still stuck the ground, but a few wooden tables had floated to the ceiling, and a giant chandelier had fallen from its chain. It gently rested on the floor, where colorful fish wove through it, feasting on sea growth covering its crystals.

They had even left old pieces of art on the walls. Snails had latched onto the sturdy frames. Everything was incredibly well preserved but for all the new life taking over—sea reeds sitting tall on the furniture, an octopus scurrying across a billiards table peppered by brightly colored sea urchins like pool balls.

The guide showed us around the main floor but asked that we not swim up to the second floor, as those areas were much tighter spaces and very dark. We drifted down a long hallway, swimming in and out of its windows, until we arrived at what used to be the outdoors. The direct light of the sun was back, making for a sunny day on the underwater pool deck. Purple and green coral reefs had started to build up all over, making it even more beautiful than it had been in its glory days. We swam down into the pool and then got out of it and pretended to dry off. I drifted into the old cocktail bar behind the pool and served Adam and June glasses full of salt water. They toasted, and then she tasted it and pretended to get offended, tossing out her cocktail in his face.

The pool deck turned into a sandy beach, and in the distance, you could see the thick cement sea wall protecting a very calm South Beach from the rest of the tumultuous Atlantic Ocean. Ned and I floated above the sand, hanging onto a rotting lifeguard tower, until a rather large jelly fish passed right in front of our faces, and Ned jolted into a panic attack.

"I'm going up," Ned mouthed and motioned to me. Then he pointed his fingers at his eyes and tried to communicate something. When he had reached the surface, Ned's voice popped into my ear—he had an open line straight to my PID. "Clark," he gasped, "keep an eye on Adam would you? I don't want him getting all bitten up by anything."

"Will do," I typed back to him on the distorted holographic keyboard popping up from my PID underwater. I looked around but didn't see him on the beach with the guide and everyone else, so I swam back over the pool deck and into the hotel. Just as I arrived, I saw Adam swim into an empty elevator shaft and head upward, into the darkness spilling out from above. I followed and swam out into the second floor. He had his PID flashlight on, and was slowly pushing his way down the dark, barnacle-encrusted hallway. I turned mine on and he turned around, noticing me.

"*Shh*...," he put his finger to pursed lips and grinned. He kept exploring. He drifted down the hallway, trying door knobs, seeing if he could get into a room, but they were all locked. A barracuda darted past us and swam out a dim window at the end of the hallway.

As Adam reached the last door in the hallway, he found it already open. He rounded the doorpost and began to pull himself through, but suddenly jumped back. I imagined a shark or a giant octopus, but Adam calmed quickly, and kept looking at what had frightened him. I pulled myself around the corner to see.

She was strangely beautiful. She glowed in our spotlights, suspended there in the darkness above the bed frame by the window. She held an array of strange objects—an old coffee pot, a golden faucet-head, an ornate wooden bedpost. Tattered cutoff denim shorts and a black lace bra clung to the olive skin of her angular body. I could only tell that her soft face seemed to wear an infinitely curious look. Around her clear mask, a mass of thick black curly hair levitated, slowly billowing this way and that, surfing to one short-haired side of her head or the other.

Adam seemed to float toward her in slow motion, never breaking eye contact with a face entirely still but for the hair that could've passed for a sea creature. When he reached her, he reached out a hand.

They were about to shake hands when a special-forces operative surged through the open window and ripped her out of Adam's reach. They had been monitoring us the whole time, through my own eyes, and I didn't even know it. She struggled as the soldier, and then a couple others, tugged her out the window and dragged her up to the surface.

Adam swam out after them, and I followed. By the time we reached the surface they had her in a boat and were roaring away from the hotel, into the man-made bay of South Beach. Adam ripped off his mask and threw up his hands. "What the fuck is going on?"

That next moment, Ned was drifting up behind us, standing on the bow of a small boat full of soldiers like a goddamn hero. "Mr. Anderson," he called out. "Are you okay? How do you feel?"

Adam turned back with a look of disgust. "I feel confused Ned. What are you doing?"

"Just doing our job Mr. Anderson. Your safety and well-being is our top priority. Did you see the speed of our response time?"

"Response to what?"

They put down a ladder. Adam and I climbed into the boat.

"It was a little too fast," Adam went on. "Who was that?"

"Exactly. That's what we were wondering. She was an unidentified risk factor, so we removed her."

"How was she a risk factor?"

"I've got the ID," one of the soldiers in the back spoke up, reading from the hologram dropping down in front of his eye from his helmet. "She works for the hotel, but this was her day off; she wasn't supposed to be here and wasn't accounted for. So we didn't have her cleared for security. That made her a very real threat, Mr. Anderson. There are people out there who want you dead. We had to do something to make sure you were safe."

"Well you're doing too much; we need to calm it down. I don't even want to know what kind of weather you just caused. Where is she? I'd like to meet her."

"We'll have her brought back for you after she's been cleared," Ned blurted. "I'm terribly sorry, Mr. Anderson. Just protocol."

"Ned, I need someone who doesn't always go by the book. You can't be like this; it's not going to help my happiness."

"Again, I apologize, and I'll do everything I can to improve. Let's start right now. What can I do for you? What would help?"

"Nothing."

"There's got to the something, what do you want? Would you like to see the yacht we brought in for you and your friends? Brand-new, 470 feet long, graciously lent to the project by trillionaire Albert Shin. He hasn't even used her yet, and I've been told—"

"Ned, I just want to apologize to this poor girl. Bring her back now; she doesn't need to be 'cleared.' She's really not a threat."

Of course Adam was right. She meant no harm. Then again he couldn't have been more wrong. She was far more dangerous than any of the threats a defense team could protect him from. He wanted far too badly to see her again. They had ripped her away, and that was the start of a reaching that would never stop.

●

N.N.N. BREAKING NEWS — *Volcanic Eruption in New Mexico*

NEW MEXICO - For the first time in thousands of years, hot lava is bursting forth from vents all over the Zuni-Bandera Volcanic Field in Northwest New Mexico. Citizens are advised to seek safe ventilation as winds blow ash west. Updates to follow.

Published at 6:17 p.m., May 15, 2076.
© *National News Network, Inc. All rights reserved.*

Ten

WHEN THE BOAT CAME BACK and met us at the docks of the Raleigh, her hands were still bound by magnetic cuffs, and her hair covered much of her stoic face.

"Take those off of her please," Adam said. They did. She stepped out of the boat and immediately ran her hands through her thick hair, pulling it back like taming a stormy sea. She looked up at Adam with a smile. "Hi."

"Hi," he echoed, taken aback by her sense of ease. "I'm so sorry about all of that. That was awful, and so unnecessary. You guys can leave now please," he told Ned and the soldiers. "And try to stay hidden. I don't want to feel like I'm in danger all the time."

"But don't you love the feeling of danger?" she said.

"The right kind." Adam laughed.

"Maybe that's what I'm here for," she mused with a laugh. She shook her hair like a dog, spraying us with salt water. "I wouldn't mind another ride in the speedboat."

Everything she said seemed to surprise both Adam and herself. I don't think there's anything she loved more than creating that odd feeling. She didn't seem to care about how this first impression came across. She possessed a dignity extending far behind and beyond the present moment, giving you the feeling that this was only the tip of the iceberg. No matter what she said or did, no matter how quirky or strange, the depths of her demeanor held it up proudly.

She wasn't wearing a PID at all, not even the rare disconnected version that straps around your wrist. Detailed tattoos adorned each wrist as if she were an old person, or just vicariously nostalgic about a time when rebellion was more than just another aesthetic. A large feather earring dripped from her left ear, and she had loaded up her right ankle with five inches of assorted jewelry, more well-worn the lower you looked—their years of experience chained her to her own spellbinding self.

Her deep brown eyes absorbed everything around her. Her nose curled up a bit, like at some point it had been afraid of her pillowy lips, but got over it. A small scar on her neck granted every other aspect of her the freedom not to be perfect. It looked like one of those scars people got from playing a lot of violin as a kid, and she had never bothered with the simple treatment to fix it.

Adam just kept looking at her until he finally remembered how to continue the conversation. "What's your name?"

"I was hoping you'd never ask."

"Oh is that right?"

"Well, to be honest, I don't particularly like my given name."

"Well, what's your favorite name?" Adam's eyebrows rose with promise.

"My favorite name...," she looked up, "I guess my favorite name would have to be Stella. Though I'll never live up to it."

"You don't know that," said Adam.

"But a star is only beautiful when it's far away. When it gets too close it's absolutely blinding."

"So what do you want to be, blinding or beautiful?"

"I'm not sure yet," she thought out loud.

"Well it's nice to meet you either way Stella." He reached out a hand. "Let's try this again."

And when she shook it, behind Adam, far off over the ocean, I saw a spider-web of blue lightening splash out of a perfectly white pile of clouds. The trouble was, I know she saw it too.

"It's nice to—" The lightning arrested her attention, but by the time Adam turned to look, it had disappeared. "It's nice to meet you too," she continued, finally letting go of his hand. "What's your name?"

"Oh," He was caught off guard by the question, "my name's Adam."

"I *knew* your name. I just thought it might be nice to get to introduce yourself for once."

"Actually, yeah, it is."

They looked at each other silently for a second. The thunder rolled in to fill the silence. Stella looked back at the ocean again. Before Adam had fallen too far into her eyes, he managed to grab hold of a question, "So what were you doing in the water?"

"Just collecting a few things for my mural," she said.

"Your mural?"

"Yes, on the wall along the side of the building, they're letting me build a piece of art out of the little old ruins I find underwater. I work here, but I get to work on my mural in my off time. I should say mosaic. It's more of a mosaic. And no I don't know what I'm doing. I wouldn't call myself an artist."

"Well I'd love to see your art anyway," said Adam.

"Hmm...," she looked at each of us, "do you want to see it too?" she asked me. "What's your name?"

"Oh." I suddenly realized I was, in fact, there with them, not just watching life unfold from inside my own head. "Right, I'm Clark. And I don't see myself living up to my name either."

"Hmm?" She inquired.

I looked to Adam, who seemed just as lost. "Like, Clark Kent."

Still nothing.

"Superman."

"Oh, right," Stella realized. "Who wants to be superman anyway? Batman's cooler."

Stella brought us around the side of the hotel, where boats could pass from the canal to the bay. As I waded through two feet of water along a ledge on the wall, I began to notice the enormous piece of art had already begun. It covered thirty or forty feet of the white stucco wall. "Wow," I said, "how long have you been working on this?"

"Three years," she said plainly. "Finding the right pieces underwater is tough."

I had never heard of anyone our age working on one project for so long. She pushed away a sliding ladder, and we swam to the ledge on the other side of the waterway to get a view of the whole thing.

An unfinished mosaic spread a spectacular storm of colors and materials across the wall, as beautiful and terrifying as an oncoming asteroid. Everything raced out from a shattered and shimmering chandelier center like the big bang. Once glorious handcrafted pieces of wood and metal and glass appeared to have soared and smashed into each other along the wall. There were busted tennis rackets and splinters of surfboards, cracked sunglasses and not-so-fine china. Even broken pieces of art mingled among the bigger picture—a hand from a sculpture, a spitting face from a fountain, and framed photographs deteriorated into strange patterns by the salty sea. Yet it all worked together cohesively, and in the finished sections, not an inch of the wall could be seen beneath the art.

In the bottom corner of the piece, a title charred itself onto a plank of petrified wood, *MJYSNBM*. We watched it in silence. I swear it moved on its own. I simply didn't know how to describe this living thing. I could have looked at it for hours, except I simultaneously felt an urge to look away. An aching sense of longing and regret overtook me at the same time, like I was being pulled forward and backward at once, stretched beyond my limits. I found myself looking down at the water, soon haunted by the mosaic's reflection in it.

"It's so beautiful, but...," Adam seemed to have lost his breath or his train of thought or both, "it's all broken. Everything's broken."

"I won't use anything that isn't. If the things weren't broken, you'd just have a bunch of objects, not a mosaic. There would be no life to it."

"But how do you make sure they all break so...I don't know, beautifully?" Adam's words split to pieces on the spiky wall and lay hopelessly at its feet.

"I don't make sure of anything. The broken things are already beautiful when I find them. I just bring them up to the light of day."

As we all stared at the mosaic, a decaying, ring-shaped life preserver slipped off a dinner knife stuck into the wall. It bobbed in the water, just shy of sinking, and began to drift away. Adam jumped back into the water and grabbed it for her.

"Should we put it back up?" he asked.

"Nah," she looked at it. "It's fallen off that knife three times today. I don't think it's meant to stay. Give it to me; I'll throw it away."

"M, J, Y, S, N, B, M," I ventured. "What's it stand for?"

"Oh," she laughed. "It doesn't stand for anything. It's supposed to say 'majoysenboom,' but after making the first letter too big I realized I wouldn't have room for the vowels."

"Majoysenboom," I said, "What's it mean?"

"Well, I'm just not sure what it means. That's the whole point."

"Where does the word come from?" I asked.

"I made it up when I was a little kid, maybe three or four years old. I used to say it all the time. I never knew what it meant, just kind of... felt it."

"What did it feel like?" Adam wondered.

"Well I wouldn't have made a whole mosaic about it if I could do it justice with words." She spoke with a resolute wonder, her voice bubbling with misplaced question marks and exclamation points. Her confidence in the uncertainty of her own words made them so assuring. "It's one feeling but so many feelings at once. It's like, it's like everything you don't know, but it feels so familiar. You forget entirely what life is supposed to be—you see what it is. And it happens so fast you don't know if it happened at all, but you long that it did, you long for it again. You just long. It feels like nostalgia but it feels like hope."

"Is it a happy feeling?"

"Oh," Stella smiled. She lost her breath a bit. "So happy it hurts."

"What caused it? When would you feel it?"

"I used to get it a lot more, when I was little and everything was new and everything mattered. But I still get glances at it every now and again when I'm not paying attention—the sight of twinkling city lights far away, or hearing my own name whispered, or, or the moment my eyes meet someone's I haven't seen in far too long. There was this one time I began to weep for no reason at all—I felt it there. I've felt it in a song. Once I felt it alone in the mountains in a thunderstorm when I was scared. I've felt it making love; I've felt it in a glimpse of a stranger across the street I would never see again. I really can't pinpoint it, but the feeling will consume me when I'm not looking once in a while. As soon as I notice it, it's gone. And suddenly I feel like a ghost."

"Why?" Adam asked.

"Because the moment before, I knew I was alive."

"Shit."

"What?"

"I just don't have a clue what you're talking about, but I wish I did."

"Do you ever feel like a ghost?" she asked.

"Yeah, sometimes, I think."

"You may know more than you think, I think."

●

I don't think Adam particularly felt the need to leave the hotel just yet, but it was quite clear that Ned wanted to show him the yacht quite badly, as if just the sight of it would secure Adam weeks of undisturbed happiness. He decided to take the whole crew, Stella included, on a sunset cruise to kick things off. We made our way out to the big boat on a smaller boat. The thing was enormous. It looked like a sleek skyscraper had laid down to float on its back in the ocean for a while. Its matte black exterior looked like firewood that had burned through all its light. If I hadn't known any better, I would've mistaken it for a warship. It rested on two enormous hulls—the largest catamaran I've ever seen. As we drifted into the tunnel between them, I felt like we were falling into a black hole. *Orpheus,* it read in sharp gold letters like lightning on the back, and the music of a live string quartet enchanted us, pouring over the water from the loading bay inside the tunnel. As the shadow of the Orpheus overtook us, I saw Stella grab Adam's hand.

●

N.N.N. BREAKING NEWS - *Sudden Sinkhole Tragedy*

YELLOWSTONE - A man vacationing in Yellowstone National Park was dressing in his rental cabin when a sinkhole opened up in the floor beneath him. The thin layer of earth that had covered a narrow volcanic tube for millennia broke loose, collapsing down the ninety-foot chute with the man. He was pronounced dead at the scene. Experts on Adam Anderson's mysterious condition are unclear as to whether

he could have been the cause or not, as no
unusual seismic activity occurred in the area
at the time.

Published at 7:30 p.m., May 15, 2076.

●

"This couldn't have been Adam, right?" Ned looked to me for some reassurance as an attendant showed everyone around the enormous, spectacular main deck to wrap up the tour of the ship.

"I have no idea, but did you have to choose the most intimidating battle ship of all time?" A server handed me a glass of champagne.

"You're saying it's my fault? This is an amazing yacht—the best. It's terrific. Fantastic. Look," he pointed to Adam, who was marveling over everything he saw, "Adam is having a blast. Couldn't be happier. What, was he frightened or something?"

"No, I mean, I don't know. It's the coolest yacht ever, and you're probably right. I'm just saying the ship was a little unsettling on the outside." I downed my glass of champagne.

"Excuse me," said the server, handing me another, "that was for the toast. Save this one."

"Sorry—thanks." I turned my attention back to Ned.

"What's gotten into you?" Ned reprimanded.

"Someone just died a very unusual death."

"If Adam even caused that, that's out of my control. This is a high-stakes job; if you can't handle it, I'm happy to send you home."

"I'm just saying maybe you should be a little more thoughtful about the little things. You might be doing too much. Adam's emotions are sometimes... out of his control. Like anyone's."

"Speak again and you're fired. *I'll* handle Adam's wellness. You do what I fucking tell you to do."

Ned walked right up to Adam as a ship attendant relayed details about the incredible ship. "Adam! Great," Ned nodded at the attendant as words spilled raucously from his mouth, "great! Good stuff. How do you like the boat Adam? Ain't she a beauty? Black beauty. Fast as the dickens."

"Yeah," Adam nodded toward the attendant, "it's really great, thanks. She's in the middle of telling us all about it right now." Adam turned his attention back to her.

"Right, wonderful. So what else do you need, Mr. Anderson?" Ned interrupted again. "Is there anything I can do for you?"

"We just got here Ned, I'm fine. Thanks," he said firmly.

"Anything at all. Anything Mr. Anderson."

"Okay ... well ... actually, there is something."

"That's the spirit," he beamed. "Whatever it is, let's make it happen."

"If you could remove ..." Adam looked down and took a deep breath.

"Remove what? I'll remove anything immediately."

"I get it Ned. Relax."

"Of course. No reason to rush. We'll remove it whenever it needs to be removed."

"If you could just remove ... I just need a new assistant."

"Don't we all!" Ned slapped Adam on the shoulder and laughed very hard in hopes that it might remove the reality of what Adam had just said. "Remove Clark?" Ned whispered. "You need more capable all-hands-on-deck assistant on the project. Understandable."

"No. Remove yourself."

"Oh, I'm not your assistant, Mr. Anderson. I'm running the project from the ground here for you."

"Whatever you call yourself, I need you to go."

"Excuse me?" Still smiling.

"I need you to leave, because I want you to leave."

"Wow." For the first time, Ned didn't smile.

"Ned, I'm sorry. You're a great guy and all, sort of, but I just need someone who doesn't bother me. This will only get worse. Why summon Mother Nature? Why wait to deal with this issue?"

"Well," Ned smiled like he had just been told he had food in his teeth, "you know, I was just thinking the same thing. Better for me to manage the project behind the scenes; that's what I really want. That was always my long-term plan."

"Good to hear," Adam rolled with it.

"I'll start looking for someone new for you, and until that person arrives I'll remain here to help you however possible."

"No, Ned…," Adam looked at him unflinchingly, "I need you to leave right now. I'm sorry."

"Who will tend to your requests?"

"I'll call you if I need anything."

"Okay," Ned looked around and tried to figure out how to handle himself. "Okay then. We'll take the chopper." Ned walked away from Adam, toward the fancy helicopter on deck.

"C'mon Clark," he called back to me. I found myself slowly following after Ned like a sheep being led to a slaughterhouse. I looked back at Adam. He waved goodbye, but I sensed some empathy in his eyes.

Ned got in the chopper. The blades were spinning faster and faster, and so was my head. "C'mon, Clark. Time to get back to the real world," he called out, motioning me in.

I was slowly moving toward the chopper, but my heart was racing the opposite direction. Those words, "the real world," they pinched something in my soul. The thought of Ned picking out my real world horrified me. The wind from the chopper was blowing in my face and an overwhelming feeling rushed toward me. I felt I was swimming in the most important moment of my life. I needed to find a way to the surface fast or I would drown. I stopped dead in my tracks.

"Clark," Ned stared me down. "What are you doing? Get over here now or you're fired."

But I couldn't move forward. Everything was happening too fast. All I could do was stand there, shaking my head, because Adam was the glitch in the system of everything I had ever known about life. How would I ever get a peek behind these closed doors again, and how would I ever quell this curiosity scratching at my soul? How would I ever stop this ache to figure out if there was some other kind of real world? This sinking feeling that I was missing it. That I was missing it. That I was missing it missing it missing it, that we were all fucking missing it. I had to know what would happen to Adam. I had to see my real world smashed to pieces and discover what was really left. I had to see the American dream awaken. I needed to see it roaring in all its decadent power and feel the vibrations in my chest and look into its eyes. I had seen happiness pursued, however feebly; I had to see it captured and pinned to the ground, forced to tell us why it had been running all this time and where the hell it was going.

I found myself stumbling backward, not knowing what I was doing, but not willing to leave. As I reached the end of the helipad I tripped and fell backward. I was laying flat on my back, staring up at the sky, when Adam walked up and reached out a hand.

"Are you alright?" he asked.

"I'm … I'm … I'll be your new assistant," I said.

Adam looked me in the eyes, and I knew he could tell exactly how clueless I was and just how little I had to offer. But he didn't seem to mind. Because I don't think he wanted anyone to search for happiness for him, but he didn't mind someone searching with him.

Before Adam had a chance to reply Ned was grabbing my shoulder, yanking me toward the chopper. "You're coming with me."

"No," I shook my head, wriggling out of my suit jacket like a little kid as he refused to let go of it.

"No?"

"I'm Adam's assistant."

"You're my assistant," Ned demanded. "You're coming with me."

"I quit."

"Excuse me?"

"I don't work for you anymore."

"You still have to come with me. You're not staying."

"Yes I am."

"Are you sure."

"Yes," I assured myself.

"Okay then. I'll have you arrested for trespassing right now," Ned looked to Adam for confirmation, but Adam didn't say a word. "He's not your assistant, is he?"

"He …," Adam began to nod, "he is."

"Since when?"

"Since right now."

"I'm sorry, Adam, but Clark here …," Ned huffed and puffed, "Clark is incredibly underqualified to manage your well-being."

"But, Ned, I don't want anyone *managing* my well-being. Clark is actually...kind of perfect. He doesn't say much. He's relaxed. He's not annoying. He's a normal fucking dude."

"Adam, Adam...," Ned pleaded, "think about this. This is a very important job."

"Clark can handle it." At that, Adam walked away. I stood there watching Ned loathe me for a second before I shrugged it off and followed Adam back to everyone else. The sound of the helicopter grew farther away, and when it had all but faded, Adam held up his glass of champagne and addressed the group. "To doing what we want," he raised his glass toward mine and started to laugh. "Clark, I would've stayed too if I were you."

And in that moment, I felt like Adam and I were just old friends embarking on a new adventure. But as the champagne in my glass disappeared, the empty bottom revealed itself. I still didn't really know Adam. I didn't know anyone around me. I found myself involved in the Pursuit of Happiness Project by sheer luck, and I barged my way into becoming Adam's assistant in a whirlwind of existential anxiety. I began to wonder if I would just be a burden to Adam, another fast friend trying to surf his wave of good fortune. That wasn't who I wanted to be, and that wasn't going to work out.

I pulled Adam aside the first chance I got. "Adam, listen." I said, "I really appreciate you having my back, but I want you to know that if you want someone else or just don't want an assistant with you at all, I totally understand. Honestly."

"Clark," he watched his drink swirl round and round, "I'll tell you something. Everything I ever had until recently—I fought for it. I didn't have parents. I didn't have money or connections. I had to fight." Finally he took a swig of his drink. He looked around, and then he looked me in the eye. "Now I don't know who you are or where you came from or what was given to you. But this—you fought for this. You get to keep this."

ELEVEN

WE SAILED ALONG the shore and watched the dusk arrive. By nightfall we were convinced a storm cloud could never set foot in the sky again. I think the shouts of those first shots will echo back at me forever. A warm breeze delivered an ever-fresh supply of energy from the ocean as we tilted our heads to the stars and knocked back round after round. Waiters always stood by with more of whatever we wanted—an endless selection of wines and liquors made before I was born. The night felt nearly as young, and it seemed we were only getting younger as our glowing ship floated so effortlessly upon the deep black sea—a contrast so bright we must have made the stars envious.

In between moments I hovered somewhere out there in the dark, over the water. My mind could only make sense of what was happening as a dream or a movie, like it was too good to be true, like we were sailing right over some unmarked line in the unlimited ocean. I could no longer tell whether life grants any value to merit or if it was just a free-for-all, a mad dash to loot what you could in a worldwide riot. I had aimlessly busted through a door and found myself in a jewelry store.

Amidst all my excitement, the fear that I would fall short like Ned haunted me to spooky silence, but only when I was alone. Around Adam there wasn't the time or even the space for it. Each moment answered to him, swept into a straight line behind him as he charged forward. He had this strange bond with himself, whoever he was, that could have made any friendship jealous, that drew all the attention to him even when he wasn't talking. But even that put me back out there in the dark, wondering if it was possible to be so whole, or if Adam had only created for himself a character so convincing that it snuck into his mirrors.

●

"*All* of this space," June hummed as she danced across the deck, twirling a few times and managing not to spill her drink. A new song filled the air with energy and every eye traced her graceful body. "All of this space to roam and play. What are we going to do with it?"

"How about we play hide and seek?" Adam looked around the enormous boat with wide-eyed wonder. "For old time's sake."

"What are the boundaries?" Steven ventured. "Can I hide in the pool?" He laughed to himself.

"No boundaries!" said Adam. "The whole damn ship!"

"But there are so many cozy bedrooms…," said Stella. "I'll fall asleep while I'm hiding."

"Okay, cabins are off limits. The rest of the ship is fine. Who wants to seek first?"

"I'll do it," I piped in. I figured this was a small way to assist.

"Count to one hundred," he said. "And close your eyes."

So I counted and heard everyone run off in various directions. When I opened my eyes, all was quiet but the music and the waves. For all I knew, I might have been the only living soul on board the big ship. I set out with the feeling of an explorer.

But I quickly found a couple people hiding under a pool chair making out. They didn't notice me. "Hey…" I ventured. They froze. "Um…I found you. So uh, you can come out when you're ready." They said nothing.

Next I found Steven "hiding" in the massage parlor, while having his back rubbed ruthlessly by a massive Samoan man. "You found me…," he barely grunted through the pressure.

"Yeah…you can just…you can come out when you're ready," I said and moved on, realizing just how little excitement the childhood game held anymore. It was strange to me that Adam had suggested it at all. I wouldn't have called him young at heart; if anything, he was an old soul.

I climbed a bunch of stairs, looking for secret places, until behind a coffee nook overlooking the ocean I discovered a beautiful little library. Cherrywood shelves full of old books and movies. Soft lighting like a warm fire. Heavy tables and obnoxiously large chairs, the kind that seem to have their own gravitational pull. I stayed quiet, maybe because I was in a library, but more because I knew someone would be hiding in there if they were smart. I crept down a book-walled aisle.

As I reached the end of the aisle I could hear voices muffled in the pages on the shelf, like the characters inside the books were whispering too loudly. I peered through a little crack between two books. On the other side, squished together in a regal chair, sat Adam and Stella. Stella had found a very old Webster's dictionary and was thumbing through it with Adam. The glass case that had been protecting and displaying it was open, and the book rested on their laps. It must have been from the 1800s. She sniffed the pages like a fine perfume as she gently cracked open a dusty new section.

"Oh god," Adam coughed. "It smells like death."

"Are you kidding?" she said. "This is the best scent in the world. Books are like a fine wine."

"A fine wine is just bad vinegar after two hundred years," he teased. "The best scent in the world is the scent of rain."

"Aw..." She looked into his eyes.

"What?" he said.

"You'd have to be sad to get it."

Adam looked at her until his eyes unlatched and tumbled down to her mouth. "So what do we do now? Just wait here?"

"Yeah, unless you wanna hide somewhere else."

"And how long do we wait?" Adam asked.

"Until they find us."

"So how do we win?"

"We win if we're the last ones found. Haven't you ever played hide and seek before?"

"Actually I don't know," he smiled and thought.

"When you were a kid?"

"I guess I wasn't much of a kid." "Maybe that's good." She looked at him. "I could probably use some adult supervision."

"Oh, no no," he professed. "There will be no adults, and absolutely zero supervision on the Pursuit of Happiness Project. Just kids like you." Adam turned his attention to the giant dictionary spread across their legs. "Now let's see," he said, "majoysenboom. Where is it?" He thumbed through the pages. Stella wrapped her arms around his neck and snuggled in closer. "It should be right here between maigre—whatever that means—and mail. But they don't have it." Adam shook his head. "I guess we're just gonna have to put it in ourselves. Got a pen?"

Stella pulled a charcoal pencil from behind her ear, where it had been hiding in a jungle of black hair.

"What? Why do you have this?"

"I always have it."

"What else do you have floating around up there?" Adam laughed as he ran his hand into her soft hair, and she swirled her head around with the motion of his hand, closing her eyes.

"Just a bunch of crazy thoughts that no one likes," she said.

"Well I kinda like 'em." He turned back to the page and started writing in the margin. "Majoysenboom," he said. "How do I define this indefinable word?"

"A terrifying happiness," she whispered in his ear. And before he could even write it, the pencil was streaking across the page and dropping to the floor with the heavy dictionary. Words fell away. It wouldn't be long before they found themselves on the floor too.

●

Well clearly I wouldn't have been doing Adam any good finding him just then, and frankly I had already seen more than I was willing to admit, so I crept out to find everyone else.

I stumbled upon a giant live chessboard on a side deck; it was made up of hired men and women in costumes to represent the different pieces. June had assembled them in such a way that it looked like someone had been playing on it and then left right in the middle of a game, yet she sat in the middle, hidden from almost all angles. I only found her because I heard her PID go off, a quick holomessage from some friend who appeared like a ghost, half his body cut off by a live chess knight.

"June," I called out dispassionately, "I found you. So, you can come out now."

"Thank god," she stood up. "I was getting really bored. Let's go find everyone else and get back to the drinking."

"Yeah."

"Have you found Adam?"

"Still hiding."

We searched on, and I made sure to steer us away from the library. We found everyone else within fifteen minutes and found ourselves among elegant foods and complicated beverages around the main pool area. But when an hour had gone by, Adam and Stella still hadn't emerged, and I wondered how much longer it would take Adam to find his missing childhood.

●

N.N.N. BREAKING NEWS - *Miraculous Apples?*

MICHIGAN — Apple farmers across the state of Michigan woke up this morning to find their orchards fully ripe for harvest, the apples having grown overnight.

"Yesterday the trees were completely barren," said George Williams, owner of Williams Orchards. "We weren't even close to harvest. Today, the trees are completely full of perfectly ripe apples. I still don't believe it. I'm not even prepared to harvest these, but whatever the Pursuit of Happiness Project is doing, I've got a feeling they're doing something right.

Farmers have found people from all over racing to their farms to pick and taste these apples, willing to pay exorbitant prices in hopes that the apples will provide some miraculous, life-giving benefit. Hundreds of people have eaten the apples thus far; none have reported feeling any different. "But they are delicious," one happy bystander affirmed. "Hands f-ing down, that was the best apple I've ever had."

Published at 10:00 a.m., May 16, 2076.

●

After two hours, everyone was asking about Adam, and I started to feel like I should know where he was, or at least look for him. I snuck off, back to the library, to make sure they weren't somehow still waiting to be found. I walked in very slowly, listening first, but heard nothing. When I looked down the aisle, they were gone. The chair had been turned over with its underside exposed, and hundreds of books lay strewn across the ground, fallen from bookshelves, split open with their pages jumbled on the floor. I wandered to the end of the hallway to pick up the poor old dictionary. There was "Majoysenboom (n.):," scribbled in the margin, but they had never written down the definition. I closed up the great book with a thump and laid it back in the glass case.

When I got back to the group, Adam and Stella had beaten me there. "I think you guys won," I told Adam.

"I think you're right," he smirked.

As the pool party disintegrated, the drunken group sprawled out on cushions by the pool or wandered off to the yacht's bedrooms. We had pulled back in front of the hotel, but no one felt like shuttling in when they could just crash on the yacht.

Stella lay asleep in a chair with Adam, but she suddenly woke up with a yawn. She stumbled out of the chair like she was just learning to walk, rubbing her eyes with ornery fists. She began to wander off until Adam stood up as well. "Stella," he said, "where are you going?"

"To bed."

"Let's go back to the room and sleep," he said.

"I think I need to go home," she yawned. "Sleep in my own bed."

"Back to shore?"

"Yeah," she said. "They'll take me back to the hotel, right? I can walk home from there."

"Why don't you just stay? You can sleep here and go home in the morning."

"I've got work tomorrow."

"Oh don't worry about that. You've already been called out by the project. Trust me."

"Oh," she whispered. "Well, I'd still like to go home."

"Okay." He nodded.

"Good night," she said.

"I'll walk you down."

"No, that's alright." She planted a kiss on his lips and hugged him. "I had so much fun tonight. I'll see you at the hotel tomorrow. Good night Adam."

"Good night Stella."

She walked away, and Adam watched every step until she disappeared around the corner. He said his good nights to the remaining few around him, and wandered off to bed. Everyone did, except for me.

I don't do a lot of sleeping, and I found myself wandering to the very back of the boat, up a long spiral staircase. A wooden platform decorated with telescopes leaned out over the great dark sea, whose massive body had curled up asleep around the whole earth, with our enormous yacht slapped onto its back like a freckle. I was staring over the water, just waiting for my PID to buzz with some alert about some crazy storm, until I heard Adam's voice behind me.

"What are you doing up here?" he asked.

"I don't know," I replied frankly.

"Well, me neither."

"Great minds think alike," I said.

"And fools seldom differ. Here." He held out a tumbler full of scotch and poured half into my empty glass. "I shouldn't drink all this, but I would've if you hadn't been here." He patted me on the back, "So thanks. I'm glad you're here bud. You're a real... you're really... well I don't know what the hell to say because I don't know you too well, but I'm glad you're here."

I had never known how Adam viewed me, but it's easy to see a person's soul spilling out when they're drunk, in between sips and slurred words, in all their squinty sincerity, and I got the feeling he saw me like a little brother. All I had done was shown up, but he was cloaked in confidence and had no problem trusting an unassuming kid like me. Suddenly I could loosen up. I swear it happened in an instant.

We leaned against the railing over the dark water. The wind was picking up and blowing into our faces from the sea. The waves had risen with it. Adam shook the railing to make sure it was secure and then sat on it, his legs swinging over the edge. "Kinda scary, huh?" He remarked matter-of-factly.

"I won't let you fall." I held out my arm to show him I could pull him back in time.

"Somehow I doubt your reflexes right now." He laughed.

"Fair. Just don't think about it and you won't fall."

"I don't mean the falling off; I'm fine. I mean the ocean—it's a little scary." His eyes raced out to sea. "Dark, and so tumultuous. Just black out there, and the waves. And it doesn't stop here. A thousand miles away from anybody—nobody to see it—those things are still crashing together in the dark, all cold and restless. It's like they're not doing this for show, you know? They really don't give a shit if anyone's watching or not. This is just how they are. Chaotic and messy and pitch black, always, and they couldn't care less." What he was seeing enchanted his drunken mind. Adam was sinking deeper and deeper into that ocean.

"But... they're waves," I ventured, hoping to pull him out of it. "That's just what they do."

"But you don't understand. I have this dream some nights. Always the same. I'm out there. And it's just like it is right now, with the choppy water and the clouds above so that you can't even see a star—you can't even pick a goddamn star to follow. It's just black, and I don't know where I'm going, and I tread water all night until I wake up. I never find the shore. I always think I will in time, but I never do. It's so endless out there. Look, it goes on forever."

I'll admit I felt the same uneasiness looking out that night; I had been feeling it before he joined me. I wish I had admitted it then, but I figured I'd better bring in something more lighthearted before he grew any more uneasy.

"Well," I said, "right now you're out of the water, on a boat, drunk, so there's that. At least you don't have embarrassing recurring dreams like mine. I always find myself naked in front of people and I never realize it until they point it out. One time I dreamt I was naked at a funeral. God, it was awful. Everyone was laughing.

Even the dead guy—he sprang up from his casket and pointed at me and laughed."

And then Adam was laughing, and so was I, and the ocean didn't feel so big anymore, and we floated on it so effortlessly. "Cheers," he bumped his glass into mine recklessly. It cracked, and he drank from the leak in the glass as he finished his toast, "To being drunk on a boat...to a party with no end in sight, and, and...to all of our favorite nightmares."

"Cheers." I laughed.

He downed the rest of his scotch. "Well, I came up here to see the stars, but it seems all the stars have pulled the covers over and gone to bed, so I guess I will too." Adam descended the spiral staircase. I stayed just long enough to see the clouds above break apart and let a star say good night.

TWELVE

"I'LL ADMIT IT CLARK," Ned grumbled a week later, popping up unannounced on my PID while I was paddle boarding out to a lily pad. "Weather's been good. A few abnormalities here and there, but nothing we can't handle. I'm not saying you're doing a good job, because your PID tells me you've been intoxicated 47.4 percent of the time this past week, but whatever you're doing, don't fuck it up."

"I have a very laissez-faire approach."

"What do you even do?"

"I'm just kind of...here."

"I hate you. But the project is going well, and Douglas is very happy with me. Jonathan Harvey tells me if we can keep Adam at this level of contentment, he thinks he can re-up his equipment over the next year or two and get forecasting back to 100 percent—a perfectly safe America again."

"How would he ever get it back to 100 percent?"

"100 percent happiness I guess, I don't know. Just keep things how they are. You do anything stupid, I'll still fire you in a heartbeat."

"Don't think you can."

"You have no idea what I'm capable of."

"I think you're capable of doing a lot of terrible things, but I'm pretty sure only Adam can fire me. He could probably fire you too if you think about it."

"You just keep the requests coming; I'll keep making them happen. You're the assistant; I'm the one in power. You're literally a set of ears that Adam doesn't mind speaking to. He could just speak his requests into the air and they would still happen without you—we're listening all the time."

"Oh, that's actually good to know. I'll let him know so that he can just say things into the air when I'm not around."

And Ned sighed a good long sigh. "Don't tell him we're listening. Don't change anything. That's all you have to do. You have the easiest job—your job is to do nothing. No change. Goodbye."

And I laughed, because at the time, I simply couldn't imagine life's greatest constant breaking into our little world. Adam was so relaxed, so perfectly stable. He was back to his old self, the one I used to see smiling above cities, rain or shine. He seemed like such an ideal candidate for controlling the weather, I began to wonder why such a strange curse had befallen him at all.

There was never a plan, and every day down in Miami felt more or less the same. The only thing that changed was when Stella showed up. She never slept at the hotel. I know because every day, at some point, she arrived. She messed around with us at the hotel or on the water, but she still wound up spending much of her days working on the mosaic, taking advantage of her time off work.

Sometimes Adam helped, diving down with her to find old relics in the labyrinth of flooded history below. She wouldn't let anyone else help. And if Adam couldn't find her, sometimes he'd go underwater looking for her and then sneak up behind her while she was digging through some old storage room and scare the living daylights out of her. When she told us those stories she was always laughing harder than anyone else.

At night we had bonfires on the lily pads and drank fine wine. We watched the colorful lights of the South Beach shoreline streak across the black water lapping up against the buildings.

More and more people showed up to party with us. Adam would give me the name, I would tell Ned, and they usually arrived within a few hours. Security would clear them and keep track of them, but other than that they were free to do as they pleased, all on the project's dime. Within a week there must have been more than a hundred people staying at the hotel. The place purred with the most wonderful, unspeakable things—it was the kind of place you could go home talking about. There was always someone dancing, always someone making a mess, always someone skinny-dipping, always boats buzzing, always people breaking expensive things, and always a few sneaking off in cahoots. There was always music blaring and champagne bursting and never one little thing to worry about. We were careless. Like money in the air. Like the last couple seconds of the old new year. Like laughter in the distance, carrying by on a breeze without caring to tell you why.

And the place began to feel busy. One day Adam and I were walking through the lobby and he ran into an old friend at the coffee bar. "Fred?" he called out, and rushed over to shake his hand. "What are you doing here?"

"Here to see you! Man of the hour, the year, the century!"

"Oh, great to see you. Thanks for stopping by!"

"I've been here for three days!" Fred exclaimed.

"Here in Miami?" Adam asked.

"Here at the hotel! Thanks for bringing me down!"

"Really?"

"Just haven't had a chance to talk to you; it's all good!"

"Oh ... oh, wow. Well have you had fun?"

"Yeah! Good to see you man!"

"You too!"

We walked away, cheery as daylight.

"Did I invite Fred?" Adam casually mentioned.

"You did," I confirmed.

"Geez. You might have to start cutting me off from inviting people after four or five drinks. I haven't seen Fred since high school. We weren't even really friends."

I don't think Adam ever spoke to Fred again after that, but he didn't seem to have a problem with Fred being there. Everyone was welcome, and every interaction was a celebration. There were dozens of outrageous guests I never even met, anonymous friends like strips of confetti gracing the atmosphere of a party. Names were not necessary for pretty people who could smile and wink.

No one ever asked Adam about the weather or if he had any theories as to why his emotions created it. No one asked Adam how he felt about the whole situation or how he was doing. No one dared ask a question that assumed anything less than perfection. There was no place for that. If there was even a place for that anywhere outside of the therapist's office, it certainly wasn't here. No, we were careless.

And it was a gorgeous irony while it lasted. Because you only get to be careless when you couldn't care less about the quality.

You can enjoy it until you notice it, but you simply cannot try to be careless. It is a sacred innocence that can never be earned or even beheld, but only looked back at wistfully.

●

N.N.N. The Anderson Affect – *Adam the Insomniac?*

After a solid week of all but perfect weather, people across the country are experiencing nightly thunderstorms, ranging in duration and intensity. Some of these storms appear and disappear throughout the night, forming and dissipating almost instantly.

The storms have been both strengthening and multiplying, raging later and later into the night. Last night alone, 72 cars crashed around the country, resulting in 41 injuries and 4 fatalities. Although the Pursuit of Happiness Project has not released any details regarding the cause of the storms, lawmakers are noting Adam's apparent insomnia, and calling out for the project to prescribe proper sleep medications. It's unconfirmed what effect sleep medications might have on Adam and the weather, or whether it is possible that Adam's dreams are leading to these late night storms. Whatever the cause, it tends to occur between 11 p.m. and 4 a.m.

Published at 9:37 p.m., May 27, 2076.

●

I swear I wouldn't have had a clue there were any screws loose in Adam's internal world if it weren't for Mother Nature telling on him. It was funny to see someone so strong, someone so face-forward, accidentally wearing his heart on his sleeve. He would have told you honestly that he was doing just dandy, but storms emerged from places in his heart he couldn't even access. At the time, the source was a mystery to me.

When the sun was out the salt water washed every concern away. They sank to the bottom of the ocean while Adam floated on top to shimmer in the sun with the pretty water and the pretty girls. But those dark thoughts crept to shore with the dusk. More and more of them started to find their way to Adam in the quiet of the night.

Weather alerts and the grating sound of Ned's nagging voice kept me awake into the wee hours. He had gotten in the habit of leaping into my ear or jumping out of my wrist completely unannounced. I lived in constant fear of Ned's stupid, reddish face interrupting me—in the middle of a conversation, asleep in bed, in the shower. There was no sacred place for me. Ned was always right behind a digital door right in front of me, willing to bust it open anytime he wanted.

I was pulling out a chair to sit down for a late dinner when, "What's the deal with these landslides in Malibu!" I jolted back in fright, flinging a full plate of spaghetti all over the girl next to me. Ned didn't even notice, drowning out my apologies with his loud voice as he steam-rolled on, "We've got road closures and some bad accidents and some homes down the chute. It's bad Clark. Bad. I'm not willing to open any of the roads again until we're confident Adam is in a better state of mind."

"Well I don't know, I'm not with him. But you blasted the spaghetti off my plate and now this girl I just met is a mess in front of everyone and she's running—she's crying now. She's crying Ned."

"You know who paid for that spaghetti? We did. And we will do whatever we need to do with our spaghetti. Where's Adam?"

"I don't think the spaghetti really needs to be involved. I don't know where Adam is. I'm not his parent; he's not a child."

"Sure he is. Here, let me connect you to his eyes."

"Ned, no. That's creepy."

"It will just help you find him faster."

"No."

"Well then go find him."

"I'll try."

"Faster!"

"Okay!"

So I found Adam. He seemed to be doing perfectly fine, sitting around with some people throwing back oyster shooters. There was nothing to address. It was a perfect scene. The only piece missing was Stella.

The next night, at four in the morning, Ned appeared again, full size, in his pajamas, in my bed, like I was cuddling with his ghost. "Clark goddamn it what the hell is wrong with Adam?" he groaned "Things are starting to get out of hand."

"Is this a dream?" I mumbled.

"This is a nightmare."

"What? What are you doing in my—"

"I'm alerting you to a tragedy. Sixteen people died in a flash flood tonight. At the exact same time, we've got these goddamn torrents of wind flying around, blowing cars off the road with two hundred mile-per-hour rogue gusts. It's insane. What the hell is going on over there?"

"I think it's a girl. This girl Stella. They were having a really great time together, but she hasn't been coming around anymore."

"So where is she? Why isn't she coming around?"

"I really don't know. She always seemed to like Adam."

"That should be illegal."

"What?"

"It should be illegal for this girl Stella to, to, to flake out on Adam like this. It's making him unhappy. It's costing lives. I think she should be punished. We need a law to prevent any woman from ever rejecting Adam in any way ever again."

"That's ridiculous."

"It's a precaution. A ridiculously smart precaution is what it is."

"Well it sounds a lot like rape, or some kind of prostitution."

"I'm a safety pimp Clark. Precautions are my whores."

"Great."

"Great."

"No—you can't just force Stella to hang out with him. *That* is definitely illegal."

"You'd be surprised what we can *legally* do Clark," Ned bragged.

"Don't try to fabricate some kind of relationship for him. It won't work. Just let it pass."

"I'll do what's best for the country," he replied.

"Do what's best for the Adam. That's what's best for the country."

"You do what's best for the Adam. Go make him feel better."

"He's in bed! Alone! What do you want me to do, barge in like you? Just let him deal with it."

"Just let him... just let him!" Ned was really throwing a hissy fit, rubbing his eyes, tripping over his groggy words. "Let him *deal* with it? And let people die? Are you kidding me Clark? He shouldn't be *dealing* with this kind of stuff at all."

"You can't expect him to be perfect."

"Why not? For god sake, it's his American duty to be perfect, or damn near perfect. And if he can't manage that under perfect conditions, we'll just find another way to calm the storm. Don't think we won't. Consider this little incident strike one."

"What?"

"You heard me," he taunted.

"But what do you mean? What happens on strike three?"

"Know anything about baseball, Clark?"

"What's baseball?"

"Are you even American? Baseball is—"

"Ned, stop. What happens if we strike out?"

"We're toying around with some ideas, more... desperate measures. I can't talk about them. And you wouldn't want to know. Do better."

●

The next night filled up Miami like a warm bathtub. It was getting hotter as the night grew darker. The air must have been over one hundred degrees, and felt like one hundred pounds smooshing you from all sides. The moon slowly mustered its way up through the dense darkness like a heat lamp hovering over us. Midnight melted into sweet drinks and sweet smiles, and not a hint that anything had gone sour for Adam, except for the fine cheeses sweating and white wines warming and the cocktail fruits decaying right on the edges of the glasses.

But around two in the morning, Adam finally stopped smiling and ducked away from the party. I followed him at a distance as he took a stroll onto the docks and dove into the water.

There I found Steven leaning over a railing along the hotel harbor with a box of cigars and three different cocktails, each as helplessly watered down by melted ice.

"Steven." I waved. "What are you doing down here?"

"Just soaking it up," Steven slurred, blowing out some smoke and breathing in the beauty all around him. "I wonder how long this can all last." He hiccupped. "I've been reading the news you know." Steven glanced at me with wide eyes. "I've been reading all the newses."

We watched Adam float around on his back about fifty feet away. When he noticed a group of people heading toward a boat, he slid under the dock so they wouldn't notice him. He looked so calm floating there, but the heat wave was only getting worse, and more widespread. Storms in the distance winked with brief flashes of lightning.

Ned would be calling any moment; I was sure of it. But before he did, Adam emerged and walked toward us. He stopped, crossed his arms, and stood there while we waited for him to say whatever he was clearly and finally ready to say. "Hey, um, Clark, listen—" A hotel worker tossed him a hot towel out of nowhere and he started to dry his hair. "Thank you!" he yelled to the man. "Tell me the truth Clark. How's the weather?"

"Why do you ask?" I replied mechanically.

"Well, besides the fact that it's hot as fuck right now, good old Douglas Powers sent me a personal message yesterday congratulating me on how great the weather has been and how proud he is and how great I am and how great this country is. He told me to keep living in the moment and enjoying the project, etcetera, etcetera, etcetera."

"So?"

"So how bad is it?" he stared.

"Been better," I crumbled. "Getting worse every night. What's wrong?"

"This should be so easy," he said, shaking his head, kind of smiling but kind of cringing. "And the project just started. This should be so, so easy. But fuck. Stella."

"What's the deal?" I asked.

"Well where is she? We were hanging out every day. Everything was so good. But I haven't seen her in three days. Yesterday she spent the whole day on her mosaic and never even came over to say hello. And it shouldn't matter, like, I'm fine, I'm great, I just don't get—"

He was about to elaborate when June and two giddy girls bounced into play, stumbling seamlessly into our conversation. June flicked her wet hair round and round so that it sprayed us with showers of laughter. She held a bottle of champagne and barely wore her swimsuit. One of the girls wasn't wearing a top at all, and held an anonymous handful of pills.

"Hey Mr. Weathermaaan." June let her words drip out slowly. "What a hot, hot night. Isn't there anything you can do about it? It's just so awfully muggy I could scream."

"Too hot for a top huh?" Adam lent his eyes to the topless girl, who giggled and covered up her breasts as if she left them out on accident.

"Oh it's much too hot to any kind of clothing," June reassured as she began to drift away, down the dock. "I doubt any of us will be wearing much of anything for long. We're heading out to the lily pads for a dip, and your presence is requested. But the boat's leaving now dear." She stepped in.

"The water's to die for." The topless one's dilated pupils met Adam's like two eight-balls.

"And this wine's to die for," the third girl raised a bottle to her lazy lips.

"Plenty of good reasons to die these days," Adam teased.

"Oh don't you know?" June called back from the boat, where she was doing one of her ballet stretches, lifting her leg high in the air. "That's how all the living happens. And we wouldn't want to die alone out there," she slowly let her leg down and looked out into the bay. "You coming?"

"Rain check," Adam smiled. "Don't have too much fun without me."

"I wouldn't mind some rain if you've got any." Wine girl tossed her arm around Adam and fed him a sip. "We can always cheer you up on a rainy day."

The topless one pecked Adam on the cheek before spinning off. "407," she whispered.

They floated away, sinking into the soft darkness.

"They've started to notice," Adam turned to us. "They've started to notice that Stella's gone."

"I mean," Steven threw up his hands, "am I the only one thinking Stella's absence might be working in your favor? There's a lot of...," he glared at Adam with crazed eyes, "*fish* in the sea, so to speak."

"Adam," I asked, "are you going out there or what?"

"I don't know..." he shook his head.

"You don't know?" Steven retorted. "What is there not to—"

Smack! The sound of Adam's ass getting slapped interrupted him. A gorgeous brunette walked by in a robe. Adam looked over, shaking his head. She winked, rounded a corner, and disappeared.

"Goddamn it," he joked, wincing a little. "Who is that? And why isn't she Stella? Why can't I just enjoy this? It's getting over-populated around here. Everywhere I look, some beautiful girl is looking back at me, and none of them are Stella. I must be crazy, but none of them are her and it's all I can think. I don't know what's going on with me."

"Adam," Steven charged, "I, I, I don't mean to be rude here, but... *fish in the sea. Fish! In the sea.* You could be having the time of your life. Living out your high school fantasies—my high school fantasies—someone needs to live these fantasies! Fuck Stella. If she's not here, that's her loss. Appreciate what you have. If I were you..." Steven buried his head in his hands.

"We don't even want to know," I replied, then turned to Adam. "You want her because you can't have her. She's the only girl here you can't have—you want her."

"Or maybe I can't have her because I want her," he replied.

"Probably both."

"Geez," Steven muttered, "you guys are too much. You're thinking way too hard." Steven turned to Adam and began etching his ramblings into stone, "Adam, get the fuck out there. June is the most magical woman I have ever laid eyes on. She looks like a fucking elf. It's not even fair how she looks. Clark, can you back me up on this one?"

I nodded. He had summed it up.

"Guys, I don't even disagree, I wish I could. But I'm stuck in this rut. It wouldn't be any fun for me. Well it would, but then I'd be worried about Stella even more, worried I'd lost my chance, and the weather wouldn't hold for second. Don't think I haven't thought about this. FOMO is part of the problem."

"Take care of the FOMO—she would never know," Steven reminded Adam. "And she probably wouldn't care. She has no right. No right! She's given that up."

"Yeah," he agreed, "but I'd hate myself if I gave up on her. I need to give it one more shot."

"Were you guys...," Steven wondered out loud, "exclusive or something?"

"We never talked about that."

"So it's casual."

"I don't know. Sure."

"So what's the problem? Keep yourself happy in the meantime."

"Well it's casual but it's not nothing. She said she wanted to take it slow. And I was glad—I didn't want to get tangled up in anything; I just want to be happy. But then she never stopped slowing down."

"So give someone else a shot," I said. "Take it easy."

"Yeah yeah I'm trying, it's just—the things she said that first night. If you knew the things she said. The things I said. She never got drunk with me again like that."

"But," I reasoned, "you guys were drunk, so ..."

"Yeah," he said, "so I wish we remembered the things we said when we were drunk and we meant them."

"What...what was it that she said?"

"That's the thing." A lonely chuckle fell out of his mouth. "I don't really remember. But I know I need to hear it again."

"You know what you need?" Steven took a deep breath, girded himself, and spoke very slowly. "You need to be reminded, one last time, that your life is, in fact, a wet dream. You don't need to hear anything, from anyone. Don't wake up. It's really actually very simple—wet dream. Get involved with it. Slap it around. Teach it a trick. Please, for us—for all of us. Take one, or a few at once, for the team."

"Maybe soon Steve, maybe real soon. Just timing is all." He patted him on the back, "But hey—they're here; you're here. Go make me proud. I'll live vicariously through you. It will bring me great joy."

"Oh trust me, I'm trying," he said. "Not all of us here can be the luckiest guy in the world. Some of us are just chubby tech boys."

"Think you're the only one," Adam quipped without thinking, covering his mouth.

"Yup," Steven said, lifting his head up and nodding rapidly, drumming on the railing while he digested this news. "Yup yup yup..." He walked down the dock. "*Yup!*" he cried as he spiked his cigar into the water and threw his arms out wide. "For crying out loud, someone make me stop eating!"

An unassuming server misunderstood Steven's loud frustrations and rushed over to him, earnestly asking what he'd like to eat.

"Oh for fuck sake!" Steven yelled. "Damn it...I'll have the swordfish sandwich. Medium-Rare. Fuck. Thank you. I'm fat. Thank you."

"Right away, sir. We're so sorry."

"That I'm fat?"

"No—" the waiter froze. "About...whatever you're upset about."

"Being fat," Steven nodded.

"Do you still want the sandwich?"

Steven exhaled a deep sigh. "Yes."

Adam walked up to Steven and threw his arm around him, calling out to the waiter, "I'll have one too please!" And as I heard Adam laughing, I could feel the air cooling down. It must have dropped twenty degrees in twenty seconds. A breeze blew in and some of the humidity floated away. It seemed Adam could breathe again, and so could we.

THIRTEEN

CLOUD NINE. That's where Adam decided he would shirk the crowds and see Stella. How perfect. But even the prettiest clouds are made of rain.

He had invited a much smaller group to make the voyage skyward. We were eating breakfast when Stella replied to his invite. "I'm sorry. I've got a lot of work to do. I just can't."

Adam dropped his fork, and I saw a void widen his eyes that scared mine shut. But ten seconds later another ping rang them open. "Wait," she followed, "I can push it back."

"Okay...," Adam thought out loud.

"Sounds fantastic," she messaged. "When do we leave?"

"Alright then. That was strange." Adam shrugged his shoulders. "Guess I'll see her in a few days. And then we'll see. We'll just see how it goes. It'll be fun. It'll be fun."

●

N.N.N. BREAKING NEWS - *Bridge Collapses in St. Louis*

ST. LOUIS - The jarring beginnings of an earthquake only lasted five seconds, but it was enough to bring down the historic Eads Bridge. Thankfully, there was no traffic on the bridge due to construction, but eight construction workers fell into The Mississippi River with the collapsing bridge. It is unlikely that any survived. Updates to follow.

Published at 11:14 a.m., May 29, 2076.

•

First we flew to Cloud Nine's current location, landing in the desert outside of El Paso, Texas, where the hotel shuttle awaited us. Getting up there, like most of our gadget-bound, digitally enhanced lives, was mainly a magic trick. We boarded a cushy rocket that burned soft and slow like a giant cigar. It pulled us comfortably straight up to Cloud Nine like an elevator, completely disrespectful of the wind.

The view got better as we rose high into the air. We passed through a cloud or two, and once we had, I leaned my head against the window to look up. There floated the palace in the sky. The elaborate foray of white blimps making up the soft underbelly of the hotel looked so much like a cloud that I couldn't notice it until we were only a few hundred feet away. Red streaks of fire shot out in bursts from different places around the underside of the blimp at different times, stabilizing the thing so perfectly it seemed to float not in the still blue sky, but in outer space, where it would remain just as unaffected by the forces of nature, by everyone and everything beneath it.

Our little ship came up through a passage in the very center and parked in the hotel. Several beautiful people greeted us with digital documents to sign. No one read them. Everyone signed them immediately. I understood this action to be signing my life away in case anything happened, like falling thousands of feet, but somehow I didn't think it was even possible.

They escorted us from the rocket bay down a hallway. It split around a circular waist-height wall that opened to the air below. Naturally, I spit into it and watched that ball of saliva until it joined the clouds drifting beneath us. They led us to an expansive deck in the sky, where cocktails, appetizers, and oxygen awaited us if we wanted it. An identical Frank Sinatra impersonator lured us out onto the deck in front of a full band, enchanting us as he sang, *"Come fly with me, let's fly, let's fly away..."* Adam took Stella by the hand and spun her around, and he started to sing the words he knew. They danced across deck before the big blue sky. *"Once I get you up there, where the air is rarefied, we'll just glide, starry-eyed..."* And just like that, it seemed Stella had fallen back under his spell. *"Weather-wise it's such a lovely day. You just say the words and we'll beat the birds down to Acapulco Bay. It's perfect for a flying honeymoon, they say. Come fly with me, let's fly, let's fly away."*

We had walked into a dream, a hallucination where we really walked among the clouds, atop man's best and brightest attempt at heaven on earth. We stood on large strips of solid wood that looked like they had just been ripped out of a redwood forest. They lined up in prettier rows all the way out to the edge, where a long arm extended into the sky like a dock in the ocean. At its end, a beautiful veranda hung over the clouds. Slowly, fearfully, we walked out. A few white ropes strung between wooden posts made up the fence on the edge of the deck and beyond that—nothing. No safety net, just air and clouds. No safety net. I just couldn't believe there was no safety net.

We walked to the very end. I grabbed the rope, trembling a little, and looked down. Puffy white clouds moved hypnotically just beneath us like a treadmill made of marshmallows, tempting me to jump into them as if this really were heaven. For a moment I forgot I stood on anything at all, like I was just another cloud passing under the bright sun to feel its warmth on my back. A tingling feeling on my neck cooled me like the crisp open sky. And with the refreshing wind in my face came the slight fear that I might never return to earth as a grounded human being.

I looked back at the hotel. Turrets and balconies climbed over each other toward a pointy peak ten stories up. The structure must have been made of only the very lightest metals, but it was painted and covered in holographic veneers to look like a stone castle from a fairy tale. Flawless, like it had never once seen the wind or the rain up there.

That was the promise after all; Cloud Nine guaranteed its guests perfect weather during the day, meaning sunny and between seventy and eighty-five degrees, or their money back. They were able to do this because the hotel was always moving, however slowly. Using the one-year forecasts, they planned routes way in advance to avoid any bad weather. If they couldn't get to clear skies, they elevated above the clouds. If it was going to be too cold up high, they descended to warmer temperatures. Of course they'd never had Adam Anderson on board, but they weren't worried—not in heaven.

I had zoned so deep into the sky, one of the hostesses nearly scared me off the edge when she spoke behind us. "Do you have any questions?" she asked. "Is there anything we can do for you? Anything at all?"

"Oh," Adam digested her words. "Well, I'm not sure. Anyone...?" He looked around. "Anyone have any questions?"

"Yeah...," Stella stared blankly over the edge, "has anyone ever fallen off?"

"Yes, people have fallen a number of times."

"Huh?" She glanced back at the hostess.

"Oh, I'm sorry. You must not have had a chance to look through the guidebook—no one has ever died on Cloud Nine. We have systems patrolling the edges and drones ready to deploy. Everyone that's fallen off has been safely caught by a drone with large net and flown back up. The equipment is on par with the latest professional sky-diving standards."

"How many have fallen?"

"Over the years? Dozens. Maybe over a hundred. People do a lot of drinking up here, and with the altitude, it hits hard. We would have safety nets if we didn't have our bases well-covered with the drones. We have seven of them. Seven people could fall at once and they would all survive. There's absolutely nothing to fear, I promise."

"Honest?" Stella raised her eyebrows.

"One hundred percent," the hostess assured.

"Are they ready right now?"

"They're always ready ma'am."

Stella slowly began stepping over the ropes like she was reaching into the cookie jar.

"Ma'am. Excuse me," the hostess blurted. "Ma'am. It's only an emergency precaution."

Stella continued creeping out until she stood completely outside the ropes.

"Ma'am! We don't allow falling on purpose!"

Stella shot back a smile that unscrunched our horrified faces and implied she was only kidding. But then she spread her arms out wide and fell gently backward into the sky.

I grabbed the ropes for her dear life and looked down, watching her tumble into a cloud.

"Stella!" Adam yelled behind me.

I wasn't looking for more than a moment when I felt hands on my back—not pulling me in, but pushing me right off the ledge—as Adam leapt headlong over my back yelling, "Wait up!"

My mind was racing faster than my body as I plummeted into the clouds, and when I surfaced on the other side of that blinding whiteness, I burst out of my panic with the all-consuming feeling of surrender. The clear air rushed into my face and crushed all my uncertainties. They could not keep up at this speed. I could see Stella below me soaring like a bird, and Adam diving after her like a bomb. The smooth red desert expanded far below and I screamed for joy at the earth. Even the birds could not feel this free. There's a feeling about falling that that I don't think flying could ever touch, the kind of thing that makes angels envious. You know that it must at some point end, and you will either splat or be saved. But you really can't control it, so you actually stop trying. There is some strange freedom in that.

And there were the drones to end this dream before it turned into a nightmare, swooping in next to each of us. The drone matched my speed exactly before extending a net out beneath me. It slowed our fall, gently wrapping me up in the net before lifting me back to Cloud Nine.

When we hovered over the deck, everyone was clapping and cheering, except for Steven, who was snorting oxygen and laughing like it was laughing gas. "I think you just cheated death," he remarked as the clapping died down. "I've never even cheated on a test."

"How did it feel?" June asked Adam. "Tell us."

"It's not a feeling I can even put into words," he panted.

"Weren't you afraid you would die?" Steven asked.

"One would think," Adam thought out loud, "I've never felt more unafraid."

"Well," Steven quipped, "I'm proud of you guys. If I did that," he peered over the edge, "I would definitely die. No doubt about it. The Cloud Nine drones would see me tumbling through the air and just think, 'Nice.' I'm more of a cloud two or three guy. Let's be honest."

And everyone was laughing, except for Steven, who was playing it straight—the comedian. But I wasn't too sure he was comfortable with his newfound role. He was churning his insecurities into something funny and spitting them out for everyone else to enjoy. It must have been grating on the inside. However funny they were, he was turning into his words.

•

As the crew migrated down the sky dock back toward the hotel, a man stood at the end, hiding behind his aviators, waiting for us to walk by. When we got close, he took them off.

It was Jonathan Harvey.

"Adam." He reached out his hand and leaned back with a shy smile. "I'm so glad you're having fun."

Adam looked at his hand for a while before he finally shook it. "What are you doing up here?"

"I come here all the time—you know that. I've invited you before. I love this place. It's my little hideaway. A place like this ... it doesn't exist without our forecasting." He nudged Adam on the shoulder like they were a team again. "They had to take it down for a while you know," Harvey caught himself before going further into it, "but that's no matter. Adam, let's make things right. I want to tell you I'm sorry. I was rude. I fell off my rocker. I was simply unreasonable. I want to start fresh—a new beginning for us— starting right now. Like old times, when the weather was easy and you were fetching the forecast."

"Okay ..." Adam studied Harvey's squinty eyes.

"You've been doing a great job Adam." He crossed his arms proudly. "Over the past couple weeks we've been right about 98 percent of the time. There were a few days—" He caught himself again. "Nothing really. I want to say thank you and congratulations on finding such happiness. You keep it up and I'll get the forecasts back to normal."

"I'm just trying to keep people safe is all. Frankly, if your forecasts are wrong, I don't care."

"I suppose I'll just have to start tracking your emotions and predict based on them," he jabbed with an abrasive chuckle.

"You do that."

"Don't think I haven't tried," he muttered as he turned away.

"What was that?"

"Just a playful joke, Adam."

"Can't we just have a peaceful conversation?"

"But we are Adam. We are. Don't worry. Look around you. How could anyone feel anything but peace up here? This is where I run and hide when I need a little more peace. I recommend you do the same, whether it's here, or some other place that keeps you calm."

"Anywhere you're not is fine with me."

"Hmm..." He closed his eyes for a moment, holding his tongue. "Excuse me," Harvey called out to hotel attendant showing another guest around. "Would you please have my things packed and get a shuttle ready? It's time for me to go."

"Right away, sir." She smiled.

Harvey turned back to Adam. "Anything for you Adam. Anything for you."

"I didn't ask for this," Adam calmly replied.

"That's right." Harvey nodded. "I did."

Adam didn't seem to understand what Harvey meant by that, but he chose not to try. He walked away, throwing his arm around Stella and falling right back into their high. I was left standing there alone with Harvey. He turned toward a bench behind us but simultaneously beckoned, "Clark."

I didn't know he knew my name. I had never actually met him.

"I'd like to speak with you," he said as he sat down.

"Um...," I felt like I was betraying Adam just by having a conversation with the man. "I gotta go."

"Stay," he said without even looking at me. "It'll only be a minute. You need to stay."

"What is it?"

"Do you see all these clouds?" Harvey asked. He paused to contemplate them. "These are healthy clouds. These clouds were in the forecast before they were in the sky. Eventually the water that makes them up will condense, and it will fall to the earth, and it will be a healthy rain, a cleansing rain, a rain that feeds the ground just as we planned, with the timing we've built our schedules around, the way we've depended on it."

"Got it," I said, waiting to see where he was going.

"Depended on it." He turned his head and looked me in the eyes. "Depended on it. Clark. I don't mean to scare you, but

Adam's happiness isn't just critical to our safety from bad weather; it's essential for this country's entire livelihood."

"How do you mean?" I sat down next to him, looking over an ocean of clouds.

"The systems are all integrated, Clark. Weather prediction, agriculture, transportation, energy systems, the market—everything. We've become dependent on precisely predictable weather. The weather is a non-linear system Clark. When we don't have it mastered, so is our society. That means we are subject to sensitive dependence on initial conditions. The more uncertainty we experience, the more this country's agricultural and economic systems suffer. If one of Adam's moods goes on for too long, we will really be hurting. These weather anomalies are not self-contained; they affect the atmosphere and create more and more weather anomalies, unpredictable conditions all over. The more weather Adam creates, the less we can predict weather everywhere. The more he offsets the system, the more dangerous conditions become everywhere. If he ever creates too much, we won't be able to keep up at all. The chain reaction will grow exponentially, and we will be at the mercy of Mother Nature. Clark, you must understand the gravity here. Already, the ripples of Adam's unhappiness permeate every aspect of our infinitely connected society. Everything factors into everything to optimize efficiency. We've built a society too great, and nothing stands that tall alone."

As I stared over the clouds, waiting for Harvey to continue, an airplane in the distance caught my eye. It was getting closer.

"What is that?" I asked.

"*That* is something you will never ever see, except up here. You're lucky one happens to be passing by." It was skimming the top of the cloud cover like a boat powering through the waves. "It's a weather bot."

"What does it do?"

"Measures. They measure everything. They gather data. Those babies allow us to predict the weather. They fly all over the world, not just here. They fly at every altitude. They're everywhere—though you'll never see them."

"Why can't we see them from the ground?"

"They're stealth, and camouflaged. Invisible essentially. The bottom holographically displays what you would see on the other side of it—sky. The top does the same. They're very hard to notice from below or above. We happen to be looking at it almost head on."

I didn't realize how fast the thing was moving until suddenly it was upon us. It buzzed beneath Cloud Nine, just a few hundred feet below and a few hundred feet away, with a muted guttural roar like a low groan of thunder in the distance. The thing was colossal, bigger than any passenger plane I'd seen, almost as big as the hotel itself.

"My god," I said. "How does it stay in the air?"

"Big boys." Harvey nodded proudly.

"Why are they so huge?"

"Some are small. Different sizes for different purposes."

"What purpose would this one serve?"

"Just measurement. Data collection."

"So why are they all different sizes?"

"Different measurements. We have machines on the ground too, machines underground, underwater. Everywhere—we're keeping tabs on everything, and it's all interconnected. These are big, complicated machines, Clark, dealing with powerful natural forces. Like we're talking about," he reeled the conversation back in. "The machines we depend on, the complex systems that make our lives so simple. It's a privilege to live like we do—simple," Harvey grunted.

"Sure," I said.

"You've got to keep things simple here Clark. That's all you've got to do for Adam—you keep things simple. Got it?"

"What do you mean?"

"Humans…we have an incredible ability to compartmentalize. One side of the mind can dominate and completely ignore the other if you will it that way. You can build a great wall to block out the bad. For most of his life, Adam was extremely good at it. But then the other side started to leak in, and then it was gushing in. And now there's a big whopping hole in the dam that constantly needs to be sealed up with new things—happy things. That's what this project is for. And you're on the front lines. Don't let the dam break."

"And how do I do that?"

"Phrase I learned in the army—" He held up his finger. "We used to—Clark, my god, we had these cold, cold nights. Long nights. Blizzards. Bad ones. Nothing we could do about the cold. Damn ice crept in every crack and corner—you were always cold. Some part of you was always cold. So we used to say, we used to tell ourselves, 'You're only as cold as your warmest part.'"

"Only as cold..." I mumbled the sentiment to myself.

"See, with non-linear systems," Harvey's eyes lit up, "one bad apple can ruin the whole batch. But not with us. If we can just focus on the good, everything else gets a little brighter, doesn't it? Everything else seems to...warm up."

"Yeah," I said. "I think so. But...don't you think maybe we are non-linear systems too?"

"Listen, Adam has some very cold parts to him," Harvey said resolutely, "and there's nothing to do but stay away from them, and keep him away from them." Harvey seemed to search me with his eyes, nodding ever so slightly. "He has daddy issues. Plain and simple. They will never go away. After I hired Adam, I actually tried to fix them. I tried to be somewhat of a father figure for him. I had a special place for Adam. Felt like I...knew him somehow. I saw something in him—this drive, this unstoppable will—that I respected. I saw myself in him. So I tried to give him some stability, whether he wanted it or thought he needed it or not. But he never really took to it. Always had an excuse not to join my family for dinner, or play a round of golf, or come out sailing, yachting, you name it—always had an excuse. Eventually I stopped trying. He had figured things out all by himself and didn't want someone coming in to tell him what's what."

"I can see that," I said.

As Harvey leaned back and crossed his leg over his thigh, I noticed that one leg was bionic. "But," Harvey went on, "even though he can't see it, he needs someone to take his hand, or he'll slip right off his peak again. He'll fall as far as you let him. I can feel it already," Harvey took a deep breath. "Clark, you are Adam's assistant. You are with him all the time. You may not realize what you signed up for, but you are a constant force in his life. You need to be mindful of his underlying issues and continually steer him however you can. Offer him the guidance he never had, the constant voice of good will. Point him to all the warmth. Remind him of the light. Don't let him search around in the darkness; he won't like what he finds. Don't ever let him feel the cold. That's what numbness is for, not feeling the cold."

Harvey left and I sat there for a while watching the sun duck under a carpet of bright red clouds. The moonless night wrapped its cool arms around the hotel in the sky. The clouds beneath stretched like an eternal quilt, snuffing out any lights that might have fogged up our perfect darkness from below. The stars glowed impossibly bright that night. I had never seen so many stars or been so close to them. No light to confuse them, just black sky, sleeping steady under a million bright eyes.

An outdoor bar hosted most of the hotel's trillionaire guests and their entourages. They mingled in the thin air, sucking down oxygen and alcohol. Adam strode energetically to and fro with Stella under his arm. Just listening to it all from my bench on the edge of the sky was enough for a while. Roaring laughter attacked from every angle. I couldn't sit for a moment without hearing more laughter behind me, and I began to laugh a little myself.

I turned to watch all of the beautiful people laughing and competing, and it took me some time to find Adam and Stella. They talked close right in the center of it all, surrounded by people but completely unaware of them.

●

P.E.A. ELECTRICAL STORMS IN THE SOUTHWEST

Highly unusual electrical storms are popping up randomly across Arizona and New Mexico. Hundreds of areas are seeing heat lighting passing between very low-hanging clouds. Some areas have reported bolts bouncing through neighborhoods.

No one has been hurt, and there appear to be only minor damages thus far.

Stay indoors, away from windows.

6/2/76 - 8:33 a.m. - Public Emergency Alert
U.S. National Safety System

FOURTEEN

WE HUDDLED IN THE WARM DIM LIGHT. A brisk breeze danced around our crow's nest perched on the peak of Cloud Nine. The small fire between us made up our collective heart, flickering and crackling to the beat of hungry souls. Smoke lifted in jagged curls, lazy lines like ballet dancers who hadn't made up their minds. Drunken laughter and the brief entanglements of eyes lent us the notion that humanity really is *good*. But that feeling can shift as quickly as the wind.

"I'm chilly." June pouted as she smacked the wine on her lips together, pulling snug her tight leather jacket and wrapping her arms around herself.

"You wanna know a little trick, Juney?" Adam asked.

"If it'll help."

"It will. So it's like this—you're not as cold as you think you are. You're just not. Your body is only telling you you're cold so that you'll do something to help prevent you from actually getting cold. You know what I mean? Your body isn't really that cold right now. You're not in danger. So the key is to remind your body how warm it is before it can tell you that you're cold."

"Okay. So how do I do that?"

"Think about your toes. They're right by the fire. Your toes are warm, right?"

"Very warm. Almost too warm."

"Just think about your toes. Don't think about anything else, just focus on your toes. Go ahead, try it."

June closed her eyes, lifting her hands like she was deeply meditating.

"You're only as cold as your warmest part," Adam said.

"I think I like that." Stella turned to Adam in the crater cushion they shared. "Where did you hear that?"

"It's something my dad used to tell me. He used to say it all the time."

"Oh my god," June blurted as she opened her eyes. "I think it's working. Seriously. I think it's really working."

"Yeah, it usually works for me," Adam replied matter-of-factly.

Stella closed her eyes and began to meditate the same way. After a few minutes went by, June noticed that Stella had completely tuned out. "Stella?" She laughed. "Earth to Stella. You asleep?"

"No," Stella's eyes opened, "I'm just trying to do this warmest part thing; it's not working for me. No matter how hard I try, I'm still cold. And I meditate all the time. It's one of the only things I know I'm decent at doing."

"Maybe that warm Miami blood can't handle the cold."

"I'm not from Miami," Stella replied.

"Where are you from?"

"The moon I guess. I don't know. Pretty much everywhere."

"Thank you for coming down to spend some time with us earthlings." June giggled ambiguously.

"I just mean I've lived a lot of places. I don't know where to say I'm from. I don't have any memory of the place I was born, and I've never lived anywhere for more than a few years.

"Alright," Adam obliged, "where have you lived?"

"Let's see…San Francisco, New York City, a small town in Georgia full of pines, Alaska, Yellowstone, Park City, New Orleans, Oregon, Texas. And that's just since I turned eighteen and left home. Oh, and Vegas."

"Vegas?" said June. "What were you doing there?"

"Nothing really. Odd jobs. Easy money."

"What types?" A greedy giggle slipped through her sealed lips.

"Nothing notable, mostly pushing really old people around in wheelchairs. The stripping actually happened in Alaska if that's what you're looking for." Stella began to laugh. At herself. With herself. And as she watched our eyes grow wide she only laughed harder, until we were all laughing.

"Why, why—" Adam struggled to get the words out. "What were you doing stripping in Alaska?"

"It sounds cold," June added.

"It was cold. It was very cold. Fuck, it was awful. I had to make all this extra money to do all the cool outdoor things I wanted to do. It was the only well-paying job available. I only lasted a couple weeks. Strange time in my life. And the weather up there—wild. Which is part of why I went, but I almost died a few times. I mean it. Tumultuous time all around. That's all there is to it."

"And what about all the other places?" Adam asked. "What were you doing everywhere else?"

"Just failing mostly." Stella smiled. She spoke with a cast-off innocence. Words rebelled, but a newness toward everything crept into the spaces between them. "I guess I went to Yellowstone to get away from all the bright lights of Vegas. I was a trail guide, then a climbing guide, then just a climber till the dollars ran out. In New York City I worked in an antique shop learning how to fix old weird things that can't be fixed by robots. I loved that, but I failed to sell my art, and I got tired of everyone over there, and I had to get out of the city again. That's when the whole Alaskan *adventure* happened. After a couple months I hitchhiked down to Oregon. I basically tried to be a hippie there, one of those people with no PID who try to stay totally disconnected. It got to be a force, and I ended up in San Francisco with a tech titan I met in the woods on one of his little retreats. He supported my art and he was cool at first. I lived with him as long as I could bear it. Ended up making some angry paintings. Now I'm poor again but much happier."

"Look at this little gypsy," June's voice splintered into unattached tones. "Honestly, I'm impressed. I wanna be as adventurous as you. I mean it. I wanna wander wild like that. You really get around, don't you Stel?" It was often hard to tell if June was being sincere or sarcastic, endearing or condescending, or both, or if she even knew herself. She just kind of took stances, whichever one felt right in that moment.

Stella barely seemed to hear what June said, but I know she did, because she quietly hummed "I Get Around" by the Beach Boys, before finally looking at June to reply, "Then wander wild. You're the only one holding you back."

"You really have done a lot of shit," said Steven. "I feel so inexperienced now. Just, in life."

"Oh no, I'm never experienced. That's why I like experiencing new things, so I never become too experienced in any one. It's kind of a problem." Her words sunk into Adam like tranquilizer darts. He was taken by her simplicity, her unrestrained yet unassuming confidence. "I'm not even done—in Georgia I was a nanny for a hot minute. I didn't mind chilling with the children but I didn't like the parents. So I went to New Orleans, where I served beverages and drank a lot of them while I was at it, and fell for this customer." Stella laughed. "Which didn't go so well once we eventually got to see each other sober. But at least he taught me the harmonica. I took that with me to Park City, where I was a poorly qualified snowboard instructor, but I got cold again and went to Miami and washed up into your life. And here I am."

"Damn." Adam smiled. "You just do whatever the fuck you want don't you? I wish I had met you when I was eighteen."

"It's probably good you didn't. You've actually accomplished some things in your twenties. I just run around breaking things and moving onto the next one."

"Why didn't you ever stay put?"

"I like change. Well, I hate change, but I really hate not to change. And I don't like anything weighing me down. What am I supposed to do? Fall in love again and try to live someone else's life? Tried that in Texas—had to run away for years to get my own life back."

"Good god girl," June gasped. "How many times have you fallen in love?"

"Too many and not enough." She shook her head. "This is why I don't like to speak in groups. I'm too honest. Everything in my head just falls right out of my mouth." She began to laugh again, and there was that careless strength. It puzzled me how someone so open could remain so mysterious, like there were still so many secrets to be shaken out of her wild jungle of hair.

"But that's what we love about you Stel," Adam replied. "Although, you're not *that* honest. You've still never told me where you were born."

"Oh right, that." Stella zipped her lips shut.

"No she did," Said June. "She's from the moon."

Stella smiled. "I don't usually tell anyone, because I was born on Soteria, the Space Settlement. Probably why I'm such a weirdo.

My parents were working and living up there. They were voluntary test subjects for extraterrestrial survival for a few years. But we moved back to earth before everything got blown to smithereens. Otherwise I'd be stardust."

"You were born in outer space?" Adam looked at her, deadpan.

"One of 392 surviving babies born in space. I was a big old revolutionary science baby."

"Seriously? Why didn't you tell me this?"

"No one ever believes me. Besides, it's not like I remember it, and it's out of my control. Nobody's given me any big awards for it, nor should they. I was just... born there, like anywhere else."

"Have you ever been back?"

"To outer space?"

"Yeah."

"I mean, no, I'm not a trillionaire. This right here," she looked around the brightly speckled black dome above us as though she were about to float, "is the closest I've come. Is it even possible anymore? I don't think it really is. Isn't it illegal?"

"It's not illegal for government sanctioned purposes," Steven piped in, clearly having researched the subject. "I mean, none of the space tourism companies are still running. But the equipment would probably still work. With enough money, you make it happen."

Adam smiled and glanced at Stella.

"Wallace Greenberg, the guy that owns this place, did it a few years ago," Steven continued, "but he almost got hit by some space junk. No one has tried it since, not for fun. It's too dangerous. Only for mining."

"Oh." Adam relaxed as the opportunity turned into pipe dream.

"I'd take the risk if I could," Stella said.

"I'd entertain it," Adam said, "but I haven't gotten bored down here yet. Might as well dodge the space junk for now."

"Easier said than done," she replied.

"Your parents," I asked, "were they scientists? Do they still work on... space stuff?"

"No, no. They were just perfectly normal people that made for a perfect case study of what it's like to live in space."

"And what is it that you do?" asked June.

"Nothing really. I'm just a hostess. I don't have any skills that a robot can't do better."

"Sure you do," Adam practically reprimanded her. "You're an artist."

"Aren't we all."

"But you are."

"Well, I've never actually sold anything. In order to be a career artist I would probably need someone wealthy to validate my work."

"How about me and Uncle Sam?" Adam replied. "He's got pretty deep pockets. And I'll validate your work; it's fucking amazing. There—validated. How much do you want for your mosaic? Just name your price and I'll buy it."

"Oh thank you, but no, the mosaic isn't for sale. I could never sell that one."

"Why not?"

"I don't know. I think that would just about turn me inside out. Just thinking about selling it makes me feel like a mess."

"Well what would you sell?"

"Nothing at the moment. Once I finish the mosaic I'll start making things that can be bought, if I ever finish it."

"You don't ever have to sell any of your art if you don't want." Adam pondered. "I'm just saying you don't have to keep working other jobs either. You should be focusing on your art. Your work is really something, I'm telling you. I'll be your ... your patron ... or whatever. I'll have the project provide everything you need just to keep working on your art. You'll have the freedom to do whatever you want. You just have to keep making art."

"Adam, that's," Stella began to tear up, "that's amazing. It's ... it's the best thing anyone's ever told me. But I can't." She stood up.

"Why not?"

"Thank you so much. I mean it. I wish I could."

"But, Stel, you can."

"I ... just ... I ..." She shook her head. She couldn't even get the words out. She stumbled away and spun down a spiral staircase from our crow's nest.

Adam searched our faces for answers, but no one had any, except for June.

"Don't worry about it babe," she told Adam. "How rude. She doesn't deserve what you offered her if she can't accept it."

"No, I—"

"It's not your fault," she continued. "Don't let it bug you; it's not worth it. You've got all you need right here."

"No, it's not that simple...," Adam professed as he began to stand up, and before anyone could say anything, he was rushing down the steps after her.

The moment Adam left, Ned replaced him in the group, popping up on my wrist. "Clark!"

"Ah!" I nearly fell into the fire. "What!"

"We have dramatic pressure changes spanning nearly the entire Southwest, including the area you are in *right now*."

"Shit, so what does that mean exactly? What's going on?"

"That's what I'm asking you. Nothing's going on with the weather yet, but it could. It's about to—that's what I'm trying to tell you—unless you calm Adam down. What's he doing?"

"He just went off after Stella. He's feeling—I don't know what he's feeling, but he's crazy about her."

"Clark, you have to find him right now and calm him down. Got it? Hurry. The atmosphere is doing very strange things and we don't know how it will shake out."

"Okay...I'll see what I can do."

I walked down the spiral staircase after Adam, not knowing what I would say if I caught him, other than apologize for chasing him down and invading his space. When I reached the main deck of the hotel, I was relieved to see that both Adam and Stella had disappeared. There wasn't a trace of them, or even a sound, on the empty deck at three in the morning.

"Have you found them yet?" There was Ned violating my ear again.

"No, but what should I say if I do?"

"Anything. Just change the subject. Just...just separate them like school kids. Hurry up."

"This place is huge. They could be anywhere."

"I'm patching you through."

"Ned, no."

"It's done."

And there on my wrist and in my ear was a live feed of exactly what Adam was seeing and hearing.

"Ned...I can't be doing this."

"You have to be doing this. You have to know where he is and what's going on. You have to be ready to do anything you need to do at any moment. You're not there for, for, for shitting kicks and giggles up on a cloud. This is a matter of national security. Do your fucking job."

I watched. Adam wandered along the back edge of Cloud Nine, on a narrow deck like a sidewalk in outer space. As he came around a bend, there she was.

Stella sat on the very edge, leaning back on her palms, her bare feet hanging into the open air. She had her head tilted back as she peered into the stars, which cast a glow on her tear-soaked face.

"Stella," Adam said as he slowly approached. She shot him a glance and then looked out over the sky. "What are you doing?"

"Look," she pointed, "I'm watching the thunderstorm."

In the distance, swirling black beasts lit up intermittently, barreling toward us like a herd of giant bowling balls.

"Can I watch with you?" He slowly approached and sat down on the edge next to her. He scanned the whole sky. "It's not just there," he said. "It's there." He pointed toward a crackling pile of lightning. "And there...and there...and there. And fuck, it's everywhere." As he spoke the very words, the storms intensified.

Now the night was flashing into day and highlighting just how dark those clouds had turned. The wind was picking up, rushing in from every direction, stronger every second.

"Go to them now!" Ned was in my ear. "It's time to break this up before things get worse."

I began walking along the perimeter as fast as I could, which wasn't very fast—unable to take my eyes off of what I was watching while trying not to get blown overboard.

As Adam watched confused clouds smash together, eventually he realized Stella wasn't looking at the storm anymore. When he looked over, she was already looking into his eyes.

"Why are you looking at me?" asked Adam.

She glanced at the storm and then back at his eyes.

"I thought you were watching the storm." Adam was blinking now.

"I am watching the storm," she said.

He paused. "Then what do you see? Tell me, because I can't see it. What do you see?" The chaos overflowed Adam's visual plane behind her.

"Those eyes, and that heart of yours," she mused, "are wilder than whatever you're making out there."

He moved closer to her face. Her black curls snapped at him in the wind. He closed his eyes as he kissed her, but only for a moment, until she was pushing him away.

"Adam, look out there!" She flung an open hand at the storms. But he just kept looking at her. Suddenly the rain came flying across the sky in heavy sheets that doused them almost instantly. "Don't fall me Adam. Don't ever fall for me. It's the worst thing you could ever do. I can't be with you. We can never have this."

"But we already do. We have *this*, right now, whatever it is."

"Well you need to stop it. You need to be with someone like June. You need to have fun."

"June? What? I've been holding out for *you*. I have way more fun with you anyway."

"We've had a lot of fun, and I would love to be your friend someday, but don't hold out for me. Please, don't hold out anymore."

"Why are you doing this? I don't understand. Just let it be what it is."

"Whatever you're feeling between us—it's just not there. I'm so sorry. I'm sorry we had too much fun. I'm sorry we made love. I was stupid. I'm sorry."

"What do you mean it's not there? I know how it feels when it's not there. It's never there for me. I never care. This is different. This is something."

"It's nothing. I'm sorry," she had to yell over the roaring wind as she turned away from him, sitting as still stone while the tempest pulled her wet hair pack in clumps like Medusa's snakes.

"Stella?" Adam yelled.

But she just kept looking out at those growing storms until Adam left. At first I thought I'd run into him on the path, but he was going the other way, and I ran into Stella.

By the time I reached her she was ducking over her knees jolting like lighting, while tears blew off her face to join the storm.

"Stella," I knelt down next to her. "What happened? What's wrong?"

"Nothing's wrong; nothing happened."

"What's the problem—you just don't like him?"

"I wish I liked him. If I liked him, this wouldn't be a problem."

"What? What do you mean?"

"I think I love him."

"You do?"

"I've loved him since the first time I kissed him. And I think he might love me too."

"So what the hell are you doing crying over here? You two could be so happy."

I waited for her answer while she stared into the storms for far too long. The wind was getting louder, and the rain thicker, and the whole of Cloud Nine was beginning to tremble in the sky. I could feel the vibrations from the deck traveling up my spine. "Stella!"

"Do you know what love is Clark?" She yelled over the rattling inner-workings of Cloud Nine, staring lightning rods into my eyes.

"What?"

"Love is not happiness. Love is honesty. Love is when you take on each other's pain. If he needs to be happy all the time... our love is already doomed." She turned back and began to weep again. "Please don't tell him," she cried. "He can't know, for his own sake. Please." She didn't seem to care that the whole hotel was beginning to blow away—we were moving through the sky like a ship in a tumultuous sea.

"Stella!" I reached out my hand to pull her up. "We need to get off of this ledge!"

She opened her eyes and stretched out flat on her back, looking up and finding the last little patch of starry sky as the black tide washed over everything. "What the fuck are you doing!"

"It's just so beautiful up here. So, so gorgeous—" she choked. "And I can never be up here again." She stared upward as if hoping any moment one of those stars might reach down and pull her to itself before they drown.

In a way, it worked. The hotel began rising through the storm. Faster and faster. She sat up as the deck began to rock and sway, boards shooting up randomly.

"Let's go!" I yelled, and we began to run along the edge of Cloud Nine, constantly dropping to our knees to stay on deck as the hotel convulsed violently. The air must have warmed to one hundred degrees in just a few moments. We rose faster and faster, so fast I could feel a wind striking me from above.

"Clark!" Ned popped up on my PID again. "Get Adam off of Cloud Nine! Now! I can't use your PID to put you through—the storm is interfering—but last we saw—"

Ned cut out as a massive bolt of lightning struck the veranda on the sky dock. It fell off and plummeted down in flames. The supporting blimps had become unbalanced and began to slowly tilt in one direction, rocking and jostling beneath us like an earthquake. In time, it would tip over like a sinking ship. Red lights ignited as sirens blared. Round holes in the floor opened up, revealing escape pods. Employees ran about the deck, yelling the same thing as the loudspeaker but in different words, "Get in the pods!"

Across the deck, I saw Adam and June get into one. Now I simply needed to reach the nearest one myself before Cloud Nine went down. Guests were scrambling out of their rooms and onto the deck in their underwear. We were rising so fast, so high, that it was becoming difficult to breathe. Another bolt of lightning crushed the top turret of the hotel, which tumbled down the side of the castle and fell away, taking a couple guests off the deck with it.

The impact jolted us all flat to the ground and the hotel tipped sideways more quickly. You could hear the sounds of the blimps underneath us bursting one by one. The hotel's ascent shifted to an ever-faster falling. Stella and I slid down the slippery deck, clawing our way toward an escape pod. Those with less room to slide slipped off the edge into the great electric sea.

We rammed into a pod. Steven reached out his hand to help pull us in. A man operating the pod closed the door, and we shot out the bottom of Cloud Nine, diving toward the earth. We fell fast until a giant parachute deployed, ripping us up into a much slower descent. Out the window, silhouetted against flashes of lightning, I could see a couple dozen other pods floating down with us.

It's a good thing the wind was strong, blowing us away from the hotel, because before we made it to the ground, I saw the whole of Cloud Nine tumble to the earth like a massive Molotov cocktail. It hit the ground and exploded with an enormous sound. And the thunder kept pounding its fists even louder, reminding us of the fundamental principle we so easily forget—what goes up, must come down.

FIFTEEN

IN THE QUIET, in the stillness of the dark, I could hear those clocks ticking again. Now the collection was displayed throughout a room dedicated solely to its timeless glory, where the watches were always whispering. As I laid back on a leather chair flipping through images of recent disasters, the sharp symphony of time rattled through my ears and into my gut.

They told Adam everyone escaped safely from Cloud Nine. They told Adam no one was seriously hurt. They told Adam a lot of things. But the hands of those clocks, they just kept reaching forward. Like flickering lights, each tick-tock stumbled and fell into the darkness forever, while an army of others marched behind it, every bit as ready to step boldly off the cliff before us, into the abyss behind us.

●

N.N.N. The Anderson Affect – *A Hellish Evening in Heaven*

EL PASO AIR SPACE, TX - Roughly half of the customers and employees aboard Cloud Nine died late last night when a severe, unexpected thunderstorm thrashed the floating palace to the earth, totaling 109 fatalities.

Short of Adam Anderson's emotions, the exact cause of the sudden microburst taking on a macro scale across the Southwest is unknown. In an early statement, the founder of Cloud Nine, Wallace Greenberg, said that Anderson had been aboard Cloud Nine during the storm, barely escaping in time. However, the trillionaire tycoon retracted

his statement after checking records, telling us Anderson left Cloud Nine hours before
the storm even began.

The Pursuit of Happiness Project released
a statement saying, "Adam is going through
a trying time during his grandmother's illness. But with a team of revolutionary doctors carefully implementing experimental
treatments, experts remain confident she
will soon return to full health, alleviating
Adam's concerns."

It is yet to be seen just how far the power
of medicine can go to relieve Adam's grandmother of her illness and Adam of the stress
caused by it. Having witnessed the horror of
109 fatalities on Cloud Nine and 57 fatalities across the Southwest due to lightning
strikes, automotive accidents, heat strokes,
and extremely high winds, we are left to
wonder what disasters may occur if Adam's
grandmother dies.

The storms that wrought such destruction have
not entirely disappeared. Heavy cloud cover
remains in the sky, and the unusual heat wave
that accompanied the violent thunderstorms has
turned into a foggy cold snap. Temperatures
seem to be rising slowly. Having reached a low
of 34 degrees an hour ago, the affected area
has climbed back up to 47 degrees.

Published at 7:07 p.m., June 3, 2076.

●

"Clark," Ned beamed himself in while power walking, so that he looked like a tiny man in a tracksuit, on a treadmill, on my wrist, "I shouldn't have to tell you last night was strike two."

"I figured," I sighed.

"And I mean strike two, and strike two and a half, and strike two point nine, nine, nine, nine, nine to infinity. That's how close I am to pulling the plug on our current emotional containment strategy."

"What's the alternative? You tried drugs. That was a sure disaster. A constant one."

"The project has some ideas you don't need to know about. The people of this country are livid and ready for a new strategy. Make sure Adam watches the press conference; it starts in a few minutes. It's designed to quell the sentiment, and hopefully improve Adam's mood. But your ice is thin big boy."

"What? Big boy?"

"You're on thin ice and you're a big boy meaning you're about to break—whatever! Go ahead; enjoy yourself. This lifestyle of yours won't last for long. Just watch the press conference."

Ned vanished. I wandered back into Adam's penthouse, where I was staying in one of ten guest bedrooms. He was watching movies and sipping bourbon and trying not to do much thinking. At least he didn't know for sure that anyone had died, though he suspected it. Either way he wore the feeling of a dog with his tail between his legs. He had become one of the most powerful people in the world, yet remained powerless to his own emotions, and not powerful enough to win what he really wanted.

Steven lay in a pit of cushions on the floor. I sat down on the other side of the massive couch to wait for the Pursuit of Happiness press conference to play on the holovision. Adam set his glass down with a loud clink and tossed lazy words around the room. "I guess I'll invite June over here tomorrow. You guys are welcome to invite whoever you want."

"No reason you and June can't have a great time," said Steven. "Imagine if you had never met Stella—you'd be so happy with June. Think of this as fresh start. Don't worry about what went wrong. That's not your fault."

"I don't want to think about whether it was my fault or not. I can't. So it doesn't matter. I just need to have a good time, and I think June can be a lot of..."

"What?"

"She was right."

"Huh?"

"June's fun. Never mind."

"The key for you Adam," Steven pontificated, "is just not giving a fuck. You should never let yourself worry about anything."

"And how do I do that?"

"Just block it out. Just decide not to worry about anything, and then don't. As soon as you feel stress coming on, just fucking forget about it. Remember that you don't need to deal with that shit."

"Simple enough. I'll give it a try."

"Give it a try." Steven held up his beer from below and feigned a toast. "And in a couple days, be sure to let me know how it goes."

"Okay, I will."

"Nope," Steven said, "no you won't. That was your first test. You don't have to be sure of anything or let me know anything. If anyone ever asks you to commit to anything, you can just say, nah."

"Okay, I'll do my best."

"Or nah, your worst. Anything goes. You can't fail this strategy."

"Great. Can you succeed?"

"Nah don't worry about it...," Steven trailed off as an advertisement managed to catch our attention. The imagery was all shapes and colors, bouncing around this way and that, and I couldn't help but wonder how they were subconsciously affecting us while the advertisement's voiceover came in.

"M-Dr. Martin Scheff," it was captioned. His old voice filled the room, as trustworthy as it was quivering, on ancient vocal chords like snapping piano strings. "Happiness," the colorful shapes taunted. "Advertisers have been trying to sell it for more than one hundred years. We Americans have been free to pursue it since our nation's birth. Now, we're free to buy it. Xuvita presents the fourth in a line of seven mood enhancement drugs: X-4, happiness." The shapes began to brighten and open up. Light beamed out from the holovision and reflected through the room. "It's not a privilege, and it isn't just for pleasure. Happiness improves energy, productivity, engagement in the present moment, and kindness toward others. Things just work better when we're happy. With a steady slow-release compound that is all-natural and non-habit-forming, X-4 is clinically proven to increase happiness 50 to 100 percent with no crash. Download this one-time X-4 sample code for your 3-D printer right now, free of charge. Live a better today."

As the shapes shrank and the ad wound down, a new voice quickly relayed the legally-required warnings. "Applies only when one maintains required dose. Do not take with alcohol or any other mood-enhancement drugs at once, including the Xuvita 1 through 7. Consult a medical professional to decide if Xuvita is right for you. Compatible with most standard 3-D printers."

The moment we were waiting for, the moment Ned made me promise not to let Adam miss, arrived. The Pursuit of Happiness Project had staged a press conference they wanted Adam to watch, where preselected, positive-leaning questions from the press would be answered. They were hoping the unrealistically light-hearted affair would ease any tensions Adam and the public might have.

It was pretty surreal when Adam's double, wearing a mask identical to Adam's face and speaking through a voice modulator, stepped into the holovision.

"Adam," a reporter spoke up, "thanks for being with us today. It's good to see you smiling up there, and we're grateful that you were able to abate your emotions before the storm got any worse. Tell us, how were you able to reverse your emotions so quickly and prevent further destruction?"

"Well," said fake Adam, "it's really about keeping things in perspective. Human emotion is inevitable, but I'm learning to remain mindful of what a great life this country has provided me, and I'm getting better and better at it. Reversing the storm was a matter of changing my attitude."

It felt like the project was trying to give the real Adam a hint. Adam laughed, watching his double up there. "Right," Adam said to us. "The real reason I regained 'perspective' is that I felt relief when we escaped Cloud Nine without dying. Actually if the hotel hadn't gone down, things might have been even worse."

The next reporter began to speak with the same chipper edge. "Adam, we all know how difficult it is to watch a loved one suffer from illness. How do you feel going forward, and how will you prevent further moments of emotional weakness in regards to your grandmother's illness."

"That's a great question," fake Adam acknowledged. "I've thought about it quite a bit. The good news is that, due to incredible new treatments, my grandmother is on the mend; so that helps. Other than that, her positivity reminds me every day how to be strong, how to not let anything get you down."

"She's not all that positive," real Adam clarified, "or I would be able to talk to her a lot more. I barely even get to anymore because it gets me down so quickly. I am relieved she's doing better though; he's right about that.

"This is all very good to hear," the next reporter harmonized with the contrived mood of the room. "One question we have here at the National News Network is—"

Bang!

Adam's double's head exploded. As the double's body fell limply to the ground, Adam leapt up from the couch, grabbing his own head, nearly pulling out his hair.

Through the holovision, we could hear the room of reporters screaming bloody murder, and we could see a handful of police officers tackle the officer who had used his laser rifle to assassinate Adam's double.

The broadcast cut out. Adam left the room and headed straight to the liquor cabinet. He must have swallowed eight shots of bourbon before he let the bottle fall to the floor. He ripped open a drawer and shoved four or five X-4's into his mouth, and a couple X-2's for peace and calm.

"Adam, that was not your fault," I tried to break through. "That was their fault for throwing a fake fucking press conference. This was not your fault."

"I know," he looked me dead in the eyes, "but that should have been me."

He rushed out to the balcony to get some fresh air. I tried to follow, but he held out his hand. "Let me be alone."

●

N.N.N. BREAKING NEWS – *Adam Anderson Alive and Not So Well*

WASHINGTON, D.C. - Officials at the Pursuit of Happiness Project have confirmed that the man assassinated at the Adam Anderson press conference earlier this evening was, in fact, a double, and not Adam Anderson himself. The identity of the double has not yet been released.

The first suspicions that Adam was still alive came when a submarine volcano erupted outside of Hawaii just as the assassination took place. The eruption itself did little damage to human life, but created enormous waves, and left a deep hole in the sea floor that led to a giant whirlpool, which took twelve minutes to equalize. A ferry boat shuttling 359 people between Hawaiian isles was sucked to the bottom of the ocean. This is the biggest single tragedy yet.

The assassin, an active Washington, DC, police officer, was apprehended immediately. He claimed to have tried to assassinate Adam Anderson in an attempt to "secure the well-being of other sons and fathers across America," having suffered the loss of his own son in the New York City hailstorm Adam created weeks ago. Upon hearing what had really happened, he tearfully mourned and said he was "just trying to do the right thing." Only the secret service had been made aware that the Pursuit of Happiness Project would be using a double for security reasons. And prudently.

The officer was not supposed to be at the press conference in the first place, due to his known bias. He colluded with a covertly like-minded officer assigned to the perimeter to gain access secretly. Both officers will be rushed to trial and charged with first degree murder and 359 counts of manslaughter. No doubt they will be sentenced to clean slate capital punishment, in other words, being blotted out. The officers have requested the punishment come as quickly as possible; both are wrought with misery, having killed the wrong man and created such a catastrophe.

Published at 8:39 p.m., June 3, 2076.

●

Strike three. That's all I could think. The project would end and then what would become of me? Would I be partially to blame for a failed mission and innocent lives lost? Or even if it continued, at what point would they say I had done my job insufficiently enough?

I'd never formed much of an opinion about clean-slate capital punishment because I never had to, but in all the chaos I began to wonder if it was only a matter of time before I would accidentally upset Adam and wind up suffering the same fate as those two officers. Suddenly I realized there was nothing I feared more than being blotted out like that. I feared it more than death—to live unaware, with a whole life locked up in my own brain, taunting me, haunting me, never revealing itself. Sure, those officers would have a fresh start from the turmoil of their mistakes, but having lost everything behind them, how would they know which way was forward? Without their memories, what redemption could they possibly find? Learning a new identity and getting a new face felt more like reincarnation to me. And here I thought reincarnation was beautiful spiritual idea. It's a scientific solution to overcrowded prisons in an age where it's virtually impossible to get away with a crime, a solution made possible by neuroscientists like M-Dr. Scheff himself.

While I tip-toed around the loft, profoundly aware of my own capacity for destruction, Adam hung out on the balcony all night, alone.

It poured and poured all over the country. A government advisory kept everyone sheltered indoors while storms roamed the night freely. And for once, I was reaching out to Ned with a question.

"Was that strike three?" I asked.

He didn't reply.

"That wasn't his fault," I said.

"Just try to get Adam to sleep as quickly as possible," Ned said. "We're going to start seeing severe flooding soon."

"I think he's already trying."

"Give him some sleeping pills. And take some yourself. Let's get this show on the road."

"What?"

"Sleep Clark. Sleep."

Sixteen

"WAKE UP CLARK!"

I opened my eyes to an enormous, drenched version of Ned projecting from my wrist, standing outside in the heavy rain, and for a moment thought it was raining in my bedroom. "Why are you ten feet tall?" I groaned.

"This is life size."

"That's ridiculous. Are you a giant?"

"Sure why not. To you I am. Metaphorically."

"I'm setting you back down to three inches where you belong. What makes you think you can change the size? And why do you still think you can just jump into my head anyway?"

"So I've gotten to your head, haven't I?"

"You literally take over my headspace whenever you want. So yes."

"It's my head-space now. Your Ned-space." Ned looked as delirious as he was infuriated. He dumped a bucket of water over his balcony, and then bent down to scoop up more. "I'm just as tired as you, and for Christ's sake crying rivers out loud I'm dealing with a flood on my own balcony. You need to get Adam to go to sleep."

"He's still not asleep? It's four a.m."

"Nope!" Ned splashed another bucket over his balcony. "He's not. Start paying attention, because the rain is only getting worse. Get on the Ark of the Covenant Clark Bell. Get on the Ark, *Moses* Bell."

"Ned, you are mixing a lot expressions and stories here. Cool your jets or something."

"I will cool my jets. In this standing water on my balcony. You mind your own jets. Go give Adam more pills."

"He took a lot earlier."

"Sing him a lullaby! I don't care. Get him to sleep, or I will."

"You will?"

"Yup."

The more serious Ned became, the harder it was to take him seriously. But oddly on edge, I wandered into the kitchen. From there I could see Adam standing out on the balcony in the pouring rain, ankle deep in water. And I could see his giant poster dancing in the wind, watching him. *"Adam, enjoy!"* his own laughing faced reminded.

I tiptoed by a sleeping Steven, passed out in the living room and drooling on the couch, while holographic music videos danced through the night all around him. I snuck past the old record collection and Adam had left the record player on. It was whispering Paul Simon's secrets again. *"Kathy, I'm lost, I said, though I knew she was sleeping. I'm empty and aching and I don't know why. Counting the cars on the New Jersey turnpike—they've all come to look for America. All come to look for America. All come to look for America..."*

Adam heard me open the porch door and glanced back. He was leaning over the railing in his soaking 1950s Levi jeans, letting a warm breeze rush past his face as the heavy rain fell on his back. He held a rare collector's stack of one thousand dollar bills in his hand. One by one, he was pushing them off the stack and watching them flutter down to the streets below. He seemed to have slipped into a glossy-eyed hypnosis. He was wearing that watch again from the wooden box, the gold one with that sad lion all out of luck.

"What's up?" I waded toward Adam.

"Couldn't sleep," he said, not turning back, entranced by the flying money. "Even took more X-6. Didn't work. Must be all the alcohol. And the X-4. And me. Look at this..."

I leaned over the edge and watched a cool grand float away. It swirled in the breeze, was hit by a drop of rain, and was momentarily propelled downward. Then it caught itself on the wind and fluttered gracefully again. It was repeatedly smacked down, then recovered, in its fight against the rain to fall gracefully. It pushed off a building or two west before I lost sight of it. When that one had escaped, Adam let another drift off into the lights of the city. We followed it as long as we could, but it too eventually vanished. Another. Another. I was every bit as hypnotized.

"Tell me," Adam let the words float carelessly out of him, "how many people died up on Cloud Nine? I'm no dummy."

"I'm a terrible liar," I said. "So don't ask a question if you don't want to know the answer."

"Somehow," Adam observed, "I think I want to know the answer more than I want to be happy. But don't tell me. It wouldn't make me very happy."

"We're a strange breed."

"Who?"

"Humans."

"Some people probably think I'm an alien," Adam said.

"That I'll tell you," I said, "I've read several articles hypothesizing you're an alien."

"I hope they're right, because I don't understand any of this."

"Do you wonder about it a lot? Do you wonder why?"

"I try not to wonder. I fail a lot but I try not to. I'm supposed to be the happiest guy in the world."

He dropped the whole stack of cash off the balcony. It poured into the streets with the rain. "Some people down there are going to be very happy tomorrow morning." Adam smiled. He raised his arm to sip on a glass of half whisky and half rain water. "It would be nice to have that feeling. That feeling they're going to have down there when they find all that money floating in the puddles for no good reason. But I'm so sure I'm going to be happy all the time I haven't found the time to enjoy myself."

"But you have all the time in the world."

"And yet I only get one moment at a time."

"I guess that's why we keep track of it—time."

"Not me." He held up his wrist to show me his broken watch. "This thing ran out of time about a year ago."

"It's beautiful though." I regarded the watch. "Can I see it?"

He took it off and handed it to me. And then I noticed his bare wrist on the edge of the wall. It was the first time I'd ever seen him not wearing a watch, and now I knew why. Hey had a peculiar scar. It looked like a little tree branch spreading across his wrist.

"What happened?" I nodded toward his wrist. "If you don't mind me asking."

"Oh this?" He grabbed his wrist. "This is just a little birthmark. That's what my dad told me. Some strange thing with my veins and capillaries in that spot. It had some kind of stress on it when I was born."

"It's interesting. It could almost be a tattoo."

"Almost." He grabbed the watch and put it back on.

"So are you ever going to fix it?"

"The birthmark?"

"The watch."

"No, no, I don't think I will."

"Why not?"

"Well, well it's not mine to fix. My father gave it to me. He can fix it if he ever gets around to it."

"Do you think he'd want you to fix it?"

"I have no idea. I barely knew the guy. Left when I was nine."

"Where did he go?"

"Like I said, I hardly know a thing about him. He hardly ever spoke anyway, from what I remember. I can't even tell you the color of his eyes. We barely ever made eye contact."

"Have you ever tried to find out about him?"

"Sure, when I was younger." Adam's eyes searched the empty city. "But it's been almost twenty years. I used to ask my grandma about him. She would always say, 'Your father was a bad man. Bad men don't deserve to be talked about.'"

"And what about your mother?"

"I imagine she was somewhat like my grandmother. Never met her."

"What happened to her?"

"My grandma and my dad, they used to tell me she died in a car accident—in a storm actually. And she loved thunderstorms. They were her favorite thing in the world. Strange, right? That much I know about her, and that's how they say she went—twenty-eight years ago in a big, unforeseen thunderstorm. That's what the police report says too. So that's what I've always told people. But I know it's not true."

"Hmm." I treaded softly, "Do you know what really happened?"

"I was the accident," he said. "I killed her."

I immediately wished I had never asked—not because I didn't want to know, but because I had accidentally opened a wound so deep, I was afraid he might bleed out until we all died. I remained silent, nodding, hoping the bleeding would stop. But it didn't.

"I overheard him on the phone," Adam said. "I was eight. He had gotten mad at me earlier that day for making a mess, and I was stubborn, so we got in a big fight. I started crying. And all the sudden ... it started raining. Thunderstorm popped up in an instant. That wasn't in the forecast. And he was about to go for a run too, and for some reason that made him so angry, so unusually livid. And he's screaming at me, telling me to stop crying. But I can't, I'm just crying even worse. So I run outside, into the rain, so that the water will hide the tears on my face. He comes out after me. 'Stop crying!' He pins me to the wet grass and I'm hiding my face. But he turns me over and he can see that I'm still crying. 'You don't cry!' he yells. 'You don't ever cry!' And then he slapped me across the head and went back inside.

I wondered if there were any tears falling out of Adam's eyes as he stopped to take a few breaths, but it was raining, and he kept telling the story.

"So I told him I was going to run away. Of course he didn't believe me," Adam continued. "But I hid, under his bed, to make him think I really had run away. Eventually, when it got dark, he started calling out for me. He was walking around the house, walking around the yard, calling my name. We had a real big house back then, full of places to hide, and the last place he looked was his own bedroom. I saw his feet walk into the room from under the bed, and I heard him call out my name again, and, and, and I heard a pain in his voice. I was beginning to think he actually wanted to find me. I was getting ready to pop out and surprise him and tell him I was sorry and hug him, until I heard him say, 'Lilla? Lilla.' He was calling my grandma; she didn't live too far away. 'Have you seen Adam?' he asked.

"Obviously she hadn't. 'Well I don't know where the fuck he is! He was suddenly so angry again. And now I was scared to come out from under that bed, see, and he just kept talking. 'What am I supposed to do?' he yelled. 'No I'm not going to calm down. Am I supposed to go track him down? If he wants to run away, he can be my guest. I don't want the little murderer in my house anyway.' And I could hear my grandma on the other end screaming something back at him. So he goes, 'No, no, of course I'm going to take care of him!' He was crying now, 'but he's been a murderer since he was born!' He was fucking wailing it out. I had never seen him cry before. He was screaming like a little boy, 'That's all I can see when I look at him, even still! All I can think about is her! I loved her Lilla! She's the only thing I've ever loved; I loved her so much, so, so much. He took that away from me—childbirth! Who the fuck dies in childbirth anymore! And now, now... well if he wasn't here, ⌐he would be here. End of story.' He was breathing so heavy I couldn't hear myself think, and then he goes, 'I'm trying to love him Lilla, I'm trying to—I don't want to hate him. I don't want to, but I just can't, I can't, I can't...' And then he collapsed onto the bed."

"Did he notice you under there?"

"Notice me? Notice me—" a painful laugh like a sob interrupted Adam's words. "No," Adam shook his head, "he never noticed me. I just froze under that bed. Couldn't move, couldn't let him know I had heard. I felt like I had disappeared anyway, like I shouldn't exist. I was practically convinced I didn't exist. My father—he never went out looking for me that night. He didn't leave his bedroom after the phone call. He wept into the bed for hours, and I hid under there, and I didn't shed a fucking tear. Not one fucking tear. I couldn't. I had to hold it all in or he would know, and that would be the end... of something. I didn't shed a tear for another twenty years after that. I just listened to his words over and over—the whole conversation kept echoing in my mind. I felt his violent weeping shaking the whole bed. I stayed under there all night. I didn't sleep, and I didn't come out until he went out looking for me the next morning. I let him find me in the yard so he would never know the monster had been under his bed the whole damn time. He told me not to run away again, and I promised I wouldn't as long he wouldn't either. He shook my little hand. He shook the little murderer's hand."

"You're not ... Adam ... you have to know you're not—"

"I know," he cut me off. But it was clear to me then that he didn't, that he was searching, that it was dark and he constantly carried the feeling that his flashlight was about to go out. Those forgetful eyes had to hide certain things to keep from looking back at them, to keep facing forward all the time. But he was beginning to remember. Memories grew like viruses clouding his mind. The more he got what he had always wanted, the less he had to look forward to, and the more he started to notice those memories. They were watching him from the shadows. Those memories had been the ones cheering him on the whole time, and at the end of it all, it was them he would have to face. He would have to finally turn back and say, 'Look at me now.' And suddenly he would find the memories no longer behind him, but before him.

I remained silent for some time. I just kept thinking I shouldn't have heard what I'd heard. It turns out the only things you really need to know about a person are the things they would never tell a soul. Not in their right mind at least. I wondered if he would remember telling me in the morning. And I wondered if Adam had bottled it all up so tight, so long ago, that it couldn't get out to make much weather—that he had never fully felt it, at least not yet. It seemed he was starting to. I wondered if, in reality, he had hadn't moved much since that moment—if he was still under that bed by himself, silently riding out the long night, waiting for the dawn to arrive and blast away the darkness. It was something darker than rejection; he was simply never noticed. And ever since, every waking moment, he had been fighting to be seen. That's all anyone really wants anyway—celebrating or mourning—to be noticed doing it. Victory and defeat by themselves are each as alone.

As we stood there in the haunting wake of Adam's story, the rain turned to snow. Adam lifted his arms up and tried to catch the flakes in his mouth. The temperature dropped fifty degrees. Now the wind was picking up, and the snowflakes were gathering into hailstones.

I quickly turned to move inside, but Adam didn't follow my lead. "Hey," I moved back to him, "this is bad. We need go inside."

"Yeah—" he said. "Yeah. Promise me something though."

"Sure, what is it?"

"Can you tell them to find my father? I need to know where he is. I need to ask him questions if he's alive. I need to know what happened. It's...it's kind of like the weather—I don't think knowing will make me happy, but for some reason I need to know. They have to know; they must be able to find out. The NSA, CIA, whatever it is, get them to figure it out."

"Of course." I nodded. "Let's go inside and talk about it."

"Okay." Adam downed the last of his drink. He wound up and threw it off the balcony as far as he could, right at his own laughing face. The glass sailed through his mouth without damaging the poster at all, because I had been wrong; it wasn't real material. It had been an elaborate hologram the whole time, fake-flapping in the very real wind. The tumbler fell in with the hail, and I thought about how the exploding glass would mingle so nicely with all the ice shattering in the streets, whenever it finally hit the ground.

We walked inside.

As soon as I entered, I felt a needle puncture my neck. I fell to the ground. And then there was nothing. Not even darkness. No memories, no present, no future in sight. Nothing. A dreamless sleep like an ocean with no bottom.

SEVENTEEN

I WOKE UP in a bland medical room lacking the comforts of a normal hospital. Ned stood before me in a black suit, feeling important and powerful. "Clark," he said. "Clark. You awake?"

"*Mm hmm,*" I grunted.

"Wake up. We need you there when we wake up Adam."

"Why?"

"Because, we need to make sure he stays calm. He needs a friendly face when he wakes up. For some stupid reason he generally usually statistically kind of does calm down around you. A little."

"I can't get up; my body feels like sand. What's going on? Why did you guys shoot me?"

"You were in the way. Hurry up," Ned ripped off the sheets.

"I also feel like I'm floating. In a big way. I feel really really high, but not really really good. What did you do to me? Where am I?"

"That information can't be disclosed. You're in a secret military research facility, underground. You'll never know the location," Ned smiled shamelessly.

"How long have I been out?"

"About four hours."

"Feels like four days. Am I really awake? Pinch me."

"We used strong tranquilizers." Ned pinched my cheek.

"Stop. Not like that. *Ow.* Where's Adam?"

"With Dr. Scheff." Ned left. Several military guards escorted me as I stumbled down long, sterile hallways, as harsh and brightly lit as logic. We entered a room that had, at its center, a large glass box, in which Adam lay. Various probes and wires and little tiny tubes of all sorts extended from Adam's body, especially from his head. He slept, breathing easy. Outside the box, silver tanks and silver instruments on silver counters littered the mostly white and black room. Holographic charts, controls, and displays surrounded the glass box. They could be pushed about the open room, floated this way and that, snapped at, slapped around, whatever scientists like to do with their machines. About a dozen men in lab coats managed them. Ned stood with M-Dr. Scheff, holding up his heavily dimpled chin with a bulbous bluish fist. "We're right here," said Ned, as if I didn't see them and wasn't remaining in the corner away from them on purpose.

Scheff was already the scariest old man I'd ever seen. In my present state of mind, he looked like a goofy monster, glaring above droopy, baggy eyes and a scraggly white beard. A speckled, red face hung deep jowls over a crinkly neck, bringing to mind a giant piece of soggy bacon. "You must be Clark," he sludged. "I would extend a salutary hand, but for various pretexts not worth explaining to you. I'm Maven Dr. Martin Scheff. I'm sure you recognize me."

"That's fine and all. But I just want you to know, I don't recognize you." Of course I did, but in my half-conscious state, I saw him like a nightmare, and so sincerely hated him.

"You must not be very well educated, and for that I am most assuredly rueful." His grubby face wriggled out the archaic words like numbers slipping off a wrinkled page.

Ned slapped his eyes onto me. "Maven Dr. Martin Scheff is the premier psychiatric expert in the world!"

"Okay, that's great, but what are you guys doing to Adam? Sorry Bacon Dr. Martin Scheff, you just look like you're ready to commit some crimes, the kind no one would know how to prosecute."

"The correct term is maven." The words seemed to burn his mouth as they crackled out like hot grease.

"I didn't mean to say bacon." I shook my head, a little ashamed but already over it. "I had bacon on the brain. It's just that right now, in this harsh lighting, well, to me, your face kind of looks like a big... you know, a little undercooked, but... a strip of..."

"*Forget* him." Ned tried to shuffle the sizzling bacon back into the pan. "Clark is quite immature."

"He's right." I opened my eyes wide and slapped my own face in an effort to get my act together. "I'm sorry. I really am. So what's happening here?"

Ned sighed and crossed him arms. "We've induced a coma. Bacon Dr. Scheff and his team have been doing numerous tests to try to determine the cause of this weather creation, searching for red flags that make Adam different from the rest of us normal human beings: genetic mutations, inhuman traits, anything really."

"Fair enough. By the way you said bacon. Were there any red flags?"

"No I didn't. And no."

"Yes you really did. Anything unusual at all?"

"No, I really didn't. And no..." Ned wiped the word off his mouth. "Well yes, in a way. Dr. Scheff was able to achieve a completely emotionless, thoughtless, dreamless state of mind—no measurable activity at all—almost like death. But the weather severely worsened, beyond belief. That's why we're waking him up. Just another minute and he'll come to."

"Wait, what happened with the weather?"

"When we knocked him out, the blizzard remained exactly the same as it had been the moment before he lost consciousness. When Dr. Scheff found the state of complete stillness...well, we'll never do it again. We're waking him as quickly and safely as possible, your job is to restore his good spirits. Smile."

●

N.N.N. The Anderson Affect − *Dark Days for the PoHP*

NATIONWIDE - The sun rose this morning like it does every day, but to date, it has never disappeared after rising. The Pursuit of Happiness Project finally released a statement on the matter.

The darkness we weathered today was part of a necessary test for the good of our nation. Scientists working with the Pursuit of Happiness Project induced a coma and brought Adam into a state of

*mind devoid of all feeling and aware-
ness, hoping to relieve the atmosphere
of any effects his emotions might have
on it.*

*The shocking results of this experi-
ment tell us that Adam's lack of emotion
does not promote our nation's safety. It
seems Adam's holistic, conscious, will-
ful emotional well-being is crucial to
our environment's health. Any emotional
state we have forced on him independent
of his genuine intention has backfired.
It seems the happiness must arise from
within him.*

In case you slept through it, at 7:38 this
morning, a thick canvas of black clouds blan-
keted the entire continental United States
so thoroughly that people couldn't see their
hands in front of them. The skies remained
entirely pitch black until 8:04 a.m.

The blizzard didn't stop, but in fact, it
worsened as temperatures dropped to unworldly
numbers. Before the completely impossible
stack of black clouds quickly vanished, not a
single area of the continental United States
measured a temperature above zero degrees
Fahrenheit. One can only imagine how low the
temperature might have dipped had these dark
times continued.

Published at 1:00 p.m., June 4, 2076.

•

Adam's glass box filled with a misty substance. The box contracted its
ceiling and lowered its walls as Adam blinked awake. We stood around
his bed. He looked around, trying to get a bearing on the situation,
noticing all the wires attached to his head and body. "Oh no...I'm
going to die, aren't I? You guys are finally going to just kill me."

Adam looked straight at M-Dr. Scheff, who removed his
glasses and made a real show of it, rubbing his eyes slowly. He
sighed for as long as his old breath would allow, shaking his head.

"You're not going to die. We needed to perform some tests. Now we know killing you is the absolute last resort."

"Oh. What did you find out in the tests?" Adam asked.

Scheff cleared his throat and looked away.

"Nothing," I answered. "You're still a total mystery."

"So, I'm not an alien?"

"No," Scheff replied.

"Superhero?"

"More of a villain," Ned mumbled.

"I had the most vivid dream—Dr. Scheff, did you record it? I'd like to see it again."

"We have had your Personal Information Device programmed to record everything for some time now. Any dreams you may have had as you came out of the deep coma will be available to you there. Personally, I have little interest in them. They are fickle, often frivolous. They are not my expertise, or really anyone's."

That was my favorite thing about the Eyes feature on the PID—it interpreted visual through the brain, not the actual eyes; so if you left it on while you slept, in the morning you could watch your dreams.

Adam began fast forwarding through all the things he saw while he slept. Images of Stella and others in his life flashed by—Goodman Washington, Steven, me, and the most random occurrences. "I don't remember any of this. Where is it?" he said. He kept pausing, trying to find the dream he was looking for. "Here, here," he paused on the image of a ladder, "this is it."

We saw through Adam's eyes as he climbed a ladder in the sky. His clothes were dripping wet, and the ladder extended thousands of feet below him into a wavy dark ocean. It was pouring rain. He looked up where the ladder reached into a billowing black cloud.

When he reached the cloud, he stepped onto it, and the enormous ladder fell gracefully away. The moon illuminated Adam quite brightly. But as he stood there, his bare feet squished into the cloud like wet mud. He started to sink. Soon he was up to his waste in dense black cloud. He began clawing his way out of it, swimming through the cloud. The faster he went, the higher he rose. He chugged along, mustering all his strength. Soon he was only knee deep, and then just ankle deep, sprinting as fast as he could along the cloud so that he wouldn't sink again.

Behind him, the sun began to rise. Beams of light turned the cloud from black to grey to white.

"I could feel the sun on my back," he told us as we watched. "It was so warm, so perfect."

As the sun rose higher, his feet weren't sinking anymore. The fluffy cloud became light and bouncy. Running was effortless. Each step flung Adam forward hundreds of yards, like flying.

The sun overcame him, and now he was running into it, constantly glancing at it but not able to look for long. The beams of light were moving with Adam now, but racing even faster than he was toward the sun, which was pulling everything to itself.

As the sun dipped lower, Adam reached the end of this massive meadow of a cloud. He stopped on the edge and looked down; there was that rough ocean again. Had he run out of room?

Adam looked around, spotting another cloud over the deep empty chasm of air. A tightrope stretched across the sky to the next cloud. Adam took a breath, looked down at his feet, and boarded the tightrope.

He carefully walked across to the next cloud. On that cloud, he started running again, toward sinking sun. But soon enough that cloud ended as well, and again he had to cross a tightrope to the next cloud. This time, the chasm was longer and the rope thinner.

When he arrived at the next cloud, he found it even smaller than the last, like a little floating boat lost at sea. The sun was about to sink below the horizon, collecting everything it had loaned to the day. A warm wind picked up behind Adam, swooshing over his head, streaming forward. The last beam of light shot past him into the sun. It was getting dark and cold. Another tightrope reached out from his tiny cloud, but it extended so far into the distance he couldn't see the end of it. Adam looked around, searching for something in the golden sunset.

Off to his right, he noticed some wispy clouds gathering into letters. "They're only vapor," the clouds read before breaking apart again.

Adam looked down at his feet. The very cloud beneath him began to evaporate. He was starting to slide through it. He had no choice but to step onto the endless tightrope. He set out, one foot wobbling in front of the other, holding his arms out like wings in the wild wind, hoping he could learn to fly.

The dream ended but the real Adam kept staring with the focus of a tightrope walker.

"Adam," I said. "Adam, are you okay?"

"Yeah, I just... I could use some X-4."

"X-4 is not what you need," Scheff replied sternly.

"But you're the one endorsing it in the commercials."

"I endorse it for people who need a functional Band-Aid," Scheff divulged, "not for people who need real, genuine happiness. There are too many variables now—human beings in the modern age require rituals to get along without needing to think so much about why they find themselves unhappy. But you, Adam, cannot lie to yourself. Mother Nature will tell on you. You cannot fall into the kinds of habits that make happiness even harder. Stay off the pills. Once in a while, they may do you some good. But please, please do not take them every day. All of the Xuvita drugs—only use them when you need them."

"But I feel like I always need them. I could always use them at least. What's wrong with a little more happiness?"

"They don't just enable more happiness, they raise the bar for your happiness. And it's a brilliant business isn't it? Because the drug works. But over time... people get used to their happiness. Now happy is just okay. Now to feel happy we need to be elated. If you take the drug the right way, if you only take it when you're feeling down and you need a little boost, it's not going to hurt you—hell, it may even improve your life. But Xuvita knows that what's not written in the fine print is printed all over human nature: we always need more. We will always abuse the drug, and they'll just keep making more money."

"But it's all natural."

"So is cyanide."

"But, they say it's non-habit-forming. *You* say it's non-habit-forming. And you recommend taking it every day to enhance life. I just saw the ad."

"Every day doesn't sound like a habit to you?" Scheff leaned in. "Adam, habits are learned like skills, not acquired accidentally like talents. Exercise is non-habit-forming, but it will become a habit people are not willing to break for any reason. Sex is non-habit-forming, but the more you get, the more you need. Memories, hopes, dreams, people—none of these are 'habit-forming,' but they are all highly addictive. The more you feed them, the more they need to eat."

Adam looked at Scheff with disgust, "so how much did they pay you to endorse it?"

"Almost enough to buy a ticket to heaven."

"Well then give me a little piece of it."

"I said almost." Scheff wagged his finger.

"I feel terrible," Adam insisted. "I was just in a coma. So I could use an X-4, right now."

Ned pulled a bottle of X-4 out of his pocket. He shrugged at Scheff, helpless. Scheff shook his head, but said, "Go ahead."

Eighteen

"DO I GET TO GO FREE NOW?" asked Adam.

"Yes, but we have to make a pit stop," Ned informed. He led us out of that strange science fiction room back into the drab hallways.

"What kind of pit stop?"

"An important one. Another experiment. But we have very high hopes." Ned took us deeper underground to an enormous room with high ceilings, full of engineers working on experimental machines, and aisles and aisles of supplies. It extended beyond visual contemplation. But right in front of us stood a table surrounded by men and women in lab coats trying not to look directly at Adam. Placed on the table were a helmet and a one-piece body suit. Adam looked around the room and then noticed the suit.

"Oh god no," he said. "I'm not putting that thing on."

M-Dr. R.W. Dobbins, one of the world's leading physicists and thinkers, and the team leader for this particular experiment, welcomed Adam with wide open arms.

"Adam, good to finally see you," Dobbins eclectically rattled. He wasn't as old as Scheff, or as much of a total piece of bacon, but he was old. He had tried to slick back his salt-and-pepper hair, but it rebelled like a misbehaving mullet. The tiny, extendable robotic microscope built into his high cheek bone was still retracting past his plain gray eyes when he reached out to shake Adam's hand. It disappeared behind fake skin before he spoke again.

"I'm Dr. Dobbins. What a privilege to meet you Adam." Behind a thin lens over his other eye, Dobbins kept blinking. "I'm sorry," he said, blinking harder. "I can't seem to get this visual modifier to—" He slapped himself in the head, and then crunched a deep, long blink. Finally the lens folded up and slipped under the skin over his temple.

"It's nice to meet you too," Adam said, "an honor. I'm sorry to cut to the chase, but I can't spend my life in that suit, if that's the plan here."

"Adam," Dobbins cringed as he spoke, "I don't mean to bust your proverbial chops, but I've been working on this suit since I found out about your mysterious condition. It's the only one in existence. There's nothing like it in the world. Ah, I must be boring you."

"No, no, please go on."

"It's clear your emotions control the weather, but we have no idea how. There must be some sort of communication going on between your body, or your mind, and the forces of this earth, and even the universe. We simply can't measure them. The idea behind this suit is that it does not allow signals, particles, or energy of any kind to get through. Short of the kind of blunt force that would break the suit, no known forces can penetrate it. So, while we do not know what forces transmit and translate your emotions, I have high hopes that this material will block it."

"Wow," said Adam, looking defeated.

"Ready to try it on?"

"I guess."

"Attaboy," said Dobbins as he extended his fingers straight outward, releasing built-in, grippy covers which encapsulated each finger. Small holograms projected upward from the back of his hand, revealing various readings and gauges.

The all black, heavily segmented suit looked simple from the outside. It was only a couple centimeters thick, but heavy—about twenty pounds. Dobbins began to talk as Adam reluctantly wormed his way into it. "You may find yourself slightly... off, socially. Nothing major. It's just that none of your pheromones will be able to escape and affect others, nor will anyone else's affect you. No ESP of any kind," Dobbins laughed, "so don't expect that late night call just when you least expected it."

"I can't imagine I'll be getting a lot of tail with this suit on anyway."

"Well, we've built in systems to safely rid you of all bodily materials excreted—all of them." He tilted his head down at Adam.

"Oh my."

"None of that will be a problem," M-Dr. Dobbins reassured.

"I still kinda think it will be a problem."

"Listen, we know it's not ideal—that's why we tried the coma and research first—but it's better than the alternative." He sealed up the suit around Adam's waist, where you could see the suit's strange accommodations toward human bodily function. "And you can wear clothes over it."

"What's the alternative?"

"Your unhappiness."

"We'll see about that. I'm still not sure this thing will work."

"Have a little faith," said Ned. He looked down at his PID to check a live feed reporting any weather abnormalities.

"Don't worry," said Dobbins as he fastened it up to Adam's neck.

"Don't worry about what?" Adam asked as Dobbins picked up the large helmet from the table.

"Just don't worry." Dobbins started to put the helmet onto Adam's head. He looked like a dog getting locked into a cage.

"Wait, wait," Adam held it up, "there's no glass. What? Am I going to be blind?"

"Virtual reality," Dobbins answered.

"So what will I be seeing?"

"You'll be seeing reality, just played live for you through a screen that you can't even tell is a screen."

"But I'll know..."

"You'll forget." Dobbins pulled the helmet over Adam's head, who fell forward onto Dobbins with its unexpected weight.

"I'd rather not." Adam's voice came through a speaker and carried a slight echo from reverberating around the helmet.

Ned looked at his PID again.

"I'm sorry. It was impossible to create a transparent helmet with all the properties we needed." Dobbins fastened and sealed the helmet to the suit. "There it is. Go ahead and feel some emotions. Test it out."

"Yeah, I'm feeling emotions alright."

"What kind?" Ned stared at his PID and listened.

"Give him a minute," said Dobbins.

Adam paced back and forth for a minute until Ned raised his eyebrows and looked up from his PID.

"Wow," he said.

"Wow what?" asked Adam.

"Okay, alright, wow. Adam, what are you feeling right now?"

"I'm scared I'll be locked away in this fucking bomb shelter my whole life, and I'm pissed off, and I hate it."

"I love it!" Ned looked up. "It's working! Dr. Dobbins, it's working!"

"It's working?" Dobbins's eyes lit up.

"I've been watching live weather feeds in a few areas. Before you sealed Adam into the suit, we were seeing dangerously high winds, severe thunderstorms, and tornadoes. But it has all stopped. The second you sealed that helmet, it all stopped!"

"You've gotta be kidding...," Dobbins said as he threw his arms out and smiled just as wide, slowly approaching Ned.

"Perfectly calm day! Everywhere!" Ned and Dobbins jumped for joy, bouncing up and down in a sloppy embrace like kids who had won the Little League World Series. Their screams of elation echoed across the warehouse, along with the whole team of men and women in lab coats slapping each other's hands and backs.

"Fuck." Adam hung a whole lifetime on the word, a whole lifetime charted out for him in an instant. "Now I'm stuck in this thing."

Dobbins and Ned didn't even hear Adam in the celebration. "Fabulous!" yelled Dobbins to Adam. "Isn't this fabulous!"

"So fabulous," Adam croaked. "Good... good for America. Guess I better get used to this." He trudged off in the great big warehouse, disappearing down a long aisle. I didn't follow. I didn't know how to react. I sat down on the cold floor.

"I have to call my wife!" Dobbins yelped.

"I have to call Douglas!" Ned echoed.

They danced around, talking into their PIDs, jabbering this and that, speaking louder and louder to overcome the other's exuberant voices on separate calls.

Until M-Dr. Dobbins fell silent and fell to the ground. I got up and ran over to him. He was breathing but unconscious. He had fainted. And now, with my heart beating harder, I felt a shortness of breath myself. "What's going on!" I turned back to Ned.

But Ned was only yelling at the hologram of President Powers, who was buckled over and trying to suck in as much air as possible. "What's wrong Douglas? What's—" and then Ned was gasping himself.

"Take the suit off him!" President Powers strained.

I got up and stumbled into the warehouse, yelling Adam's name. The louder I yelled, the more of my own oxygen I drained. I ran down the main corridor as fast as my legs would take me, but my body felt as heavy as Adam's suit without fresh oxygen in my bloodstream.

I glanced down each aisle as I moved deeper into the warehouse. "Adam!" All I saw were scientists and engineers on the ground between the aisles.

Finally, there was Adam, looking at some strange equipment at the very end of one of the aisles. "Adam!"

He turned nonchalantly, having his own supply of oxygen from a carbon dioxide converter in the suit.

I couldn't yell anymore. I motioned for him to take off the suit as I fell to the ground. He clumsily barreled toward me. When he reached the main corridor, he noticed all the people gasping on the ground. "How do I take it off!" he screamed. "How do I take it off!?"

The only people who knew were unconscious.

I looked around and desperately pointed at a small engineering robot rolling toward us down the aisle. "How do I take this off!" Adam screamed at the little thing.

It couldn't identify the suit or Adam's words, and it calmly began to say, "Pardon me, sir, what was it you said? I'm having trouble—"

"No!" Adam picked up the robot by the head and began smashing it against his own helmet in a spot where it connected to the bodysuit. As it broke apart on his helmet, rougher metallic edges exposed themselves. He continued hitting the same spot until I heard a crack. The helmet opened up at the neck just enough for Adam to wedge his fingers in and pry it off.

A thwarping mass of air and pressure knocked Adam off his feet. We could breathe again.

●

"Doesn't get much worse than that," Dobbins drew deep breaths as he helped Adam get the suit off. "I knew you were a force of nature, but my god, there's just no way what just happened is possible. Ned, did it happen everywhere?"

"Yes, that looks to be the case."

"The oxygen, it just...," Dobbins trailed off, rubbing his forehead. "I hope nobody died." He started pacing and panicking around the space. "What have I done? As if physics could have had anything to do with this. How could I have thought...? I'll be put away; I'll be blotted out. Surely people died. Likely many. They'll blot me out! I deserve it. This is the end for me. What have I—"

Adam grabbed Dobbins by the shoulders firmly and looked into his eyes. "Dr. Dobbins," he spoke calmly, "you're a good man. You tried to do a good thing. They asked you to try. If anything happened, it's not your fault."

It was amazing how much M-Dr. Dobbins calmed down, like Adam had hypnotized him. "Your eyes...," M-Dr. Dobbins said incredulously, "I know those eyes. Your, your whole face—I know that face."

"What do you mean?"

"Was your father, by chance...was his name Paul?"

"Yes."

"Cal Tech?"

"I believe so," Adam said. "Yeah, that's right."

"I knew your father," Dobbins said. "I always thought you looked familiar in a strange way, always, ever since I first saw you on the weather. I knew your father. He was a student of mine."

"Really?"

Ned was tapping his foot so hard I could hear it. I could see his eyebrows furrow in and his lips tighten as if he was doing everything in him not burst out and inappropriately cut off the conversation.

"A long time ago," Dobbins thought back, "I taught a few courses at Cal Tech. Your father—he had an incredible mind. I bumped him into a higher level on the first day of class. The kid was nineteen. Looked a lot like you."

"Did you know him well?"

"Only for a few weeks, but he left an impression."

"How so?" Adam leaned in.

"Well, he was a-once-in-a-lifetime sort of student. I saw that right away. I saw myself not just teaching him, but working with him someday, maybe even learning some things from him. What a strange and bright thinker he was." A bitter nostalgia melted over Dobbins's face.

"So what happened?" Adam insisted.

"Dropped out. His parents were killed. Shame. One of the very first attacks on our soil—both of his parents, your grandparents, they died in a surprise bombing in San Francisco."

"So he just left? That was it?"

"He dropped out join the military—said he needed an outlet for his rage. I tried to get him to stay. Begged him to stay—begged him not to waste his brilliant mind in battle. I would have mentored him. But he was dead set on serving his country. On vengeance, really. Who could blame him? He was furious. He wasn't just sad—he was out of control. He only showed up to class one more time after that conversation, but he couldn't contain himself. Couldn't concentrate on what we were learning at all. He was a mess. He sat there biting his nails and scribbling furiously in his notebook, though I don't know what. He left in the middle of class. I never saw him again."

"And...," Adam stared blankly while he struggled to process Dobbins's words, "and what happened after he left?"

"I have no idea. Never heard from him again. You tell me," Dobbins rubbed his eyes. "What did he do? After the war."

"He was some kind of chemist," said Adam. "Worked for a pharmaceutical lab. I don't know much."

"Pharmaceuticals...," Dobbins murmured. His train of thought stopped abruptly. "Hmm."

"Hmm?" Adam asked.

"That's good. I'm glad. I wouldn't have put him in pharmaceuticals, but I'm sure he had good reason. Makes me wonder what kind of discoveries he must have made; his work is probably saving lives. He was good man, Adam—an afflicted young man after what happened, but a good man at heart."

"A good man...what field would you have seen him in?"

"Such a young mind, he hadn't specialized yet. He could have done anything. But you never know what people will do; they don't even know. It's been a long time, but I used to wonder how he weathered the war. What was he like?"

"Very quiet," said Adam. "Hardly said anything at all, except when he was mad."

"A lot of anger." Dobbins nodded.

"His wife died as well, when...shortly after I was born."

"Oh," Dobbins choked on his words, "oh, I'm so sorry. How's he doing now?"

"You tell me."

"We've got to be going now," Ned interrupted before Dobbins could apologize or ask anything else. He forced some brisk hand-shakes and brief goodbyes before whisking us away.

"Let's talk again soon!" Adam shouted back to Dobbins as we left. We waved as the door closed behind us. We walked down the hallway a few steps when Ned stopped.

"One second, I left my hat." Ned turned around and headed back in.

Adam and I waited there in the hallway for a minute. "How long does it take to grab a hat?" Asked Adam.

"Hold up, I'll get him." I ventured back in.

A ways off, near the table, Ned was whispering to Dobbins. But as he got angrier, his voice grew louder, and the sound carried swiftly across the warehouse. "Were you planning this little moment of yours?" Ned demanded. "Did you know the whole time?"

"No, no. I swear to you, it's just something I realized! Something I realized when I saw him in person for the first time!"

"Great. Wonderful. Smart. So smart of you Dr. Dobbins. What are you gonna realize in front of Adam next, some things about the Venice Project?" Ned grabbed old Dobbins by the collar and shook him.

"No! I refused to be a part of that for this very reason, so I wouldn't have to deal with this kind of nonsense! Let go of me! I know nothing!"

Ned let go. "Then stay the fuck out of it. And stay out of Adam's life. You 'realize' anything else and you may find yourself inexplicably suffocating again." Ned pulled a small device with a needle from a case in his pocket and held it in front of Dobbins' face. "Or falling asleep. Forever. Waking up not knowing who you are, sitting around an old folks community playing chess and wondering why you're so damn good at it." He turned and started walking toward the door, noticing me standing there for the first time. "Clark! What are you doing?" Ned called out.

"Just waiting for you."

"How long have you been standing there?"

"Just a second."

"I was just reprimanding Dr. Dobbins for the faulty suit he built Adam. It's just part of my job trying to help protect this country. I'm sorry if you had to see that."

"Okay."

But when Ned reached me at the door, he whispered into my ear, "Did you hear any of that?"

"No."

"If you realize you did, or start to think you're realizing anything else, think about your life, and how little it matters to me."

Ned slapped a smile onto his face and walked out the door. I followed at a distance, realizing just how entrapped I'd become in the PoHP's web of lies, whatever they were. Adam was sitting against the wall in the hallway waiting for us. "Where's your hat?" He asked Ned.

"I realized it was in my bag the whole time," he pulled it out.

"Ned, listen" Adam said as he stood up. "I've been thinking, and I told Clark just before we got conked out that I need you guys to find my father. I need to know what happened to him, where he went, why, where he is—everything. Got it?"

"Sure ... ," said Ned not so surely.

"But will you?"

"We will do everything in our power to find the answers you're looking for."

"I just want the real answers, whatever they are, even if he's dead or did something horrible. Can you get some sort of manhunt going at one of the government's intelligence agencies?"

"Of course, as soon as possible, Adam. But we have another strategy to try first."

"You can't possibly tell me there are more experiments."

"This one is easy," Ned smiled proudly. "It's my own brainchild."

"Were there any birth defects?" asked Adam.

"No, just common sense," Ned grumbled through his nostrils with a snort or a burp or something. "To be honest, Adam, this is probably the best—" he accidentally interrupted himself with gnarly hiccup, "idea—s'cuse me—best idea yet. Most logical catch-all—" enter horrible hiccup, "solution."

"Gross," Adam replied and then faded behind with me as Ned walked.

"What?" Ned stopped.

"Just ... ," Adam filled the silence, holding out his hand, "walk by yourself if you're gonna do that."

"I have the hiccups; what do you want me to do?"

"Take a shower or something." Adam shook his head. They were very dirty sounding hiccups that bellowed up from all of the broccoli and health supplements Ned constantly inhaled.

NINETEEN

THE BLUE SKY grew darker and darker. And then I could see the stars and the curvature of the earth. And finally, the blue-green sphere we live on fell behind. The endless emptiness overcame us, and only glimmering blackness filled my field of vision. It was the most unsettling moment of my life.

Without warning, my body tore loose from the grip of gravity. We burst freely into orbit around our planet. I could see Stella's hair expanding like the universe in the passenger seat in front of me.

The captain's voice warmed my heart and chilled my bones. "Ladies and gents, you are now free to float about the cabin. Welcome to the rest of the universe." She sighed for joy. "Good to be back on the final frontier, folks." And at that, she turned on the music. There was Sinatra again, *"Fly me to the moon. Let me play among the stars. Let me see what spring is like on, ah, Jupiter and Mars."* I know Adam hadn't asked for it to play himself, the way his eyes lit up when the song came on. Elated but almost embarrassed—it was too good to be true. It seemed that against all odds, the very stars were conspiring in his favor. *"In other words, hold my hand. In other words, baby, kiss me."* Adam glanced over at Stella and she couldn't quit smiling, and they couldn't quit studying each other's eyes as the song went on. They unfastened their seatbelts and began to levitate, bumping into the walls and each other like billiard balls. The captain dimmed the lights and the stars leaked through the windows. *"Fly me to the moon..."*

●

We had left our planet in hopes of removing Adam's weather from it. First Ned had tried sneaking Adam out of the country, hoping that his disasters would stay within foreign borders rather than continuing to plague our own nation alone. But when Adam stubbed his toe at the airport in Thailand, errant lightning set forest fires all over the Sierra Nevada mountain range.

"Just get him off the planet; maybe that will do the trick," Ned thought. Mother Earth wouldn't dare reach outside her jurisdiction. It was the Pursuit of Happiness Project's last big idea to alleviate the Anderson Affect. Having lived through the fiery demise of the space tourism industry, Ned wouldn't join himself, but sent us up in a retired space tourism vessel.

Of course Adam invited Stella to outer space, and how could she resist? We told him it was a bad idea. "Oh, it's a terrible idea," he confirmed, "but what better way to test my emotions up there?" He got what he wanted. Adam was a wise man with a foolish soul, and he knew that Stella liked stars even more than he did.

●

As our small group explored the small cabin, we split up into the two viewing bays. Adam and Stella drifted to the side that looked out into space, while poor Steven took to the earth-viewing window with me. "So tell me," he mumbled, shaking his head. "Death. Do you think we're about to have some of that up there? Do you think there's a bit of space death about to go down? I'm trying to enjoy this, but I've got death on the mind."

"Nah," I said, "I think all the people down there are in more danger right now than we are."

"You don't think this will work?"

"Nah."

"Woah...check it out!" Steven lost his breath as he pointed above the earth. However many miles away, a giant asteroid orbited the earth, just like us. "That might be where Adam's going if it does work," Steven said.

"That's definitely where he's going—one of the asteroid mines. My god, look at that thing." The way such an enormous slab of rock hovered above the earth, floating so gracefully—I kept thinking it would just drop whenever the hell it wanted. You could see its sharp edges catching the sunlight, and red lights of mining stations flickering like fires in the dark valleys. The asteroid cast a little shadow moving quickly over the earth. "How do they know it won't fall?"

"Because it's already falling," Steven replied. "It's falling around the earth, no maintenance required. It's in orbit, chillin' balls, probably having a blast."

In the distance I could see some sort of space shuttle moving from the asteroid down to earth. It dove gracefully toward the ocean until it was too far away to see, and it brought my attention back down to that gorgeous globe. It hung there on nothing, in the middle of nothing. Pitch-dark, mind-boggling nothing. Nothing had ever looked so full of life as that twirling green-and-blue sphere. Behind it, a trillion hopeful stars winked. I pressed my forehead against the window and peered out. Just a clear rectangle separated us from eternity, and I winced at the beauty of it all. Words failed and conversation died.

With no sign of any unusual weather, Ned's hopes rose again. But I quickly put them down—I'd never seen Adam so peaceful.

I could hear him and Stella talking from across the galley. They floated together right in the presence of the stars, soaking the brightness into their souls. They talked softly, like the universe was eavesdropping and they didn't want it to hear their precious, trivial thoughts.

"For some reason," said Adam, "I just can't get over the fact that this all goes on forever."

"Forever…" she hummed.

"Forever."

"Well, it doesn't go on forever. At least not this universe."

"I thought it was endless."

It's always expanding, but it runs out, at least right now," she said. "It won't be endless until forever. But forever never happens—it's always forever from now."

"So what does forever even mean? Is there such a thing?"

"I guess that depends on if you believe in time," she answered.

"Do you?"

"From time to time." She laughed, and rested her head on his shoulder. He wrapped his arm around her, and they levitated there together, gently bouncing between the edges of the big window.

They must have forgotten there was a window at all. "It's so beautiful my eyes hurt," Stella said. "I wish we could stay up here with these stars forever."

They stared out silently for a while. "Stella...," Adam turned her name over in his mind out loud. "I don't blame you for going with Stella. I always liked that you picked that name."

"Picked?"

"The day we met. You picked it as your favorite name. You said you didn't like your real name. Remember? But I've been wondering about the real one."

"It's Stella."

"Yeah, yeah, I got you. But... your given name."

"Still Stella."

"So?" Adam inquired.

"Oh I'm sorry," she smiled. "I didn't mean to trick you, I just like being tricky sometimes. I don't like my name because I wouldn't ever want to live up to it. My parents named me after the stars. Stars are perfect."

"But you said it was your favorite name."

"It's my favorite because it's my own. It's the only name I have. Plus, maybe if I stay up here long enough, the stars will rub off on me a little."

"I like that theory," said Adam, "because I may be stuck up here for the rest of my life, mining a fucking asteroid, circling the earth, round and round, looking down from above, forever."

"Forever." Stella's dark eyes glowed like shimmering stars. "It sounds amazing."

"Maybe for little while, but it would get pretty lonely up there, and boring. I've looked into it already. The mining is all automated. There's almost no need for people at all. They only keep two people up there to supervise all the machines or something, living together on a giant rock in a tiny station."

"I'd be the other worker. I'd join you."

"What?" said Adam, because now it seemed the universe had whispered something.

"I said I'd join you. I would." Stella nudged herself toward the other side of the cabin, slowly drifting away from him.

Adam tried not to hear it, but that was tough, perched up in space like that, just a shouting distance from the stars. "Would you really? Why?"

Stella gently bounced off the other side of the cabin and slowly sailed back toward Adam. "Yeah," she said, "I think I really would. So you don't have to worry about being so lonely up there."

And now Stella was closing in on Adam in the air and there was absolutely nothing she could do to change her direction, until they were bound together effortlessly. But she didn't kiss back, not really.

"What's wrong?" he said.

"Nothing." And now she looked away from him, back out at all of the little specks of light.

"You just said you'd spend your life on an asteroid with me ..."

"But we're not on asteroid, alone under the stars together without a care in the world."

"Do you see a care in the world here? Do you see the stars we're under?"

"I see them now, but they run out eventually." Her eyes scattered into the abyss all around them.

"Don't you see?" Adam held her shoulders and pulled himself in front of her "You just ... you make me happy. That's all."

Stella stared into his eyes for a few moments, as they slowly spun together. "Do I?" She pushed off the window and swam across the galley to our side, where she could see the earth, and she didn't like what she saw.

A dark cloud expanded over the Pacific Northwest like the black plague, gaining hundreds of miles every second. Adam rushed over, and seeing his first storm growing, another enormous cloud took shape over Nevada—a sandstorm. We watched the powerful natural systems crawl across the land like gods up there, until Adam suddenly backed away, slamming his fist against the wall. A red hot meteorite flipped through our line of sight and down into the upper Midwest. I watched with wide eyes as it roasted through the atmosphere, and thankfully burned away.

I turned back to Adam. The rage in his eyes settled to sadness as he said, "It didn't work." He pulled himself back to the space window, wishing upon a star, or a few thousand of them, while we watched his storms ravage the earth.

●

The storms wore out by the time we were coming back around again, and Ned sent us back down. I strapped into the seat next to Adam. We could feel the boosters roaring, pushing us closer to the earth, as we got ready for the final descent.

"Why do you put yourself through this?" I broke in. "You don't have to give her this much of your attention, your energy, your happiness. I don't get it."

He didn't respond. He looked at her, across the cabin, looking out the window as we fell faster and faster toward the earth.

"Hey," I said, "You're gonna be okay."

"No," he smiled with a beautiful singleness of mind, the way anything looks beautiful sailing through the air until it smashes into the ground. "It's too late for that."

"What do you mean it's too late? It's never too late."

"You don't understand. I didn't know why I was so upset to see those storms at first, to see that the space experiment didn't work. I should have been relieved, but I wasn't, and I realized that in that moment, I wanted more to be stuck on asteroid with her, than back down there, with all of the everything in the world." He looked over at me. "I'm fucked."

"She's great, but Adam, you don't even know her that well."

"You're right," he said. "But I feel like I can size anyone else and their intentions up in about a second—she's a fucking mystery to me. I don't have the slightest clue why, but I have to have her."

We dropped quickly. The enormous earth grew and grew and seemed to swing at us like a wrecking ball. We splashed through the blue atmosphere. Fiery waves roared over the wings with noise so heavy we could no longer talk, or even scream, but only fall. The question was how long it would last, and if somehow Stella would be waiting at the bottom to catch Adam.

Why it had to be her, the one woman smart enough to stay away from him, I had no idea. I suppose some people you like because they're pretty, and some people you like because they're funny, but some people you just like. And some people call that love.

TWENTY

ADAM WAS FINALLY FREE to do whatever he pleased, and was once again a slave to his own happiness. They were done with him—at least for now. We boarded a hover jet with unlimited possibility and not the slightest idea where to head next.

"Well, where do you want to go Stella?" Adam asked.

"I just need to go home," she said.

"Okay," he nodded, "we'll fly you there first, and then we'll go home."

"Thanks," she said. But she knew he was buying time and trying to figure out what to do with it.

We soared into a mostly overcast evening, and no one mentioned the pretty sunset. No one was talking at all. I stared silently out the window at the spaces between tears in a blanket of clouds. City lights like quivering embers kept the earth warm as the cool night came down. They slipped behind us as we flew over the dark desert, leaving us to our cold thoughts.

But in the distance, a mound of lights rose high above the clouds like a pile of fallen stars.

"What is that?" Stella perked up.

"That," the pilot replied through his bushy mustache, "is Sky Grove—biggest farm city in America. A skyline more impressive than Manhattan with a population of maybe a hundred employees." We crowded up front to get a look out the cockpit window.

The nearly soulless, diamond-shaped city rose gradually from the outside to the center like a giant pine tree, the buildings getting higher and higher toward the center. An endless array of golden lights dotted that mountain of metal and glass, shining with all the hope of the bright future we inhabited.

"Let's go there," said Adam. "Let's check it out."

"Can we do that?" asked the pilot. "Security is very tight in farm cities; I've never been allowed to visit one myself."

"Now's your chance. Head in there. Clark, get this cleared."

The shimmering city drew us in with a million winking eyes. But as we neared, gliding high between the buildings, their starry-eyed promise fell away. The bright light washed us out, and we could no longer see anything but light. That beautiful brightness was gone. The stars know better; they allure us just the same, but never let us into their light, lest we forget just how bright they are, set against all the darkness of outer space.

Now we were in the cold harsh light, but a warm breeze pushed in from darkness beyond the city. We landed softly and walked down the clean, empty streets. A forest of skyscrapers hummed lowly all around us, vibrating a little through the chest. The shiny roads were designed to reflect the sun's light back up into the towers' solar windows. Each tower looked identical but for their incrementally increasing size. The sides of the buildings angled out ever so slightly. They hung above us as if falling over on all sides at once. The top of each building took a pyramid shape, making the whole city look like an arrangement of giant silver daggers.

Only employees could get in due to an electric fence—not to mention a mile-wide perimeter of spiky, slanted reflectors pouring extra light into the city. Employees monitored the farm towers, riding up and down in little glass elevators on the corners of each building, but manual maintenance was rarely needed; they lived at peace.

Advances upon advances in vertical farming meant extremely efficient food. Cows on one floor ate grass and then shat, which fertilized vegetables on the level below, whose waste provided food for fish in tanks on the next floor, whose shit fed different plants below that, whose inedible parts were eaten by pigs below that, and so on, and so on. All the towers worked together to create even more energy than they used. They looked like sharp new office buildings until you saw the not-human herds through the windows.

We felt like explorers on a strange new planet, seeing a farm city up close for the first time. Adam noticed an employee stepping out of an elevator onto the quiet street. "Sir? Excuse me, sir?"

The middle-aged man, surprised to see outsiders on the farm, silently walked over. He looked at Adam in a daze for quite a way, vaguely smiling for no apparent reason, saying nothing. I had a feeling he was ever-made, though I'd never met someone like that in real life. X-4 had only been on the market for a few years, but there were rumors and videos starting to circulate about those who severely abused the drug, that they always "had it made," so to speak. They'd taken happiness pills for so long that the chemistry of their brains had permanently changed, and they were stuck in that state forever. Even without the pills, no matter what they were saying or doing or trying to express, they always seemed happy. Like a mask that you can never take off.

"Hey there. I'm Adam." Adam shook the man's hand.

"My name's Phil," he nearly sleep-talked. "What are you guys doing here? Wait... I've seen you." His mouth hung open and his blank eyes latched onto Adam.

"Yes, yes, we're just here to explore. It's like a field trip. Would it be alright if we used the elevators, sir?"

"I guess I can't say no..." He squinted as if peering through a heavy fog, then smiled wide and stupid, words loosely leaking out of his mouth. "Because, because you're that guy, right? You're that guy whose emotions make all the weather that's killing everybody. That right?"

"Um," Adam was dumbfounded by the man's benign bluntness. "Yeah... it's not quite what you think."

"How about that," he smiled. "I never met anybody so famous before. And so... so ev—" Phil's whole face suddenly scrunched together. Something was trying desperately to wriggle out of that twisted expression. "So evil," he finally said. But by the time he looked back up at Adam, his face was melting into some strange sigh of relief. "You got some kind of curse," he laughed. The dull euphoria took back his voice. "You think the people is bad—you, you should see the crops. We got some floors dead as doornails. How many people you killed so far? Thousands? Well the crops is millions. Tragic. Magic. Tragic but I never seen anything like it. Magic." He didn't seem like he was really talking to anyone but himself. Life had become its own satire.

"Shit...," Adam turned away. "Okay. We gotta go. We'll just—"

"Whole system too," he blurted. "Rough on the system. Tough." The brutal battle deep in his mind came to the surface again for a moment. His face smooshed up like a wrinkled photograph before unfolding back into that surreal smile. "Rough and tough, rough and tough. Tough and rough. Never done so much maintenance in my life you're puttin' me to work you are."

"Sorry to hear it." Adam hurried. "We'll be off now. Thanks." Adam walked away briskly and we followed. But he came to a brief halt. "Oh my god," he gawked under his breath.

"What's is it?" I asked.

"If things don't change for me," he glanced back at the man, "I'm gonna be him one day."

"Adam, don't be ridiculous. You're going to be fine."

Adam shook it off and kept walking. When I looked back Phil was still watching us, and still smiling, but simply his emotions were not tied to reality. His happiness was an entirely separate constant, trouncing and squashing anything else he felt, so that he never really knew how he was feeling at all. Ignorance, they say, is bliss. If only it were that simple.

We rounded a corner, heading toward the center of the cone-shaped city. I think Stella could see the guilt welling in Adam's eyes as it wrestled to move from his head to his heart, where it would create monsters we'd have to deal with outside. Stella smiled at Adam and then took off running into the city. "Race you to the top!"

Stella knew exactly what she was doing, because in a moment, if only for a moment, Adam forgot everything and chased her down the street. Their yelps and footsteps echoed back to Steven and me as we followed. "I'm too fat for this!" Steven yelled, lagging behind. "I haven't run since high school!"

"You're not even that fat!" I yelled back. "You're just size large. Suck it up!"

"I am too that fat! I'm family-size! Do you jiggle like this?"

"It's a graceful jiggle! Think of it as a dance! You're really not that bad off man!"

"Just let me think I am so I can keep eating! I'm going to crush these farm towers."

Stella reached the very center of the city—a tower bigger and taller than any skyscraper I had ever seen. She hopped into a glass elevator and Adam caught her just before it closed. They waved down at us as they ascended together.

Steven and I jumped into the other one. There were no buttons. "How do we get to the top?" I asked, and the elevator must have heard the key word. We launched upward like a rocket. As we got closer to the top, the other buildings descended in order below me like falling dominos. I started to notice military planes hovering all around the city and remembered how much security secretly tailed Adam at all times. They were always watching. Like anything else, we got used to it.

When we reached the very top level and stepped out onto the glass floor, there was no sign of Adam and Stella, only Ned in my ear.

"Clark, there are immense storm clouds building in the Southeast. Adam and Stella got out on the sixty-ninth floor for the love of god. Go back down and find them. She's too much. At this point we're ready to let Stella get out of Adam's life like she wants, and let him get through the loss before he goes any crazier. I need you to slap on a smile and third-wheel them, hard, until we can get everyone back on the plane and drop off Stella."

Steven stayed there on the top to wait for them, and I headed down. "Sixty-nine," I said to the elevator. When the doors opened, I walked into a field of giant corn stalks twenty feet high. "Ned," I ran in, "there is no way I'm going to find them. Let's just let them be for a while; I think Adam needs this."

"The atmospheric pressure is actually subsiding a little bit," Ned told me. "But I'm patching you into Adam's eyes. This is very high risk—being alone with Stella. If anything starts to happen you need to *accidentally* burst in on the scene to break it up and distract Adam from what he's feeling. Essentially, cock-block him."

Maybe I had gotten to used to the kind of hover-parenting the government was always doing anyway, but I had to keep track of what floor they were on and where, and I couldn't take my eyes off of what Adam was seeing anyway. They were springing through the cornfields, laughing. They batted the husks away and the dirt flung up from the floor onto their previously clean clothes.

They burst out the other side of the cornfield and into another elevator. They came out on another floor that wasn't lit. When

Adam turned on his flashlight, a wall of water showed up behind a pane of glass in front of him. A tuna as big as great white shark swam by, "Holy fuck," Adam said as fifty more swam by. Stella clung to Adam in the eerie darkness as they watched. Her hair moved in front of his eyes when she leaned against him, but he didn't bother adjusting to see the fish again.

They jumped back into the elevator. On the next floor, they found a sprawling, wet, muddy garden. Adam hesitated on the edge, but Stella stepped into the mud. "There's blackberries over here," she called out to Adam and he ran over. The bushes were full of shiny black blackberries; they plucked them faster than they could eat them. "These are the freshest blackberries I've ever eaten," Stella spoke with her mouth full and her lips dyed purple. "They're my favorite."

Adam heard a rumbling in the distance. "What's that?" He turned around to see a rowdy herd of pigs running at them, pigs that had only ever known people to feed them. "Run!" he yelled.

Stella burst out laughing so hard she could barely run at all. She buckled over into the mud. As Adam tried to pull her up, he slipped and fell into the mud too. Before they had a chance to scramble away, the pigs were overtaking them. They curled up into a ball together in the mud while the squishy pink creatures surrounded them, practically trampling them, oinking and ramming their noses into them in search of food. As they screamed and laughed, the pigs oinked louder, like the herd was there to hold them in the mud and tickle them to death.

Eventually the pigs realized they had no food to offer and scattered enough for Adam and Stella to run away, covered head to toe in mud.

The next time the elevator doors opened, a dense grove of citrus trees greeted them. The sprinklers were on—it was raining in there. "*Mmm*," Stella purred, "it smells amazing."

"It's perfect," Adam said as he smiled in wonder. He grabbed her hand and they ran through the grove, letting the rain wash their mud away. Adam plucked a few massive oranges, and they sat down together against a tree trunk. They tore away the thick peels.

"Why do we always have to have such a good fucking time together?" Adam looked at Stella as she bit into an orange.

"I wish we didn't." She smiled. "I'm going to miss you."

"Why don't you hang around for a while?"

"I already told you Adam," she looked away, to some far off place. "On Cloud Nine I told you. And we can't let that happen again—please, please, let's just keep enjoying this moment. This is all we have, all we'll ever have. Just enjoy it." But now the moment had changed entirely.

"But why? Just why. Why did you even come to Cloud Nine in the first place if you don't want to see me?"

"Do you really want to know?" she asked.

"Yeah."

"They..." She looked down, digging her fingers into an orange, ripping up the peel as the juice ran over her fingers and down her wrists. "They made me. You invited me, so the project made me go. They couldn't risk you being unhappy. They thought it would be better for me to accept your invitation than stay away. They were wrong." Her fingers bust in between the sections of the orange so that the whole thing unfolded in one messy moment. "They didn't know you'd fall in love with me."

"Fuck," Adam deflated. "Look at me," Adam said. But she couldn't bear to. And through his eyes, I could see Stella's hands moving onto another orange, tearing and tearing and tearing.

"Stella, look at me."

She finally looked into his eyes.

"This," he said, pointing at her eyes and his own. "You can't hide those eyes. When I look into your eyes, I know something I didn't know before. I know something you're not telling me."

"Well I don't know it," she shook her head.

"Then what can you tell me? Say something. Give me something. What's going on underneath it all? What's going on in your heart?"

She stared into his eyes for quite some time without uttering a word.

And now Ned was saying something, "Clark, we're seeing earthquakes all over the place; they're getting worse and worse. Find him, make it stop! They're on the hundred twenty-first floor!" But I had been so engrossed in what I was watching, I had wandered somewhere into the middle of the cornfield and had absolutely no idea where I was or how to find the elevator. I ran through the fields recklessly, getting thwacked by husks of corn. Finally I found a wall, but no door. And finally Stella was responding.

"I just don't have anything else to say," Stella relented, finally breaking her eyes away from his, back to the oranges. "My heart is a lockbox Adam without a key. The only way to find out what's inside is to smash it wide open. That's not something we can do. This whole thing...I mean...we must be creating natural disasters right now. Can you imagine the ones we would create down the road? We could break each other's hearts. We would wreak havoc on this country."

"What do you mean? I'm not going to break your heart. You're not going to break mine. We have nothing to lose."

"A good heart is always breaking."

"Well fuck, guess I've got a good heart then."

Stella said nothing. She couldn't get any words out. She looked like she was about to cry.

"Because you were right..." He nodded. He looked into her eyes. "I think I'm in love with you."

"But you can't love me. You can't. How can you?"

"I can't help it. I tried as hard as I could not to." She could not seem to break her eyes away from his. They grew like hot air balloons, sucking in every word that left his mouth, letting it swirl violently inside of her, until a tiny tear snuck out of her eye.

"But can you?" She leaned in and her eyes burrowed into his like the oranges. "Can you really love me? Could you...could you cry with me? Could you love me when I'm sad?"

"I could...well, I could—"

"What if I was really angry about something?" Stella let the things that ravaged her heart run free. "Could you stand up for me? Could you get mad for me? Could you even worry about me? What if something happened? Could you mourn for me? And could I really tell you my darkest secrets? The things that would bother you, the things that would deeply grieve you if you really loved me. Can you really love me as I am? I'm a human being. I'm not always happy. Sometimes I'm violently sad, and I don't even know why. Sometimes I'm lonely without any reason. Sometimes I long for things I don't have, and sometimes I hate the things I do have. Sometimes I hate myself; sometimes I hate others. Sometimes I'm arrogant as fuck, and sometimes I don't think I'm worth shit. And that all comes out. All of it. If you really love me, I will smash your heart again and again and again, though I will never mean to. I'm just human. And humans are natural disasters. Breathtaking natural disasters." She slouched back against the tree, crying great gobs of tears. "You can't love me. So I can't let myself love you."

As Stella collapsed under that tree and wept, Adam came to realize it was all true. He could never have her. Never truly. Never for more than a moment. In fact, moments were all he could have. No past, however sweet, that might bear the pangs of nostalgia in his present. No future—hope for something might bring the emptiness of not having it yet, or the pain of failing to realize a dream.

Adam began to think his entire pursuit was for naught. In isolating happiness, he could never truly have it. His whole life was a real sham and the pursuit of happiness a genuine oxymoron. Adam could hardly breathe. His soul folded up in inside of him, and he stood up in a panic.

He looked at Stella, gasping in agony. The second she looked at him, he turned away. "Stella, god, when you look at me, I just fucking die." He walked away.

"Where are you going?" she asked.

"The roof," Adam stumbled under the orange trees. When he got to the elevator he looked back. Tears blurred his vision, but after blinking a few times, he could see that she was already looking at him. Just before the doors closed, she suddenly stood up.

I ran along the walls as fast as I could until I finally found an elevator. I jumped in and headed straight to the roof.

●

The door opened onto the flat ledge around a transparent, pyramid-shaped roof. I scrambled up the glass, over the silhouettes of vegetation beneath, to get to the top. On the other side, I saw Adam standing right on the edge, holding his arms out in the wind.

"Ned!" I called in, whispering. "I really think he's going to jump Ned! Can security save him?"

"We don't have equipment for that down there. We never anticipated this. If he jumps, he's dead. We all may be dead too. Stop him!"

I slid down the glass toward Adam, but before I reached the ledge, Stella came out of the same elevator he had taken. "Adam," she cried, "wait!" She ran down the flat edge of the building toward him.

"Don't touch me," he said.

"What are you doing!"

"Oh nothing," he swung one foot out over the edge, "just getting ready to jump."

"Adam stop!" she screamed, falling to her knees. "Please come back here!"

"Adam!" I yelled, "You don't have to do this!"

"I'm not doing this because I want to die! I don't want to die! I'm doing this so that you don't die." he pointed at me, "and you," he looked at Stella, "and Steven, wherever the hell he is. I'm doing this for everyone I've caused to suffer so much. I've got to end this before I kill thousands more people."

"But you can't Adam," I said. "You don't know what will happen if you die. We could all die!"

"I've wondered—if I could manage to do it myself, maybe the weather would stop. It's the only possible solution. We've tried everything else. I could save so many lives here; I could prevent a whole lifetime of disasters. Otherwise...I'm about to explode, and the weather will too. Check the weather—it's already starting, and it won't stop. I don't want to destroy things anymore Clark. I don't want to kill people anymore. I can't do this; I don't see myself finding any happiness anytime soon. I wish I could get past this and live, but I'll wreck the whole fucking world before I do, so I better jump now," he looked down and then over at Stella one last time.

"Grab him," Ned was in my ear. "Pull him off the ledge!"

But Adam was leaning so far over the ledge that if I were to make any movement toward him, even frighten him, he could fall. I was afraid the wind would push him before he even tried to jump.

"But, Adam, this will pass so much sooner than you think," I begged. "I promise you. Just take a deep breath. Imagine all that you can do; you have everything ahead of you!"

"And it will mean nothing to me. I imagine everything with her. Maybe it will pass eventually, but I'm going to spiral down until I hit rock bottom, and I can't let that happen."

"Just please!" Stella screamed. "Don't jump!" As Stella watched Adam fall apart, something became clear to her—for him, losing her was worse than losing everything. It smashed her to pieces, and it freed her. "Please Adam! Please!"

"Why?" he asked sincerely.

"I've loved you since the day I met you."

"Stella...," Adam searched her crumbling eyes, trying to figure out if this was real, or just another hollow attempt to keep him happy.

"I've always loved you Adam!" she cried. "Resisting has been the hardest thing I've ever had to do. But if I mean this much to you, fuck it, let's do this. We can wreck the whole fucking world together I don't care."

Adam shook his head. He wanted to believe her so badly, but how could he now? It felt too late and too good to be true. He peered over the ledge and stretched his arms out again.

But then Stella stepped up to the edge, holding her arms out in the wind just like him. "If you jump, I jump."

"Stella! Stop!" He looked over at her, reaching out.

"If I have to watch you fall," she choked on a sob, "I'm going to have to fall with you."

Adam inched toward her until they stood on that ledge face to face. "We don't have to fall," he looked into her eyes, "if you really mean it... if you really—"

"I really, really do."

"If you really," a little smile broke across Adam's face, "really want to come fly with me instead."

"No Frank, I don't want to fly." She laughed through her tears. "It sounds exhausting. I just want to fall and fall and fall, to some freeing place near certain doom." She kissed him.

He held her there as their lips slowly unlocked. "Certain doom?"

"Just the freeing place on the way," she said, and then whispered, "falling never ends well."

"But what does? It all... ends."

She peered over that ledge and an updraft blew her hair back, "From here the ground looks so far away I can hardly see it."

"Until then, we can fall."

TWENTY-ONE

YOU COULD CALL IT a honeymoon stage, or just a long dream. They lived an unfairly happy life in an unfair world. Everything felt like magic and they questioned nothing.

●

N.N.N. The Anderson Affect – *Some Answers for an American Dream, a Few Questions Remain*

The Pursuit of Happiness Project had turned into a bona fide nightmare until mid-June, when the weather took a sudden turn for the better. It seems the sun finally came out for Adam, and he hasn't looked back since. Since June 10, a night forever marked by a horrific slew of earthquakes, flash floods, tornadoes, and hurricanes that caused trillions of dollars in damage and claimed more than two thousand lives, we've hardly witnessed any unpredicted weather.

This morning, Ned Norman, head of the Pursuit of Happiness Project, finally dispelled this theory in a press conference when he made the following statement:

> *Adam underwent a very tumultuous time of internal struggle, but it bore the perfect weather we've been experiencing six weeks now, and I don't think it's stopping anytime soon. Adam has fallen deeply in love and is happier than ever before. We're grateful for the new relationship that has brought such peace, both to Adam and to this country, and we*

will continue to provide whatever Adam
and his partner need to thrive.

As millions of Americans continue recover
from the disasters and tragedies that led to
this relationship, we're just hoping those
love bugs don't bite.

Mr. Norman declined to comment on the
identity of Adam's partner, saying that she
and Adam would like to keep that information
private.

Jonathan Harvey, who heads up the National
Weather Commission, was present to answer
questions among a few other consultants to the
PoHP. National News Network reporters asked
Mr. Harvey about the three strange aircraft
that crashed during the events of June 10,
but he declined to offer any comment on the
matter, stating that inner workings of the
National Weather Commission and their relationships with the Depart of Public Wellness
and the Department of Homeland Security are
entirely private, for unspecified security
reasons.

First responders at the crash sites were
shocked by both the size and capability of
these unusually shaped, unmanned, unnamed,
completely stealth aircraft. Oddly, two of
the three crashed behemoths exploded, but
not on impact. The first vessel crashed in
an empty valley in the Rocky Mountains and
exploded within a minute. The second vessel
went down in a forest just a few blocks from
a crowded highway. As the traffic grid had
completely shut down, some passengers who
saw the aircraft crash ran to the scene in
hopes of helping anyone that might have been
on board. The aircraft exploded before most
arrived, but flying shrapnel injured seven
and killed one.

The third aircraft crashed in the small
town of Hutchison, Texas, which also suffered
some of the worst tornadoes of the night. The
impact destroyed several small buildings,
killing fifteen people, but the plane never

exploded. A large Department of Homeland Security team arrived at the scene within the hour, securing a two-mile perimeter around the aircraft until they could "safely remove" all elements therein. While doing so, they blocked any view of the aircraft from the sky with large tents. The removal process took several days, and the DHS didn't allow local emergency services to help in any way, except to establish a secure perimeter around the accident and discourage citizens from trying to take photos or videos.

Why these aircraft exploded, why one of them didn't, and why the government rushed to secure the scene so quickly and thoroughly, are all unclear. Government officials have only said that the aircraft were important weather-prediction tools taken down by the storms and that their technology must remain undisclosed, once again for unspecified security reasons.

Published at 12:00 p.m., July 25, 2076.

●

I swear the stars shone brighter that summer, and a mystical whiteness poured down from the moon like misty fog. There was rain only when needed, and just in the right amounts. Other than that, the sun shone. All of Adam's cares felt as far away as the stunning mother-of-pearl clouds twenty miles up in the stratosphere. They channeled sunsets through ice-crystal prisms like rainbows in milky pastels.

I didn't see quite as much of Adam and Stella because they spent all their time together. And they always wanted more. Stella's unlimited creativity could not be met by anything but Adam's endless forward motion. If she could think of it, he already held the bright eye to believe in it and the will to make it happen.

Strange cloud formations appeared in the sky some days, and people would gather together just to watch the clouds and guess what they looked like. They constantly changed, shifting and morphing and growing and shrinking. Those clouds would streak and swirl as if they had been painted by Monet, ending the day with a giant sunset masterpiece. Even birds flew in interesting formations beneath those clouds like synchronized swimmers in the sky. Those dream days didn't report a single animal attack on a human in the wild, not even rowdy dogs or angry cats or even a bee-sting.

With the Pursuit of Happiness Project at their fingertips, Adam and Stella had no limits. Imagination became life. There were no authorities to tell them what they could and couldn't do. The president was happy. The people were happy. Ned was Ned-like once again, returning to his overabundance of cheesy smiles. And nothing seemed boring to Adam and Stella because they did everything together. One day they tried to get bored but only ended up laughing at how hard it was; it was the hardest thing they'd tried to do yet. I suggested they move to separate rooms if they really wanted to be bored. "No way," Stella said, "we want to be bored together, as a new experience." But that was impossible.

It didn't feel like Adam was even trying to be happy anymore. The happiness chased him down. It wrestled him and Stella to the ground and tickled them till they couldn't breathe. We traveled to the rarest and most beautiful places, and we took everything we wanted. We stayed in an underwater hotel, spied on beasts in the deep jungle, explored ancient ruins, summited brave peaks. We even camped out with friends, sleeping under the stars on warm nights. I even met a gal that liked to travel around with us, a friend of Stella's named Stacy. She had these bright yellow-green eyes like lemons not quite ripe. She was clean and she always smelled like sunscreen. The bright sun burnt her shoulders anyway, and left a growing galaxy of freckles on her sun-kissed face. All she ever did was laugh or make me laugh. And suddenly there were four, and we were so content no fifth wheels felt comfortable latching on—sadly not even Steven. Our little group was the envy of the world's four corners.

The sparks between Adam and Stella could be seen high above us. Meteor showers painted the night sky constantly, as if the heavens could not grant them enough wishes. They scraped away the earth's black ceiling to reveal reds, greens, blues, oranges, whites, all popping and fizzling through the darkness. When Adam turned over to look at Stella, he could see the colors dancing on her face, and her smile killed him time and again. He died happy every night into her arms. That honey moon smiled down on them with its bucktooth crater mouth, and Mother Earth loved Adam as her own.

I remember spending America's 300th birthday in New York City. We had been going wild all day like the rest of the country, when late at night, it began to pour. Thunder warned us otherwise but we felt the need to head outside. We ran through Central Park in the middle of the storm like we were indestructible. "I didn't even cause this," Adam yelled for joy. "I miss these!" Lightning flooded the air, and we dove into a fountain to swim with bygone heroes who'd turned to stone and frozen in time just to catch a glimpse of moments like these.

And I remember trying to stop for a second and breathe and just take it in. Everything felt so right and moved so fast, I barely had time to store a memory. We tried to intercept beauty at its poignant passing. Tried. Real moments leave a note on the fridge to tell you they've stopped by. They do not knock on the door. They do not wait for you to notice them. Each one I knew I'd never see again, not through telling this story or looking at mental photographs, not through any amount of pining or pushing to make them happen once more.

I remember them all so clearly, but the moments lose their luster in the warm hues of nostalgia. Their beauty carried forever past us before we ever knew we had them, but we were too careless to notice, or care that this couldn't last forever.

Adam thought he could find a nice cloud to call his own, stick a flag in it, and live a life aloft. But he had forgotten something: Clouds change. A weatherman ought to know, they can fall down as water and snow, or crash into each other and groan with thunder. They can bruise black and blue, or burn away in the hot sun. But you never can tell till you're looking back.

●

When Adam was ready to stay in one place for a while, the project told him to pick any place he wanted, as if his high-rise penthouse weren't enough. He wanted somewhere that would stay a little warmer in winter.

"Any place?" he asked.

"Any place. You pick it; we'll get it for you."

He picked it alright. He picked the most elaborate estate in America, the one that had belonged to the richest man that ever walked the earth, the world's first trillionaire, Randolph Williams. It was The Museum of American Opulence now, but the glass cases would be removed, the "Do Not Touch!" signs would be taken down, and Adam would break in all the old treasures like new.

The estate ran a few miles deep along the coast of South Carolina. The mansion crept into sight as we rolled down a long brick road lined in giant old oaks, sheltered by hanging Spanish moss. The sweet fullness of the air wafted through our windows.

The house sat heavy on the earth like a mountain. It crouched against giant white pillars burrowing into an elegant porch, behind which rose a giant wooden door carved with the wild whispers of the South. The historic plantation had been enormously renovated and expanded. It was impossible to tell the difference between what had stayed alive all these years and what had been resurrected.

A shaft of light sheared through the vast entrance, cutting a bronze path through air saturated with the dim comforts of very old money. A long, wide hallway of sorts spread out before us, twisting up a grand marble staircase as if rising and stretching after a long sleep. It landed on a second floor that wrapped an indoor balcony around the whole space. On the walls hung dozens of giant mirrors, so that the giant mansion looked even bigger. The double reflections across the open space stretched into infinity.

Bronze pillars separated sections of wall, and each section bore a large painting of an animal. On the floor beneath the painting lay a rug of that animal's skin—whole beasts, their outer shells sprawled out to be walked on. A grizzly bear, a polar bear, a cheetah, a lion, a black puma, a zebra, even a giraffe with its long neck crawling up the side of the painting's frame.

"This is…," Stella petted the lion's soft furs as if she could bring it back to life, "this is so sad."

"I wonder if they were hunted or just died," he said. "But I'll get them out of here for you either way."

"No," said Stella, "I love them."

"I thought they made you sad."

"They do, but they're so beautiful. They're already dead; at least let them be beautiful."

We moved throughout the enormous place and all its unnecessary spaces. The mansion had far too many rooms to see. It was the kind of place you could honestly get lost in, really, and looking back, I imagine Adam only wanted to do just that. The magnitude of the place scared me. Its vast emptiness hollowed out a space in me, one I could shout into without ever hearing word back from my echo. An army of rooms and their ghosts kept secrets. They hid the skeletons of a long, wealthy parade through time, and you could feel it. But I loved the place because it had things like light switches and faucets that you turned on yourself, cruder technologies that made life feel more tactile.

It was golden hour in the backyard, which was about as big as the ocean at the end of it. It was perfectly manicured from the polo grounds to the golf course to the race track to the great pine forest. A lazy river flowed from the pool all the way to the edge of the beach and back around again, so that you could simply float your way around the estate. Adam leaned down to feel the water.

"It's so warm," he said. "It must be ninety-five degrees."

"It's lovely." Stella reached in and splashed Adam.

"Hey—" He laughed.

"We can make it even warmer if you like," the butler showing us around spoke up. "We can make it like a hot tub. And we can turn on the bubbles too. It makes the river into little rapids."

"Oh no," said Stella, "no bubbles please."

"No bubbles?" Adam chuckled. "Who doesn't like bubbles?"

"I don't like bubbles, that's who."

"What did they ever do to you?"

"They always pop."

●

The one and only Goodman Washington was waiting for Adam in the backyard because Ned, whose name no longer terrorized us, had asked Adam if he would be willing to let the people of this country see his smiling face again. It was almost like a transaction, the way Ned had proposed it. In exchange for using the estate as a private residence, Goodman would get to record Adam arriving, capture the excitement of his life, and ask a few questions. Adam obliged with ease.

"Adam," Goodman smiled as they strolled among the fountains and statues decorating carefully curated gardens. "The rise to fame that somehow came to this—the charm, the happiness, the pristine weather—do tell us, what's it like to win so big?"

"What's it like?" Adam asked.

"How does it feel?" Goodman clarified.

"Well, I guess it feels ... happy."

"Of course!" Goodman cried. "Happiness! You've finally found it. You embarked on the great pursuit, and you've caught it."

"Yeah," Adam smiled sheepishly, "I guess I have."

"So here's the question—" Goodman's electric eyes bowed before Adam. They worshipped him like a sun god. "The only question—what's next? You've clearly met the most magnificent woman in the world. You've moved into the most magnificent home on the planet. What on earth are you going to do now?"

"I don't know," Adam wondered out loud. "I guess we're just going to live here. We're just going to live our lives, that's all."

"And what will that entail?"

"Well," Adam was really thinking about it, and he had no idea what to say. He stared into the blank eyes of a pure white porcelain angel spreading her wings over a giant rose garden. "I don't really know."

"A whole lot of shenanigans I suppose! How about some more sunshine?" Goodman celebrated.

"You got it," Adam nodded sarcastically, but Goodman laughed sincerely, proudly, like he had really just granted Adam all the shenanigans, and now the sunshine would rain down forever.

But Adam smiled a little nervously, like was he on display in a glass case with everything else in his museum mansion, like he was some historic American accomplishment. "The Final Capture of Happiness," it would read. He looked like he wanted desperately to break out, and that's when it began to rain. Right there, right on the interview, it poured.

"Oh—oh my," Goodman exclaimed as the droplets grew larger.

"I'm so sorry," said Adam. "That," he shook his head, "that wasn't in the forecast. How strange."

"Oh no. I hope I didn't jinx you," Goodman jabbered.

"Jinx me? No." Adam inhaled the air through his nose. "God I love the smell of rain." He stepped off the path and into the soft green grass in his bare feet. He closed his eyes and took a deep drag.

The rain let up.

"Hmm." Adam looked up.

It began to rain again.

"Shit, there I go," said Adam.

But the smell of the rain came back. It must have brought him to some innocent place, some ethereal moment when he smelled the rain for the first time. The scent consoled him. The rain stopped.

But then that smell was fading again and Adam was back with whatever feeling was haunting him. So the rain started up again, and things went on like this until the interview had entirely lost focus. The rain fell when he was sad, then stopped as soon as he enjoyed it. Sadness made a door for joy, but joy only opened it back up for sadness. He couldn't beat it because it's only the natural order of things. Food tastes better when you're hungry, right? Sleeping is sweeter when you're tired. Cold water is most refreshing when you're too hot.

And why is the sun prettiest just before it goes away, or right when it starts? No one admires the sun right in the thick of it, full and soaring high in the sky. Funny how a thing gets so bright we can't bear to look at it any longer.

Adam looked out at the pink clouds over the sea, and he told Goodman that would be all for now. He sauntered back toward the mansion towering over him. Stella stood by the door, in the rain, waiting for him. "What's going on in there?" She gently knocked on his head with her knuckle. "This is the first time you've made any weather in a long time."

"Nothing really," said Adam.

"Nothing? It's got to be something."

"No that's the thing; it really is nothing. I was just thinking about those bubbles, how they always pop."

"Those poor, pretty little bubbles." She kissed him gently like the rain. "Don't worry about them. They're full of nothing anyway."

TWENTY-TWO

AUGUST DRIFTED IN like a warm breeze, and so did Adam's twenty-ninth birthday. His grandmother called him to wish him the best and report that all was going well on her end. Adam was happy to hear her voice, as he did every couple of weeks, but on his birthday he wanted to see her smiling face. She asked Adam to give her a few minutes before connecting via hologram.

But then she wouldn't answer his calls and didn't call back for another hour. Finally she appeared, smiling.

"Grandma," said Adam. "There you are! How are you?"

"Having a lovely day darling. How's your birthday going?" Her words tiptoed around her teeth.

"Speak up a little grandma. Are you tired?"

"I'm just perfectly alright," she said. "Tell me about your birthday dear."

"Couldn't be better," he smiled. "I just wish you could be here for it. We're throwing a big party tonight, probably too big."

"That's wonderful, honey, you deserve—" she burst into a coughing fit that shook her body like an earthquake, and a wig fell off of her head. She was completely bald.

"Grandma..." Adam froze. "What's going on?"

"Don't worry your little head—just a bad cough. The baldness—it's just a side effect of the treatments. I'm perfectly fine. We're just finishing up a round of treatments. It's really not a problem at all."

"But I thought you were already doing better. You don't seem well."

"These are just temporary nuisances, I feel fantastic—better than ever Adam. The treatments are working wonders." As she went on I could see Adam's face slowly relaxing—he eventually believed her because he so badly wanted to. "You should be celebrating! And not just that I'm getting better. It is your birthday, after all. You have countless reasons to celebrate."

●

And countless guests to celebrate with him. They ran in like a river and flooded the estate. Adam had invited everyone he knew and then some—people he just wanted to meet or felt like having around, knowing he wouldn't have time to meet everyone. No one was off limits unless they were dead. And no one was dead if Adam thought they were alive. He invited an old classmate who had, unbeknownst to Adam, died in one of his earthquakes. The PoHP decided to send a perfectly executed double to make an appearance at the party so Adam never had to learn the truth.

The estate had already become quite full, though Adam remained hidden, when I walked over a mile from the grand entrance to the front gate to bring Stacy in.

Carriages pulled by unicorns—pairs of pure white horses adorned with spiral horns and wings—ushered guests from the gold-plated gate to the party. "Where have you been?" Stacy asked as we boarded one. "I haven't seen you in … days. Maybe a week."

"I've been here," I said. "Busy helping the project ready the place for tonight."

"What did they need to do to get it ready?

"Oh there were lots of things. An overwhelming number of things." I gestured to the absurdly real-looking unicorns as they pulled us down the lazy lines of trees.

"But wasn't this place supposed to be already be … perfect?"

"No yeah, it was already perfect. I guess there are different kinds of perfect, and we keep finding them and realizing we got the wrong kind. With an estate this outrageous, not an inch of the whole thing can be less than stunning. It's horrible. The project had hundreds of workers here redoing the yards, decorating the house. I don't even know. It was all the details no one notices unless they're off. There wasn't enough Spanish moss hanging on some of the trees, but look at all of it now. Isn't it glorious? They needed to bring that in and install it as organically as possible."

"Needed." Stacy laughed as she leaned out the window and let the low-hanging moss welcome her with a passing hug. Halfway down the road, we could already hear the chirping of a whole lot of people preparing to lose themselves in the bursting pressure of all their desire.

At the front door, a gang of gorgeous ballet dancers greeted us with party favors. Inside the antique tin boxes were two things. First, a surprise pocket pet—mine was a lion the size of my thumb, roaring like a cricket in a tiny cage. Stacy found a tiny elephant in hers; it was trying to using its trunk to dig into the other part of the goody bag—the aromatic drugs, for making damn sure everyone was ready to party.

They were sweet little innocent candies. Though the project had provided them, these were illegally reinvented combinations of the Xuvita drugs. Everything from classic party pills to happy hallucinogens featuring concentrations of the X-7 dream drugs you weren't supposed to take without X-6 to make you sleep.

Hundreds of people had gathered in the backyard to watch the sunset, while nearly as many servers carried colorful trays. The pool sprawled out whimsically, sometimes beneath bridges or around pool bars. It shallowed out and dried off in Bermuda grass like a putting green, which spilled all the way to the beach, following an old stone wall that predated the Civil War. The sun sank into the Atlantic and left some golden light to evaporate into the night.

"Have you seen Adam?" Stella tapped me on the shoulder, looking around like everyone else.

I pointed to the silhouette of a man playing golf in the distance. "Don't tell anyone."

"When's he going to come to his birthday party?"

"The bigger the mansion, the tardier you must be to your own birthday party."

"Is that the rule of the land?"

"That's what the experts are saying."

People practically ran around the party, bouncing between groups with their heads on swivels, looking for Adam and wondering when and where he would come out. Though waiters moved about with exotic food and curious cocktails, though the band sang in full swing, the party had clearly not yet begun. So everyone was talking about the weather, and in the presence of the weather himself, for once that kind of small talk wasn't boring.

I found it a little strange that the weather had become so perfectly predictable again. There were a few times, trying to get the mansion just right for the birthday party of his dreams, that Adam got frustrated about something, or frustrated with himself for how ridiculously high his expectations had become. The Pursuit of Happiness project had allowed Adam to raise the bar so high he could barely reach it. Adam was very, very happy, but that couldn't ward off all pain and frustration, however light and rare. That's what it is to be human—to be capable of suffering in the best circumstances and thriving in the worst, to be contained by the walls of our own brains. Surely those human moments should have been creating some weather, however insignificant. But up until that birthday party, nothing unpredicted entered the skies, nothing since the time it rained during his interview.

No one at the party seemed to find that strange, or if they did, they decided to believe what they wanted—that a man, under such perfect circumstances as these, could achieve a clean and thorough happiness that didn't miss a spot on his soul.

To everyone watching, Adam was damn near perfect. In snide grins at the reception of compliments they thought he was even humble too. But I started to catch a hint of resentment in it all. He was beginning to hate his perfection. It left no room for improvement. And Adam loved to improve.

With months of perfect weather, his radiance had become too bright to look at directly. But from my front-row friendship, I got to look a little deeper—glances here and there until my eyes hurt. And when I did, I think he kind of nodded, as if without admitting it, he was glad someone was really looking. He wanted to see if my eyes would really burn, and he hoped they wouldn't, so that he could desire again. You see, Adam's dreams belonged to him, but he desperately wished to belong to his dreams again.

●

A small hover jet flew over the mansion and touched down on the landing pad on the side of the house. The whole crowd broke into a murmur, and then into an all-out run, stampeding around the house to greet Adam when he stepped out.

But it wasn't Adam. It was David Webb, the world's greatest dreamer, literally, and he'd probably never witnessed a crowd so disappointed to see him. This was one of the people Adam had always wanted to meet and invited to his party. The man pioneered dream films and had become the world's foremost expert in lucid dreaming to do it. He built entire worlds while he was sleeping, impossible places one could only imagine in a dream state, and wove storylines through them. When he woke up, he would edit the recordings and work on dreaming up the parts he still needed. It usually took him a few years just to make one film, but few would disagree they were the best films being made.

He stepped out of the jet and nodded at the silent crowd. His sharp swirl of bright white hair fell over his face as he reached back into the jet and pulled out one June Dafney. She stood on the edge of the platform scanning the crowd for a minute before stepping into it. She actually hadn't been invited to the party—Adam hadn't let her slip back into his life since Stella saved it. She was David Webb's plus one, and I had a feeling she wanted Adam to notice.

When we all walked back around to the main area, Adam was simply waiting there for everyone, watching the band alone. He turned to the migration nonchalantly, and they slowly began to realize it was him. "Where were you guys?" he called out, and the lovable smile we all knew from his days as a weatherman broke across his face.

For a moment everyone forgot everything—the kind of moment you remember. The crowd rushed at Adam and practically trampled him with love. Somehow it seemed the same music we were hearing before became irresistibly rhythmic. All the movement turned into dancing, and suddenly Adam was surfing the crowd in his tuxedo.

Dancers dissolved into drinkers and eaters and talkers and laughers. The band rocked on, and a group crowded around a miniature racetrack for the pocket pets. A cheetah the size of grape was racing a horse the size of a strawberry toward a finish line filled with some sort of tiny food. That was when David Webb walked up behind me and said, "What the fuck? Am I dreaming?" When I turned around he was taking his glasses on and off, blinking, and searching around behind him for something, because I think he was serious.

"Clark!" It was Adam now, quickly walking past me, with Stella riding on his shoulders, feeding him champagne straight from the bottle. "I heard there were monkey butlers, is it true? Where are they?" I pointed up to the chandelier, where three of them swung around. The party had gotten too rowdy for them down below. Adam and Stella laughed like little kids and pushed off carelessly into the sea of revelry, trying to pour champagne into people's mouths as they swam through the bubbling crowd.

●

Just before midnight, Adam ran up to me. "Start the countdown at thirty seconds!" He bolted up the stairs.

I stood up on tables in all the main rooms, making announcements with a voice amp to move everyone outside. I barely got most of the masses out there in time. We gathered around the pool and throughout the backyard. I climbed to the top of a ten-foot-tall, oversized analog alarm clock. Standing between the two bells, I got everyone's attention again. "Thirty seconds until Adam turns twenty-nine! *Thirty* seconds!"

The crowd began counting down, watching the giant second hand tick toward midnight. I saw hundreds of heads bobbing this way and that, each person looking for the birthday boy and thinking they were the only ones who hadn't spotted him. "*Three! Two! One!*"

From the roof, Adam sounded an air horn. Everyone looked up as he bounded down the diving board he had put up there. He bounced off the end and went flying into the air, flailing wildly in his tuxedo all the way into the pool. The crowd fell silent as he splashed into the deep end, but few seconds later his head popped out of the water with guttural cry of celebration. Everyone lost their fucking minds.

The enormous alarm went off. Giant hammers banged in the bells. The vibrations and noise knocked me clean off into the bushes, but I couldn't have cared less. Everyone jumped into the pool in tuxes and gowns, and I was no stranger. We filled it to the brim with high-end fashions and humans happy to shed those threads for a moment much grander. Enormous fireworks boomed above us and the band broke into a rocky rendition of "Happy

Birthday." With one voice, the drunken crowd belted it out. Adam floated on his back in the pool, soaking it all in. People surrounded him, spinning him in circles while he watched fireworks like giant chandeliers falling through the night sky. Colorful rain doused us with warm light.

Adam and Stella wrestled in the water. And when the sky finally went silent, if you looked farther out, you could see a meteor shower painting the darkness. In fact, I was later told people all over the country could see those sparks skipping through the sky. The night was warm and full—they went outside to feel the same way.

Adam tilted his head back and shouted into the stars, "Let's dance!" He scooped Stella up into his arms and boarded the unstoppable train of his own momentum. We all made a mad dash for the grand ballroom after them. We threw our clothes into big wet piles and championed the dance floor in our undies, free to unite in the irresistible rhythms pounding through our bodies. The party had reached a new high, so far beyond our reach that we lost sight of ourselves entirely. Stacy and I morphed into the hypnotic jams populating the dance floor for God knows how long. There was no keeping track of time, only that timeless madness. And with the lights and the loudness and the bursting crushing roaring moment, we all knew what it was to be an exploding chandelier in the sky.

●

It was when Adam and I finally stepped outside for a breather that we saw Steven for the first time that night. He was standing all alone on a third story balcony with a pile of giant watermelons. Evidently he had gathered them and brought them up one by one. He rolled one over the edge. It exploded on the pool deck. I don't know what he had taken that night, but he laughed hysterically and then grabbed another. *Splat!* We moved close to the drop spot and suffered through the shrapnel to make sure no one walked underneath one and died.

"Steven!" Adam yelled, "Good to see you! What are you doing up there?"

"Adam!" he yelled. "Happy birthday! Have you seen the size of these watermelons? It's like dropping fucking nuclear bombs!"

He let another plummet down. It smashed to smithereens. Adam found a chunk of watermelon stuck to his forehead and ate it. "It's pretty good! How the hell are ya? Sorry I haven't caught you yet! We were all wondering where you were!"

"I've been in my happy place," he said as he tipped another bomb over the balcony. *Splat!* "Oh, and I got you a birthday present! But I have no idea where I put it. You'll find it eventually. It's very..." Another bomb dropped. "interesting!"

"You didn't have to do that! What is it?"

"Well I did, and you'll have to find out for yourself! Then I'll tell you all about my theories."

"You're too good to me! Get down here and hit the dance floor with us!" Adam yelled.

"I can't dance! And I don't know anybody in there!"

"Neither can we!" I yelled up. "You know me and Adam! And Stella and Stacy!

"No no no," Steven fired back. "I'm like a fucking wrecking ball on the dance floor!"

"That sounds perfect. What's wrong with that?" Adam shot back.

"Like a big fat wrecking ball, you don't, you don't under— everyone dancing down there is in their underwear, and being all sexy and shit, and..." Steven's laughter broke into heaves of tears. He was trying to suck them all back in, but to no avail. All the emotions had come out to play tonight.

"Steven, Steven...did you really think any of us ever cared about that? That doesn't even matter, it never has. And if that matters to anyone here, then fuck 'em. We love you man."

Steven didn't really believe what Adam was saying, so he didn't know how to respond. He just cried even harder. But Adam waited there while Steven cried, while he let it all out, and after a few moments, it was pouring rain. Steven could feel it on his back. He finally looked at Adam, "Adam, you can't be out here with me. Look at this!" He extended his arms to feel the rain. "I'm a complete buzzkill, see? Go have fun!"

"Nah."

"This is the night of your life, don't stay with me like this! I'm a mess."

"Nah."

"But it's your birthday! Go back to your party—don't worry about me."

"Nah. It's my party and I'll cry if I want to. I'm going to stay out here with you until you feel better, and if everyone else has to deal with a little rain because of it, well, they'll just have to deal with a little rain. Or even a torrential downpour. I'm not leaving you until you're dancing your balls off."

"No, look at your audience—nobody wants me bouncing around out there, just admit it."

"Steven, I don't care who's at this party or what they want. I don't care how they look. I don't care how famous they are. And I especially don't care for them if they don't care about you. You're the best guy here, and probably the most fun person here too, and you need to know it, and so do they."

"But I can't. Honestly, it's too much. I would but I just really can't."

"Sure you can. When you see those people, when you think those thoughts, you just say 'nah,' and keep going. You're going to come down here, and you're going to cut yourself loose like a runaway train. And you know what—" Adam paused. He started laughing to himself. "You don't have to worry about the dancing part, or even the underwear thing. We're going streaking."

"You can't be serious." Now Steven was laughing again. "Adam, you've gone full madman-rich-guy; you can't actually be serious."

"It's only right I get to wear my birthday suit tonight. And it's about fucking time you faced your fears and got through this bullshit. We are going to wreak havoc on this party. We are going on a naked rampage through every dance circle we can find. They are all going to see you, in all your fucking glory, and they will never forget it."

The rain let up. A smile split across Steven's face like a sledge hammer, crushing every concern. He jumped right off the balcony, over his watermelon wasteland and into the pool. When he emerged he had already shed his briefs. "Fuck it. We're doing this." He bent down to pick up a chunk of watermelon and eat it, then turned to a girl not far off who had noticed his nudity. "Oh, I'm sorry," Steven kindly mentioned, "are you seeing what you think you're seeing? Congratulations you're welcome and yes thank you what a pleasure." He grabbed his belly fat and started shaking it around, turning to another onlooker. "Oh, excuse me ma'am, does this bother you? Are you wondering what exactly this is? This is just some extra body to be naked with. Nothing to worry about over here." Steven broke away pieces of a watermelon so that he only had the rounded top end. He put it on his head like a helmet. "Gentlemen," he addressed us. "It doesn't look like you're ready for battle. You'll need to put on your watermelmets and shed everything weighing you down."

We were a Flying V of nudity. We charged naked through the crowds like pasty white lightning bolts. Clumsy ones at that, striking shrieks into sweaty people as we bounced between them like greased pigs. The brave joined our cause. A growing nudist colony rumbled about the party, and Steven led the way. No one knew why they were chanting *nah, nah, nah!* as they ran behind Steven pumping his fist; they only knew that they were singing Steven's anthem, and it cried freedom. Call him crazy, but I had never seen a man set so free.

●

It was around five in the morning that I heard Ned's voice in my ear while I drifted down the lazy river, having a smoke with Stacy and a few wonderful strangers. The dance floor had not settled, but people had scattered randomly to every corner of the estate.

"Clark," Ned sounded serious but confused. "We've got a storm system slowly building over large portions of America's heartland. Rain is beginning to fall, and it's slowly getting heavier. Adam is wandering aimlessly around the garage. You need to find him and see what's going on. You may just need to help sober him up—that's what we're hoping."

Off I went, hurrying down the river, back toward the house, more out of curiosity than fear. When I stepped into the garage, Adam was so far to the other end of it, I could barely see him. It held the world's largest rare and antique car collection. There were thousands of them, some dating as far back as cars go. There were even a few Model T's, and old military vehicles from every major war.

Adam strolled down an aisle of gorgeous red Ferraris, grazing his fingers on the hoods. "Adam!" I called out. He looked up when my voice reached him. "What are you doing in here?" I jogged toward him on the cold cement floor in bare feet, like most people still in my underwear. In addition to his underwear and dress shoes, Adam had found a leather racing jacket to throw on. We were an absolute mess. When I caught up to him, we continued walking down the aisles and looking at all the gorgeous cars from every decade. He was scanning, looking for something.

"So what are you doing in here?" I asked again. "Everyone's still having a great time back there."

"Oh, I know," he said. "I am too. I'm just going to go for a little drive."

"Do these things still run?" I looked over the section of cars from the 1960s in front of us.

"Why do you think there's a race track around the entire property? Sure they run. They're perfectly maintained. That's what Mr. Randolph used to do for fun here. He raced these cars around the track. Though I doubt he had the chance to try all of them."

"So you're going to go for a drive around the track?"

"Not around the track, no. Ah, there she is!" Adam hustled over to the slickest black bike I had ever seen. "See this baby right here?" As he patted the motorcycle's leather seat, I could he was wearing his father's watch again. "This is the Vincent Black Lightning. 1949. Handmade. They only made thirty of them—just a few left in the world now." Shiny chrome pipes and a beautiful slim black body twisted together, holding tight a gritty heart of pistons and gears. It was crowned with a gold stripe.

"It's what," I broke in, "almost a hundred and thirty years old? That's older than Dr. Scheff. She's a real beauty, but you can't possibly trust that thing to drive."

"No, no. See, this…this is timeless. She still looks so young. They restored her to perfect condition. She's timeless. That's exactly why I'm going to drive it."

"But you don't even know how to drive."

"I learned how to ride a bicycle a few years ago. Fucking Harvey gave me one and I learned. And I've driven some of these old cars with the manual shifters. That's good enough for me." He hopped on the motorcycle and started studying the controls, trying to figure out how to get it going.

"Even if you could manually drive, Adam, you're not in any condition to, not even close."

"Oh I feel fine," he insisted with a relentless determination in his eyes, the kind that can only look forward. "Just took a focus and an energy; I feel great. It's time to face it. I've got to face it."

"Face what? What are you doing?"

The engine roared like a lion, and he smiled. "I've got to make it to the sunrise." He looked at his PID and then at his broken watch. "I've only got an hour to get there."

"To get where? There will be a sunrise right here. We're on the ocean. You don't need to go anywhere," I pressed, and he nodded understandingly, but my words weren't sinking in. "Come on back out; we're all here. I mean it. Stella's out there looking for you. It's your birthday! We all love you. Everyone's here."

"Not everyone," he said. He drove the bike right off the blocks and almost toppled over as he turned down the aisle toward the garage door.

"Adam!" I ran after him. He gained more balance as he picked up speed. "Adam! You'll crash! Where are you going!"

"Garage open!" he yelled. And by the time he hit that opening, he must have been zipping fifty miles per hour through the garage.

I ran outside and stood there in my underwear, searching the clueless night. I watched his single headlight pierce a bright path through the tunnel of old oak trees, gaining speed down the long brick road. The sound of the engine howled over the thumping bass beats and distant crowd's chatter behind me. The light became small and dim. Someone whistled from a balcony at the distant growl of the engine, and loose laughter followed like champagne spray after the cork has popped for good.

Adam was gone. A warm gust of wind shook indecipherable secrets from the leaves on the trees, and that was all. The darkness hung heavy and I was left listening to the silent, scheming world.

TWENTY-THREE

BEFORE I EVEN MOVED, a hover jet was landing in front of me. The door opened, and there was Ned in a stupid Hawaiian shirt. "How could you let him go!" he yelled. Then he waved me inside.

"How are you here right now? And why the Hawaiian shirt?"

"I'm always close. And I was ready to blend into party if I needed to go in."

"It wasn't a luau. You wouldn't have—"

"Whatever. We need to bring Adam back right away. Get on a call with him. I've already tried; he won't answer mine. I'd force it through, but I don't want to scare him into an accident. He's moving over a hundred miles per hour." The hover jet lifted above the estate as I waited for Adam to answer. A few dozen guests must have heard the noise of the jet landing. They watched us fly away.

"Yes," Adam answered.

"Where are you going?" I asked.

"A place I know on the coast."

"But why?"

"I told you—to watch the sunrise. There's an old hiking trail by the beach there. Beautiful place. Perfect for this sunrise. Perfect."

There was silence for a moment, and I didn't know what to say. Ned was about to speak when I held up my finger to make sure he didn't. "Listen, Adam," I said, "I'm in a hover jet coming after you. This is really dangerous. You need to come back; you're freaking me out."

"I'm freaking myself out," said Adam. "But I kinda like it!"

We caught up to Adam. He ripped down a massive highway on the Black Lightning with only his single headlight to guide him.

There were no streetlights on the highways—automated cars and trucks didn't need them. The same darkness that hung over the rest of the big empty night poured onto the highway, which wasn't so empty. The biggest of freight trucks raced efficiently down the road at about a hundred twenty-five miles per hour, giant monsters that would gobble cars whole if they ever got a chance to see one in daylight. These were the kinds of trucks that could transport airplanes. They were moving faster than Adam, who was glancing back and changing lanes to make sure he didn't get swallowed up.

Ned couldn't take it anymore. *"Adam!"* he yelled, "This is madness! You're going to die!"

"I don't care!" Adam yelled back as he sped forward.

"You need to get off the highway now and stop!"

"I can't just get off the highway. I have to get away from these freighters!" Adam gained speed and caught up to the forty-eight-wheeler in front of him. He whipped recklessly around it into the next lane.

"Adam!" Ned shrieked. "Move to the shoulder and slow down!"

Adam topped the Black Lightning out at almost a hundred fifty miles per hour, threading between two more gigantic barges. As he broke free, he screamed for joy. "Why don't they make 'em like this anymore!" He was conducting a thrilling symphony of fear and joy, producing the feeling a good roller coaster can give— the euphoria of still being alive when your body is convinced you should be dead.

"Okay, shut down the traffic grid!" Ned yelled into his PID, where apparently someone had been awaiting the word. Suddenly all the giant trucks slowed to a halt, pulling off to the right side of the road. Adam raced freely down the far left lane.

"Thank you Ned!" Adam yelled.

"Fuck you!" Ned yelled back. "You still need to slow down!" Adam said nothing, but kept cruising until Ned spoke again. "We spend billions throwing you the greatest birthday party of all time you're about to fucking kill yourself."

"And it was amazing! Thank you so much!"

"Is it not enough? What else do you want? You already have your fairy tale ending! The girl, the money. Your life is perfect! What more could you want?"

"A motorcycle ride!"

"Are you not happy?" Ned begged. "Because if you're not happy now, we're fucked."

"I'm happy!" Adam screamed and felt the rush of the wind in his face. "I'm so fucking happy it hurts!" The night was fading into a moody dark blue. The sun would be up soon.

"No you're not!" Ned railed. "There are severe rains all over the country. High winds are taking down homes. Hurricanes are forming! What am I supposed to do? You think you're happy, and you already have everything! I'm out of options!"

"I know Ned! That's the problem! I've hit the peak! I've hit the fucking peak. What am I going to do now? I need to keep making things better, but things will never be better than tonight!"

"But, but, how is that—"

"Have you found my father yet, Ned?"

"What?"

"I asked you to do a search months ago but I haven't asked—have you found him yet and not told me? Have you found anything?"

"What does it matter?"

"How long do I have to keep waiting? I've been waiting for twenty years now! How long will time keep ticking? How fucking fast does my life have to move to keep up?"

Ned and I stared down at Adam from above as he chased a beam of light through the eerie morning twilight, hoping to find the sunrise before the engine gave out.

"I have to know! It all needs to make sense somehow! You've gotta find him, okay?" Adam pleaded. "You've gotta find him or this is all a wash!"

"What's all a wash?" I broke in. "Adam, tell me what's going on."

"Quit following me; I need to do this." He hung up.

●

We faded back out of sight, but we didn't quit following. We watched through his eyes now. Adam eventually peeled off the highway and turned down a series of narrow streets into a park. He rode the Black Lightning down a bumpy hiking trail through the forest. When he reached the beach, he cruised right onto the sand and dismounted. He sat down on an old wooden bench sticking out of some reeds in the sand. The air was bright. The sun was about to come up. Dark clouds were building high in the sky and moving toward the horizon over the ocean.

I had Ned drop me off at the mouth of the trail. I wasn't sure Adam wanted to see me, but it's easier to know what we want than what we need, and I was pretty sure he could use a friend.

When I reached the other end of the trail, the image I saw burned into my brain forever. The burning sun was hauling itself over a perfectly clear horizon, but an enormous mountain of black clouds was closing in from above, ready to squash the sun like a steamroller. Adam squinted straight at that narrow golden gap of between the blue and black. He didn't notice me until I sat next to him on the bench.

"You're here," he said.

"Couldn't miss the sunrise."

We didn't say a word for a while, just watched the sun try to tell us a new day was starting. And when the chaotic mass of clouds ate the sun like an orange, Adam finally turned to me, "Pretty spot isn't it?"

"Yeah. It's gorgeous. How'd you know about it?"

"Been here before."

"When?"

"I was nine. It was my birthday."

"Not a bad way to—"

"My father brought me here," he blurted.

"Wow." I didn't know what to say. "How come?"

"He took me on a surprise trip for my birthday, completely out of the blue. It was the first time he had ever taken me on a trip, or really done anything for my birthday. I couldn't believe it. First he took me to the Randolph Estate. We did the whole tour together. It was the most amazing thing. The place completely… captivated my imagination. And then we camped out in the forest behind the beach here, and we looked at the stars. He told me about different constellations and taught me how to find the North Star. And then we got up to watch the sunrise right here. Right here on this bench. He pointed out different kinds of clouds. Well this sunrise had the most colorful clouds; it was the most vivid sunrise. It was the greatest birthday."

"Better than this one?"

"No, not better than this one; it didn't end so great. After the sun had risen, he told me he had to go. I asked him where, and he just said to wait for him. I asked him why. 'We do what we have to do to have what we have to have,' he said. 'In time, you'll understand.' And then I asked him when he'd be back. 'In time,' he said. He told me to look at this sunrise and remember it. He goes, 'Look at how beautiful it is. Someday we'll do this again.'"

Out over the ocean, you could tell it was pouring rain. The rain hadn't made it to us yet, but the air grew anxious, and we watched lightning splashing into the ocean.

"So that was it?" I asked.

"No, he gave a birthday present to open after he left. He told me to make sure never to lose it."

"What was it?" I asked.

Adam held up his golden lion watch. "This," he said. "He used to wear it every day. But he had wrapped it up in a little box and he gave it to me and then he walked away. walked away, back into the forest. He didn't say goodbye. He said, 'Wait for me.' So I waited. I opened the present and put on the watch, and I waited on this bench that whole day for him. And then all night. And when the sun came up the next morning, I went looking for him. But I never saw him again. And I've been stuck with this damn watch ever since. He wrote a note in it. I must have read it five thousand times."

"What did it say?" I already knew, but I wanted to know which parts he would tell me.

"Some bullshit. He signed it 'love, dad.' I wish he hadn't. I didn't know the damn word was in his vocabulary. And it said not to become the weatherman. He knew that was my dream, my childhood dream. I got it from him. The weather was just about the only thing we ever talked about. And it's the one fucking thing he told me not to do."

"So you did it...," I said. "I would've too."

"Of course I did," Adam was impassioned now. "I said to myself, I said, 'I'm going to become the best weatherman in the goddamn country someday, so that wherever he is hiding from me, he'll have to see me every day on the weather, on his PID, on the city screens, on every fucking thing there is, and see how great my life is, how I'm not waiting around, how happy I am without him, how happy I am—how fucking happy I am.'"

Adam breathed heavy. The other storms had been slowly fading. Now I was getting alerts about earthquakes buzzing my PID, alerts I was hiding from him.

"I wanted him so see me up there, smiling up above the cities, and wish he could have that with me. Wish he hadn't left me. And regret," he teemed, "deeply regret. And wish he could come back. Wish he could come back to me ..."

"I'm so sorry," I said, and that's all I could say. I patted him on the back and just sat there with him. We felt a distant earthquake shaking the ground beneath us, vibrating the little reeds and making the grains of sand jitter. He put his hands into the sand to feel the tremor, and then he picked up a mound and watched it slip, slip, slip through his fingers.

"But I guess I became a different kind of weatherman, didn't I? And who knows the fuck how or why, but now I'm even happier—I'm the happiest guy in the world! Right? I'm the most famous, happiest man on earth, and he's still hasn't noticed. That's why it's all a wash."

"What's a wash?"

"Everything."

"What do you mean a wash? Your life—you're winning Adam. You're winning."

"Yeah. I finally won. Only to realize life's not a game. Because here I am, sitting on this stupid bench watching the sunrise again. I hate sunrises. I *hate* fucking sunrises."

"I'm so sorry," I said again. "I can't believe he left you here."

"What's so hard to believe about it?" Adam quipped. "I wasn't surprised at all. He wanted to get rid of me since I was born. I didn't even cry when he left. I knew the whole birthday trip was too good to be true. I didn't cry when the facade faded. And I don't need this. I don't fucking need this! What the fuck am I doing here? It must be the drugs." He stood up and kept diluting his words with more words. "Let's get back to the house. I need to sober up, or maybe get drunk again. People must be partying. Stella's probably worried about me. Let's go. I hate this fucking place. How do we get back? I can't ride this bike all the way back, not after it's been in the sand. Where's that hover jet?"

Before I even called Ned, the thing was lowering onto the beach in front of us. We walked toward it. "Sorry about all that," he said. "I'm so sorry; I don't know what got into me."

"It's perfectly fine man. I'm here for you."

"No. I'm perfectly fine. But thank you," he dismissed my statements, hoping that would make them unwarranted, hoping that meant he had never said the things he said. "Let's get back to the estate; let's get back to our friends. It's my birthday. This is the best birthday. This is the best birthday I've ever had. I'm honestly doing great. I couldn't be happier. I'm very happy."

He was and he wasn't. The happiness and the ever-growing darkness lived side by side in his soul. He was perfectly happy, and he wasn't. It was two things, not one or the other, not even two things alternating. It was two things at the same time, always, whether he knew it or not. Sometimes he couldn't access one, but it could always access him, spilling over when he let his guard down. He was happy and unhappy, empty and full, tired of being so tireless. He was a walking contradiction, wiggling to stay atop his tightrope between the clouds, trying to move gracefully from one high to the next. Happy and unhappy, all at the same time, and he knew it but he didn't.

The thunderous clouds over the sea faded like distant voices. The earthquakes around the country let up. And the giant rain-cloud Adam had created over America's heartland shrank almost all the way down, but it never went away.

It drifted about the country aimlessly, raining wherever it went. And somehow it never ran out of rain. It never went away, no matter how happy Adam felt. From that point on, it only ever grew.

TWENTY – FOUR

I PUSHED THE HEAVY DOOR of the mansion open just enough to step through. A miniature monkey swung around the door post, bouncing off my shoulder on his way to the ground. Adam stood with his hands on his hips, proudly surveying the wreckage as if it were a newly finished work of art.

Half-awake half-alive one-night-friends winked and blinked their way through the tail-end of a riotous party, struggling to carry on after the sun had come up and burnt out all their illusions. Dozens of people laid asleep on the floor in cuddly clusters—the ones who hadn't managed to nab a bedroom or a couch. Others snored peacefully on the floors of bathrooms and closets. David Webb walked among the ruins, stepping over people as he took photos with his eyes and notes on his PID. Pocket-pets that had escaped or been forgotten roamed freely, climbing over the sleeping bodies. A girl's curly hair spilled from her sleeping face across the floor, and pack of lions slept in it like tall grass. Webb picked up a hat to reveal a bear that had crawled in through the snapback hole as if it were a cave. I heard a faint, small roar.

A tiny golden retriever sprinted out from a side room, followed by a fast-approaching tiger, followed by a scrambling Stella. Adam stepped out and scooped the little dog safely away. Stella tried to grab the tiger, but got distracted by Adam's return, and the tiger darted off on little legs.

"Where the hell have you been!" She beat Adam's chest and embraced him all at the same time. "I've been up all night worried sick about you. I called a million times."

"I just had to be alone. I had to go for a little drive," he said nonchalantly. "I'm so sorry I didn't tell you."

"People told me they saw you dart off on a motorcycle. Adam, you could have died! What were you thinking? How could you be so selfish?"

"I really don't know. I don't want to think about it," he relented, just as confused as she was.

"We can talk about it later," she rushed. "Keep that little dog safe. I'm running around the house trying to catch all the predators. People didn't bother to put their pets back in cages and some of them are trying to eat the others!"

At that, Stella ran off. "I'll guard him with my life," Adam called out and then almost kissed the tiny golden retriever but didn't because it was smaller than his lips. As Adam tucked the critter snugly into a pocket in his jacket, David snapped a close-up.

"Gathering material?" Adam asked.

"Some of the best," he replied. "Whenever I see strange things I like to document, review them later, give them a good chance sink into my mind."

"And then," Adam was very intrigued, "and then you find that those things manifest in your dreams?"

"Sometimes, yes."

"I thought you controlled the dreams. Can't you make them appear?"

"I could, but it wouldn't be authentic. I control the dreams, but it's more like suggesting, guiding. I don't like to control too much or it's no different than imagination. I try to coerce the deepest and most confusing aspects of my subconscious out into my dreams."

"Do you, um..." Adam hesitated, "do you think you could teach me? Do you think this is the kind of thing I should try?"

"It's a highly emotional endeavor. I could teach you my tactics, but it's a real process. You'd have to have lots of very vivid dreams that are out of your control, before you could consistently lucid dream. It took me months to achieve that kind of awareness while remaining asleep."

"Surely some of the dreams would be fantastic though, right? Happy?"

"Oh, you can't even begin to imagine—paradise, Adam. Paradise. I mean, these were places like you see in my films. But it's no relief. I used to wake up in agony. Sheer heartbreak. Because what I experienced felt so real, but it didn't last. And the bad ones, you don't want to deal with those Adam. Deep dreaming often presents us our own realities, heightened. Did you catch my flick with the vicious beast that lurked in the heart of that impossibly large, living garden?"

"I did."

"That was me dealing with guilt from time I cheated on my girlfriend when I was nineteen. And there are much bigger monsters I haven't even touched. They're all living in my subconscious, messing around behind closed doors."

"But… those things are in the past. They can't—I mean, can't you just focus on the present?"

"The present is just the tip of the iceberg we call the past. But you're right; it does have one advantage. It can breathe."

"So the past is always with you?"

"I didn't say that. But it's always right there behind you. The second you stop moving it will catch up. It will be there waiting for you like an old friend or a relentless enemy. It is always reaching out until it has something to grab onto. It's yearning for balance as the whole universe does, longing to be reconciled with the future. But the present keeps taking over, and not always the way the past imagined. It's tricky. That's the funny thing about time. It's born every second, but as old as the hills."

"Born every second…" said Adam. "I like that. Always new chances streaming in."

"I couldn't agree more. And presence is a beautiful thing, maybe the most beautiful thing. But Adam," David grabbed his shoulder, "you of all people need to understand—it's not as though the future is gracefully falling back into the present. We want the future flying in swift and fast, and we want it just as we believed it would be, but the future doesn't exist. There is only ever present. And the present is only an ever-growing snowball made up of the whole frozen past, crushing everything in its path. Bumps in the road break the surface, flinging the past forward like a blinding blizzard. The things behind the mind, the things you don't always see. You may not even know how they're affecting you. That's why I like to dream. It's healthy. It lets me get a look at the monsters."

"But what do you think I should do?" Adam asked.

"For you ..." He looked Adam in the eyes. "Just get a plenty of good sleep. You'll dream as much as you're meant to. I like to think it's Mother Nature's psychotherapy."

"Sleep isn't always so easy for me," said Adam. "I may need a little help in that department as well. How do you get to sleep?"

"For me it's different. Sleeping and dreaming is my job, my expertise. Over the years I created this door in my imagination. I close my eyes, and when I walk through it, I fall asleep. I dream lucidly, and when I want to wake up, I walk back out the door. It's always there behind me if I look for it, no matter what's happening in the dream."

"So you can just sleep for as long as you want?" I asked, envious beyond belief.

"The longest I've ever gone is eighteen hours. That's when the door started to fade. I figured I'd better head back to the waking world before I found out what would happen if the door disappeared."

"Well what do you think would've happened?"

"I've got no idea. I don't know if I would ever wake up. I've always been wary of the door. It took me years to set it up, and once I got it working, it was working even better than I thought it would. It scares me."

"Oh c'mon," said Adam, "You'd wake up. The door would disappear, and you'd wake up. It's not like you'd be dead."

"You could be right, and I could be paranoid. I just don't know. If I can ever get that door not to fade, hell, I'll dream for a month and see what I find. Until then, I can't break the rules."

"But you make the rules," said Adam.

"Exactly. That's the problem. We all set our own rules whether we know it or not, and we follow them to a tee—core notions like impenetrable walls in our minds. My mind has some kind of rule; it says you can only dream for so long or it ain't dreaming anymore, and I don't want to find out what it is. I'm at the mercy of my own rules. Nobody can punish you like you can punish yourself. We build stories in our heads and we stick to them until we finish them or they finish us."

"And that's it?" Adam's eyes flashed wide. "No escaping the story?"

"Escape the story? You are the story."

"So I get to decide where my story goes."

"Sure, but stories are paths to truth. You'll always find the truth of the thing at the end of it."

"But we can build new stories."

"We can. And you can keep starting over all you want, but you'll keep telling the same old story until you finish it. Until you face the ending, whether you like it or not."

"What's to stop a person from changing the story?"

"It's difficult because you can't change the past. That's where the story started. We need to feel some kind of harmony with that. We need to win, or we need to lose. We only want the wins. We have all these loose ends and we think we need to tie them up all pretty But life is a loose end. Adam," David stared into his eyes, "don't try to tie it up too tight. Some loose ends just need to be cut off. And it's not pretty, and it doesn't feel like riding off into the sunset. I'm telling you all of this because I want you to think about the stories you're telling yourself. Find the endings, and you'll find some fresh beginnings. They don't have to be perfect. Neither do you. Perfect stories are only in dreams. And perfect people belong in bad movies."

Adam nodded. This was a lot more than he was ready to hear.

"You'll be okay," he patted Adam on the back. "Enjoy yourself. You deserve it. The conscious mind is here to make shortcuts. It's the boat floating you across the top so you don't have to swim through all the muck. The subconscious will splash up when it needs to, just don't be afraid of it. If you don't dip in once in a while, the waves can get so rough they'll toss you in—drown you. Can you do that? Can you dip in?

Adam froze. "A dip sounds nice." He smiled. "Let's hit the pool."

●

Adam, David, and I strolled out to the pool. There were still a few people playing drinking games on the pool deck. Underwater, all of the band's instruments had drowned and lay shimmering at the bottom. But above the water, on a raft in her lingerie, June slept soundly in the morning sun.

"Juney!" David called out. "Dear lord, you're asleep in a pool."

"How did I ... ," June said, crinkling her nose and grabbing her head as she sat up.

"June, I didn't even know you were here," said Adam.

"Hi," she said.

"I brought her," David interjected. "June, why didn't you tell me you knew Adam?"

"Maybe it's because I don't know him well enough," she glanced at Adam and then wiggled into a wake up yawn, stretching her beautiful body on the raft, "but I do know Adam. So there. How's that?"

"Good work." David nodded. "Why are you sleeping in the pool? I've been looking for you."

"Because," she replied, "look at how easy it is to shower when you wake up." She rolled off the raft into the pool and then swam underwater to the edge, surfacing right under Adam. "Feels amazing."

"You've got the right idea," said Adam. He jumped into the pool without even bothering to take off the leather jacket. "This is refreshing," he said. "I'm exhausted." Adam ducked under water again.

As the wake of Adam's splash crossed the pool, it slid into a dense congregation of pool toys floating in the very corner. As they bobbed up and down, I noticed a pair of feet hanging down underwater. There was a man hidden between those rafts and balls, floating face down.

"Oh god," I exhaled in quiet shock. David looked at me. I whispered into his ear about the feet just barely visible. David squinted at it for a moment and inhaled a gasp so loud it frightened Adam and June, then looked at me with wide eyes.

"What's wrong?" asked Adam.

David blurted, "There's a—"

"It's just ... ," I cut him off, "Calm down David. It's okay; David was just mentioning how shocking it is see all those expensive instruments at the bottom of the pool."

"Hmm ..." said Adam, looking for something more. But I held my ground. "Crazy," I said, looking over at David, who nodded vigorously and then looked down and started scribbling on his PID.

"Wild," Adam remarked, pushing off from the pool wall and drifting on his back across the middle of the pool. He bounced off the pile of pool toys, and he was just about to turn and grab one when Stella crept out of the house, sneaking up on some animal too small to see.

"Stella," he called out, "do you want some help?"

"Yes please!" She reached down, evidently missed, and ran after it back into the house.

"Oh fuck," Adam said, realizing he was already supposed to be protecting a little creature. He reached into his submerged jacket pocket, pulling out the tiny dog. He laid it on the side of the pool and kept pressing on its little chest, hoping it would wake up. But it didn't. Adam covered his mouth with his hand, and that tiny animal cost a few lives in Montana, where a rock slide barreled through a small retreat center.

"How sad," David rattled nervously, still fighting not to glance back toward the pool toys. "but don't worry about it too much Adam. I've been doing some research; these pocket pets only have life spans of a few weeks at the most anyway. Which is also very, very sad. Sorry."

Adam seemed a slightly consoled, but not enough to prevent the rain that sprung a flash floods in Utah. He ran inside, hoping to pay penance by saving some of these animals with Stella, who wouldn't be happy if she found out what had happened—and that would probably cause another weather event. As soon Adam disappeared, I sprinted to the corner of the pool. But before I got there, two camouflaged soldiers emerged from the bushes. They quickly dragged the large body out of the pool and back into the bushes with them.

"Oh my god!" June screamed.

"*Shh*!" David stared her down, whispering, "he can never know!"

"But I've been in here the whole time with a dead person!" she screamed.

"This isn't about you June! He was Adam's best friend!"

It was Steven. Several guests around the pool had also seen, and after the party, everyone knew who Steven was. They stood shocked, frantically looking around, whispering to each other, not knowing what to do. A few moments later Ned walked out from around the corner of the house in his Hawaiian shirt. He held some kind of badge, and the needle device I'd seen him use to threaten Scheff. He approached each person who saw and threatened them to silence.

Adam could never know. No way. Not about his childhood best friend. At the time I didn't know exactly how Steven died, but the levels of Xuvita and alcohol in his system were found to be very high. I had to mourn silently, and I mourned for Adam because he would probably never be told about Steven's death. Never get to cry. Never get to remember. It would just seem like he'd left without saying goodbye. And we would be stuck keeping Adam in the dark, continually pushing him on to the next moment, hoping moments have no memory.

The government was prepared to play Steven for as long as they needed to, even intercept any holographic calls with a double in a Steven mask. As long as they could avoid in-person contact, it was unlikely Adam would ever know.

●

The days seemed to pass even slower than the sun moved through the sky. There was nothing to complain about. Everything was easy.

"How long are you going to let everyone stay here?" Stella asked Adam as we walked into the kitchen in our swimsuits to get another drink. "There must be twenty people still wandering around, partying. It's been more than a week."

"It's a such a big house, I hardly notice them. Might as well have them around, right? Are you annoyed?"

"No, not at all, it's fun. But, what do you want to do? What do you want to do next?"

"I don't know. Nothing yet." He cracked open a vintage-style glass bottle of beer and took a summer swig.

"Well," she said, "I want to go back to Miami and work on my mosaic."

"Yeah, for sure, let's do it."

"But when?"

"Whenever we feel like it." Adam sipped his beer. "Don't worry, we'll get around to it. Let's stay here for a while; we're having so much fun."

"We are, but this is important to me. I'm starting to feel an urgency about it. We can't just party and chill forever."

"Why not?"

"Well, I can't." She searched him. "I need some purpose."

"I'm all for that. It just that...," he shrugged, "well, my purpose is to be happy. And that's important too, and not just for me. I've been having a pretty good time, so I don't want to mess with that. At least not yet."

Stella sighed. "I know."

"Have a drink. Come out and play." Adam tried to cheer her up, twirling her in for a hug and offering her a sip of his beer.

"I can't," she said.

"What do you mean you can't?"

"I just can't. I don't feel good—too much partying I think. It's alright. I just need to take a nap."

"Okay," he said. "I'll come check on you later." We headed back outdoors and hopped onto a trolley to the ocean, where David Webb and June and a handful of others were waiting for us to play beach volleyball. "I miss Steven," said Adam. "Where is that guy?"

"I don't know," I mumbled.

Adam sent Steven a message.

What a night man. And so good to see you, it had been way too long. I found a few really cool birthday presents but I'm not sure which was yours! We're still hanging around the estate, come join whenever you like, stay as long as you want.

Dead Steven responded immediately.

It was fancy champagne! I think we already drank it. I have to get back to work for a while. I have an important project I'm very excited to work on. I'll talk to you when I'm free. Thanks anyway!

"I didn't think Steven liked champagne," said Adam.

"But you like it," I replied.

"Yeah, I guess. Still though, strange."

That's when I started looking around the mansion for the birthday present Steven had misplaced, because if I knew one thing, I knew it wasn't champagne. I was checking on top of every counter, under every table, in every guest bedroom, all over the grounds. I spent almost a full day sneaking around, and found ten other unopened presents along the way. Finally I found it in the garage, inside of an old World War Three tank. I only looked in there because I knew Steven would've been checking it out.

I figured I wouldn't be able to give it to Adam and risk another text or call, so I unwrapped it.

Steven had geeked out and gotten Adam a vintage science and tech magazine. It was a beautiful, mint-condition copy of *WIRED* from November 2031, well before the war.

"**The War on Nature**," read the front cover. The subtitles further explained, *"Global warming is even worse than we thought. Can we crack open the Kardashev scale in time to save the planet? An interview with conceptual physicist R.W. Dobbins."*

I brought the magazine to my bedroom, but I went down to the kitchen to grab a drink before settling in to read. When I got back to my room, the magazine was gone. I called Ned.

"Ned, what happened to the magazine on my bed?"

"What magazine?" he replied calmly.

"The one Steven was going to give to Adam for his birthday. It just vanished."

"I can't explain to you how or why you lost some old magazine."

"How did you know it was old? I can't pretend all of this isn't very strange. What are you hiding?"

"Would you like the psyche Adam has built up to crumble to pieces? Is that what you want?" Ned paused. "Clark, I hope you don't think you're realizing anything. You know what happens to people when they think they are realizing things. Oh, and by the way, thanks for finding the magazine for us." He hung up.

And now I was really starting to realize some things, and wishing I could read the magazine they had taken from me. I looked online for the article, but it was nowhere to be found. It had been blotted out of American history. I don't know where Steven had found that old hard copy, but I wished I could've asked him about it. And I wished he had never found the magazine in the first place. I wanted to call Dobbins, but I didn't want anything to happen to him. Or me.

●

I awoke to an earthquake shaking so violently—I was afraid the whole mansion might come down.

It was late. I fell out of bed, made my way down the hallway, and stumbled down the stairs. Everyone in the house was doing the same, scrambling to get to safety. I ran outside to get out of the house.

I lay flat on the lawn as the tremors intermittently rumbled beneath me. Mainly I was just hoping the ground wouldn't open up and swallow me alive.

But from the garden, I could hear Adam and Stella arguing. I could see they were steadying themselves by clinging to a heavy statue that, in the dim light, looked like a silent third party hovering over the conversation.

"Almost three months?" Adam was baffled. "So why didn't you tell me almost three months ago?"

"I didn't know! My PID isn't connected to my body like yours. I just thought I felt funny."

"I don't understand how this could've happened. I mean, who the fuck gets pregnant by accident anymore? What is this, 1950?"

"I know—that's what I'm trying to say. It's like a miracle."

"You mean a freak accident?"

"Adam!" she screamed.

"I'm sorry—I didn't mean that. I'm just, I'm not nearly ready for this. How could this have even happened? Have I even known you for three months?"

"It could have happened the first night we met. I'm on birth control; it's implanted. So are you. The chances that this would happen are like…one in a million. Adam, I think it's meant to be. I really do. I really, really do. Because I think it's exactly what we need. I want to raise this baby boy with you."

"Just hold up a second; we need to give this some serious thought. I love you, but we've only known each other a few months. This is absurd. Just think about this."

"I've given it a lot of thought. I've suspected it for a week, and I've known for five days. I was just afraid to tell you."

"Why?

"Because of this!" The ground was shaking as Stella clung to the statue. It tipped over and smashed into a few clunky pieces. Adam and Stella fell to the ground. "Will you just calm down so we can talk about this! I'm not even three months pregnant. He's not going to pop out tonight. Just breathe Adam. Just breathe."

Adam fell silent. He stretched out on the ground, reaching his arms out to feel the rumbles as he stared up at the stars. Within a few minutes, the tremors were gentler and briefer.

"I really don't think I can do this," Adam said. "Let's be honest. Having a child does not fit my lifestyle, the lifestyle I need to have. It's a whole lot of responsibility and a whole lot of concern. We'll bring one new life into the world, but I'll end up destroying thousands with my fucking storms."

"What makes you think this is the lifestyle that you 'need' to have?"

"I guess because it's the one I want to have. Because it's carefree. It's easy. It's happy."

"How happy is it?" she asked sincerely.

"I don't know. How do I answer that? Stella, look at what's already happening. You've just told me about the pregnancy, and the thought of this baby has already caused massive earthquakes. Who knows what damage I've done. I might have just taken down a city somewhere for fuck sake. But I can't even know about that kind of thing either! I can't have these kinds of concerns! Right now I can't be responsible for anyone's happiness but my own. My own happiness is already more than enough to deal with."

"But I want this baby." Stella began to cry. "He's meant to be; I just know it Adam. He wasn't in my plan, but he's meant to be for us, I can feel it." She wept into his chest, and he held her, and he began to cry too. The earthquakes ceased, but it began to rain.

"Stella, it's bad enough just caring about you." He held up his hands to feel the rain. "Look at this. Can you imagine adding a baby into that mix? Caring for a little crying, screaming, frustrating, adorable baby. Can you imagine the weather? I can't bring another love into my life."

"But how long can you go on with this lifestyle? How long will it keep you happy? It's already wearing away. I can see it, even if you can't. You think you're feeding yourself—you're eating yourself alive. This isn't easy for me to do. I'm not doing this for me. I'm doing this for *you*. I'm doing this for us. I think we need this baby."

"But it will be so hard," Adam pleaded. "How could you want this right now?"

"Because I can see more than a few days ahead. Because all this close focus on ourselves is making me dizzy. Because I want to bring someone new into this world, someone I helped create, and now seems like a good time. Someone that will have different talents and strengths and traits than me. Someone who will be able to do things I could never do. It's a new life, Adam. It's new life, for all of us. Yes, it will be hard—so is everything worth anything. Is all this doing it for you? Because this is all very easy."

"What? I don't know. My life is good. Just let me have that."

"Is it good?"

"I'm having a pretty fun time, and I need to keep it that way."

"I know it's fun. Is it good?"

"What the fuck is the difference Stella? When I'm having fun, people are safe, and I can rest easy."

"Easy," she echoed.

"Yeah, easy! Why is this suddenly all about you? Don't you understand my moral responsibility to be happy? Everyone benefits when I'm happy. My greatest responsibility is self-interest. I've just got to do what makes me happy."

"I do care about your happiness. I care about you more than anything in the world. But what don't you understand about happiness? If we just keep chasing it, we'll never catch it." She stood up, and started walking toward the beach. "I need to be alone and think."

"Stella...wait. Just wait. Please wait for me. I'd love to have a kid with you someday if possible. But we both need to be ready. I'm just not. I'm still searching for happiness. I have to look for it everywhere I can, moment by moment. I need to figure out how to find happiness first, and I need you on that pursuit with me."

"But, Adam," she looked back wistfully, like she could already see the solid ground fast approaching and knew the falling was just about finished. "You'll never find happiness by looking for it."

TWENTY-FIVE

"I KNOW IT'S HARD BABY," June consoled Adam a few days later, late at night while we sat around the living room watching stupid shit on the holovision. Stella had gone to bed, as had David Webb. "I know it's hard," she went on. "But I'm here for you if you need anything. Have you done much thinking about your decision?"

"I can't think about it," he said blandly. "Just thinking about it stresses me out. The second I let it enter my mind, I'm overwhelmed with anxiety. No thinking. I just have to go with my gut."

"I can't imagine. I can't believe she would put that on you. I'm so sorry. I promise I'm here for you. I know it must be so hard baby. Let me know if I can do anything to help."

"You can stop calling me baby, and stop reminding me of it." Adam shook his head. He left.

I was left alone with June, watching her watch him walk away. Now she sat there with anxious pursed lips, wondering how soon she could leave the room without me realizing she had only been there for Adam in the first place. "June," I said, "listen, I really don't think you should be asking Adam about these intimate emotional things."

"Well I...I just think maybe he needs someone to ask him about it."

"Maybe he does," I said, "but it's definitely not you."

"I," she held up a finger like hoisting the letter high into the air, "am closer with Adam than you think."

"June, you should have left a few days ago."

"I'm here with David, and Adam asked us to stay. He wanted his friends to stick around to keep his spirits up. I," she drew out the letter again, "for one, am not going to let him down."

"Just say 'I' normally," I muttered out.

"What?"

"It's a fucking one-letter word. It should be quick."

"Clark, 'I' is the biggest word there is," she took on a philosophical tone. "It means you're taking a stand, expressing your very self. You should be proud to say that little letter."

"Can't make yourself any bigger no matter how long you draw it out."

"Do you think that little of me?"

"I don't know June, maybe you're right." I stood up to leave. "But my grandma used to say that old phrase all the time, 'me is a very small word.' And I don't think anyone's ever bothered to tell you that one."

"You're right, nobody has. But I guess ignorance is bliss. Ever heard that one? I like that one myself." She taunted with a bite of laughter. "Silly old me."

●

N.N.N. The Anderson Affect - *An Early End to Summer*

It was on Adam's birthday that the weather turned again during a rumored extravagant birthday.

While most of the weather events ceased the next morning, the dark cloud formation Adam created late that evening still has not dissipated. While first it shrunk to just a few square miles, since Tuesday, the rainstorm has grown to roughly the size of Colorado and taken on a far more violent nature, bringing heavier rains, higher winds, and more frequent lightning. The cloud first formed over Oklahoma, but it has since moved to Indiana, down to Georgia, and currently hovers over large parts of Louisiana. The rain pouring from Adam's loyal cloud without stopping proves completely impossible, but has yet to let up anyway.

While a series of misplaced earthquakes around the country late Monday night damaged dozens buildings and homes, the fierce gusts of wind have done far more damage and taken twice as many lives—that number being 57.

Yesterday afternoon, extremely high winds near Palm Springs, California, spun a field of dated, giant wind turbines so fast, the blades came off the hinges. These enormous propellers, some of them hundreds of feet wide, flew across the area in the wind like helicopters. Some of them ripped into buildings and homes, while others sped down the freeways, wreaking havoc as people ran for their lives.

As usual, the Pursuit of Happiness Project has declined to comment on the issue, hoping perhaps that this will all blow over soon. But it seems summer has ended early for most Americans, who now stay indoors as much as possible, plot escape routes for anywhere they're going, and are always preparing for the kind of destruction we saw in June.

Published at 3:57 p.m., August 18, 2076.

●

"We need more time!" Adam's voice echoed down the great hall to my room. Stella was walking right out of the house, not too fast and not too slow. He caught up to her at that giant wooden door just as she cracked it open. "We need more time to think about this Stella."

"Adam, I've done my thinking." She turned back to him, pulling her small bag of belongings up over her shoulder. "Life is happening; this child is happening. If you're not on board, I'm leaving. There's no in between. There's no 'thinking about it.' It's all or nothing."

"So you're just going to leave right now? You're just going to walk out into the world?"

"Yeah."

"Where will you go?"

"I'll find a way back to Miami," she said. "To work and eventually have my baby. And to work on my mosaic. It's still hanging there, unfinished. It's just begging me to work on it."

"Why is this mosaic so important to you that you would rather be there than staying here with me? It's not like I'm kicking you out. I'm just struggling with this stuff. We can work through it together."

"It's pretty clear you have to work through this one on your own."

"But why don't you just stay here?"

"Because ... what are we doing here? Nothing. I'm getting tired of all this happiness. I want to work. I want to struggle. I want to be free to fucking fail. I want my life to create something. I want to leave something behind, something that wasn't there before and never would've been there without me. Even if it's just for a few unsuspecting people passing through that little waterway in Miami and seeing my art. Even if it means raising a baby boy all alone. If you can't live that kind of life, the kind of life that makes something, then I can't live it with you."

"But I love you Stel. I mean that."

"I don't doubt you mean it," she said. "But you don't love me."

"What do you mean I don't love you?"

"I mean you can say you love and you can really mean it, but if you're not loving me, it doesn't mean anything to me."

"I'm loving you as best as I can. I have to be happy and I have to be happy now, but I love you, and I always will. I thought this was forever."

"Whoever believed in forever?" Stella's voice crackled, her heart splintering into sharp pieces as it tried get out her mouth. "I would love you forever but there isn't enough time. If you want to love me, you have to love me now."

"But you've changed," Adam relented.

"Yeah." She nodded. "What did you expect? People change. And never gracefully. They must constantly be broken and refit together again."

"Like a mosaic." Adam nodded, and the tears rolling down his face began to acknowledge he couldn't love her, not really, not as she was now.

"Like a mosaic," she echoed.

"I want to love you," he whispered. "So badly. I do. I love you so much. I just can't, I can't—"

"When you can," she wiped tears from her face, "I'll be waiting for you. I love you." She kissed him one last time and walked out the door.

"How, how—" Adam could barely get the words out as he began to break down, calling out to her. "But how will I ever—how can I?"

"Don't you see the difference between you and me, Adam?" She looked back at him. "You're still trying to fly. I've only ever wanted to fall."

Adam shut the door with a thud that reverberated throughout the mansion, "Someone bring me X-4!" he yelled out.

As I walked down the grand staircase toward Adam, a butler arrived with a pill on his palm. Adam popped the pill into his mouth. "More. I need more!"

"More X-4!" The butler called out. "Quickly please!"

Another butler arrived with three pills. Adam shoved them all into his mouth and started grinding them up with his teeth like he could bite the pain away.

"Adam! That's too much!" I ran up to him.

"It's not enough." He stood up. "It needs to hit me faster! It needs to hit right now!"

Adam surged through the grand hall toward the kitchen. June sat the top of the stairs, staring with wide eyes and covering her mouth with trembling hands.

"What the fuck are you looking at?" Adam yelled to her and then shouted back to the butlers, "Where is it! I need more of it!"

"Adam, stop! This isn't helping!" I ran after him.

"It will!" he shouted at me. As we entered the kitchen, a cook stepped back in fear. "Where are the pills!" Adam yelled.

The cook quickly pointed to a cabinet and ran out of harm's way. Adam grabbed the bottle and dumped them on the counter. He started chopping them up with a knife and then pounding them to a dust with a heavy, cast iron pan, crushing the counter in the process.

"Adam, what are you doing!"

"Faster!"

He ran his face along the counter, snorting up sharp flakes that had his nose bleeding immediately. I tried to pull him away, but he shoved me to the ground like he didn't even know me.

"Adam, stop!" June was at the doorway now. "You're going to hurt yourself!"

"*I need to be happy!*" Adam snorted up more. "*Happy!*"

June wrapped her arms around Adam. She dragged him away from the counter and pressed her body against him, holding him up against the fridge.

"I loved her," he whispered into June's face. He was breathing heavily, deliriously, and blood was running from his nose into his mouth. "Now I fucking...I fucking hate," he choked on drugs and tears, coughing and snorting, "hate," pain piled up behind Adam's quivering eyelids and he shut them, "hate her."

"It's going to be okay, baby. It's going to be okay," June's voice rattled and tears ran down her face. "I'm here. I'm here. It's okay. I'm here." She wiped the blood from his face. "It's okay. I'm here."

He looked up into her soaking eyes. "You're here," he repeated, pulling her in a little, so that her open lips brushed up against his cheek. Loneliness washed all around him like an ocean. He looked like he was stranded at sea, fighting for his life in the cold waves, struggling for every breath. He grit his teeth together. "I can't breathe."

"I can help you breathe baby."

"I need you. I need you right now," he exhaled. "I've always, always...," he could barely talk. He was sweating, shaking. "I need you."

His mouth slowly opened as his eyes squinted shut, as if he couldn't bear to watch what he was doing. He was crumbling into her, squeezing tighter, trying to hold himself together against her. His lips melted onto hers. He pulled away for a second. She looked into his eyes, and a look of sweet self-destruction lay claim to his. Now he fell back into her with abandon. They stumbled off together.

●

P.E.A. CLIMATE VIOLENCE, TAKE SHELTER IMMEDIATELY

Sudden heat waves reaching 150 degrees across California are sparking dozens of forest fires. Widespread landslides in the Rocky Mountains have pulverized Highway 70 in Colorado. Tornadoes have broken out in Wisconsin and Minnesota. Extremely high

```
winds, thunderstorms, and flash flood warn-
ings remain.
    Find secure shelter immediately. Updates
to come.

8/19/76 - 1:46 p.m. - Public Emergency Alert
U.S. National Safety System
```

●

David Webb walked in through the patio door, having been on a run at the beach. "What's going on?" he stammered. All of the anxious friends and workers were staring straight at him. "I heard Adam freaked; I'm seeing the news. Did Stella leave?"

"Yeah," I said, "just about fifteen minutes ago."

"Why are you all looking at me? Where's June?"

"I don't know."

He began to walk into the house. "Don't go looking for her!" I pleaded. But that only made him move faster, and now I was running after him. "Don't! David!"

"What's going on!" he yelled. He sprinted up the stairs.

"Don't go up there!"

But there was no stopping him. "No, no," he muttered as he ran down the upstairs hallway. "This is a nightmare! No!"

At the main doors below, I could already see a security team storming in, guns ready.

Webb burst through the double doors into Adam's master bedroom. "What the hell is going on?" he stammered at the sudden sheet-ruffled silence. Adam peered around June's naked body. She scrambled under the covers.

"Adam!" he screamed. Webb leaped headlong over the bed, colliding with Adam. They tumbled to the floor like boulders, grappling with each other's flailing limbs indiscriminately. Webb grabbed Adam's face and shoved his head to the ground. Then he landed a heavy right fist on his left eye.

"Stop it!" screamed June. "Stop!"

Webb landed a destructive blow on Adam's other eye, but Adam got his leg loose. He hiked his knee into Webb's face, sending him crashing into a bedside table. Webb grabbed a half-empty martini glass fell and smashed it over the back of Adam's head.

By then the soldiers were bounding through the door. They shoved Webb against the wall so hard it crushed the drywall. They dragged him out of the room and all the way down the hallway, down the stairs, through the grand hall, and out the main entrance. All the while, he screamed bloody murder from his bleeding mouth, "Don't blot me out! Don't blot me out! Please! Please! Don't blot me out!"

A team of medics rushed to Adam. They fixed up his bloody face, and shot him up with drugs to negate the X-4 overdose.

"What have I done?" Adam mumbled before lying back into bed. He asked June to leave, and he lay there alone for a few hours.

When he finally surfaced from the fog, Adam specifically asked Ned to make sure David wasn't punished in any way, especially not blotted out. He said it was all his own fault. But it was too late. He had been blotted out within the hour. They hadn't even bothered with a trial.

Adam never saw June again. Never said goodbye. He felt too terrible about the whole thing. Seeing her face would have been torture. She had gotten what she wanted alright, it just wasn't what she really wanted. I had to ask her to leave for him.

She walked out the door with her head held high. And for that, in a strange way, I admired her.

But after she closed the door I looked out the window. In the short walk to the car waiting for her she collapsed onto the marble driveway. "Do you need assistance?" The car asked, sensing a fallen pedestrian. "Do you need assistance? Emergency services are two minutes away." She wept on the ground as it repeated the words in its unsympathetic voice, over and over again. Finally she stood up and wobbled into the car.

That must be how she does it, I thought. That must be how she holds her head so aggravatingly high all the time. When no one is watching, she falls apart like a Jenga tower. By the time we see her, she's rebuilt, and we start the game all over again.

As for the weather, things calmed down quite a bit that same day, but the casualties that occurred along the way numbered in the thousands. It was Adam's thick raincloud, grown to the size of Texas, hurling lightning everywhere and pouring without stopping, which quelled all the forest fires a few days later.

Twenty – six

WE HAD TO SPEED UP to a pace that couldn't possibly be sustained. "The fast lane," they'll say. The only trouble with the fast lane is how quickly the road runs out. Adam's heart had swollen with big dreams that vanished when he woke them up, leaving it both bigger and emptier than before. He started spending a lot of time making memories he couldn't remember, and all of life spun out in ironies.

●

N.N.N. The Anderson Affect - *Fresh Start or Swift End?*

After a week of intermittent, violent storms and natural disasters that began on August 19, President Powers held a press conference last night to make the following announcement:

> *While ending Adam's life is still completely off the table due to previous experimental findings, we are entertaining the idea of giving Adam a full identity replacement treatment.*

For those unfamiliar with the technical term, that means clean-slate capital punishment, or put more colloquially, blotting out Adam.

> *In the meantime, the Pursuit of Happiness Project will be doing everything it can to help Adam get back into good spirits,*

*providing him opportunities to try a
number of new psychological well-being
techniques from all fields and walks of
life. In addition, I am opening a public
forum to receive new ideas for keeping
Adam happy or for curing his inexpli-
cable condition. Anyone may submit an
idea, but we are not looking for shot-in-
the-dark, hocus-pocus theories. Rather,
we are seeking reasonable, thoughtful
solutions. I have set up an operation
to filter through every submission and
select the most promising. We are a
nation of pioneers. That is why I'm urg-
ing you, America, to reach higher. We
need our best and brightest thinkers on
this, because if we want it badly enough,
there's nothing us Americans can't do.*

*Adam's ability to restore and maintain
his former happiness will factor heavily
into the decision we make regarding the
proposed identity-replacement treatment.
While I am in favor of this plan, I will
not be making an executive order, though
it is within my power in the interest
of National Security. This is an enormous decision. If we elect this option,
there is no going back. It is only a last
resort. The House and the Senate, repre-
senting the people of this nation, will
take time and consideration to come to
a decision on the Anderson Identity Act.
Don't expect immediate action, or even
close to immediate action.*

Americans have grown extremely fearful,
both of the daily weather and of this impending decision. People are equally divided
over the issue, as are their lawmakers. Many
wonder how it is that Adam hasn't managed
to maintain his happiness already, and in
light of his statement on the matter, hold
out hope that he will soon. The President
decided it was important to let Adam know
identity replacement is being considered,

publicly saying that he was "hoping to bolster (Adam's) gratitude for the life he currently has, as he will be able to keep it if he only appreciates it enough."

Adam responded with this statement:

I'm deeply sorry to tell you all that after separating from the woman I loved, I've been going through a very difficult time. In the end, the separation was mutual, but still hurts.

Some have suggested punitive action toward my ex-girlfriend, who will remain anonymous. There will be absolutely none of that, as it would only make me far more unhappy. She deserves nothing but happiness.

There are no words to express my condolences for the loss of life and destruction I've caused. I almost feel ashamed to tell you how sorry I am, because I know it will not help. I can only tell you that I will do my best to keep things on the up and up from here on out. The breakup is behind me. Things will get better, and stay that way. I promise.

But if they don't, it seems clean slate capital punishment is our last hope. The question no one can answer is this: Would blotting out Adam mean a fresh start for this country, or would it mean a nasty ending?

Many politicians and thinkers believe that, based on the experiments done thus far, the results of blotting out Adam would be catastrophic. However, an equal number of others acknowledge such risk, but under the present circumstances, have deemed it a risk we must take. If we can give Adam a completely fresh start with a clean mind and a new identity, they believe, we can teach him a healthy mental and emotional outlook, something he wasn't fortunate enough to receive as a boy, having grown up largely parentless. Some congressmen and psychologists have gone on record saying they believe the residual damages to Adam's psyche are simply too large for Adam to overcome and that a completely new identity is the only way Adam will achieve consistent emotional stability, a healthy core with a positive outlook that maintains his happiness and our safety. It may take weeks of immense destruction to arrive at this new state of mind, but it may be better than letting Adam create natural disasters for a lifetime.

Whatever decision is eventually made; Americans are presently applying for immigration to other countries in droves. But our acrimonious, post-war international relationships are not helping. While some are getting into the UK, by and large, American visas have been rejected. There are simply too many applicants. For the first time, Europe and some Asian nations are experiencing an American immigration crisis. While plenty of countries around the world have extremely loose borders, none of those countries are safe for Americans, leaving most of us nowhere to go.

Early reports estimate around 80 percent of the super-rich have taken to large yachts and private islands offshore and away from the danger. If only we could all escape the sinking ship that is our nation and float out to sea.

Published at 1:00 p.m., August 26, 2076.

●

I didn't blame them—the super-rich. I just hoped they were bringing people with them. People had to do what they could, and families and friends banded together to find safety. You just never knew when and where severe weather would strike. My family took to a ranch out in the countryside with my uncle's best friend. They had a solid storm shelter there—like other prudent people, they'd started building it months ago.

Those staying at the mansion with us had a real sense of carpe diem about them, an urge to live it up while they still could. Some people left all the fun for safer parts of the country. Even Stacy went off to hide out with her family in the Midwest, a place that at least wasn't susceptible to hurricanes and tidal waves like the estate. I was left to try to deal with Adam's loneliness all alone.

For weeks, while unfortunate civil servants filtered through millions of submissions, shot-in-the-dark hocus-pocus was about the only thing that floated to the top. We were so desperate for a solution, Adam was willing to try anything.

Someone tried to rid Adam of a voodoo curse. Then someone tried to curse him with voodoo. An articulate nerd tried to unleash Adam's superhero powers and train him to control them. Various intelligent fanboys with various superhero doctrines did different things. Others rubbed strange substances on his forehead and said things. Someone hypnotized Adam and eventually slapped him in the face. There was a commercial health guru who thought Adam could eventually just sweat it out if he ingested certain natural substances and took a sauna for long enough. He fainted. Fitness experts and yogis provided plans of all kinds, and they helped, but they weren't exorcising his demons.

Mysterious mystics had Adam try a series of strange, ancient drugs. Psychedelics and the like. We were lucky he never had a particularly bad trip, but people always ended up dying when he would try that stuff. Leaders from every major religion, and a bunch of very minor ones, came to pray over Adam or try to heal him or make him fly or what have you.

Nothing did anything.

And eventually, old M-Dr. Scheff was slowly hobbling through that giant door. He could barely get it open, and it took him fifteen minutes just to get to the other side of the house, only to find Adam floating down the lazy river in the backyard. It was a sunny day, and we hadn't seen one in a while.

Adam saw Scheff just as he was floating around a bend that would lead him back out toward the beach. "Dr. Scheff!" he called out, "I'll be right with you! Frederick," he signaled to a butler, "would you please fix Dr. Scheff one of our margaritas? And turn on the bubbles so that I come back around a little faster." Adam disappeared down the river.

I waited with Scheff at a table in the grass. The butler placed the margarita in front of him. "I'm allergic," he told me.

"To what?"

"At this point," he sighed, "pretty much everything. Oh, what the hell." Scheff started to drink the margarita. "It's been years. This is delicious." He took a deep breath and leaned back in his chair. It was the first time I'd seen Scheff somewhat relaxed, like he'd already given up on Adam, and could rest.

Twenty minutes later, Adam was drying off and sitting down, while Frederick refilled our margaritas, even Scheff's. "Adam, thanks for having me in today, though I don't believe I'll be of much help, and clearly I do not belong in this picture." He chuckled, glancing around at all the fair-weather friends drinking and dancing by the pool. "Tell me about your daily routine."

"You're looking at it. I do what I feel like."

"So the drinking, the partying, the women, and I imagine you're still taking X-4..."

"Well, this batch of margaritas is spiked with it, if that answers your question. But it doesn't affect me too much anymore."

Scheff regarded his second margarita. "I'm afraid you're simply less surprised by the same effects."

"But aren't they nice?" Adam raised his glass with a wink and bumped it into Scheff's. "Cheers."

"And here I thought I was feeling so free and easy all by myself." Scheff shook his head, but he took another drink. "I never much believed in karma," he mused, "but maybe I'm due for it. Maybe self-destruction is inevitable. Yours and mine, the whole world's."

"And here I thought we were having a nice time for once," Adam replied.

"We are Adam, we are. But there's an end to all of this, and isn't pretty. You're numbing yourself. Not just the pills. The alcohol, the sex, the spending and wasting and building and destroying, the mindless frivolities—your entire lifestyle. Everything you do is geared toward squelching pain with pleasure. But the pleasure carries diminishing returns, and pain's poignancy grows.

Burdens are heavier the longer you hold onto them, so you're piling on more and more pleasure to keep the pain down, but when the balance flips, it will flip all at once. You're storing it all up for one catastrophic, bottle-bursting breakdown, and I don't want to see it happen. I know better than anyone the mystery and the depth of human emotion, and I don't want to know what you're capable of. Your lifestyle may seem like it's helping you now, but it cannot last forever."

"And why not?"

"To put it simply, you can't numb the bad stuff without numbing the good stuff."

"But what other options do I have? It's my duty to be happy, and it's not fun anymore."

"I told you I wouldn't be of much help," Scheff paused. "It's very tricky. There's nothing I can do for you neurologically. There's nothing I can prescribe that we haven't tried. I would put you in therapy, but you can't fully deal with the failures and shortcomings of your past—those are the disasters we're trying to avoid. My hands are tied. So for now, I'll tell you is that it is possible to remain presently happy without numbing yourself." Scheff nodded. "The best thing I can recommend is meditation. Mindfulness. Concerns about the past and the future needn't dominate your mind. If you can learn to remain in the moment and remain grateful, and if you can manage to love yourself, you can find a great deal of happiness."

"How do I love myself?"

"Accept yourself."

"Without any of my past?"

"Acknowledge it and let it pass. It's all gone anyway. There is just no way to stay *always* happy except by staying in the moment, and recognizing those moments are beautiful, however transient."

"But what if I want to remember? What if I want my memories to be part of my present?"

"Sometimes that's fine. We have only the present; we will always yearn for the time we do not possess—the future, the past. Hope is good. Memories are when we reach for moments we want to see again. Maybe we like them. Maybe we don't. Maybe we want to respond, to retaliate, to redeem them. But they are fixed, and we are bound to react, one way or another, and that chain of reactions is our present. So the memories that hurt have to be viewed for what they are and nothing more—sunk costs. If anything, Adam, anchor your present to your future. Your future is wide open. Look forward."

"What am I supposed to look forward to? More happiness? Now that I've had it, now that it's here, it doesn't feel like looking forward anymore. And that was always the best part."

"Don't lose hope. Anything can happen Adam. You can do *anything* you want. Anything can happen; nothing can last. Remember that, and remain in the moment you have."

"Listen, everything you're saying—it sounds wonderful. And it's all true, I'm sure of it. It just feels a little impossible sometimes."

Scheff let out a long sigh. He leaned back. He took another swig of his margarita. "They may kill me for saying this—then again I may die in my sleep one of these nights—but you're right. Eventually, for a time, it may be impossible. In fact, it will be. That's the burden, the burden of being human. But we do our best. What else can I say?" Scheff threw up his hands. "We do our best. Do you know, do you know something I heard when I was a boy in a synagogue in Brooklyn, Adam? Over one hundred years ago now—and it's been stuck on a wall in my brain all these years like a strange painting I can't throw away, always haunting me, always freeing me..." He looked up to recall it, "'I have seen the burden God has placed on man. He has made everything beautiful *in its time*. Yet he has set eternity in their hearts.'"

Adam stared at Scheff until Scheff spoke again, "What a damn tragedy—nothing ever lasts, yet we can't shake this longing that it would." He paused. "Some strange torture, isn't it? Time. Adam...enjoy the beauty you have, now. In all my expertise that's all I have to say to you at this point. Sometimes it jumps out at us and sometimes it does not, but we do our best to find the beauty. Always try to find the beauty. Even if it makes you look ugly."

●

Adam never heard from M-Dr. Scheff again after that. He passed Adam off to the best mindfulness and meditation coaches he knew, and Adam spent the next five months trying to stay in one moment at a time.

Sometimes Adam meditated a couple hours each day. He was learning to appreciate the present, and doing everything he could to surround himself with the kind of distractions that would fill every moment with excitement. And it worked alright for a while. There were days, even some weeks, where we saw real improvement in the weather.

But it wasn't easy. And every time he slipped, he knew he had he created a disaster, he knew more casualties occurred, and he wondered. Those nameless ghosts haunted him all the time. Every emotional falter was accompanied by more than enough guilt and regret to create another. He slowly spiraled downward, even without knowing it. People were always encouraging him to let go of his demons, but it seemed it was the demons grabbing onto him, not the other way around. No matter how hard Adam worked to stay in the moment, no matter how well he might do it for a while, his giant raincloud wouldn't quit growing while his demons, unchecked, grew inside of him. Strange sinkholes all over the United States slowly opened up, swallowing homes and eventually whole towns. Temperatures dropped as summer turned to fall, and that raincloud brought early blizzards to the country.

On a daily basis, Adam had nothing to be unhappy about, so he pretended to be pissed about a lag on his PID, or frustrated with how long the 3-D printer took, or indignant about an antique race car's engine that wouldn't start. He fooled himself, holding up a plethora of externalities to block any view of the inside. His perfectly normal mind edited everything to the beat of his surroundings, because minds do not observe; they perceive. Suddenly the things that didn't matter were the only things that did matter, and errant lightning spat out of the sky. Trivial bouts of anger spouted serious volcanic eruptions. Annoyances caused avalanches. And it all welled up from some place Adam couldn't even see.

I used to wonder why people cry over spilled milk. Now I understand that it's never about the spilled milk at all. Now I wonder how their mini meltdowns contain themselves as much as they do. With Adam I could see under the surface, how the real things, the invisible things—they scratch and claw all the time, searching for the slightest tear in our psyche, through which they will burst forth like a leak in a dam. The things we have hidden deep within ourselves—they will kick and scream until we notice them. Our miseries will make fools out of us until we give them company.

Other than the little things Adam rarely seemed upset, but optimists never think they're depressed. Almost every day, at some point we would be crushed with rain at the estate. We'd all huddle together, and Adam would try to cheer up. If he'd been off alone, he'd come find us to lift his spirits. If he had been with us, he'd go be alone. Sometimes he'd run off with a girl. Sometimes he'd run off from a girl. Sometimes he'd drink and take drugs; other times he'd try to sober up. And sometimes he wouldn't do anything, because he already thought he was happy. There was no rhyme or reason to it. His life had become a shallow introspection, like trying to feed a real hunger by licking the icing off a cake.

●

It was one of those days where the whole space between waking up and going to bed just felt like an interruption. We had been living a variation of dreams. When my eyes opened in the morning I did not wake up, but simply moved into a different fantasy, and drifted about the estate like a ghost. The largeness of the mansion only reminded me how lost we were inside of it, how it ran us around its edges until we were spread as thin as the paint on its walls. I kept looking for something to land on and there was everything and nothing felt quite right.

I remember ambling through the grand hall and stopping dead in my tracks, having completely forgotten where I had intended to go or where I should go or if there was really anywhere I had wanted to go at all. I sauntered in circles watching myself get tossed back and forth between the massive mirrors—a million reflections staring back at me like strangers crowding into the house, inescapable strangers never close enough to touch never loud enough to hear never thinking for themselves anyway.

Night fell like a black brick and I found myself heading up to the roof for relief. That's where I bumped into Adam. He was tinkering around with a giant telescope, twisting different knobs, moving it across the sky, blinking and shifting between his eyes, trying to get it right.

"Hey," I said from the darkness behind him.

"Woah!" He startled, banging his forehead on the telescope. "Ow. Hey."

"My bad—didn't mean to scare you." I chuckled. "What are you doing up here?"

"Seemed like a good place to get away from everyone." He rubbed his head. "What about you?"

"Had to get away from all the mirrors—everywhere I look in this house there's a giant mirror getting involved."

"No kidding." He looked back into the telescope, trying to focus it again, struggling to deal with a high-tech machine he wasn't nearly prepared to use. "Why don't you have them replace them with paintings? I'll start collecting paintings."

"Sounds good." I laid back on the roof under the clear night sky.

Adam kept adjusting the telescope until exasperation overtook him. "Fuck it. I can't find shit. I'm never getting this thing to work." At that, he tipped the telescope right over the edge of the roof. He watched it plummet down onto a stone pathway with a loud crash that had every guest and butler on the estate trying to figure out what had blown up. He exhaled a deep sigh of relief.

"Geez," I said. "That was ... that was something."

"Yeah. It's a little troubling how satisfying that was."

Adam laid back on the roof and we just looked up into the stars for a while. I felt like I was up there in space again, with that same unsettling feeling. Only instead of being all around me, it was a part of me. Like a space just as pitch black was expanding within me and would never stop expanding, just like the universe. I had never felt so detached from anything and everything as in that moment. Like an astronaut whose rope had been cut, toppling into the abyss and never once stopping. I thought I'd have changed or matured or discovered something by now in all this, but if I had, I couldn't tell. I thought I might have found myself along the way, hiding somewhere in all the incredible experiences the project provided, but it seemed my search had only grown more desperate. Was I to define myself by my fondest memories and best hopes? Should I pretend to be my interests? Will it work to mingle with my favorite things and activities and people until I can no longer tell the difference between them and me? Am I just some blender full of ingredients? I only knew that I was spinning, and felt as though there are no solid answers out here in the existence of things. Just questions, and the feeling of floating. Just space, and stars too bright to ignore but too far to reach.

After a while I looked over at Adam—he had begun flipping through mental photographs on his PID, reminiscing about all the great times he'd had over the summer. Times with Stella. Times still crystal clear in the videos, but nowhere else. When he noticed me looking, he quickly shut it down. "Shit," Adam seemed to realize, "I can't be doing this."

"I wouldn't worry too much about it."

"No, it's too much. I need to stay present. I think I've been getting better at it. Except when I go to sleep and I'm a hostage to my own mind. My memories have been creeping into my dreams. Sometimes I can't tell the difference."

"Like what?"

"I see Stella almost every night. Last night I was seven years old; I was with my dad."

"What happened?"

Adam pulled up the dream on his PID to show me. Him and his dad were laying in the grass in their backyard. They were watching fluffy piles of white clouds pass through the blue sky.

"What do you see Adam?" Paul asked.

"Um...I don't know," little Adam replied.

"Well, what do you want to see?"

"I don't know, why?"

"Because we see whatever we want to see. Try it. Decide what you want to see, then look up into the clouds. You'll find it. It may take a little time, but you'll find it."

Adam looked over at his father, and he was smiling. And there was wonder in his voice.

"Go ahead. Pick anything. What do you want to find?"

"A lion."

"Let's look."

Adam's eyes scanned the sky for a minute, and sure enough, there it was—a great, vague, pile of lion. Adam pointed up at it. "There!" he said.

"Well look at that." Paul laughed. "No doubt about it. I can see its mane hanging down in the front and the little legs growing out at funny angles and its tail curling up in the back. He's a goofy lion, but isn't he a beauty?"

"He's the best cloud in the sky!" Adam couldn't hold back his excitement.

"But there's the catch," Paul said. "Don't look for too long. Once you find it, it will fade away just as fast. It will morph into something else."

Of course Adam continued to watch his lion anyway. As it drifted across the sky, it warped and spread thin. Before he knew it, Adam couldn't tell how it had ever been a lion at all.

"I can't find it anymore," Adam mourned.

"Now we're forced to see it for what it is."

"What is it?"

"Vapor. Vapor in the wind." He paused. "Onto the next one! What do you want to see?"

●

But Adam didn't know what he wanted to see anymore. He had seen it all. Everything had its moment in the sun and burnt off. The immense happiness he once felt loomed over him. The good life grew dull. Adam began to feel bored as hell, because he actually believed he could find heaven on earth.

I think we spent those days in the mansion because it was the only place big enough to hold all of Adam's stuff. He started collecting fine art and old wine and other rare things that he so desperately wanted to care about. He was hoping to replace himself with simpler possessions and growing just as dead. There was always a crew of workers delivering something or building something or renovating something that didn't really need to be changed.

Adam would take meetings with all kinds of charities—he wanted to use all the money he had access to for helping people. Of course it wasn't his own hard-earned money he was giving away, so it didn't feel much like sacrifice, and didn't make him feel any different. So he tried helping people directly, doing volunteer work like visiting kids in hospitals and seniors in nursing homes. But that kind of happiness wasn't so neat and clean. The weather wouldn't hold because compassion too often hurts before it feels good.

Ned and I scrambled to organize entertainment every day to keep the party going. Professional athletes and sports teams competing right on the estate, musicians and dancers of all kinds, circus acts, magicians, comedians, artists, masseuses, naked synchronized swimmers—anything you can imagine.

Months escaped as Adam tried to become terribly forgetful. Girls came over. New ones all the time. That was never difficult for Adam. They all wanted their shot at saving him, at making him happy and saving the nation, if only for a minute. Some days I would see them streaming in and out of his bedroom.

All focus slowly slipped away as he lived moment to moment. Even the most basic delayed gratifications, like working out or intentionally going to bed, became overbearing obstacles. He could not sit still in his own skin. Every ordinary hour needed to generate some kind of high, because high was ordinary. The guy had logged enough massage hours to be considered premium Kobe beef, and his pelvic muscles were probably the only part of his body still in great shape.

Exuberant friends roamed the estate freely, staying God knows where within the mansion, always smiling whenever they appeared. Women often came with certain notions about what kinds of things might happen, but Adam couldn't possibly notice all of them, and sometimes they turned their attention to me. I was swept up in cheap ecstasy with breathtaking women I would never see again. And it was all too wonderful, but all too easy, leaving me all too much time to think—and slowly realize it might be nice if one of them cared about me a little bit. But I didn't know I had any real morals until I bashed them to pieces. I never had a problem with playboys until I became one. I never had anything against drugs until I fell in love with them. I never said never until never wasn't an option for me anymore. I floated aimlessly, pushed this way and that by the winds of my own whims. Life became a rabbit trail, a chase after our addictions, an intoxicating sweetness that built up a poison in us.

No matter what he did, Adam couldn't seem to make climate conditions better. They only ever got worse. Earthquakes rumbled all over like the whole country was getting ready to unhinge. Adam's black storm cloud grew impossibly large, covering more than half of the continental United States. As December blew in, sometimes the floods would freeze over, leaving whole towns stuck in three or four feet of ice. Blizzards spat huge hail while tornadoes batted it across the sky like cannonballs.

Lawmakers debated furiously over the Anderson Identity Act. Getting a majority had been dragging on for months, but they were getting very close. Americans were about as angry with the government as Adam was at himself. He had to look at himself so much, he grew to hate what he saw.

He couldn't even visit his grandmother in the hospital, though they always said she was doing well. And they made her say it. They caked her in make-up and loaded her up with energy every time Adam wanted to check in holographically. He had no idea how close she was to death, and he couldn't bear to think about how close he might be to getting blotted out.

TWENTY – SEVEN

"NO! NO! I'M NOT READY!" Adam's voice echoed down through the mansion. Faces of fake friends popped out of doorways as Adam screamed, "I need more time!"

All over the house, people feebly approached or backed away from Adam, each as unready to quit partying. "Everybody out!" Adam screamed. "This is all over!"

The mansion began to shake, as if quivering at Adam's words. The decorations were still up from the holidays we had hardly noticed, and now the ornaments were shattering on the floor. It was New Year's Day, but there had been no celebration the night before, and there was no reason to celebrate.

The rumbling grew more violent and the floor began to break apart. The great animals fell off the walls of the great hall.

The car collections crashed into each other. The ancient sculptures crumbled to pieces.

Adam had heard the announcement. I wasn't supposed to tell him, but I did.

●

N.N.N. The Anderson Affect - Anderson Act Vote Date Set in Light of Horrific Conditions

The increasingly violent weather plaguing this country may take a turn on January 6, for better or worse.

But with the vote on The Anderson Act less than a week away, lawmakers in both the House and the Senate remain equally divided. There is no telling which way this historic, potentially catastrophic decision will go, as 12 senators

and 34 congressmen remain admittedly unde-
cided. It's no easy choice. Many of the lawmakers who have already made their decisions say
they are simply going with their guts.

The conditions Adam creates this week could
have a serious effect on the vote. Adam's
enormous storm cloud now blankets 60 percent
of the country in snow, including Washington,
DC. A sinkhole in Mississippi more than 20
miles wide continues to grow and shows no sign
of slowing down. Perhaps worst of all, the
severe weather damage to farm towers and the
widespread lack of sunlight during the last
few months has led to a 71 percent decrease
in agricultural yields, increasing expensive,
inefficient imports of food by more than 100
percent and causing the government to tap
into emergency food stockpiles.

The transportation industry at large remains
in no better shape. After three commercial
airplanes went down in sudden, violent storms
last week, only a dozen commercial flights
have even take off. There are no customers.

Slingshot lines have all but shut down in
the wake of the massive rock-slide that took
out the Appalachian Line in West Virginia,
along with 479 passengers.

As people search the country for a safe
place to hide, it seems they prefer their
own automobiles, where at least they can
pull over and get out of the vehicle in an
emergency.

Published at 9:36 a.m., January 1, 2077.

●

"Ned," Adam screamed into his PID, "Tell me right now before
it's too late; have you found out *anything* about my father!"

"This really isn't the time—go to the roof!" Ned was screaming.

"Fucking tell me!"

"Look, there's just no word on him yet!"

"How is that possible? It's been months. You're hiding the
truth. How the hell can you not know yet?"

"We're doing our best. Get to the fucking roof now!"

"The clock is ticking Ned! I need to know! My life needs answers!"

The earth shook the mansion like a Christmas present, and a giant chandelier fell from the ceiling. It crushed a guest to death just as he looked up to see the thing falling. "No!" Adam screamed, but there was no time to react—icy water rushed through the mansion. We sprinted up flights of stairs as all the great collections of great things that once meant something to great people washed away below us.

From the roof, we could see the tidal wave rushing in, swamping the entire estate. It swept up everything in its path, no matter how beautiful. Beautiful cars and beautiful people and even the beautiful oaks lining the long beautiful drive. They were all washed away indiscriminately.

The hover-jet descended, shaking as it attempted to hover steady in a crushing wind. A rope ladder descended, whipping around like a jump rope until Adam managed to grab it. As soon as we clung on, they were already flying us away. We hung there looking back at the others on the roof until the soldiers pulled us into the plane.

"Go back for them!" Adam screamed.

"We're sending another plane," Ned said. "We need to get you to a safe, calm place."

"Take me to Chicago," Adam demanded. "I want to see my grandmother."

"That's not something we can do."

"Why not?"

"It's not going to improve your emotional condition."

"I don't care." Adam fumed. "I haven't seen her in months. I have one fucking week to live. I need to see her."

"You don't know that!" Ned erupted. "And if you want to help your chances of the vote swinging your way, trust me, you don't want to see her!"

"So you've been lying the whole time?" Adam shook his head. "She's not getting better at all, is she?"

"We've been protecting you the whole time!"

"I need to see her! How bad is she? I need to see her now!"

Ned said nothing. They wouldn't be able to hide it anymore. We rerouted for Chicago; it was the only way to calm down Adam.

"Okay," I urged Adam, "okay. You're good now. We're good. We're going to see her. You can calm down. It's time to calm down."

"It's time to start tying up loose ends Clark. There's no time to calm down." He looked out the window, down at the great army of waves storming the whole coastline, surging right through neighborhoods.

"I need to talk to Steven," he said.

"What?"

"Loose ends. I need to talk to Steven."

Adam tried to beam himself in on a holographic call with Steven.

"Why won't he answer?" Adam asked. "Why won't he ever fucking answer anymore? I haven't seen his face since the party."

He called again.

"Maybe I wasn't the greatest friend in the world, maybe I wasn't totally consistent," Adam went on, "but my god, I did everything I could for him."

He called again.

"Stop calling!" Ned burst out. "Why do you need to talk to him so badly?"

"Because he's my friend, and I need his opinion on the vote."

"Why would you need his opinion?" Ned retorted. "Why the fuck would his opinion matter?"

"Because I grew up with him. Because he's smart. Because I trust him." Adam's brow furrowed as he looked into Ned's anxious eyes. "No," Adam shook his head. "No. What else are you hiding from me? Why can't I see him?" Adam called Steven again. "This doesn't make any sense. He was never angry with me. Why haven't I seen him Ned?"

And finally, the Steven double was ready to quell Adam's concerns. His fake face appeared on Adam's wrist. It was startling how accurate he was. There was no way anyone who hadn't seen Steven floating face down the pool could tell the difference.

"Where the fuck have you been man?" Adam pleaded. "I haven't seen you in months."

"I've just been busy," fake Steven replied. "I'm sorry."

"Busy with what? The whole country's been falling apart."

"Busy with work."

"Are you wearing a tie?" Adam asked. "Since when have you ever worn a tie?"

"Oh," the double said, "I only wear them to work."

"Are people even going to work these days? Plus, you work from home," Adam said.

"Umm, not anymore."

"Okay, whatever. Listen man, I'm sure you heard the announcement. I need to know what you think. I need to know if you think I should be blotted out. If you were a senator, and you didn't know me, which way would you vote? Be honest."

"That's a really tough question," the double said. He leaned back and looked away from Adam for moment, somewhere else in the room, wherever he was. And when he did, part of his body entered the holographic field. "But, I would definitely vote against the act. I think we're much better off letting you be. I know things will get better in time. Besides, if you can just—"

"Steven, have you lost weight?"

"Umm, a little bit," the double replied. He'd never met Steven in real life; he'd only seen his pictures on *Fix*. And on *Fix*, Steven had always edited his pictures to make him look quite a bit slimmer.

"Back up," Adam said. "I want to see."

"What?"

"Back up."

"Okay..." The double leaned back, and Adam's eyes grew wide.

"What happened to Steven?" Adam turned to Ned.

"Nothing." Ned shrugged. "Nothing that I know of. He lost weight. You lost weight, didn't you, Steven?"

"I've been working out," the double said.

"How much weight did you lose?" Adam asked.

"Umm," the double stalled as he tried to think of a safe answer. "About ten pounds. Ten or fifteen pounds." But he looked about forty pounds lighter than Steven.

"*Take off your fucking mask!*" Adam screamed. "What happened to Steven?"

"Nothing!" Ned yelled back. "He's right there."

I glared at Ned, and now Adam was glaring at me.

"He's dead," I said. "He died at the party. I'm sorry. I'm sorry I hid this from you. He's dead."

"What? How could that—"

"He drowned," Ned interjected. "He had too much...too much...everything, and he drowned."

"I was..." Adam shook his head. "I was planning on spending so much more time...is that it? That can't be it. It can't be. He's just gone? No goodbye? No making up for lost time? How can that be it?"

"But how could he have even drowned like that? His PID should've have sent out for help if he was drowning. There were paramedics nearby—they should've have been there within a minute and saved him."

"He wasn't found until the morning."

"But why not? You didn't want to cause a scene?"

"He just wasn't found."

"Say it! You didn't want to ruin my precious fun!"

"Okay! We were waiting for a chance when nobody would see and start a big fucking fuss and we never had that chance until Clark had already found him!"

"But you let him die..." Adam began to tear up with rage.

"Tell the whole truth Ned," I said.

"That's the truth. Why would you say that!"

"Because I can't keep lying! Because you killed him! He knew something and you found an opportunity to discreetly kill him at the party."

"We didn't kill him! Why are you trying to—"

"I saw the fucking magazine Ned! He knew something in that magazine, and you killed him!"

"He *thought* he knew something!" Ned burst out. "He knew nothing! And he was going to send Adam on a wild goose chase with the lies he was starting to believe! An emotional nightmare! He would've created chaos! We didn't want to kill him, it was risky! We killed him because we had to!"

"What did he know!" Adam leapt across the aisle and grabbed Ned by the neck. "Tell me the truth Ned! I just want the truth!" He squeezed to the point of choking. "I won't quit! Tell me!"

But a soldier put Adam in a headlock, squeezing harder and harder until Adam let go of Ned's neck. Ned pulled his trusty needle from his pocket. He held it right next to Adam's neck. "Do not threaten me. Do not ask questions that don't have answers. One prick and you're out cold, in deep sleep from which you will never wake. All I need is an executive order to blot you out, and trust me, I can get that after the fact. You've made such a mess this morning, President Powers is already thinking about making the order before the vote. It could happen any moment."

"Let me go. Let me see my grandma."

Ned pulled back his needle and stared at it. "Any moment Adam." He nodded to the soldier, who let Adam go.

Adam fell back into his seat, just trying to focus on his breathing. He sucked in deep, strained breaths, inhaling the pain into a heart already on the verge of bursting wide open. "My whole life is sham. Everything is a fucking lie. I have nothing real." He shook his in disbelief, holding it in his hands as if to keep it from squishing under the impenetrable grayness pressing from all sides. "I have nothing. It's all vapor."

Adam fell silent. Everything was snowballing to something too big for his frigid soul to hold. He stared out the window as we cruised above an endless table of dark clouds, spewing flashes of lightning with all the ice and snow. The plane shook so much we had to strap in to keep from being tossed around like rag dolls.

●

P.E.A. *FIND IMMEDIATE SHELTER, DISASTERS IMMINENT*

Adam will now be grieving the reality of his dying grandmother for the first time. Go to your nearest bomb shelter or storm shelter immediately. Prepare for the worst.

1/1/77 - 1:17 p.m. - Public Emergency Alert
U S. National Safety System

●

The shaking didn't stop in the hospital. Even in Chicago, we could feel distant tremors shaking the building. Out the window, I could see massive waves beating against enormous mounds of ice on the shores of Lake Michigan. A horrifying blizzard blew furiously through the city.

"Grandma..." Adam choked back tears. She lay in bed as machines beeped her along the fringes of death. Most of her hair had fallen out. Her lips were blue and chapped, and like most of her frail body, looked already dead. She struggled to keep her eyes open. He slowly cracked forward like a shattering frozen lake, until he reached her bed and kneeled beside it, shivering.

"I'm so glad you came to see me honey," her voice hummed quietly.

Tears formed as Adam shook his head in disbelief. "How long do you have?"

"Who knows," she said. "Maybe a week. I hope I live long enough to see you happy. That's all I want, to see my sweet boy happy." She reached up a cold hand and touched his face. "I love you so much Adam."

"Grandma," he rubbed his hand across the few hairs on her bald head. "I'm trying. I'm trying so hard, but I don't know how that's going to happen. I've lost it. I'm going to get blotted out, and none of it will matter. I don't understand Grandma. I don't understand why this all happened to me."

Tears soaked his face, and she began to cry dry sobs that reverberated through her body.

"Why? Why is this happening to me? Why do I have this curse? Why?"

"I can't be sure *why* honey, but…there's something—Adam, before I die, there's something I've wanted to tell you for a long time. The government threatened to kill me if I ever did. You would've had no one."

"Grandma, it's okay. I already know. I know it wasn't a car wreck; I know it wasn't a storm. I overheard dad on a call with you. I know she died in childbirth with me. I know you lied to me. It's okay. I understand. It's okay."

"All this time you've been believing a lie," she wagged her head, peering into his eyes, "I never lied to you. Not about the storm or the wreck. I just didn't include the details of how she died—your father threatened me. He said you could never know. An early childbirth was part of her death, sure, but there was something else. Something much stranger. He blamed you because he couldn't face how much he hated himself."

"What? What happened?" Adam begged. I know Ned so desperately wanted to stop her, but it was too late now. What would he do, knock her in front of him? Cutting her off and leaving Adam an inch from some kernel of truth would have been even worse.

The dam was bursting. Ned was all out of options short of that executive order.

"Your father, Adam," she looked afraid, "was a very powerful man. He swept my Sofia off her feet so quickly. And he was so ... mysterious. Never even knew what he did for a living, but he had money. I trusted him because I could see how much he loved Sofia—that wasn't a mystery at all. Clear as day. He really, really loved her. Well you know how your mother loved thunderstorms. They were always her favorite. Ever since she was a little girl, we would curl up and watch the storms roll in over Lake Michigan.

"Your father, he loved storms just as much. It's how they met—they were both running in the rain. So they started running together whenever it rained. They fell in love that way.

"And as they did, as they fell for each other, well, once in a while, he would surprise her...with a thunderstorm." She stared into Adam's eyes. "He would create them, Adam. Your father, he would command these things. He was brilliant. He could touch a few buttons, and a few minutes later, a thunderstorm would appear right in front of them. Can you imagine? And he told her that in the beginning, he had been creating rain just to have a reason to call her to go on a run together."

Lilla began crying, remembering it all. Her pale hand surged with blue veins as she grabbed Adam's hand. "That kind of power, that kind of magic, for her. Can you imagine how your mother felt? It'd be hard not to think the guy was a god. It was, it was monstrous, but there was something so sweet about it. And she was always a little apprehensive, but he told her creating these storms was harmless, that he was very careful. And it was just for her. He never ever did that for anyone else." She gasped to catch her thin breath. "Of course I wasn't supposed to know. It was top secret. But she told me. She couldn't hold it in. Can you imagine?" Lilla began to weep again, and I was afraid the tears would kill her right then. "He really loved her, Adam. More than anyone I have ever seen, he loved her. Your father was a bad man, but he loved even worse."

"So what happened?" Adam leaned in to hear her shrinking voice.

"A thunderstorm," she said. "She was eight months pregnant with you. It was their anniversary and they went on a little road trip. Well they were in the middle of nowhere, and all of a sudden, he pulls over to an overlook, a gorgeous overlook with a big valley and lake. It was a perfectly calm day, but he says to her, he says something like, 'I got a feeling there's gonna be a thunderstorm here.' And sure enough, a big old, mean old thunderstorm, full of lightning, formed right in front of them. They sat high and dry, but there it was. It was the best surprise she could've asked for, Adam. And he told me it was the most powerful thunderstorm he had ever created for her. They watched the sky dance, and they were...happy," Lilla burst into tears again.

"But Adam, she was so in love, she was so excited by it all, she went into labor. They had to rush to the nearest hospital. But on the," she couldn't get the words out, "on the way, the storm followed. He'd made too big a storm to handle, and there were side effects in areas he hadn't foreseen, byproducts. The storm was out of control. It met them on the road so suddenly. Lightning struck a tree in front of them and it fell onto the road. This great, giant tree. They slammed right into it. They survived the crash, but now they were in the middle of the storm, and they needed shelter. She was already in labor, but there was nowhere to go. The car was full of smoke. So Sofia, she said, 'lightning never strikes twice,' and she ran over to the base of tree trunk that had been struck. Of course, your father knew that old saying wasn't true, but he knew it was still unlikely that lightning would strike there again, and the fallen trunk provided some semblance of shelter, and he decided let her believe the comforting myth. So they ran to the base of the fallen tree and waited there for help.

"But help wasn't coming. The road was shut down—the whole traffic grid was down. Nobody could get to them. So she pushed and pushed and she had you. Right there in the storm, she had you. And she got to hold you there. She got to look into your sweet little eyes." Lilla's tears sent her into a coughing fit.

"But Adam, the lightning—it struck again. It struck her right there with you against the tree trunk. It struck you both. She had bundled you up in her and your father's sweaters and jackets. She was holding you, curled up around you, protecting you from the cold and the rain. It's the only reason you survived, with no damage but a strange little electricity scar." Adam pulled back his broken watch to look at it.

"She didn't survive," Lilla mourned. "Not after taking the brunt of the strike, not with the labor and the blood loss. Her heart stopped. Your father did CPR for twenty minutes waiting for his machines to get rid the massive storm he'd made. When the ambulance finally arrived, there was no bringing her back. But you, Adam, you're some kind of miracle."

"Did you know?" Adam asked. "Did you know my emotions would control the weather?"

"No, honey, I didn't. Not until you did."

"Did he know? Is that why he left?"

"I don't know if he knew, and I don't know why he left. But he made me promise never to tell you any of this. He said it would be easier for you that way, simpler. He was never the same after she died. He loved her more than anything. He went into shock, became a different person. For years, he barely even spoke."

"He hated me for it. You must have too. She was your daughter."

"No, Adam, he had no right. I could never hate you. I have always loved you so much. I fought for you. After your father left, I fought to take you in as my own."

"What do you mean?"

"Legally, I was not supposed to have you. Your godfather was supposed to take care of you. I had to fight to get you, because I could tell immediately he wouldn't care for you, not like I would. I didn't trust him. He was so coarse."

"Grandma, what was his name?"

"Oh I don't remember. It was over twenty years ago. I only met him the one time, and he never took off his sunglasses. He seemed very shut off. A real tough guy. He was your father's old friend from the war. And he had a bionic leg. That's all I remember."

"Harvey..." Adam exhaled. He straightened up, staring into her eyes, shocked to his core with a wave of anxious energy. "Grandma, I, I have to go. I love you so much."

She clutched him tight as he wrapped his arms around her.

"I want to stay, I love you, but I need to find—"

"Go," she said, fighting through another coughing fit. "Go and face the storms that made you." She held Adam's hand again. "You cannot run from them any longer. Face them. You cannot run from them or you will never lose them. Find them, and they will lose you."

TWENTY-EIGHT

TEARS FLOWED DOWN Adam's face as we tore down the hospital hallway. Adam barreled right over Ned as he stood up from a bench to stop us. Earthquakes tossed us against the walls and had us jumping over fallen nurses like an obstacle course.

I think Adam knew that was the last time he would ever see his grandma, and like the crumbling of an invisible pillar that had always been holding him up, her goodbye left him profoundly unstable. The rumbling in the ground became so severe, we couldn't take ten steps without falling down.

"Where are you going!" Ned crawled out the hospital door after us. We didn't look back. Surely they would chase, but it wouldn't be easy in the middle of a panicking city in the middle of an icy Armageddon.

We sprinted and slipped down city streets caked in ice as we made our way toward the National Weather Commission building. Extreme winds ran a race course between the skyscrapers, spraying ice and snow into our faces like bullets. I didn't know if I would freeze to death or split into a million pieces first.

Suddenly Adam peeled off the street into a cafe full of people crowding in for warmth, and I thought he was doing the same. But he had only gone indoors because Stella was calling. For the first time since she'd left, Stella was calling. Adam wrapped his jacket over his face so that no one would recognize him. We pushed through the people to the bathroom and locked the door.

"Stella!" He finally answered her third call.

"Adam," she gasped. She sounded exhausted. "I went into labor."

Hurricanes silently swirled in Adam's wide eyes.

"Did you hear me, Adam?" she said. "I'm having our baby boy."

"No, no, it's too early," he stammered. "It's way too early. I need more time Stella. I'm not ready!"

"Neither am I," she said. "But it's happening, and there's a huge hurricane hitting shore in Miami right now. It's insane. I heard the announcement. I know this must sound impossible, but I need you to try, to really try to calm down, so I can have this baby."

"Are you okay?" His voice was laced with panic.

"I'm okay right now, but I'm scared. I'm really scared Adam. I'm inland at the hospital, but it's getting worse and worse. The levies have all failed; the flooding is crazy. And the wind—every window at the hospital is broken. My whole apartment building is gone. The hotel is gone."

"Completely gone?"

"It's wrecked. Everything's collapsing into the water."

"No, no," Adam broke apart. "Stella—your mosaic."

"It's okay Adam. That's the last thing you should worry about."

"But I've wrecked it. I've wrecked it all."

"It was made from wreckage anyway."

"So?"

"So it feels right enough. I just hope a few people appreciated it while it lasted."

"But all that work, the years—you'll never get it back."

"Adam, it's really okay. I was getting close to finishing it; it was time to begin again."

"What?"

"I'll make a new one."

"So, what—the old one is just a sunk cost?"

"Sunk cost? Huh? Sure it sank, but there's no such thing as a sunk cost. It's still floating around in my head at least. I'll resurrect the wreckage and I'll find some new pieces and I'll create a new one. And it will be even better, even more broken and more complete."

"Stella—"

A pounding on the door hushed Adam to a quiet. "We know you're in there! Open up!" It was Ned and a few of the soldiers. "Open the fuck up Adam! The whole country's blowing up!"

Adam stood up on the toilet and busted through a small window with his elbow.

"You've done enough!" Ned screamed. "We have an emergency executive order to blot you out. Come out here and get it over with! Now!"

I helped shove Adam through the shattered glass into an alley, then he pulled me through. The freezing wind funneled through that narrow alley so powerfully, we could only move in one direction—but very quickly. It thrashed us to the frozen pavement and we slid along like hockey pucks, until slamming into a brick wall at the end of the alley.

"They're just going to keep tracking us!" Adam yelled. He looked at me, gritting his teeth, and without warning he bit down on his wrist. He wedged his teeth deep under the ridges of his PID and ripped the thing out with his mouth. He screamed in agony as the small square tore out a chunk of flesh behind it. Bloody wires and tubes that had been attached to his veins and nerves hung out of Adam's mouth. He spat it out and clutched his wrist, writhing in pain. "It's the only way," he nodded at me. "You with me?"

I had to do it before I had a chance to think. It felt like tearing off a part of my body. We chucked our PIDs down the alley to the side and ran the other way. I saw Ned pop his head out the window from which we had escaped. He tried to come out after us, but he got stuck, blocking all the soldiers behind him as well. Turned out he was too fit to squeeze his muscly shoulders through the small window.

The only trail we would leave now was the blood leaking from our wrists. We each had to take off a layer to wrap our wounds tightly, making the bitter cold twice as bad. The Weather Commission building was just a few blocks from the hospital, but those conditions made them impossibly long blocks. We ran out the alley, back into a biting wind, and found ourselves waist deep in snowdrifts. We trudged down the street in the crippling cold.

When we finally rounded the block and turned toward the Weather Commission, I looked back. In the distance, through the blurry blizzard, I could see dozens more soldiers pouring into the alley we had come from. Once they found our PIDs, they'd have to figure out how the hell to find us.

We began running down the final stretch, but a great screeching noise in the air stopped us in our tracks. We looked up, trying to find the source. An enormous weather bot fell out of the black clouds above us, spinning as it fought to stay afloat. It was far too big to fit between buildings, destroying several structures as it bounced and bashed its way to the ground.

A massive pile of twisted steel filled up a whole city block. There was absolutely no way around the wreckage to the Weather Commission building. As the wind cleared away the smoke Adam began running toward it again.

"Adam, wait!" I yelled. "It could blow up any minute!"

"Then hurry up!" He yelled back, and kept running.

I could feel my whole body vibrating as we got close. The machine emitted a deep humming noise punctuated by popping sounds with showers fiery sparks. One of the broken wings had torn through a building and set it ablaze. The slightly more intact wing sprayed chemicals into the air, and leaked rivers of bubbling fluids that cut right through the thick ice in the street, and even the concrete beneath. The air between the buildings was filling up with a dense reddish hue, the temperature warmed to what must have been a hundred degrees. I began to feel very lightheaded. And with the chemicals in air, I felt like my skin was burning off. Yet it provided some much-needed relief from the cold. As we climbed over the hot metal, I could feel its interior components crackling and shifting. "*Warning*," a damaged robotic voice boomed. "*Stay one thousand feet back. Warning.*"

"C'mon!" I screamed to Adam as he stood atop the fuselage, surveying the behemoth. We slid down the side into the piles of melting snow and hauled off. Another block and we ducked into the beautiful National Weather Commission Building, standing tall against all the chaos.

We jumped in the elevator and zoomed up toward the top floor. Halfway up, the boom of the weather bot self-destructing rattled the whole building.

•

Harvey was standing at his panoramic window when we walked through the open door. He had been watching everything unfold from above. No one else was up there on the top floor—just him, like a captain prepared to go down with his ship. All was quiet but the sound of the howling, crushing wind, and the ice pounding the windows.

He didn't hear us walk in. Through the window we could see another weather bot tumbling out of the sky. "No! No!" Harvey banged on the window. The aircraft crushed a historic brick building a few blocks away. Harvey let his fist slip off the window and his head fall down.

When he turned around, Adam was standing right behind him. Harvey looked at him like he had come back from the dead. Adam pinned him against the window. "You knew my father."

Harvey said nothing. Adam put both hands on Harvey's neck and pinned him up higher against the black sky behind. "You're my fucking godfather! And this is all your fault!" Adam screamed.

"My fault?" Harvey choked. Fear scaled over his eyes.

"You've been controlling the weather! No wonder you're so good at prediction. You and my father. And I am paying for your mistakes!" Adam let go. Harvey slid to the floor in a heap. He slowly lifted himself with the help of his onyx desk.

"My mistakes...," Harvey muttered, indignant. "Remind me, who's the one throwing a fit here? How the hell is any of this my fault?"

"To think the two of you were close friends..." Adam crept right up to Harvey's face. "Just tell me what happened Harvey. Just tell me the truth."

"The truth..." Harvey shook his head. "Why? Why Adam? Why can't you just accept the life that you have, the fairy-tale ending you've been given? Why bother with the truth?"

"Because what else is there? What is there but honesty? There is nothing else, because everything else is nothing. So fucking tell me something Harvey! Tell me what's going on! Because I can't escape him! He cursed my whole life! Where is he! What happened to—"

"Your father was a great man!" Harvey exploded. "Your father is the reason any of this is possible!"

"Any of what?"

"You want to know about your father? You want truth?" He slowed down. "For god sake, your father won us the war. He was the goddamn Turing of World War Three. The weather control you're so mad about—your father invented that. He was a genius Adam. When he joined the Venice Project, his mind took over our entire operation. The advances he made in weather creation won us the war. Understand? The power he was able to harness from nature is mind-boggling. He tapped into the next level of civilization. No one thought what he created was even possible. Still they don't know it's possible! The sweeping sandstorms that hit at just the right time, the tsunamis and hurricanes that wiped out entire naval forces, the relentless heat waves that struck whole armies helpless in days, the earthquakes that brought nations to their knees—those were not the convenient results of global warming. Those, Adam, were the ungodly acts of God that your father created. Those were what we achieved with the Venice Project. And you won't hear about it in the history books. Your father won the war, and no one will ever know his name."

Adam stood stunned.

"And you have nothing to say. Of course."

"I don't know what to say Harvey. It sounds like a war crime."

"*War* is a crime. Sure, we skirted the convention. It was a fucking world war, not a game. Everyone was breaking the rules; we broke them best. Broke them brilliantly. With Mother Nature—a weapon as deadly as nuclear bombs without the radioactive effects. We ended the war without starting a nuclear Armageddon that would've ended the whole word."

"How could you get away with it?"

"How could we not? The world was in a panic, fighting over resources in the face of the most extreme climate conditions in human history. Any catastrophe, however strange, could be seen as the latest and greatest effects of global warming. It was simply a matter of directing the disasters toward our enemies, harnessing the volatile energy already ravaging the earth."

"And after the war, the two of you just kept the weather bots running?"

"Of course we did. We started the commission. We kept improving the technology, building more of it, using it for defense instead of offense. We started protecting this country from the horrendous impacts of climate change."

"And what happens to everyone else?"

"Adam, relax. Ninety-nine percent of what we do is just fore-casting. Big data. We only manipulate what we have to. The big storms. The hurricanes and hot spells and droughts. The worst blizzards. The biggest earthquakes. The things that would really endanger people. We simply keep the climate under control, main-tain the status quo."

"But what happens to all that energy?"

"Nothing notable."

"Well you can't just get rid of it."

"It's essentially diverted."

"So you're just passing off our worst natural disasters to other countries."

"It's not so simple. We do as little as we can. The energy is redirected, reshaped. At worst, we create something elsewhere to prevent something worse here. We negate, deflect. We police the earth to protect ourselves. The energy is spread around the rest of the world. It manifests in all kinds of ways. Their weather is bad enough—they could never know the difference."

"But they pay the price for our safety."

"They pay for the world they created! For the war they started! They made choices. We made better ones. Now we are safe, and they are not. We won the war and saved the world. We found the antidote to the climate change. We get to use it. Did you really believe that our little utopia came at no cost at all? Of course there's a scapegoat! But no one can know that. No one can face the cost or they won't be able to enjoy what they have. They wouldn't be happy." Harvey glared at Adam.

"You should have told me Harvey," Adam pushed Harvey back. "You should have told me all of this a long, long time ago."

"As if you wanted to know! You don't ask; we don't tell. That's the deal. You know what happens when you know? You know what happens to our engineers? They get a little chip implanted into their necks so that if they ever spill our little secret we can kill them instantly. Intelligence agencies don't even know except for a few top officials. Homeland Security barely knows. The President doesn't even know the extent of what we do and how we get it done. He chooses not to know! They all do, because they're smart; they know what you don't. The truth is a pest. It ruins the happy ending."

"This is sickening."

"We do what we have to do. Your father did what he had to do. You, on the other, are destroying everything he created. *You,* are bringing it all back on us."

"Just tell me what happened to him already."

"It was his own fault. He started to get…emotional." Harvey stared out the window. "We did what we had to do."

"What the fuck Jonathan!" Adam grabbed him and thrashed him to the ground. "Where is he!"

"Okay okay!" Harvey put his hands up. "I'll tell you. At this point, what's the difference?"

Adam stared into Harvey's eyes, fuming, until finally Harvey got up and started in. "Well first he fell in love, and that was all good and fine. But then he started tinkering around with the weather. Having fun with it. He got too brilliant for his own good. He was Mother Nature's master. He would create storms just so your mother could watch them. It was our bots that would create them, and our bots that would clean them up and clean up all the other aftermath. We had to make a million adjustments to the whole atmosphere, the whole system, to accommodate the one little storm he had created, so that it wouldn't affect our other forecasts. Cost us billions every time he did it. But who could stop him? He was in charge—he and I. But he was the hero. Everybody owed him something. We still do. But I knew," Harvey shook his head, "and I warned him. I said he shouldn't be messing around like that. But he didn't listen. And then you came around." Harvey looked at Adam in disgust. "You and your weather."

"How long have you known?"

"We've been adjusting for the weather you create since the day you were born! It didn't take your father long to catch on. Anomalies popped out of nowhere all the time. At first it was hard. The system couldn't possibly negate all of your weather. But the system got better and better. Your father was competing against you, and trying to teach you not be…such a crybaby." Harvey smirked. "He figured Mother Nature had dealt him some payback for stealing her thunder, but he wasn't going to back down, not

after she took the love of his life. He was going to show her who
was boss. And he did, for years, as you got older. After he left, we
had no problem making your weather disappear before it ruined
the forecast. You weren't creating too much. We had plenty of
bandwidth. We were always a step ahead. And then one day you
appeared in my lobby. Hell, I would've hired you the first time you
asked for an audition, but I couldn't mess with the streak. You were
so happy with your hopes."

"Eventually you got impatient, and I could see it in the
weather. One day we had a particularly close call and I caved. Gave
you the audition to lift your spirits. And I then I hired you. 'Great,'
I thought, 'I can look out for him. I can make sure he's happy.' It
worked wonders for a while. But there was a tipping point somewhere along the line. A peak. And after that it was all downhill. It
wasn't enough for you anymore. Nothing was enough. The longer
you worked for us, the more energy it took for the system to offset
what you were creating and keep people safe. I had no choice but
to fire you, just to kick you out of your rut. And then the goddamn
dam burst. The weather anomalies became too powerful and too
sudden for us to control anymore, as if you woke up from a very
long slumber. The bots got so busy fixing your effects and the endless ripples of those effects to match the forecast—we lost control.
Now we were always a step behind. It became difficult even to stop
the small stuff. And here I thought your father leaving had a nice
stunting effect on your emotions."

"So why the fuck did he leave already?" Adam teemed.
"Where is he? He said he would come back. He promised. He said
he would come back!"

"I told you, he got soft. That anger, that edge…it wore away.
He got spooked. He started to worry about you and your strange
curse, about everything. He decided to take a trip around the
world, and see what kind of collateral damage he was creating. We
tried to stop him—he didn't like what he saw. He was going to try
to take down the system, to 'make things right.' He had a whole
plan to destroy everything he had created and flee the country. Of
course, we couldn't let that happen."

"What did you do to him?"

Harvey paused. His eyes zeroed in on Adam's. "We blotted him out." He glanced away. "Sad, really, but it's what we had to do. I was there when it happened. I saw his eyes go as blank as a newborn baby's. And then he was sent off to a re-identification clinic somewhere—we don't even know where. That's the whole point. We never will. It's a new identity."

"But," Adam's fingers clutched at his hair, "but, no. You have to, you must know where he was sent. You can't possibly—"

"No. Even the blotting out was covert. No one could ever tell you because there's no record of it. Even if there was, he's off the books completely—randomly, anonymously, independently given a new identity. A new name. Even a new face. No one will ever know who he used to be. That's part of the whole deal—a clean slate! Not even the government can locate him. Paul Anderson doesn't exist anymore. Don't you see?"

"No!" Adam's eyes darted everywhere, looking for answers nowhere to be found. "No, no, we could still find him. He's out there. He's not dead."

"Don't be ridiculous Adam." Harvey chucked darts into Adam's heart and enjoyed it. "He may be alive, but he's not your father anymore. His memories are all burnt up. He's about as good to you as a pile of ashes in the wind. He's never coming back for you. You'll never find him. Even if somehow you did, he wouldn't recognize you. You'll never get to know who he really was, and he'll never know who you became. Maybe he even saw you on the broadcast, on your talk shows—but I can guarantee he didn't notice it was you. He doesn't even know he has a son. You'll never get your payback. He'll never hurt. He'll never regret. He'll never apologize. He'll never tell you he loved you. He'll never tell you he didn't. You'll never even know the difference. You'll never know why he abandoned you, why he left you with this curse, all alone. You'll never know if he cared for you at all. You'll never know. Never, never, never! So get the fuck over it!"

Adam looked dead ahead as if he had never heard it. It wasn't easy accepting the one answer he hoped not to find—that after all of this, and all these years—there was no sure answer to all his striving, all his pain. No justice, no harmony, only a dissonant chord that would drone on forever. He could keep trying to change its tune, or he just wail with it.

"Did you hear me?" Harvey berated. "Is that good enough for you? He's never coming back! It's time to get over it! Let it go!"

"Let it go..." Adam moved closer to Harvey. "Let it go? Do you really want me to let it go, or are you just asking me to keep avoiding it? Because I'm ready to let go."

"What's the fucking difference?"

"I've never been able to let go because I've always been avoiding the truth. To actually let go...well I have to embrace my losses before I can let them go."

"No, you don't embrace! You don't lose! Look outside! The whole country is underwater. My weather bots are dropping like flies trying to fight this shit. Hundreds have fallen! If things get any worse, the entire weather safety system will collapse! People are dying! All the time, people are dying! You may have difficult things in your past—great, so do I. Suck it up! I don't care what you have to do; kill a man if you want, but get happy! We've given you the whole world. Just enjoy your happy fucking—"

Before Harvey could finish speaking, Adam barreled into him, pinning him to the floor. "How's this?" Adam swung with all his might and punched Harvey square in the face. His head banged against the marble floor so hard, I wondered if he was dead. But as the blood came out of his smashed nose and the back of his head, Harvey opened his eyes. "That felt pretty good," Adam said. "Want me to do it again?"

"No, no, please!" Harvey spat and shook. "Please!"

Adam slapped Harvey across the head and stood up, but he quickly fell back down. The entire building was swaying in an earthquake.

Out the window, Adam watched in horror as one building buckled at the waist and toppled into another. Both fell into a heap of ruins.

Over Lake Michigan, a fiery meteorite cut through the dark clouds and the white blizzard. It smashed into the lake, pushing a thick wall of water and ice toward the city. The massive wave barged through the streets of Chicago. In an instant, roads became rushing rivers thirty feet deep. Icebergs like runaway yachts crashed into buildings.

Adam stared out the window. His worst nightmares had come to life. Little did we know Harvey had gotten up and pulled a gun out from under a vase in the corner of his office.

"Maybe I should just kill you right now." Harvey wiped the blood streaming from his nose. "Maybe it's the only chance we have."

As Adam dropped to the floor behind Harvey's desk, Harvey fired off a shot. He missed, and the bullet shattered the giant window. The blizzard blew in and smacked Harvey against a bookshelf. He lost his gun and fell to the ground. We went tumbling past him out the door and down the hallway. The elevator wouldn't work; we had to take the stairs, jumping down four or five of them at a time.

When we reached the third floor, we couldn't go any farther down. The windows of the large office space looked like a giant aquarium. Some had broken and the water was rushing in, filling up the office and pouring down the stairwell. A shivering woman in a soaking wet suit was running toward the stairs when she looked up and saw us. It took a moment to register. She pointed a shaky finger with no words on her lips. A disheveled man behind her noticed. "That's, that's Adam Anderson!" he cried. A fierce revulsion overcame his shock. He sprinted toward us. Four other men and the woman instantly followed.

We booked it back up the stairs, bounding all the way to the seventh floor, hoping to find it more vacant so we could hide. But the more offices we ran through, the more angry people joined the mob chasing us. There was no escape.

We hit the end of line in a big corner office. We locked the glass door, but the mob was piling up against it, banging on the glass, gnashing their teeth behind lips quivering with hatred. There must have fifty of them pointing and screaming at Adam, all wanting him dead, even if that meant they died with him.

I found an autographed baseball bat hanging on the wall and used it to smash a big hole in the floor-to-ceiling window. We stepped up to the edge and looked down. A raging river hustled giant ice cubes between buildings forty or fifty feet below. At this point, the water no longer rushed in from the lake. It was rushing back out, and could swiftly carry us to our frozen deaths. I stumbled back with a dizzying feeling. But upon turning around,

I quickly realized there was no other way. The mob was making room for several men to use a heavy sculpture as a battering ram to shatter the glass door.

As they burst inside, we jumped. I fell fifty feet, legs flailing, clinging to that baseball bat, hoping we would beat the iceberg speeding toward our landing spot. We splashed in just in time, and the strong current ripped us away underwater. We surfaced way down the block, breathing big gasps against the freezing water, and sped through the deep canyon of skyscrapers. Whirlpools sucked whole cars underwater into the flooding subway system, and pieces of the river peeled off into perpendicular streets where the water slowed.

Adam pointed out the fast-approaching Michigan Avenue as our only hope. We swam furiously to dodge the grip of a whirlpool and make it in before the river carried us away. We flung ourselves from the top of a streetlight to catch the inlet. Rocky rapids carried us down Michigan Avenue toward the Hancock building, where Adam had his penthouse.

"There it is!" he screamed over the rushing water.

We swam to the very side of the side to make sure we would hit the building. We smashed right into it and clung to the edge of a window. Adam held me steady as I clubbed it with the baseball bat. We burst in with a wall of water, washing up on the carpet of an office like waves on a beach. We scrambled from the flooding floor into a crowded stairwell. But as we climbed against the grain, people began to notice Adam again. "That's Adam Anderson!" a man screamed, and that's all it took to create another angry mob.

People higher on the stairs began to notice what was going on, and now a waterfall of people was pouring down the stairs toward us. We bolted onto the tenth floor, into the elevator bay. Adam clicked furiously, while I stood there with the baseball bat, swinging at anyone who came near us.

The elevator door opened and Adam yanked me through it by the back of my shirt. I stood at the edge of the elevator doors with the bat above my head, ready to crush anyone who advanced between them until they closed. "Penthouse!" Adam yelled, exhausted, freezing, and enraged beyond anything I had seen before. The elevator recognized his voice and shot us up to his loft.

Twenty-nine

"ADAM," HIS OWN LAUGHING FACE still beckoned above the city, *"enjoy!"* As Adam watched the giant hologram flicker on and off in the storm, his reflection floated in the billowing black clouds behind the window, and it told me that he loathed what he saw. His eyes grew old until his breath fogged up the glass.

The government still didn't know where Adam was, and in conditions that made flying, driving, and moving on foot impossible, no one could even try to find him, even if they weren't busy just trying to survive the chaos unfolding across the country. Certainly no one wanted to be on top of a skyscraper like us. America was crumbling to pieces. Adam had survived so far, but he had no idea what to do now.

He turned around and began pacing—pacing, pacing, pacing. The screaming hail and wind rattled the building. Thunder exploded every few seconds. Over the lake, a cyclone bigger than a skyscraper twisted toward the city.

Suddenly, Adam stopped moving and stretched his arms up, clenching and unclenching his fists, like he was literally trying to hold it all together, trying to hold up the whole falling sky. He coiled up into himself and then burst open. "What do I do Clark! What do I do? There's no happy ending here! It's all fucking loose ends! My whole fucking life! This will always be impossible! But life's still going and somehow I have to be happy! How am I supposed to fix all this?" The thunder crashed outside, punctuating his unbearable question. "How am I supposed to be happy? I'm stuck right here, right now! Time won't fucking stop! I need it to stop!"

But time would march on, whether or not he ever fixed that golden watch on his wrist. A million others were all still ticking, reminding him over and over that he could never go back, that they would always rush him forward, ready or not.

"What do I do?" asked Adam as the rage turned tearful. "What the fuck do I do?"

"You can try," I said. "You can try! You can try to relax and step back and just forget about everything. You can try to calm down. You can try to find happiness someday. Please Adam, try!"

"Try?" he erupted. "I have been trying, and trying, and trying! It never works! Don't you get it? She was right! It doesn't matter what I try. Trying is the problem. When I look for happiness, it hides."

"Just, quick, try this for now," I panicked and grabbed a glass decanter of Scotch off the table. "It's something at least. Just have a drink," I held up the booze, "maybe it will help ease your mind."

He stared at me blankly.

"Here." I tried to toss the decanter to him. He didn't move. It sailed gently through the air and smashed onto the crystal coffee table next to him. Both shattered into nothing, splashing Adam with tiny shards of glass. As he tried to wipe shiny specks off his arm, red lines dripped to the floor.

"Shit I'm so sorry!" I blurted. "What can I do? How can I—"

"Nothing! Stop trying to fix it! I want the sadness! I want the anger! I want a real life! I want the pain. I don't want to be happy; I want to be free. The things I want aren't easy. They're too beautiful for me and they're fucking heartbreaking."

"But, Adam...Adam..." The entire building began to bend and creak, and I was so scared, I was still trying to make him feel better. "Adam, there are still so many good things you can have—maybe not the hard things, but good things! Think about those things!"

As he shook his head, tears fell off his face. "But Clark, you're only as warm as your coldest part."

"Adam, no!" I grabbed his shoulders. "Don't think that way! Don't give up; you can't give up. Don't let go!"

"Let me go!" Adam screamed. He grabbed my collar and began pushing me across the loft. He shoved me right out the door and slammed it shut.

I didn't know what to do. I couldn't upset him even more. I stayed there just listening for a minute. Hateful mumblings sputtered through the edges of the door. I pressed my ear up against it and hoped he wouldn't open but hoped he would. The mumbles morphed into loud screams, which released into smashes and blows. I heard things shatter and break, bang and thud. I felt the vibrations from impacts on the walls. And everything he was doing in there would happen to us.

"Adam!" I yelled through the door over the noise. "Adam let me in!" Louder. "Adam!" I knocked while I yelled. "Adam Adam Adam!" I banged on the door for all I was worth. "Adam you need to stop!"

He kicked open the door so hard it knocked me unconscious. I don't for how long. I only know that I fell swiftly out of time while he continued to battle it.

You see, Adam was right; when everything goes to shit, time ticks on anyway. But our failures and losses are behind us, right? We can't go into the past to change them, so why worry about them? It would make sense to let them go, without a care, and happily move on. Like yesterday, they are gone.

Yet we feel them. Their ghosts beg us to resurrect them all the time. Because we never really believe in sunk costs, do we? In the end we believe the world is whole, and the missing pieces are out there somewhere. All those ships that sailed away—they will eventually float back to us, one way or another, to tell us where they've been and why. They will deliver us from the tumultuous sea, set us squarely on their backs, and sail us safely to shore.

The trouble is, some ships sink. They rest on the bottom of the ocean, while we are left to battle the pounding waves in the dark. And we will kick the shimmering waters until they drown us or scream at the cold stars until they lift us, but we will not remain in limbo, not for long. We will always sink or rise, because we ache for an end to the story. Because tears spring like soothing rain at our lowest and our highest. Because in the end, we just want to feel, all of it, to know we are alive.

•

When I woke up, I crunched back into the loft on a floor of broken glass. As I looked down, hidden within the shiny shards, I saw Adam's father's watch. Its face was smashed in. It had been hurled at the heavy door.

A gaping hole in the picture windows opened up to a busted statue on the balcony. Enormous chunks of hail bounced through it, and an icy wind as heavy as wet cement funneled into the room. Overturned chairs with missing legs made the loft an obstacle course. Giant mirrors lay in jagged ruins, cutting eerie reflections across the floor. Various plants and their soil forested the carpet. The faucet was running, and the kitchen sink flooded half the place with a few inches of half-frozen water. Brightly colored fish from the shattered tanks struggled to swim on the floor. The record player had been smashed to pieces, while many of the records had been broken in two, or whipped across the place like Frisbees.

Elegant watches crept around the room like cockroaches, appearing everywhere I looked. They wiggled in place as thunder rocked the building. Some watches were lodged in the drywall and others had smashed through glass cabinets into mountains of broken plates. Many were cracked to pieces. Most littered the floor aimlessly, but for the ghosts of watches, who dug empty graves in the windows, and were probably still falling through time.

Across the room I spotted Adam. He was watching the breaking news that had taken over every station, or trying to watch it, through all the burning fear and anger and sadness and disgust and regret and loneliness in his eyes.

"Adam, no!" I called out. "This is not what you need!"

"It is."

"It will only hurt you."

"I have to see what I've done."

"It's not worth it and it's not your fault!"

"But it's mine," he said, "and I need to see it."

Goodman Washington hunched over his desk with a bandaged forehead. "Now to Manhattan, where we have live footage of the events." A row of building stood against the wind and water.

The sea walls had broken. Boats flew off giant waves, pushed by the wind, and slammed into office buildings. Entire harbors of boats tumbled into the city. A massive steel cargo ship surfed a giant wave, barreling into skyscrapers like bowling pins.

Adam and I watched in complete silence, mouths gaping, tears flowing. It was too much to believe. The scope was too big. The pain entirely overwhelmed him.

"Adam, you have to stop watching."

"I have to know!" he yelled.

"As you can see," Goodman went on, "chaos erupting across the country. A Category 5+ hurricane landing in Manhattan, followed by tsunamis making shore across the East Coast. Let's move Northwest, to Seattle." A wide shot of the city revealed a dense shower of ash pouring down, while fires made certain areas of the volcanic fog glow. "Mount Rainier has exploded in the worst volcanic eruption in American history, sending fiery debris into the city. Heavy ash rains across the greater area, but worse—lahars, immense walls of super-heated volcanic mud, have already swallowed small towns, and are racing downhill toward Seattle and Tacoma. Both will be destroyed within the hour. The death toll is ... incomprehensible. And now to—"

Goodman paused to read something new. "This just in—government sources report Adam was last seen fleeing defense forces on foot, into the streets of Chicago, where soon after, a wall of water due to a meteorite in Lake Michigan rushed in. There would be no feasible way to survive. Adam is assumed dead. His death is assumed the cause of these catastrophes far greater than anything his emotions have ever created."

"Earthquakes," Goodman pushed on, "are destroying our cities' foundations. Let's move to St. Louis." The arch had broken in two pieces and fallen into the Mississippi River, whose flow was temporarily reversed. Wild rapids spilled over its banks, and new rivers cut through the city in the gashes left by the earthquakes. The entire city lay in ruins. "Multiple earthquakes on our nation's biggest fault have numbered eight point six, nine point eight, and nine point seven on the Richter scale. Surviving authorities estimate that more than 90 percent of buildings have collapsed. Cincinnati, Louisville, even Chicago, all greatly affected by the earthquakes and their aftershocks. The number of tornadoes around the country is far too many to cover, but let's now move to—"

An epic burst of thunder pounded my chest and the holovision cut out. The building's power went out and left us in darkness. It was getting very, very cold.

A football-sized chunk of hail smashed through a window, just barely missing me. Then another, and then another. It wouldn't quit. The whole massive window came down, and we were exposed to the fullness of the blizzard on the balcony. I ran into the kitchen to duck behind the island, but Adam didn't react; he didn't care. The only storms in his world raged inside him.

"Adam!" I yelled. "Over here! Take cover!" Instead, Adam began walking onto the balcony. "Adam, what are you doing!"

"She was right!" he screamed. "About everything!"

He walked boldly to the edge of the balcony. The glass wall had shattered and nothing separated him from the unforgiving ground but one thousand feet of chaos. I ran out to the balcony after him, kneeling behind the edge of the frozen hot tub. "Adam, don't do it!" I cried.

"I should've done this a long time ago!" he yelled back. "I need to end this now!" I jumped up and started moving toward him, but he raised his hand out at me so decisively, I was convinced if I came any closer, he would just jump. I just stood there in front of him and stared into eyes swollen with complete abandon. The giant water spouts whipped into the city behind him. He didn't cover his head when ice zipped by it. "I'm done with it," he told me. "I've got nothing left," he wheezed like a dying man.

Behind Adam, some of the clouds began changing to a crystal color. They turned into enormous chunks of ice and fell out of the sky like freight trains. An immense crushing noise enveloped the city as icebergs smashed into buildings a few blocks away, splitting into the flooded streets. Adam whipped around at the sound. He banged on his chest so hard he could have stopped his own heart. He screamed at the collapsing city, "I can't do this anymore! I don't want to be happy anymore!" He threw his hands halfway up, and I thought he was going to jump right then, but he slipped and fell to his knees. He looked down over the ledge. "I just want to be miserable!" Adam threw his arms out wide and his head back. He stared straight up into the dark sky. "I hate this damn happiness!" The sky kept falling. The deafening sound only made Adam louder, "Why can't I just be miserable!"

While he slowly but surely crept over the edge, he dropped his head and let his body fall into a heap over his knees. He had run aground on the invisible fringe of things and simply couldn't go any farther. His face fell to the ground. He was shaking, convulsing, drowning in his misery. It was all washing over him, every last tear, and he was already falling a million miles before he fell over that edge.

His hands gripped the slippery deck. His knees slid over the ledge and wobbled in the wind. Before dropping into the abyss, he leaned his head back for one last ugly scream into the sky. He let every last bit of himself out into the storm.

And from an onyx cloud hanging not far above, a bright white bolt of lightning electrified Adam. He uncurled limp and lifeless, hanging half over the edge.

The giant hail stopped in an instant. The wind died. The lake calmed. Everything found peace, except for a baby boy in a flooded Miami hospital room, who came crying into a terrifying world.

I dove down to Adam, yelling I don't know what. I didn't know if he was alive. He didn't respond. I grabbed his arms and pulled him off the edge. Smoke lifted off his body. If he hadn't been soaked from the storms the lightning might have set him on fire. His hair was burnt. His shirt was singed to rags, barely hanging off his shoulders. And all the electricity coursing through Adam's body had left a fresh scar dancing across his back. It was just like the one on his wrist but far bigger. It looked like a giant tree. Its trunk started near the center, and the branches extended in all directions, weaving intricate patterns all the way across his neck and shoulders.

As I turned Adam onto his back I could see that he was still breathing. "Adam!" I shook him. "Adam! Wake up!" He started to regain consciousness, coughing and gasping for breath. His eyes burst open like bright suns. He inhaled the whole sky, and slowly came back to reality.

Sitting on the ground there, Adam peered over the city, observing it as if for the very first time, taking it all in, all the unthinkable destruction. And it crushed him. He fell back onto his back and turned his face in agony, weeping again.

But the clouds began to break apart. Beams of sunlight widened over a glistening city in ruins. The light shone down on a man in sweet disarray. He could feel it warming his back. Adam pushed himself up just a little and paused. He listened. He heard the stillness. He pushed himself back onto his knees. He kept his head down and breathed.

Finally, Adam tilted his head back and looked into the sky again. His eyes brightened as clear as the new day, because he realized what had happened. His emotions weren't controlling the weather anymore. A terrifying happiness spooked all his ghosts away.

He laughed great heaves of joy. They burst out in clusters that fell over the fallen city, and the sun doused everything in light. He started crying again, but these were tears of a different kind, like stars pouring from his eyes. I had never seen anything so whole as the feeling cutting through that broken man. It wasn't happiness but it gave him so much. He wasn't staring into the sun anymore, only to be blinded by its brightness. No, he looked out over the beautiful broken earth, and the sun struck him.

Adam fell onto his back, watching the golden light blot out the clouds.

"Where's my son?" he asked. "Where's Stella?"

Adam stood up. He was alive.

N.N.N. The Anderson Affect - *Adam Alive, Questions Arise*

As intelligence agencies continue to search for Adam Anderson to bring him to justice, President Powers has called on fellow Americans to offer any assistance possible, stating that, "Information leading to the arrest of Adam Anderson will be rewarded with a cash sum of one billion dollars."

Mr. Anderson was last seen by disaster survivors in Chicago as he escaped the city on foot. While many believe Adam to be dead due to the sudden calm in our climate, dozens of eyewitnesses have reported otherwise.

Americans continue to struggle in the wake of the impossible destruction Adam created on January 1. Since then, the National Weather Commission can point to no known weather abnormalities. But the commission currently cant point to much of anything; they lost all forecasting abilities during the disasters, when thousands of weather bots fell out of the sky, and almost all of their systems were destroyed.

At first, Jonathan Harvey and the commission held that these enormous flying machines only collected data to predict the weather. But after thousands of them crash-landed for people to find and study, the government cannot possibly continue keep the technology secret. While most of the bots self-destructed, over 100 of them failed to explode after crashing.

Citizens are finding these weather bots not only have prediction capacities, but also seem to possess immense weather creation capabilities. Hundreds of scientists inspecting the planes around the country are convinced that they went down while struggling to combat the catastrophes that destroyed this country a couple weeks ago.

It stands to reason that all this time, the National Weather Commission has been able to predict the weather so perfectly by manipulating it to their liking. If confirmed, this

exposes one of the largest government cover-
ups in history, explaining why we, until this
year, had been "fortunate" to experience less
violent weather than most of the world, and
supports conspiracy theories asserting that
the United States used weather as a weapon
during WWIII.

Stay tuned as we investigate the government's alleged weather control and what
connections it may or may not have to the
Anderson Affect.

Published at 5:00 p.m., January 16, 2077.
© *National News Network, Inc. All rights reserved.*

Epilogue

THAT'S ABOUT ALL I can say for now, except that I have found myself in a strange and beautiful new part of the world. We are drifting at sea as I write, yet for the first time in a long time, I don't have the feeling of floating.

Every morning the ship treads closer to the horizon, and every evening it remains as far away. Sometimes the waves keep me up all night and sometimes they rock me to sleep, but they never go away. When my eyes open I wake up and I am at rest. I go straight to the window; I try not to bother with the mirror—I can see myself better in footprints and shadows. I think I'm happy here. Not because I think I am. Not because I'm here. But because I'm looking out across an ocean so big I could never see all of it, and who I am hasn't got all that much to do with who I am.

I don't know exactly where we are, and I don't really know where we will end up. Not all who wander are lost, but some are. And if you ever find me, please don't tell me where I am. See I'm hoping to discover things I wasn't even looking for.

THE WEATHER MAN

ACKNOWLEDGEMENTS

First, I want to thank my mother Stephanie and my brother Josh. They have been so loving and supportive, through and through, even when things weren't going so well. I want to thank my late father, Warren Hayes (1947–2010), who always loved me, believed in me, and encouraged me to chase my dreams.

I'm so grateful for the support of so many friends throughout the long journey of writing this novel, from starting it back in college, to all the growing and rewriting out in LA, to doing a Kickstarter and seeing so many friends and strangers come together to help bring this book to life.

I have a whole lot of people worth thanking, and I'm going to try to thank them all, so here we go.

I'm so thankful for my agent Lacy Lynch, who has believed in me, invested in me, and has pushed me to be a better writer since 2012. Thanks to everyone at Dupree/Miller who has made this possible: Dabney Rice, Shannon Marven, Jan Miller. Thanks to my editor Jerusha Rodgers for some incredible insights, and my copyeditor Jen Charat.

I want to thank all the designer, artist, and filmmaker friends who helped create an amazing Kickstarter and all the other fun stuff that comes with launching book: Abigail Mitchell (Cover), Elliot Matson (Poster), Natalie Seitz (Street Signs), Graham Hauser (Artwork), Chentell Stirritz (Mugs). Filmmaking & Beyond: Joel Lopata, Zared Shai, Jono Senef, Alex Beh, Dan Stowell.

I'm thankful for the teachers that taught me to love storytelling, teachers that went above and beyond to help me grow: Dr. Roy Joseph (1973–2014), Dr. Roger Lundin (1949–2015), Dr. Brett Foster (1973–2015), Dr. Read Schuchardt, Faisal Mohyuddin, Sharon James Ledbetter.

Lastly, I want to thank a number of friends who have been a big help, whether it was reading the book and giving me feedback at any point, proofreading last minute, going out of their way to help me promote the Kickstarter through their own social networks, or just supporting and encouraging me in a really big way. So thank you Margot Atwell, Eric Albaugh, Sam Barnett, Samantha Becker, Martha Bowman, Caleb Bragg, Heather Coates, Nicole Cogan, the Dehuffs, Nina Dobrev, Josh Doppelt, Daniel Downey, Amanda Forth, Jason Geick, Amanda Glassman, Simon Goldberg, Mike Greenhill, Rebecca Griffin, Nate Hinton, the Hayfords, Austin James, Scott Jemison, Kyle Johnson, Georgia Mae Lewis, Joel Lopata, Matt MaLossi, Tim McCrary, Donald Miller, Bruce A. Miller Jr., Kirsten Miller, Ryan Miller, David Royer, Izzy Rubinstein, Nolan Saup, Austin Stowell, Dan Stowell, Ryan Stowell, Kenneth To, Bobby Tunberg, the Ullenbruchs, Parker Willis Young.

But wait, there are still more people to be thanked—*almost 600 of them.* These are the names of every Kickstarter backer, in alphabetical order from the first name they provided (some first names only). This book wasn't possible without you guys. Thank you!

Kickstarter Backers

Aaron, Aaron Becker, Aaron Schilling, Adam, Adam Cook, Adam Matherly, Adam Pines, Alaa Madison, Alberto, Alejandro Rodriguez, Alex Beh, Alex Dooley, Alex Lavin, Alex Song, Alexandra Hooven, Alyse Liebovich, Amalie Krøldrup Hoff, Amanda, Amanda Azadian, Amanda Dunton, Amy, Amy Kirchgraber Berger, Ana Maria, Anastasiya Tsekhanovich, Andrea Coombes, Andreas Meier, Andrew Hoffman, Andrew Kilgore, Andrew Mulder, Angelika Lohoff-Gaida, Ann Hamel, Anna & Tony, Anna Kristie, Anna Ziętkiewicz, Annalise Kelly, Arek M Porczynski, Arkady Chepniyan, Arron Perks, Arthur Huang, Arvin Lee, Aubrey Brown, Aubrey Swander, Austin James, Authentic David William Christians, Babs K Crump, Barb Brink, Beant Kaur Dhillon, Bek Stone, Ben, Beth Viner, Bharath Holla, Bo DeHuff, Bob Dickman, Brad & Amy Herzog, Brad Peterson, Bram Prawira Gani, Brandon Parrott-Sheffer, Brandon Rodriguez, Brendon Yost, Brent Madison, Brett Smith, Brian Carter, Brian Goedde, Brooke Martens, Bruce A. Miller Jr., Caleb Winchester, Cara Ademe, Carla, Carlos Anthony Camacho, Carolina McVeagh, Carolyn Dun, Carrie Ullenbruch, Casey Janke, Cayt Landis, Charles Verner, Charley Carey, Charlie Cardella, Charlotte, Chase Pashkowich, Chelsea Callahan, Chelsea O'Donnell, Cheryl Eng, Chris, Chris Graybeal, Chris Hudson, Chris Kotson, Chris Lentino, Chris Mann, Chris O'Brien, Christine Choe, Christine Dolejs, Christine Rogers, Christopher Trendler, CJ Vinson, Claire Pearson, Clarke Demchy, Claudia Fua, Clint Woosley, Coby Gesten, Cody Fry, Cody Lawrence Wilson, Cody Newton, Colson Hauser, Conor Flaherty, Cory Lowery, Cru Ennis, Curtis Chow, Daina, Dan, Dan Della Gatta, Dan Forbes, Dan Mitchell, Dan Stowell, Dane, Daniel Barth, Daniel Downey, Daniel Gordon, Daniel Jackson, Daniel Kan, Daniel Lundgren, Daniel Teoh Yong Liang, Danny Greenhill, Dante Cosentino, Darcy Carmela, Dashiell, David Abiera, David Girandola, David Glawe, David Mudrak, David "50 Weeks" Royer, Deanna Johnston, Dee Dee Prince, Delaara, Derek Scott, Devan Ruthra, DeVonne Esposito, Diana, Diana Merslich, Dimitri Pilotto, Dina campbell, DJ Bentley, Dominick Mascitelli, Dominik Leitner, Donald Miller, Donta Baker, Doug Astor, Doug Boyd, Drew Daum, Dylan Leifeld, Dylan Waller, Ed Feng, Eden Roberts, Edmund Brown, Edric Subur, Edward Chan, Eirik Norbye, Eléonore Merdrignac, Elin Raun-Royer, Elise Vadnais, Eliza Spear, Elizabeth Phelps, Ella Grossman, Ellie Hemicker, Elliot Matson, Emily Covington, Emily Garcia, Emily Keena, Eric Brown Albaugh, Eric Damon Walters, Eric Gibb, Erik Eclov, Erin Karson, Ewan, Fancy Boy, Fatima Iqbal, Felix Ramos, Finn-Niklas Lüben, Flo Lloyd-Pötscher, Frank Frank, Froze, Gabriel John Rodriguez, Gabriel Vasquez, Garrett Miles, Garth Warren, Gary Curran, Gary Ladewig, Gearsoul, Gemma Neeleman, Georgia Gerasimos Kouloumpis, Georgia Mae Lewis, Gerry Kehler, Gertjan Scholten, Glenn Grigsby, Grace Bell, Grace Bunardi, Graham Rouse, Greg, Gunnar Agrusa, Gustaf Bjorklund, Hank Clifton, Hannah, Hannah Voyta, Hannah Poirier, Hannah Small, Harry Scott, Hayden Patel, Heather Coates, Heather Silhavy, Henry Tan, Hilary Bosa, Humza, Ian Isaacson, I.c.w.w.b., Isaac Spear, Jacelyn Yap, Jack Crowe, Jack Sneed, Jacob Galbraith, Jacque Nodell, Jacqueline Camero, Jacqueline DeHuff, Jade, Jade Mitchell-Ross, Jag Bahra, Jake Cannella, James Burke, Jamie, Jamie Nicole Minyard, Jamie Oliva, Janine Amberger, Jann Lynch, Jason Geick, Jayson Clarke, JB Wiese, Jeff Ullenbruch, Jeff Atkins, Jeff & Julia Royer, Jeff Shiflett, Jeffrey, Jeffrey Fralick, Jeffrey Radloff, Jenessa Duval, Jenna Bellovich, Jenny Eldridge, Jenny Morrison, Jeremi, Jeremy, Jeremy Browning, Jeremy Keys, Jeremy Popper, Jessi McLaughlin, Jessica, Jessica Enfante, Jessica Eppen, Jessica Foust, Jessica Homer, Jill Gillmore, Jimmy Sawczuk, Jme Smith, Joan Kurtz, Jochen, Joe Gutilla, Joe Friend, Joel Lopata, Joel Wilbur, Joel Mollman, Joel Sorge, Joey Marrazzo, John Anderberg, John Avedisian, John Battaglia, John Cavey, John Dietzen, John Kasserman, John Lamar, Jon, Jon Maas, Jonathan André, Jonathan Hippensteel, Jonathan Solomon, Joni Rodgers, Jonny Hofner, Jono Seneff, Jordan, Jordan Christner, Jordan Davies, Jordan Hinson, Jorn Straten, Joseph Aiello, Josh Hayes, Josh Hobbs, Josh Doppelt, Josh Mccarthy, Josh Ng, Joshua, Joshua

Cheung, Joshua Peace, Joshua Rawe, Joyce, Judd Bonamino, Julian Jacobsen, Julie Hwang, Julie McCrary, Justin Leow, Karen and George DeHuff, Kartikeya Shukla, Karyn Besaw, Kasper B, Katelyn Kirkland, Katie, Katie M, Katie Tyler, Katy Hillary, Keba Jackson, Keith Palau, Keli Bjorklund, Keller Schlueter, Kelsey, Kelsey stulken, Kelsey Ullenbruch, Ken Arvidson, Kenneth, Kenneth Ogilvie, Kerri LaPratt, Kevin Alban, Kevin Bae, Kevin Brock, Kevin DeHuff, Kevin Engel, Kevin Puett, Kimia Hangafarin, Kina Crow, Kodee Cahill, Kristi Marie Karrenbrock, Kristian Rosenberger, Kristin Morris, Kurtis Manke, Kyla, Kyle Bedell, Kyle Lindsay, Kyle David McCray, Kyle Ward, Lacy Lynch, Larry Eclov, Laryssa, Laura Olander, Laurel J, Lauren Creek, Lauren Schaeffer, Leilani, Leonel Cortez, Leslie Weaver, Lewis Lawrence, Lily, Lindsay LaPlante, Lindsay Solfelt, Lisa Gordon, Livia Guérin, Liz Dolinar, Liz Losoff, Liz Mansfield, Logan Arney, Lori Kornack, LS, Lucy Solorzano, Luis Cardenas, Luis Rangel, Luke, Maasai Colour, Mae, Maggie, Marc, Marcia, Marcus Söderberg, Margaret St. John, Margot Atwell, Margret-Ann Natsis, Maria Anderson, Maria Krump, Marie Juarez, Marina, Mario, Mark Corapi, Mark H Webert, Mark Kassen, Mark Sommerville, Mary & Caleb Bragg, Mary Iwinski, Matt, Matt Boothe, Matt MaLossi, Matt McCrary, Matthew B., Matthew Bashford, Matthew Davies, Matthew Wolf, Matthias Schweizer, Matty Vallevand, Maxim Veksler, Mea, Megan, Megan Brandewie, Megan Davis, Megan Russell, Mekenzie Hayford, Melvin Poujoulat, Michael Curzi, Michael Greenhill, Michael & Thomas Mauriello, Michael Thuneman, Michelle Andujar, Michelle Christine, Michelle VanSetten, Michiel, Mickey Gervase Franson, Mike Woodruff, Miranda, Molly Hennessy, Mona Jiveh, Monique Park-Smith, Mr. Turing, Myles Howard, Nairee Bedikian, Natalie Tolbert, Natalie Warther, Nate Horowitz, Nate Reinders, Nathan Hinton, Naxin Nancy Wang, Nehemias, Neithan Levi, Nermeen Zia, Nicholas Hunt, Nick Cartwright, Nick Coffeen, Nicole, Nicole Navarrete, Noah Medeiros, Noah Schnaubelt, Noah Thomas Nolan Saup, Nora Alrajebah, Olivia, Olivia Akl, Olivier Moreira, Otto Cedeno, Paris Marx, Paul, Paul Doppelt, Paula Price, Paula Tran, Pearly, Peter, Peter clifton, Peter Jenkin, Peter Tse, Phil Gorman, Philip Martin, Quinton Moore, Rachel Tinker, Radha Kura, Rafael Pacheco, Ragan, Rajeevan, Ralph Loielo, Rasmus Von Beissenhertz Harild, RC, Reenie Erwin, Ren Oh, Rex Lam, Richard A. Roberts, Richard Margaritondo, Rick Zhang, Ritarsha Y. King, Rob, Robert "Burns" DeHuff, Robert Goodman, Robert Tunberg, Rod Blackhurst, Rod Mearing, Romain Tahon, Roy & Joanne Schwarcz, Rozzie Sanders, Rudolph Crane, Ryan Bydder, Ryan & Ned Miller, Ryan Stowell, Saish Dabholkar, Sam, Sam Butler, Sam Chastain, Sam Medeiros, Sam Miller, Sam Tran, Samantha Duda, Sammy, Sara Sista, Sarah, Sarah Cathey, Sarah Lebaigue, Sarah O'Kane, Sarah Ullenbruch, Scott Clifton, Scott Dolejs, Scott Jemison, Sean Lawrence, Sean McCormick, Sean Valant, Steven & Chentell Shannon, Shawhin Mosadeghzad, Shaylin Riley, Shelby, Shelley Katsuki, Shirley, Simon Goldberg, Sopon Supamangmee, Stacy Lam, Steph Bong, Stephanie Hayes, Steve, Steve Atkins, Steve Ivester, Steve Zwolinski, Steven Brunwasser, Steven Moore, Steven Victor, Summer Lynn Holeman, Susan Downd, Susan Wechsler, Suzanne Wilson-Higgins, SzuTsung, Taboo Portillo, Tee Hongda, Tejas Sharma, Terence, Teresa Ruminski, Theo Frastus, Thomas Bull, Thomas Egbert, Thomas Hooper, Tieg Zaharia, Tim Kroesbergen, Tim McCrary, Timothy E. Little, Tom, Tom Burggraf, Tom Cannavino, Tom Sum, Tom Van Der Spek, Tony Abiera, Tracie Belsanti, Trey H. Butler, Troy, Trystan Vel, Tyler Cosma, Valeria, Vanessa, Vanessa Flores, Varinder Singh Bal, Veronica Benitez, Victor, Victor Chang, Victoria, Vineeth Nalla, Virgilio Joselito Guevara, Virginia L. Samuelson, Warintorn Phanichkul, Wayne Brink, Wenting Guo, Whelana, Windi Bergeron Larson, Xidle, Yael Kaufman, Yi Qian Tan, Yuri Beekman, Zach Coan, Zach Fallon, Zachary, Zared Shai, Zoheb Davar.

Made in the USA
Lexington, KY
14 January 2017